FUNERAL DAZE

Dorian Box

FRICTION
PRESS

FUNERAL DAZE

ISBN 978-1-7346399-4-0

For my daughter Caitlin, my inspiration
for Jessica Jewell and so much more

And a child shall lead them.
—Isaiah 11:6

SUMMER
2000

Before

April 2000

THE MIAMI SUN burned hot and bright on the inaugural graduating class of the Frogleman School of Law as Bennie "Fink" Finkel stepped up to the microphone. His curly red hair fluttered beneath his mortarboard cap in the humid breeze like the fronds of the surrounding palm trees.

"Welcome future lawyers of America!" The greeting boomed through a massive sound system erected for the post-ceremony celebration, headlined by a classic rock band that had two legitimate hits in the seventies and featured one of the original roadies.

A few lazy whoops. The graduates lounged in various states of intoxication on blankets and chairs scattered across the law school plaza. Many had broadly interpreted *Florida Casual* on the invitations to include swimsuits, although *No Nudity* signs spoke to the solemnity of the occasion.

Danny Teakwell stood to one side, blending easily with the crowd. Tall, tan and blond, he wore board shorts, flipflops and a *Nine Lives* tee, his surf shop on Hollywood Beach, a few exits north of Miami on I-95.

Watching Fink mop sweat with the puffy sleeve of his black robe, he still couldn't believe his childhood chum was on the verge of becoming a real lawyer. When they reunited five years ago during the summer of mayhem, Fink was already running a fulltime law practice—without a license. He ended up representing Danny in a murder trial, failing to mention he never bothered to attend law school.

They hadn't seen each other since Sari's funeral more than a year ago. Danny had been preoccupied with sinking to rock bottom since she lost her battle with breast cancer.

"Distinguished ladies and gentlemen," Fink said. "And also my fellow graduates." He stopped and struck a pose like Henny Youngman waiting for a rimshot. No one laughed. He frowned and continued.

"It is my great honor—" A Frisbee bounced off the speakers and hit him in the face. "You'll be hearing from my lawyer about that," he said, rubbing his cheek and readjusting his round wire-rimmed glasses. "*Me.*" Again, he paused. Crickets.

"As I was saying, it is an honor to be your class speaker for this historic event. I'd like to begin by thanking everyone who helped me get this far. First, my parents. I know you're hiding here somewhere."

Finally a couple laughs. They appeared to come from the leafy branches of a ficus tree.

He proceeded to recite a list that included his life-coach, pharmacist, and auto mechanic, who all had the same name, and his "good friend" Bruce Springsteen, which drew oohs and aahs. "And, of course, we're grateful to our generous sponsor, Thomas T. Frogleman."

"Who the hell is Thomas T. Frogleman?" said Grady Banyon, standing next to Danny, half a foot shorter and wearing a tattered skipper's cap that reined in his wiry white hair. He owned the Tradewinds Bar and Grill on the ground floor of Danny's condo building on Hollywood Beach. "The only Frogleman I know is the pest control company with the idiot who does the commercials dressed like a rodent."

"That's him," Danny said. "Toxic Tommy. He donated five million bucks for the naming rights."

"You're kidding. Is this law school accredited?"

"Still pending," Danny said.

Fink was getting wound up on stage, bombastic oration being one of his strengths. "My fellow graduates, in these past three years we have been like family. We broke bread and raised glasses together, laughed and cried together. When disagreements occurred, we sought medical treatment together."

"You suck, Fink," someone yelled to applause.

"Yes, I do. Not as much as you, of course. That would be impossible. Allow me to be honest on this joyful day for reflection. We all suck."

His first cheer of the day, from the ficus tree again.

"That's why we're at Frogelman. I say take pride in it! We spent our entire lives surrounded by annoying overachievers. Then we stepped into these hallowed, well-fumigated halls and learned the true path to success. Skating by."

"Same old Fink," Danny said.

Grady nodded as Danny's name blasted through the loudspeakers. He looked up in surprise to see Fink pointing at him.

"There he is, my best friend. The very paragon of what I'm telling you. Danny Teakwell has been an underachieving loser and washout for most of his life. But did he let that stop him from winning the Florida Lottery or being acquitted of first-degree murder? He did not. Everyone, give it up for former lottery winner and murder defendant Danny Teakwell!"

The throng hooted and hoisted drinks in Danny's direction. He forced a smile and waved.

Danny's greatest life accomplishment in Fink's view was a distant afternoon at a convenience store where he picked six numbers on a Lotto ticket. He won five million dollars, a fortune he squandered years ago.

"Brothers and sisters," Fink said, turning somber, eyes downcast, chin dipped. "As we prepare to set out into this cold, cruel world, hear my final message to you. Never forget—"

No one heard the conclusion because a guitar tech for the classic rock band plugged in a Les Paul for a sound check and hit a power chord that ignited the crowd. Fink slumped offstage.

Danny and Grady caught up with him on the way out.

"Danny! I haven't seen you since ... Sari's funeral. How have you been doing? Stupid question. I should've called more. I've been so wrapped up in law school and ... hell, that's no excuse."

"No problem. There's never anything good to say."

"Thanks for coming."

"How could I miss seeing my former attorney graduate from law school? Congratulations."

"We'll see how the state bar feels about it. I not only have to pass the bar exam, they have to approve my *character*," he said with air quotes.

"The practicing-law-without-a-license thing?"

"Yeah, that. I was expecting it. I knew they were going to hold a grudge. They're jealous of me. Do you know how many so-called real lawyers ever successfully defend someone in a murder trial?"

"No idea. How many?"

"I don't know either, but it's rare."

Fink patted Grady on the back. "How are you doing, captain? Good to see you too. How's the Tradewinds?"

"Fine, fine," he said, scowling. "A law school named after a guy who jumps up and down on TV in a rat costume?"

"What can I say? It's the only one I got into."

Grady muttered something and strolled away to complain about last night's Marlins' loss to a passerby in a teal jersey.

"What are your plans?" Danny said. "Do you have a job?"

"I had one, at Frogleman Pest Control, interning in their legal department. I was hoping for a permanent in-house job, but they fired me."

"What did you do?" Danny said, although he wasn't sure he wanted to know. Fink's history of erratic behavior was long and checkered.

"Absolutely *nothing*."

"Nothing nothing? Or something nothing?"

"They assigned me to respond to customer complaints. One day a woman called to say she got sick and had to go to the hospital after the service technician left. She asked if the pesticide could be responsible. I said, of course. It's poison. What do you expect? She asked what she should do and I suggested hiring a lawyer."

"I can see where the company might have an issue with that."

"Not me. They told me to keep the customers happy. She got a six-figure settlement and even sent me a thank you note. How much happier can you get? Anyway, I'm moving back to Hollywood to open a solo practice."

"Happy ending. It will be great having you back."

A staccato keyboard riff shattered the calm as the band opened with their first hit. The graduates went wild.

Fink shook his head. "I can't believe that guy ruined my speech. *I* was the rockstar up there. I had them eating out of my hand. You liked it, right?"

"It was, um, unique. So you're pals with Bruce Springsteen? How did I miss that?"

"Saw him in the back of a cab once, pretty sure."

"What was your unforgettable final message?"

"First you have to pretend you're in the audience listening."

"Alright. I'm pretending."

"Ready?"

"And waiting."

He spread his arms and declaimed, "Never forget, my dear friends. The ambulance you chase may one day be your own."

"What does that mean?"

"*Du-uh*, it's a metaphor."

"For what?"

"If it's too deep, there's no point explaining it."

"You have no idea, do you?"

He shrugged. "I liked the way it sounded. Profound. Hey, I hope you didn't mind me bragging on you out there."

"Mind? Why would I mind being called a loser and washout in front of a large group of strangers?"

"Not that part. I mean about winning the lottery and getting off on a murder charge."

"Fink ..."

"What's wrong?"

"Never mind. Congrats again. I have to run Grady back to Hollywood to open the Tradewinds."

"What about Nine Lives? How's your surf shop going?"

"It's going." Down the drain. He hadn't been there in a month. "Don't be a stranger when you get back to Hollywood."

"It might be a while. I have to study for the bar exam. No way to fake it."

"Good luck on it."

They did a handshake-hug and Danny walked away to find Grady.

"Call me if you need a lawyer!" Fink shouted after him.

Chapter 1

Two Months Later ...

DANNY WOKE UP on the couch. He could see the microwave through the open bar to the kitchen. The clock said four p.m. He barely slept the night before. Having counted down the days, he thought he was prepared. Then midnight arrived and kicked him in the head. Sari's birthday.

He crossed the living room and pulled open the patio doors. The knob came off again. Like the rest of the crumbling Seabreeze Towers his penthouse had seen better days.

But the view was there. The whole reason he used the lottery money to buy the place. The ocean he grew up on and in, since he was three-feet tall as Buffett would sing.

He took deep breaths of the healing sea air. Even from the fifteenth floor, he could taste the garlicky seaweed left behind by the afternoon tide. Out on the horizon, far past the limey shore water that turned dark over the reefs before stretching deep blue, a sole cargo ship seemed to stand still.

The vista usually brought him perspective, even peace. Today the glare just hurt his head. The bourbon he overconsumed last night to induce sleep wasn't helping.

He went to the kitchen and filled a glass with water, careful not to spatter any on the photos of Sari spread across the countertop. The last time Grady came up he suggested it was time to put them away. Danny told him to mind his own business. A five-by-seven took him back in time. Sari in a checkered dress, smiling with teeth too big for her face, shiny brown hair parted in the middle and tucked neatly behind her shoulders. He recognized her mother's handwriting on the back. *Sari, 5th Grade.* The year they met.

They were childhood sweethearts before he committed an unforgivable sin in his sixteenth year of life that still weighed him down. He lost Sari over it. Getting her back took a twisted twentieth high school reunion and body-strewn search across the Sunshine State.

He dreamed of marrying Sari his whole life and wasted no time asking her. At their wedding, downstairs in the Tradewinds, he was flooded with gratitude, for getting a second chance at happiness, at life itself. Then she was gone again. Forever this time. He'd been stumbling in a haze ever since.

He set down the picture and picked up the stack of mail accumulating on the bar counter. Bills and more bills. One from the condo association reminded him that if he didn't catch up on his HOA fees quickly, they'd have no choice but to put a lien on his place.

The broke lottery winner.

At the bottom of the pile laid a cream-colored envelope addressed in loopy cursive written with purple ink. The return address said *Slagger-Jewell Funeral Home.* Another blast from the past. What could it be about? His last contact with the Jewell family was five years ago.

He thumbed open the envelope and pulled out a stiff card bearing a headshot of a toothless old man with an impish grin and strands of white hair that stood straight up on his otherwise shiny dome.

Please join us to celebrate the life of

Jarrod Jewell Sr.

April 4, 1902 – July 10, 2000

**We'll gather at the Slagger-Jewell Funeral Home,
the institution he co-founded, to laugh and cry and
share our memories of this truly unique man.**

Below was more of the loopy purple penmanship:

*Please come, Danny. My grandfather really liked you.
My dad too. And especially me!*

*Yours very truly,
Jessica Jewell*

*p.s. Don't forget you promised to be my first customer
when you die.*

The postscript made him laugh. A genuine out-loud laugh. He couldn't remember the last time.

Junior mortician Jessica Jewell. They met when he visited the funeral home to investigate a grave robbery as part of his mad hunt for Sari. The kid was only seven at the time, but already following in her family's footsteps. She gave him a helpful tutorial on embalming.

The invitation's description of her grandfather as *unique* didn't do him justice. He napped in a casket and collected the organs of old friends as they passed away. As mementos, he said. His hobby in retirement? Putting make-up on corpses.

The whole family was a piece of work. He checked the date. The memorial service was tomorrow.

He stuck the invitation to the refrigerator with a pelican magnet and considered his options for the night. Sit at home obsessing about Sari or go down to the Tradewinds and drown his sorrows. Easy choice, but he needed a shower first.

On the way, he passed the room where Sari spent her final weeks on a rented hospital bed, their former home office. She insisted on keeping the guestroom free for her parents and refused to let their bedroom become a *sick room.*

When it got to where she couldn't eat or drink, he fed her spoonfuls of ice chips. He put balm on her drying lips and helped her change position every hour. He did anything and everything he could, but still felt utterly helpless.

Sari stayed upbeat and strong, disguising her suffering. Visitors sometimes commented she seemed to be improving. Danny knew better. One look in her truth-telling eyes said it all.

Even after they moved her to hospice, she fought to hold on. A social worker told Danny he needed to let go, to tell Sari it was okay to let go. She said it was the most loving thing he could do for her.

He did it through a veil of tears. He didn't know if she could hear him, but the next day she stopped breathing while he held her hand. His last words were, *Thank you for loving me, Sari.*

* * *

Entering the Tradewinds, the first thing Danny noticed was a pair of lacy pink underwear skewered on the sword of a dust-encased blue marlin mounted next to the door. Tom Petty's *Free Fallin'* played on the jukebox.

"Ahoy, Danny," Grady said from inside the rectangular oak bar, tipping his cap.

"Oh, *Dan-nee-boy.*" The D'Angelo brothers. They'd been greeting him in barbershop-style harmony since the first time they met. "Get over here and let us buy you a beer."

"What the hell took you so long? I've been waiting since noon." John the Diver.

He waved and planted himself on a barstool. PBS Newshour host Jim Lehrer was interviewing presidential candidate Al Gore on a muted TV at the end of the bar. Grady set a pint in front of him without him having to ask.

"Grady, about my tab."

"We've already argued about it, son. You lost."

For all his other shortcomings, Danny had never been a deadbeat. Before he won the lottery, he worked too many crappy jobs to count. He lived paycheck to paycheck, but always paid his bills. Now? He was an embarrassment to himself.

His only hope for financial survival was Nine Lives, his surf shop. Over the years he gained a following in the niche world of making custom boards. Some of his best sold for more than ten grand. Then Sari died and he let the shop wither along with the rest of him.

The first time he raised the tab issue, Grady sat him down. "Son, one of the big reasons you're broke is you wasted your lotto money buying rounds for every Tom, Dick, and Harry who came through that door. You probably singlehandedly kept me in the black for ten years. My turn now."

He didn't try to relitigate the issue tonight. Just said thanks and quietly sipped the beer, lost in thought.

Shannon Briley stopped by to peck him on the cheek on her way to serve a table of broiled tourists recounting their day of deepsea fishing. She'd been part of the Tradewinds family since working her way through community college. Now she was married with a kid, but still picked up shifts for extra cash. Being a former Broward County Miss Teen winner didn't hurt her tips.

John the Diver brought over a petite woman with wild dirty-blonde hair and a blot of red and purple ink on her bicep that said *Resistance Is Usless*. The typo added a certain flair to it.

"Marlena, this here is the legendary Danny Teakwell I told you about. Danny, this is my cousin, Marlena. She's in town for a few days looking to have some fun," he said with a wink.

Danny got the message, but said only, "Nice to meet you. I hope you have a great visit."

J.D. shrugged at Grady and led Marlena back to their booth.

That's the way it went all night. Danny did his best to act upbeat, but all he wanted was to be left alone. As the early crowd filed out, Grady confronted him.

"What's the matter?" he said. "And don't say *nothing*. I'm sick of hearing it. I know you're hurting, but I also know you're good at shining it on. Not tonight. Three different people asked me if you were alright."

"You know. Same old thing."

"No, something's different. Worse. Why?"

"Sari's birthday."

"Ah."

"It triggered a lot of memories."

"Understandable," he said. "But last month it was your wedding anniversary and before that—"

"I know what you're saying. I just miss her. It's as simple as that. I'm empty. I have nothing left."

"You're wrong, son. You have friends. Look around you. These ol' pirates love you, in no small part because of everything you've done for them. Who gave the D'Angelo boys five grand to fix their boat just in time for tourist season? Who spent six months helping John the Diver rebuild his house after Hurricane Andrew tore it apart. That man would give you his liver, not that you'd want it."

"I love them too. It's just that nothing's the same. It never will be."

"You're right. It won't. Glad you recognize it. Next step is to accept it and get back to living. There's a big difference between remembering Sari and wasting away feeling sorry for yourself."

Danny slammed his glass down. "I don't feel sorry for myself. I could care less about myself. You know that. I feel sorry for Sari."

Grady gazed above his head chewing on an unlit cigar, an improvement over the three packs of cigarettes he used to smoke daily. "Do you think this is what Sari would want for you? To disintegrate? Because of her? If so, you're a bigger fool than I thought possible."

Danny deflated and said softly, "No, I don't think that. She told me to do just the opposite."

It happened the day before she moved to hospice. She was propped in the rented hospital bed. Her hair was gone from the chemo. Blue veins showed through her skin like a roadmap. She had lost so much weight he could see the outline of her skull.

She asked him to sit on the bed. He knew something was coming. Like always, her eyes said it all.

"We need to talk. I'm going to die soon. Look at me, Danny. You know how they always talk about dying wishes? I have one."

"Anything, Sari. If it's humanly possible, I'll get it done."

"So glad to hear that," she said with the sly smile he knew well. "You're a beautiful person, Danny Teakwell, even if you're too thick to realize it sometimes. I want you to be happy, to go on with life and meet someone else. I don't want you to be alone."

"Please, Sari. Don't."

"Too late. You just said name anything and you'll get it done. You have a big heart, Danny. *The Heart of the Heart*. Remember?"

The poem cut out of construction paper she gave him when they were kids. "Of course."

"My wish is that you save a space in it for me—"

"I will, Sari. Forever. You don't have to worry about that."

"I wasn't finished. Save a space for me, but keep your heart open. Be willing to let someone else in. A heart has room for more than one person. Promise me."

"I'll try, Sari. I swear."

Grady refilled his beer glass. "What did you she tell you?"

"She said her dying wish was for me to be happy. She wanted me to promise to keep my heart open for someone else."

"Did you?" Grady said.

"I promised I would try."

"Try harder."

Stumbling into his condo near midnight, he went to the kitchen for some Gatorade and saw the invitation to Jarrod Jewell Sr.'s funeral service on the fridge.

The eccentric geezer helped him back when he was desperate for answers. So did his son, *Junior*, as the old man called him. Little Jessica too. He remembered how much he appreciated all the people who came to honor Sari at her memorial service. He'd stop by and pay his respects. He owed them.

He slept fitfully, dreaming he was being chased by a dark thing he could never see as he ran toward a bright light he could never reach.

Chapter 2

THE FUNERAL HOME looked the same as it did five years ago, an august edifice to death, with a marble façade and four imposing Corinthian columns. Chiseled above them was *Slagger-Jewell*.

Danny stood beside his beat-up Hyundai straightening his tie and tugging the lapels of his navy blue suit, the only one he owned. Sari insisted he buy it for their wedding even though it took place in the divey Tradewinds.

He rolled his shoulders and made his way up the brick walkway that sliced through the well-manicured St. Augustine lawn, hoping the funeral service didn't trigger an avalanche of bad memories.

A blast of laughter and animated conversation surprised him when he pulled open the door and stepped onto the plush burgundy carpet. Frank Sinatra was belting *That's Life* from speakers mounted in the ceiling. Lavish buffet tables with white tablecloths lined one wall.

The invitation didn't exaggerate. It definitely looked like a celebration.

"Danny!"

Jessica Jewell ran to him balancing a plate of celery sticks and an empanada missing one neat circular bite.

"It's me, Jessica! Do you recognize me? I'm twelve years old now. All grown up."

"Well, hello. Of course I recognize you." She was a lot taller than at seven, but had the same round face and hazel eyes. Her blondish-brown hair danced back and forth in a chin-length bob.

"Thanks for coming. I didn't know if you would. Most people find a million excuses to avoid a funeral. And you even wore a suit. That's a surprise. You look nice."

"You too." She was wearing a sleeveless black calf-length dress and black flats.

"Thanks. I looked better before. I started out with a veil, but couldn't see and almost knocked over my grandpa's casket. Dad got all annoyed and made me take it off. Speaking of gramps, let's go see him!"

She set her plate on a side table and dragged him by the hand through the crowd to another room, where Jarrod Jewell Sr. laid at rest in an open casket. He was headed to his final resting place in a lobster-themed silk sport shirt and white pleated pants with a sharp crease.

One stiff hand held a reddish-brown cocktail with two cherries floating in it. Looked like a Manhattan. His pruney face was a picture of bliss.

"See that smile? I molded it myself," Jessica said. "Gramps taught me how. Smiles were his specialty. The tricky part is the jaw suture. If you don't sew or glue it shut, a dearly beloved's mouth will hang open. That's what we call corpses here. Sounds more upbeat than dearly departed."

She let her jaw drop and stuck her tongue out to demonstrate. "Not a good look. Dad doesn't let me practice on clients because I don't have a license, but gramps let me do it all the time, starting when I was young."

He nodded along with the twelve-year-old.

"I finally convinced him that gramps would want me to do his smile."

"It's a, uh, very nice smile. I'm sorry you lost your grandfather."

"Yeah, I already miss him. But, you know, he was ninety-eight and had a good life. No one lives forever. I was raised not to fear death. It's just a part of life."

She waved her pea-shoot arms at the surroundings. "He's still here, somewhere. We're never really gone. Do you believe that?"

Danny didn't know what he believed when it came to dying. "I'm not sure."

"Look at it this way. When you see a wave in the ocean and it goes away, do you think it's gone?"

He'd wasted major portions of his life sitting on surfboards waiting for waves that dissipated before they arrived. "Yeah, I'd say so."

"Wrong! It's still part of the ocean, isn't it?"

"I guess that's right." The kid had been wise beyond her years even at seven.

"Plus, gramps loved taking naps in a casket. So I think he's happy."

"I remember your dad mentioning that back when we met." *Swears it's more comfortable than his own bed.*

"Speak of the devil," she said as a pudgy man with curly brown hair approached from the side. "Just kidding, Dad. You remember Danny."

"Of course. Welcome, Danny." They shook hands.

Her father didn't look well. His clothes were disheveled. Red patches blotted his face and neck. His rheumy eyes rested on puffy half-moon circles.

"Thank you for coming," he said. "Jessica insisted on inviting you. I hope she isn't pestering you too much."

"I'm not pestering him. I'm his friend." She looked up at Danny. "Right?"

"You bet. Jarrod, I'm sorry about your father."

"He was one of a kind. How about a drink?"

That sounded good to Danny. The whole scene was disorienting, everyone partying around the old man's corpse as Frank sang *That's Life* over and over from the ceiling. He followed Jewell to an open bar and asked for a gin and tonic. Jessica tagged alongside.

Jewell asked how he had been doing. A white-haired woman leaning into a speeding aluminum walker saved him from having to lie. She rammed Jewell in the backside, intentionally it appeared to Danny.

"Junior," she said. "While you're standing around blathering, I'm about to pass out. Where's that plate of food?"

"I'll be right with you, Rosie." He turned back to Danny. "I have to move on. Glad you came. The old man took a real liking to you. Said you were the only person ever willing to drink brandy with him out of a formaldehyde beaker."

"Junior!"

"Coming, Rosie." He followed her as she bulldozed a path to the buffet with her walker.

"That's my cranky Great Aunt Rosie," Jessica said. "So, I would ask how Patches is doing, but hamsters only have a lifespan of three years. And that's if they're lucky. I hope you held a nice funeral service for him."

Five years ago, when he was recovering from gunshot wounds, she dragged her father to the hospital to visit him, bringing the hamster as a gift. Said she didn't want him to be alone.

"Funeral service? Oh, well, it was nice. Not fancy, but nice."

"Danny, tell me the truth. Did you throw Patches in the trash?"

"No, no. I buried him on the beach."

She nodded. "That's not bad. Are you finally married? I don't see a wedding band."

He wore it for six months after Sari died before putting it away. He opened his mouth and nothing came out. It was coming back how unnerving the kid's directness could be.

She studied his face, slitting her left eye. "Never mind. Let's get some food. Wait until you see the cupcakes I ordered. They're the cutest. Little caskets with white icing."

They sat in the waiting room balancing plates on their laps. Danny went with boiled shrimp. Jessica opted for three of the cupcakes. *That's Life* started over again.

"I take it your grandfather really liked this song."

"It was his favorite," she said. "He always told me that no matter what knocks you down in life, you have to get back up and keep going. As for the song, it's okay, but I'm ready for something else."

"Tell me about you," Danny said. "What grade are you in?"

"I start seventh in a month."

"What's your favorite subject?"

"Mortuary science, but they don't offer it. Do you believe not one of my teachers has heard of Wilhelm von Hofmann? Not even one."

"I have to admit, I'm drawing a blank."

"I'm surprised. He discovered formaldehyde. It's pretty basic."

"Do you still play softball?"

"Yeah, but I'm stuck in right field even though my dad's the coach. That's where they put the worst player."

"How is he, your dad?"

"Not well. Couldn't you tell by looking at him?"

"Losing someone you love can be tough."

"If it's that tough, I've been lied to my whole life. He and gramps taught me death is no big deal, just a passage to the next place. I took them at their word."

Chapter 3

AS SHE WAVED GOODBYE to her one and only friend, Gloria, who hated her name and liked to be called Gigi, Jessica coasted her bike down the driveway contemplating how suddenly her world had been turned upside down.

She and Gigi had spent the afternoon watching their favorite movie. *Invasion of the Body Snatchers.* The original, of course. She was so busy fretting about her father she missed her favorite scene, when Kevin McCarthy kisses Dana Winter and realizes she fell asleep and turned into a body snatcher. The worst!

Last week her biggest concern was the state of her summer vacation. She started it with three goals: run five miles a day, read twenty books, and master the guitar. She hadn't laid eyes on a guitar, ran only to catch the ice cream truck every afternoon, and read one book, although it was long. *Embalming: History, Theory, and Practice.*

With time running out she decided to skip the running and books, but find a guitar and dominate it before seventh grade started. How hard could it be?

Then gramps died, her hero and best buddy. She missed him much more than she was allowed to say. She wasn't supposed to get upset about death. Her father told her that a million times.

Then he started falling apart and was getting worse every day. Not eating or sleeping, and being grumpy. Like when he took away her veil at the funeral. That was uncalled for.

Maybe she really had been lied to. Maybe death was a big deal after all. Not a transition, but a terrible ending.

She had never been more confused in her life, not even the time she woke up in a dark casket as a toddler and wondered if she was dead. Her gramps put her there for a nap and someone accidentally shut the lid.

Then last night happened and she began to suspect her father's breakdown wasn't about gramps dying after all. His voice woke her up. She crept out of her bedroom to find him pacing the living room in his pajamas and bare feet, talking into his cellphone.

He didn't say much and she couldn't hear the person on the other end. What he did say added more confusion, and worry on top of it.

I can't.

Please.

No no no.

His last word was *Okay,* like he surrendered to something. She slinked back to her room and had trouble getting back to sleep.

Purple streamers fluttered from her handlebars as she zipped around the corner and closed in on home. A shiny black SUV was parked in the circular driveway.

She stowed her bike on the porch as the front door swung open. A man wearing a black suit came out, tall and thin with a cadaverous face. Jessica figured he was a new assistant director at the funeral home. Who else wears black suits in Florida in the summer?

Then a second man followed, also in a black suit, carrying a briefcase. He definitely wasn't an assistant funeral director. They don't wear eyepatches or have jagged scars running down their cheeks. He was one of the biggest men she had ever seen. Not tall, but wide. He had to open the double door to fit through. A sideways giant.

She said hello, but they passed by her like she didn't exist, climbing into the SUV, the tall one holding the passenger door for the thick one.

She thought about the late-night phone call and entered the house with a bad feeling. In the living room her parents sat on the sofa doing absolutely nothing. Not talking, not watching TV, not even moving.

"Hi, honey," her mom said in an upbeat voice, eyes red and kneading a tissue. Her mom was good at a lot of things. If you gave her a glass of wine, she could twist a hula-hoop on one foot and sing *How Great Thou Art*, but she was a terrible actor.

"Hello, Jessica," her father said, staring at his knees.

"Who were those two men?"

"Sit down, sweetheart," her mom said, patting the sofa. "Your father has some big news for you."

"That's okay. I'll stand. What's going on?"

"Well," her father said. "We made a big decision. It was very difficult and I hate to spring it on you like this, but we've decided to sell the funeral home."

"That's not funny, Dad."

"It's not a joke."

"Of course it is," she said. She looked to her mother, who gave a twitchy nod of confirmation.

"We're selling Slagger-Jewell? That's crazy! Why?"

"There were a number of factors."

"Such as?"

"It feels like the right time. We've been family-owned business since the beginning and with your grandfather gone—"

"With gramps gone we're still a family. He wouldn't want this. He spent his whole life building the place. And what about me? I'm part of this family. Why wasn't I consulted? You raised me to think I would be taking over someday, like you did for gramps."

"There were other factors," he said. "We decided it wasn't healthy for a child to be raised around so much death."

"It's a little late for that. I've been helping in the embalming room since I was five. It hasn't hurt me. Does this have something to do with that phone call last night?"

"What phone call?"

He knew what phone call. She saw it in his eyes. Her own father was lying to her. She never would have conceived it was possible. "I can't even believe this is happening!" she said.

He asked her to calm down and lower her voice.

"You calm down," she said, which didn't make a lot of sense because he was already practically comatose. "What about all the people who made preneed arrangements with us? They trusted us to be there. They signed contracts."

"The buyer agreed to take over those contracts."

"What about our employees? They're family. Norma Pollinuk started there when you were my age. Are they still going to have jobs?"

"Unfortunately, the buyer is bringing in new staff, but everyone will receive a severance check."

"Who is this buyer?"

"A new company called *Snowbirds in Paradise Funeral Services.*"

"Tell them you changed your mind and they are *un*-buying it. You're just overreacting because gramps died. We'll get over it."

"I'm afraid we already signed the papers. There is one more formality." He slid a single sheet with a pen attached to it across the glass coffee table separating them. "Your grandfather left you a thirty-percent interest in Slagger-Jewell in a trust in his will. We had to include it in the sale."

"You sold my interest? Can you do that?"

"As joint executors and trustees, the will gives your mother and I discretion to use the assets for your health, education, and maintenance. That's what we're doing. Don't worry, your share of the funds will be deposited in a custodial account in your name."

"I don't care about *funds.* I want our funeral home."

He ignored her. Her mom did that sometimes, when she was worn out, but never her dad. "Nevertheless, the buyers said they would feel more comfortable with the transaction if you signed this consent form."

"No way. I don't consent to any of this."

Nothing made sense. She thought back to *Invasion of the Body Snatchers*, weighing the possibility that the people in front of her were, until recently, pods from outer space.

"Please," her father said. "There's no other choice."

"Yes, there is. I choose not to sign."

"Jessica," her mother said sharply. "Do not make this any harder on us. There are other factors we are not able to discuss with you."

"I deserve to know. That health, education, and maintenance stuff is baloney. The only problem with my health is the heart attack you just gave me. I go to public school, so my education is free. And I don't need maintenance. I'm not a car."

Her mother lost it, burying her face in her hands and sobbing.

"Sweetheart, you know we love you," her father said. "Please trust that even though you don't understand it, we're trying to do the right thing for all of us."

Right thing? Not even possible. The paper said, *Consent of Minor to Transfer of Trust Assets*. She didn't bother to read it. They just told her she didn't have a choice. She snatched up the pen.

"Where do I sign?"

Her mother pointed a trembly finger at a line marked with an X. She scribbled her name, misspelling it in case it mattered. *Jestica Jellwl.*

Chapter 4

DANNY GOT UP early and fixed the patio doorknob before hitting the ocean, paddling out on one of his custom boards. The morning sky was still pink, the clouds chalky. Another waveless South Florida day. Didn't matter. The ocean was his antidepressant, his spirits rising the moment he hit the water.

He'd done a lot of thinking since the night Grady tore into him at the Tradewinds. Grady apologized, but Danny said it wasn't necessary because he was right. He woke up on a mission, gathering the piles of Sari's photos from the kitchen counter and putting them in a box.

He did the same with the framed pictures scattered around the condo, leaving out just one. It stood alone on a side table in the living room. The last photo of them together. They were standing barefoot on the shoreline at John the Diver's annual lobster bash, smiling and squinting into the late afternoon sun. The wind had whipped Sari's sundress around her long legs.

He buried the box in a closet, realizing when he emerged he had been holding his breath the whole time. If hiding Sari in a closet was a mark of progress in the grief process, it didn't feel that way. But at least he had done something.

Tonight would be a good distraction. Fink called with the surprising news that he passed the bar exam.

"Made it by one point," he said. "Take that, *suckers*. And I moved back to Hollywood, out west. I'm sharing office space with another lawyer."

"So you're officially an attorney?"

"Benjamin Finkel, Esquire. That's me, although I still have that character fitness hearing to get through."

"What are you going to do to celebrate?"

"I don't know. Maybe order a pizza and watch some porn."

"You can do better than that. Come on over. We'll celebrate at the Tradewinds."

*   *   *

They sat on barstools at a shaky round table stabilized by a thick wad of napkins under one leg, a design feature shared by most of the Tradewinds furniture.

Danny sipped a beer. Fink slurped a piña colada through a straw with a pink parasol attached. He was preparing to explain "a slight mishap" that occurred at the bar exam.

The drinks were on Danny, thanks to a surprise sale of one of his custom boards that morning, cannabis-themed with tailfins resembling jagged marijuana leaves. It had been gathering dust in his workshop since the original buyer, a pot dealer, got busted before paying. A guy in California came across it on the Nine Lives website and snapped it up. Already sent the money. He used it to settle his tab with Grady, catch up on his HOA fees, and still had a little left.

"So what was this *slight mishap*?" Danny said.

"There was a guy in front of me whose nose made a whistling sound every time he breathed. It was crazy loud, like being trapped inside a jet engine. I couldn't concentrate. So I tapped him on the shoulder."

"Here we go," Danny said. "What'd you say?"

"Nothing bad. I explained I'm ADHD and couldn't concentrate because of the extreme amount of noise coming from his nostrils. I asked if he could please—I said please—breathe through his mouth during the exam."

"O-kay. So you asked a man to change his breathing for, what is it, like six hours?"

"Yep. That's all. Guess what he tells me? *Go fuck yourself.*"

"Ouch," Danny said.

"Well, one thing leads to another and now we're standing in the aisle. He tackles me and I fall on a woman and all three of us start wrestling around on the floor until security comes and pulls us apart."

"This was during the exam?"

"With two hundred test-takers looking on. It turned out okay though. They moved the nose-whistler and gave everyone thirty extra minutes because of the disruption. People thanked me at the end."

Danny picked up his beer. "That's wild, and you still passed. Amazing."

"Cheers to that," Fink said, and they tapped drinks.

"How does it feel to be back in Hollywood?"

"Not bad, but I need to find some clients. That's the problem with being solo. I just got my first one. My new office partner threw a case my way, which means he thinks it's a dog."

"What kind case?"

"Products liability. My client was using soup cans to make explosive devices and one blew up in his face, got a shard of metal in his eye."

"Who's he suing?"

"The soup company."

"On what ground?"

"No warning label."

Before Danny could ask one of his many questions, Fink picked up his piña colada and gave him a sudden head-jerk.

"What's wrong?"

He pointed with his eyes over Danny's shoulder.

"Danny?"

He turned to see Jessica Jewell, unmistakable in her Slagger-Jewell Funeral Home softball jersey and cap. One hand gripped the straps of a bloated backpack resting on the floor.

"Jessica?"

"It's me."

"Well, what a surprise. What's up?" He scanned the bar. "Where are your folks?"

"Could I talk to you?"

"Of course. Come on over and have a seat."

She dragged the backpack across the grimy floor and climbed onto a bar stool. "I'm here on my own. I asked someone in the building where you lived and they said the bar."

Nice. "How did you get here?"

"Walked."

"By yourself? What's in the backpack? It looks heavy."

"Just some stuff. Like I said, I need to talk to you."

"Talk away. This is Fink, my friend and former lawyer."

"Bennie Finkel," she said, surprising them both. "I saw you on the news during Danny's murder case. Nice to meet you. Could you please leave us alone? This is private."

Fink looked at Danny, who shrugged. He got up and said, "Fine. I'll be at the bar. Celebrating."

"What's wrong?" Danny said. Something, obviously.

"I'm in trouble and need someone I can trust. An adult."

"What kind of trouble? What about your mom and dad? You can trust them."

"No, I can't. Not right now."

"I don't understand."

"I'm getting to it if you'll just listen."

"Sorry. I'm all ears."

"Here's the situation ..." Sitting ramrod straight, hands folded on the sticky table, she explained her parents' surprise sale of the family funeral home.

"They didn't even tell me about it until after it was done. My whole life they raised me to believe it was my destiny to be the *Jewell* in Slagger-Jewell when my dad retired, like he did for gramps."

"That does sound strange," Danny conceded. "Why do you think they sold it?"

"They said it was *the right time,* whatever that means, and about gramps dying and me being around too much death. I think it was all bullcrap. They acted scared. My mom was crying and my dad didn't even sound like himself."

"Any idea what scared them?"

She told him about the late-night phone call and arriving home the next day to confront the two men in black suits leaving the house.

"They were scary just to look at. One guy was a tall goon and the other one had a long scar on his face and an eyepatch. He was so big he could barely fit through the door."

"Do you think it was some kind of extortion?" Danny said.

"Nope. I think they scared my parents into selling."

He resisted explaining she just defined extortion.

"My dad would never sell that place on his own choice. My gramps started it seventy years ago."

"Have you talked to them about it? Did they call the police?"

"Ha! In the last week, the only words I've heard more than *I'm sorry* are *Whatever you do, don't call the police.*"

Shannon came their way, swaying to Al Green on the jukebox. "*Let's stay together,*" she sang as she wiped the table with a bar mop, which did nothing to reduce the stickiness embedded over decades. She set down a bowl of pretzels.

"Thanks, Shannon," Danny said.

"Who's this lovely lady?"

"This is Jessica. She's, uh ..."

"His friend."

"Well, hello there, Jessica. Any friend of Danny's is a friend of mine. Can I get you anything?"

"Just water, please."

"I'll have another beer," Danny said. He waited until she walked away. "I don't know what to say. That story is a lot to digest."

"It gets worse. Two days ago my new *pod*-parents sent me to my Great Aunt Rosie's and informed me I would be staying there until further notice."

"Where did they go?"

"Nowhere as far as I know. They said it was important to them that me and Rosie get to know each other better, which is ridiculous. She doesn't want to get to know me. She hates kids."

"What makes you think that?"

"She complains every time I blink. *Don't change the channel. That's not how you pet the cat.* And she can't hear because she never wears her hearing aids. She keeps the TV so loud I have to stick wads of toilet paper in my ears."

"That doesn't mean she hates you. Maybe it really is important to your parents that you get to know each other."

"What would be the point? She's ninety-six. She'll be dead by the time I get to know her. I think they did it to try to protect me."

She scooped a handful of pretzels from the bowl. "I'm here because I need your help."

"What kind help?"

"To investigate what's going on."

"Me? Sorry to disappoint you, but I have absolutely no qualifications to be an investigator. I wouldn't know where to start."

"Don't worry about that. I have ideas. But I need an adult and you're the only one I trust."

"It's really a job for the police."

"I already told you. My dad said a million times not to call the police."

"I remember. It's just that—"

"Danny, I'll be frank with you."

Frank with you? He hadn't heard that since he was sixteen and got kicked off the high school baseball team for skipping practice after Sari broke up with him. He was an all-state pitcher. *I'll be frank with you,* his coach said. *You don't know what you've thrown away.* Danny knew, and it had nothing to do with baseball.

"I'm desperate and don't have any other place to go," Jessica said. "I thought you'd help me. But if you won't, fine. I'll be on my way." She reached for her backpack.

"Hold up. I'll listen to what you have to say. Go ahead."

"Not here," she said. "Too many people. I have another favor to ask. Can I stay with you?"

"Stay where?"

"In your condo."

"Uh, *no*. Sorry. I don't have room."

"That's a lie. The woman who told me you lived in the bar also said you have a penthouse."

"Okay, you're right. It was a lie. The truth is I can't let a runaway girl stay with me. Nothing personal."

"I'm not going to hurt you."

"That's not my worry. It's hard to explain, but society frowns on grown men taking in minor runaway girls."

"A, that's stupid if they're trying to help, and B, I'm not a runaway."

"You need to go home and work this out with your parents. I'll give you a ride."

She rolled her eyes. "Don't you listen? I told you, they don't want me at home. That's why they sent me to Aunt Rosie's. How about this? We'll call my parents and if they say it's okay, you'll let me stay with you. If not, I'll go. Deal?"

He agreed only because he was one-hundred percent certain her parents would never go for it.

Chapter 5

"I CAN'T TELL YOU how much we appreciate this, Danny," Jewell said. "Jessica likes and trusts you. We all do, including the old man."

"But I'm basically a stranger."

As he talked to her father on the cellphone he recently gave in and bought, Jessica sat across the bar table with her arms crossed, a smug smile stamped on her face.

"That's actually a good thing under the circumstances," Jewell said. "I'm sorry to be so cryptic, but there's less likelihood anyone can find her this way."

"Who's looking for her?"

"Probably no one. We're just being extra careful."

Jessica read the situation right. He sounded scared.

"Listen, Jarrod. She told me what happened, at least what she knows, about selling the funeral home. It's not for me to say, but it didn't sound kosher. If you're this worried, you need to call the police."

"We can't do that," he said quickly. "And *please* don't think about doing it yourself. We expected the whole thing to be behind us, but apparently there's a legal snag in the transaction that has to be worked out. It's just better she be out of the picture for right now."

"I'm not a bodyguard. I'm a surfboard maker. My most dangerous weapon is a Skil planer."

"We would never ask you to put yourself in danger. If you could just look after her for a couple of days, I'm sure this thing will be wrapped up."

"Isn't there someone else you can ask?"

"Just her Great Aunt Rosie. That's where she stayed the last two last nights. It wasn't working out. Needless to say, we would insist on paying you."

"It's not about money," he said. He looked out the front windows. Night had fallen. Then at Jessica, mouthing, *A deal's a deal.* "Alright. I'll make sure she's safe for tonight, but that's it. Call me in the morning. First thing."

"I will. Thank you, Danny. I'll let her aunt know. May I speak with her."

He handed the phone to Jessica.

"Mm-hm ... Yeah ... Don't worry, I'll be good. Bye," she said and handed the phone back. "Told you."

"You heard what I said to your dad. You can stay tonight. That's all I'm promising."

"I knew you wouldn't let me down."

Fink waddled over from the bar. "Danny, no offense to your little pal, but we're supposed to be celebrating."

"Sorry, Fink. Have a seat." He turned to Jessica. "Mr. Finkel just got his license to be an attorney."

"He just got it? How was he your lawyer in your murder trial if he didn't have a license?"

"You're not the first person to ask that question. In any event, I think you should let me tell him what's going on. He might be able to help."

"If you trust him."

"I do. Fink, here's the situation." Danny unpacked Jessica's story with her filling in the gaps.

"What's the name of the company that bought the place?" Fink asked.

"Snowbirds in Paradise Funeral Services," Jessica said. "Which is a weird name if you ask me. They must be new. Their website says *Under Construction.*"

"Maybe the funeral home story was made up," Fink said. "They probably want the property to develop it, for condos or a shopping center."

"Possible," Jessica said. "But I did see their name on the legal paper I signed."

"*You* signed?" Fink said.

Jessica explained about her parents making her sign the consent form giving up her thirty-percent interest in Slagger-Jewell that her grandfather left her in a trust.

"That's bizarre," Fink said. "A minor doesn't have the capacity to execute a binding legal agreement. Even I know that."

"My dad said the trust gave them discretion to sell my interest for my health, education, and maintenance, whatever that is."

"I barely passed Wills and Trusts in law school, but that sounds fishy."

"Can you research it?" Danny said.

"Sure. I need all the clients I can get. I can also poke around the state's corporate records department to find out more about this Snowbirds outfit. Who's paying my fee?"

"Unfortunately, Fink, I don't have any money right now."

"I have some," Jessica said. "In my savings account. Four-hundred and twenty-three dollars and sixty-three cents."

"That'll work as a retainer."

Danny smashed his knee against Fink's under the table.

"*Ow*—on second thought, no fee. This will satisfy my pro bono requirement, maybe even help me in my fitness hearing."

"Thank you, Mr. Finkel," Jessica said.

"You can call me Fink, kid."

"Okay, Fink. You can call me *Jessica*."

Shannon returned. "Another round, gentlemen?"

"Lamest celebration of my life, but I gotta drive," Fink said.

"I'm good," Danny said.

"More water, Jessica?"

"I'm fine. Thank you."

"Man," Fink said, watching Shannon walk away. "I haven't

seen her since your trial. Didn't you say she's married with a kid now? That's amazing. She's still a total babe. What a nice pair of—"

"Fink!" Some things never changed. Fink's boob fetish dated at least back to high school.

"Uh, shoes," Fink said. "Nice pair of shoes.

Jessica took note of Shannon's thick-soled server shoes with Velcro straps.

They parted with Fink on the boardwalk. He said he would start researching and Jessica announced her plan to conduct visual surveillance of the Slagger-Jewell Funeral Home, explaining transportation was a big reason she needed an adult's help.

She asked if Danny had binoculars. Given his spartan personal belongings, it would have been a silly question except for the fact that, like most people who live on the beach, he actually did own a pair.

A man and woman who ran a smoothie stand not far from Danny's surf shop passed them. As they exchanged waves he overheard the woman say, "I never knew Danny had a daughter. She looks just like him."

*   *   *

"So this is where it all happens," Jessica said as they crossed the threshold of Danny's condo.

"Not much happens here, but, yes, this is my place."

"I expected a penthouse to be fancier."

"It's an old building. Dump your backpack wherever you want and make yourself comfortable. I'll order the pizza."

On the elevator ride up they agreed they were famished and that a pizza would be the perfect cure. Jessica prowled the living room while Danny called in the order from the kitchen on the cordless landline. "That's right. Large veggie. Thin crust. Fifteenth floor. Thanks."

"Who's this?" Jessica called out.

The last voice he heard coming from the living room belonged to Sari. His stomach clamped as it sunk in what she was asking about.

"I mean, obviously that's you on the left," she said. "Who's the woman? She's pretty."

He exited the kitchen to find her holding the framed picture from John the Diver's beach party.

"That was ... *is* ... my wife."

"Is she dead?"

WTF?

"I'm asking because one of the most common difficulties our customers face is when to use the present or past tense in referring to their dearly beloveds. Or maybe you're just divorced."

Heat rose in his chest. "Yes. She passed."

"I'm sorry for your loss, Danny. No wonder you acted weird at my grandpa's funeral when I asked if you were married. I'm also sorry for saying *dead*. I could tell you didn't like it. Gramps taught me *passed* is just a word we use to avoid facing the truth."

"Pizza's on the way," Danny said. "Why don't you go get settled? The guestroom and bath are down that hall to the right."

"You look so happy," Jessica said, still studying the photo. "I've never seen you look happy, not that I've seen you that many times."

He snapped the frame from her hands and laid it face down on the table. "I'll show you the room," he said, snatching her backpack from the floor. It was heavy enough to tweak his back. "Follow me."

"What's behind that door?" she said as they passed Sari's room. He hadn't been in it since the day two workers showed up to take back the hospital bed.

He stopped and whirled. "Why do you have to know everything? The only room you need to worry about is the one I'm about to show you. Alright?"

"Sure. Obviously, I've already annoyed you and I've only been here, like, five seconds. Maybe it wasn't Aunt Rosie's fault after all. One of my teachers wrote in my progress notes I can be *difficult.* I don't do it on purpose. Dad says I'm just being true to myself but I think Mom agrees with the teacher."

Feeling like a jerk, Danny said, "My wife's name was Sari. She died of breast cancer, just over a year ago. That's the room she stayed in until she went to a hospice. It's a sensitive subject for me."

"I can tell," she said.

"Great. We have an understanding then. That topic is off-limits."

"No problem. Let me know if you want to talk about it."

Danny massaged his temples. What was he thinking when he agreed to this?

"This is your bedroom and through that door is your bathroom. Do you need anything?"

"Nope." She unzipped her backpack and dumped the contents in the middle of the bed, a cylindrical lump that expanded as it decompressed. "Can I use that dresser?"

"I don't think that's really necessary. You're not going to be—"

He stopped. She was already holding a hair dryer and armful of clothes.

"Yeah, go ahead."

The pizza arrived. They ate at the dining room table. Danny got real plates out of the cabinet and washed them.

"I like this pizza," Jessica said. "Nice and crisp. So, tomorrow we begin our visual surveillance of Slagger-Jewell."

"Hopefully your father will call before we need to do that."

"I wouldn't hold my breath."

"How exactly are we supposed to conduct this surveillance?" He should have objected when she mentioned it out on the boardwalk.

"There's a Denny's across the street with a perfect view."

"What are we looking for?"

"For one thing, we should be able to tell if it's really being used as a funeral home."

"Then what? You said you had *ideas*—plural."

"One idea always leads to another. That's the way it works. Don't worry."

Worry? Why would he worry? Just another day, stalking a funeral home with a twelve-year-old whose own parents are afraid to have her around. He checked the time.

"It's getting late. What's your bedtime?" Danny said.

"Whenever I feel ready."

"Well, I hope you're feeling ready because I was up surfing early and I'm tired."

"Can I take a shower first? I sweated like a pig walking from Aunt Rosie's. She lives near Young Circle."

A three-mile hike. "What did she say when you left?"

"Nothing. She was asleep. She drinks three vodka and tonics every day at four o'clock and goes to bed."

Danny washed his face and brushed his teeth while she showered, then waited in the living room watching the nightly news. Tiger Woods became the first golfer since Ben Hogan to win three majors in one year. Only twenty-five years old. That kid was something special.

Jessica emerged from the guestroom wearing black pajamas with tiny skulls on them.

"Ready," she said.

"Great." He stood and turned off the TV.

"There is one thing I need."

"What's that?"

"A hug. My mom and dad give me a hug every night before I go to bed."

"Hug? Um ... well ..." Danny leaned forward and awkwardly tapped her shoulders.

"Seriously? Even Aunt Rosie hugs better than that. Goodnight."

Chapter 6

"WOULD YOUR DAUGHTER like another refill?" Brenda asked. She wore the standard Denny's uniform, black pants and a polo shirt with the logo on one side, name on the other.

She just topped off Danny's coffee. Jessica had already polished off two cups. Since when did kids drink coffee?

He supposed the assumption they were father and daughter made sense given the lack of other reasonable explanations for why a grown man was hanging out with a tween. Their light hair made for a superficial resemblance.

They were at a window booth across the street from the funeral home. The chiseled *Slagger-Jewell* above the Corinthian columns was still there, but a newly erected sign at the corner announced *Snowbirds in Paradise Funeral Home*. A banner tied below said, *Coming Soon!*

Jessica was under the table with the binoculars.

"Jessica," he said. "The server—"

"Hold on. Well, *that's* interesting."

"She's fine for now. Thanks," Danny said and Brenda walked away.

Jessica climbed up and onto the bench with red raccoon rings around her eyes from the binocs. "Discovery!"

"Can't you just watch from up here?"

"Don't you think it would look a little strange for me to be staring out the window with binoculars all morning?"

As opposed to eating breakfast on the floor under the table?
"What did you discover?"

"First, we've already learned from the new sign that they really are planning to use it as a funeral home. But I've been watching the strangest thing. A truck backed in and some really big guys came out and started unloading caskets."

"What's strange about that? It's a funeral home."

"They were huge. Standard caskets are twenty-seven inches wide. Some of these looked almost double that. Same with the depth. Standard is twenty-three inches, but these looked thicker. Maybe longer too. I couldn't tell for sure."

"Don't some people, big people, need bigger caskets?"

"Not that many people. We would special order oversized caskets when we needed them, but I counted two dozen being unloaded. That's not all. See that hearse parked in the driveway?"

"Uh-huh."

She unwrapped the binoculars from her neck and handed them to Danny.

"Take a close look at it."

"Do I have to get under the table?"

"Very funny, Danny, but now isn't the time for jokes."

He focused in on the hearse. "It's a Cadillac. Looks brand new."

"We could never afford anything like that, which means these people have a lot of money. But that's not what's strange about it. Look closer."

"What am I looking for?"

"It's oversized too, with extra-wide doors and heavy-duty suspension. So we have two dozen oversized caskets and at least one oversized top-of-the-line hearse."

"Well, obesity rates in America are rising," Danny said.

"That's very true, but it's odd that the first thing they would do is load up on so much oversized equipment."

"I'll take your word for it. Can we go now?"

"Go? We're just getting started. Remember how I said one idea always leads to another? It did."

Danny glanced at a wall clock above the cashier stand. Her father hadn't called yet. "Let's hear it," he said.

Idea two in her investigation was to walk across the street and pay a visit.

"That way we can get an inside look at what's going on."

"And what might be our reason for popping in?"

"We're interested in making preneed arrangements for your death. I'm your daughter."

"What if someone recognizes you?"

"They won't. Dad said they fired everyone, even Norma Pollinuk. She'd been there since my dad was a kid."

Danny remembered the schoolmarm receptionist. She took an instant dislike to him when he came snooping around five years ago, pegging him as a troublemaker.

He paid the check while Jessica waited outside. The funeral home was at a busy intersection. They waited for the lights to change and used the crosswalk.

"Are you sure you want to do this?" Danny said as they reached the brick walkway. "It could be painful for you seeing a bunch of strangers running your family's business."

"I'm sure. Let me do the talking."

"Bad idea. No twelve-year-old would do the talking about her father's funeral planning."

"Danny, what do you know about preneed funeral contracts?"

"Nothing."

"Exactly. I know everything about them."

"I'll do the talking," he confirmed. "Chime in if necessary, but it's going to be suspicious if you come across as a funeral industry expert."

"Legit point," she conceded. "Just make sure you say preneed *burial* arrangements. That will get their attention better than cremation. That's where funeral homes make most of their money."

She marched to the front door and yanked the handle. "Locked," she said.

"I see that."

"The front door isn't supposed to be locked." She pounded the glass with her fist.

"Easy, easy," Danny said. "We're supposed to be prospective customers, not angry previous owners."

"I'm not previous."

"Someone's coming. Remember, I do the talking."

A short man in a black suit, with a square face and jaw to match, studied them through the glass before unlocking the door. "Whaddaya want?" he said, poking his head out.

"Hi, I'm here to see about making preneed burial arrangements," Danny said.

He looked Danny up and down. "Why would a strapping young man like you be worried about dying?"

"I'm the kind of person who always likes to be prepared," he said, which in fact was the exact opposite of him.

"Sorry, amigo," the man said. "We're not open for business yet. Come back another time." He started to close the door.

"Hold it!" Jessica said. "Since you're a new business, we were wondering if we could come in and look around, just to see if we feel comfortable here."

"Like I said, some other time."

He pulled on the door, but Jessica's foot was blocking it.

"Could we at least see your casket selection? Do you have anything in an extra-large? My dad's tall, as you can see, and a little claustrophobic."

"Move your foot or I'll break it."

Danny pulled her back and stepped chest to chest with the man. "Hey! Don't talk to her like that."

"You a tough guy?"

"Not me. But like you said, I'm strapping." It was true. Danny's muscles were ripped from a lifetime of surfing. At six-two, he towered over the man, who proceeded to slam the door in his face and relock it.

Jessica shook her head as they made their way back down the brick path. They crossed the street and got into the Hyundai before she spoke.

"I appreciate your standing up for me. It was a very fatherly thing to do. But it wasn't very smart. I doubt he would have really broke my foot. He'd go to jail. Now we won't be able to go back. We'll have to figure out another way."

He pulled onto U.S. 441, heading south toward Hollywood Boulevard.

"Something fishy is definitely going on there," she said. "You don't turn away customers in the funeral industry. Some funeral homes are losing money because too many people decided to start getting cremated. And you don't greet people by saying, *Whaddaya want?* You say, *How may we be of assistance today?*"

"Again, I'll take your word for it."

"Hey, look! It's Fink."

Sure enough. A giant-sized Fink in round gold-rimmed glasses and a three-piece suit, red hair slicked back, grinned down at them from a new billboard. A banner across the top blared, *Injured? Arrested? Think Fink.* At the bottom: *Bennie "The Hammer" Finkel. Free Consultations. Call Today.* With a number.

"The Hammer?" Jessica said. "Oh, brother."

Danny wasn't thinking about Fink or the funeral home visit. He was wondering why they hadn't heard from her father. Danny had told him to call first thing in the morning. It was almost lunchtime.

"So," Jessica said, "we made a little progress in our investigation. Now the question is what should we do next?"

"Let's call your parents."

"They're not going to be any help."

"Not for the investigation. I'm sure they miss you. Probably ready for you to come home. Here, use my cellphone." He handed it to her.

She punched in numbers and chewed on her cheek. Fifteen seconds passed, then twenty. She turned it off.

"No answer. That's weird."

"They're probably just out."

"We have an answering machine. It should have picked up. Can we go over there?"

"Excellent idea. Where do you live?"

"Not far from here. Emerald Hills."

"We're on our way." He made a U-turn.

* * *

Emerald Hills sat west of I-95 off of Sheridan Street adjacent to Topeekeegee Yugnee Park. When Danny was growing up, it was one of the neighborhoods where the rich kids lived.

"Right there," Jessica said as they approached a long low-slung cinderblock home with a two-car garage and circular driveway. Double dark-wood doors with panels of etched glass and a clay tile roof added some curb appeal.

"Park in the driveway," she said, and leapt out with keys in hand the instant the wheels stopped turning. She was already inside by the time Danny reached the door.

"Mom! Dad!"

Danny stepped into a gray-tiled foyer, the air hot and stuffy, like the AC hadn't been on for a while. He waited as Jessica sprinted back and forth across his view frame: an outdated living room with a chrome coffee table and overstuffed recliner. She ran into the garage and came back drooping.

"No car. They're not here," she said. "Wait! The answering machine."

He trailed her into a kitchen of dark oak cabinets and yellow floral wallpaper.

She held up a cord, a wall wart swinging at the end. "Unplugged. Why would the answering machine be unplugged?" She plugged it back in. "Something's wrong. Come on. We have to check around more carefully. Don't touch anything. You take that side and I'll take this side."

"What exactly are we checking for?"

With a sigh, "You were right that first night, Danny. You really aren't cut out to be an investigator. We're looking for *crime-scene* clues."

"Crime-scene?" he said. "Just because they're not home and the answering machine is unplugged? I wouldn't jump to conclusions." She had enough worries without assuming the worst.

"Do we have to argue about this now?"

He was beginning to give credence to her teacher's progress note. He reminded himself she's under a lot of strain and wandered off to explore his assigned portion of the house. One bedroom and an attached bath with wood paneling and gold shag carpet. Nothing looked disturbed.

"Danny! I found something! Quick!"

He backtracked through the living room to find her in the master bedroom pointing at the top of a walk-in closet. "Look."

All he saw was an empty closet shelf. "There's nothing there," he said.

"Exactly. That's where they keep their suitcases. They've flown the coop. Abandoned me."

"Come on, they wouldn't do that. I'm sure there's a logical explanation."

"That *is* the logical explanation. Nothing else makes sense. Maybe I've been looking at this whole situation wrong. Maybe they took the money from the funeral home sale—including my thirty percent—and went on the lam."

On the lam? What did she watch for entertainment? Fifties gangster movies? "That's not what's happening," he said. "They were scared. Remember? We both could tell that."

"Yes, but maybe they were scared of *me*, that I would figure things out before they could pull off their evil plan."

"Alright, that's enough. You don't believe that. Your parents are good people."

She squished her lips. "Yeah. For a second I liked that theory better because my other one is that someone sawed them up and stuffed them in the suitcases to carry away."

"That didn't happen either."

"How do you know?"

"Because there's no blood anywhere."

She looked around. "True. Okay, maybe you're not a terrible investigator."

"There are lots of reasons why their suitcases are gone. Maybe they moved them to the attic or lent them to a friend. When's the last time you saw them in the closet?"

"I don't remember. Long time ago."

"See? Do your parents have a cellphone we could call?"

"Dad got one for funeral home business a few months ago, but I don't know the number."

"I'm sure they're just out," he said.

Although he was getting less sure. Maybe they took off and went into hiding. But how could they do that without taking Jessica? Like she said, things didn't make sense. "Let's leave a note asking them to call as soon as they get home."

"Okay." She picked up a marker and wrote on a dry erase board mounted next to the fridge. *Mom and Dad — Call your daughter as soon as you can. You know how to find me.*

"I wrote it so it didn't leave any clues about my location."

"Very clever. Let's go."

Chapter 7

BACK AT THE BEACH, Danny spotted Grady inside the Tradewinds cleaning fish on the bar. He'd watched him from the balcony that morning, wading into the ocean with his favorite surfcasting rod. Surfcasting was to Grady what surfing was to him. Church.

"Let's stop in the bar for a minute," Danny said. He knew Grady would be wondering about the girl from nowhere who showed up last night.

"Already? It's barely noon."

"Just to say hello."

The place was empty. Scratchy Gaelic folk music played on a portable record player under the bar.

"Morning, captain," Danny said.

"Morning, mate. Who's this?"

"Jessica," she said. "Danny's friend."

"Hello, Jessica. I'm Grady."

"Nice to meet you."

"Likewise. So you're a friend of Danny's, huh?"

"That's right. We go way back."

Grady scratched his white whiskers. "That so."

"She's the little girl from the funeral home," Danny explained. "I told you about her back when everything happened."

"The hamster kid?"

"If that helps you remember."

"What's she doing here?"

Danny looked at Jessica, who vigorously shook her head. "Her family is having some issues and her parents asked me to look after her."

"Why you?"

He shrugged.

"Hell, I don't need to know anything," Grady said. "Any friend of Danny's is a friend of mine."

"That's what everyone says. I guess you can tell him, if he can keep a secret. But no one else."

*   *   *

When they returned to the condo, Danny opened the patio doors to let in the ocean breeze. A seagull basked in the sun on the balcony railing.

"Look, a seagull," he said.

Jessica stood stoically in the center of the living room, gazing at the ocean. "Whoop dee doo. Only the nine-thousandth one I've seen today."

"Well, they don't usually fly this high."

"As you like to say, I'll take your word for it."

Her mood had declined since they left her house. His too. He was stuck with her until her parents called back. "What would you like to do?" he said.

"I don't care."

"Have you ever tried surfing? I could give you a lesson."

"No, thanks."

"It's pretty fun stuff. Do you like the ocean?"

"Not really."

"How come?"

"Why do you have to know everything?" she said sharply.

He was taken aback until her smirk reminded him he said the same words when she asked about Sari's room.

"If you must know, I'm afraid of drowning," she said. "And now you're probably thinking I'm a liar because I said at my grandfather's funeral I wasn't afraid of death."

"No, I wasn't thinking that at all."

"*Death* and *manner of death* are two completely different things. I'm not afraid of dying, but I don't want to go by drowning. Not being able to breathe is my biggest fear."

"Did you have some kind of incident when you were younger?"

"One time an undertow sucked me under the water and my dad barely had time to rescue me from certain death."

"Yikes. How deep was the water?"

"About two feet."

"Oh."

"I have news for you. A person can drown in two inches. It's happened. If you don't believe me, look it up."

"I believe you."

"What's your biggest fear?" she said.

"I'm not sure. Maybe myself."

"What in the world is that supposed to mean?"

He didn't know. It just popped out. He wasn't afraid of death either. Sometimes he wished for it. Maybe that was it. "Nothing. Do you know how to swim?"

"Of course. I took swimming lessons. I'm not afraid of pools. Just the ocean. It's too big, and there's waves, and that undertow is the worst."

"I could guarantee you wouldn't drown. I'd be right there with you."

"You can go. I'll stay here."

"And do what?"

"Watch TV or something."

His phone rang. Let it be her parents. But it was just Fink.

"Danny, I wanted to give you an update on my research about Snowbirds in Paradise. Can you meet at the Tradewinds at five?"

"Yeah, we can do that."

"We?"

"Me and Jessica."

"She's still with you?"

"Mm, yeah."

"Alrighty then. I'll see you there."

Chapter 8

"SO WHAT HAS *The Hammer* learned?" Danny said.

They opted for a booth this time, Fink complaining the bar stools were defectively designed because they didn't accommodate his lopsided posterior. Danny and Jessica shared one of the benches.

"You saw my billboard?"

"Hard to miss."

"That's the idea. You have to advertise in this business to stand a chance. It's cutthroat, and expensive. I had to take out a bank loan for the billboard. Did you know Florida has more than a hundred thousand lawyers?"

Shannon strolled up in white shorts and a tight black top with a scoop neck. "Oye, gang," she said. "What's it going to be?"

Danny was studying the beer list when she said, "What are you looking at?"

He raised his eyes expecting to see Fink getting busted for sneaking a peek at her cleavage, but she was talking to Jessica, who was examining her feet.

"Your shoes," she said. "Fink really likes them and I'm just trying to figure out why."

They were the same Velcro-strapped server shoes she wore every shift.

Fink coughed. "Well, they just look really comfortable."

Danny went with a beer. Fink got a margarita. Jessica ordered coffee.

"Maybe you shouldn't drink coffee at night," Danny said. "It'll keep you awake." She already had the two cups at Denny's that morning.

"Fine, *Dad*. I'll have the usual. Water."

"Here's what I found," Fink said. "I searched the state's corporate records to see who's behind Snowbirds in Paradise. Corporate records are public in Florida, but Snowbirds used a loophole to keep their address and officers anonymous."

He explained it involved hiring a registered agent to file records and using the agent's address as the business address.

"To hide the officers' names, all you have to do is form two LLCs, limited liability corporations, each one listing the other as manager. And it's perfectly legal! Is that not beautiful? How can anyone not love a legal loophole? I mean, not in this case, but as a general principle."

"It stinks," Jessica said. "So that's what you found out? Nothing?"

"I'm just getting started. When did your grandfather die? Was it more than ten days ago?"

Jessica did the math. "Eleven including today."

"Florida law requires that a will be filed with the probate court within ten days of death. I checked the county clerk's office this morning and nothing's been filed."

"What does that mean?" Danny said.

"Not sure. As executors under the will, her parents would be the ones obligated to file it. No idea why they didn't. In any event, the kid said—"

"Jessica," she said.

"Noted," Fink said. "Jessica said her grandfather left her a thirty-percent interest in the funeral home in a trust and her parents sold it to Snowbirds relying on their discretion to use the trust assets for her health, education, and maintenance."

"That's what they told me," she said.

"I talked to an estate lawyer who said that language is common in a trust, almost boilerplate. But she also said it's intended for unforeseen expenses over time, not as an excuse to liquidate the trust right off the bat."

"Interesting," Danny said. "Her father told me there was a *legal snag* in the transaction that was holding things up and that's why he was asking me to shelter her for a few days. Maybe that's the snag."

"Could be. Once the will gets filed for probate, a judge could rescind the Slagger-Jewell transaction over it. Jessica might even have a claim against her parents for breaching their fiduciary duty to her."

"Sue my parents?"

"Not saying you should, but families get in legal disputes over wills every day."

He vacuumed the remains of his margarita with a straw. "That's all I have right now. I'll keep working on it. I also came by to see if you still have that *Time* magazine with the picture of you and me after we won your murder trial."

"Maybe in a box somewhere. What do you want with that?"

"My fitness hearing with the state bar is in a few days. I thought it might impress the judges."

"Come on up with us and I'll look for it."

In the elevator, Jessica claimed dibs on pushing the PH button.

Danny had to climb the pulldown ladder and crawl through his attic space to find a box labeled with a thick marker, THE MESS, under a snowy layer of dust.

"Here," he said when he wrangled it down the ladder steps. "You can take the whole thing. I don't know why I kept it."

Jessica yawned and said, "This is boring. I'm going to my room."

Danny watched her disappear down the hallway. "I'm worried about that kid."

Fink threw his hands in the air. "Earth to Danny. How long do you intend to let this go on?"

"What?"

"Having an unrelated female minor living with you. In case you weren't aware, it's a bit dicey from a societal point of view."

"I know. Believe me. I don't know what to do with her."

He had snuck away to call her parents twice during the day. The answering machine picked up both times. He left messages to call back, saying it was urgent.

"I was hoping to unload her today, but her parents disappeared."

"Well, you'd better do something, fast."

Danny walked him to the door. "Thanks for your help. I owe you one."

"Then see if you can fix me up with Shannon."

"She's married, with a new baby."

"Details, details."

"You're disgusting," Danny said.

"Of course."

Danny went to the master bath to take a shower. He twisted the nozzle to get the massage blasts. His muscles were tight as cables. Fink was right. He needed to extricate himself from this arrangement. But how?

When he came out, the condo was quiet. The door to Jessica's room was shut. He went to the kitchen and microwaved the leftover pizza from the night before.

"Jessica," he said. "You up for some soggy pizza?"

No response.

"Hey Jessica," he said louder.

He walked down the hall and knocked. "Jessica?" He knocked again before easing open the door. The room was dark. He turned on the overhead light.

The bed was neatly made. Her belongings were gone. Panic wasn't part of Danny's makeup, but that's exactly what he did. He was responsible for her.

He ran through the condo, even checked Sari's room, closed for more than a year. Dark, musty, and empty.

The balcony. One of the doors was open. Could she? Would

she? He ran out and gripped the railing, scanning below. Nothing, but then where?

There. Down the boardwalk, almost out of sight, heavy backpack bouncing on her shoulders with each determined step.

"Jessica!" She didn't look back.

He darted out the door in bare feet, poking the elevator button like he could will it to go faster. When it didn't work, he took off down the stairs, ramming his toes into the railing post on the sixth-floor landing. She was nearly to the paddleball courts at Garfield Street by the time he caught up with her, panting and squeezing his screaming foot.

"Jessica. Hold up."

She kept walking.

"Stop. What's going on?"

She wheeled, hands on her hips, eyes burning. "If you wanted to *unload* me, all you had to do was tell me to leave. Not talk about me behind my back. I thought you were my friend." The sadness in her eyes was heavy enough to sink a ship.

"I'm sorry. I don't want to unload you. I used the wrong word."

"What's the right word?"

"All I want is for you to be back safe with your parents, where you belong. But until that happens, I'm telling you right now, I'll do my best to ... be present for you."

"*Present?* Should I take attendance?"

"*Here* for you. Is that better?"

"What about *society?* I heard everything."

"I told you before, it's an unusual situation."

She stretched her neck closer, squinting like she was trying to read him from the inside.

An elderly couple, part of society, paused their evening stroll to observe the spirited encounter between the wet-haired man in bare feet and young girl wearing the swollen backpack.

Danny smiled and waved. "Can we *please* go back?" he said.

"Only if you're sure."

"I'm sure."

"Swear?"

"Yes."

"Okay. Just remember, my parents were the ones who wanted you to take care of me. It's none of society's business."

He offered to carry her backpack. She said she was fine.

Chapter 9

DANNY PEEKED IN her room the next morning to make sure she hadn't taken off during the night. She was already up and in the kitchen.

"Danny," she called down the hallway. "How do you like your coffee? Did my parents call last night?"

"Black is fine. No, they didn't call."

He called them three times after she went to bed, getting the machine each time, not bothering to leave more messages. Hours of tossing and turning brought him to a shockingly obvious conclusion: *Call the police.*

"Here," she said when he entered the kitchen, handing him a white mug with a black-lettered inscription. *Thoughts that do often lie too deep for tears. — William Wordsworth*

"I bet Sari gave that cup to you. That's why I picked it," she said, sipping from her own steaming mug. "Who's William Wordsworth?"

Danny gave the cup to Sari. She was a poet, a real one, working on her fourth book of poems when she died. The day they met at age ten, when her family moved from New Jersey into the house next door on Sand Dollar Lane, they awkwardly agreed "to play."

What do you like to play? Danny asked.

I like to write poetry.

Poetry? What else do you like?

Sari laughed and they ended up playing ping pong in her garage. In the years after he lost her the first time, he came to appreciate the poet's gift for expressing feelings that, as Wordsworth
put it, were too deep for tears.

"An English poet," Danny said and changed the subject. "How
long have you been drinking coffee?"

"Not that long. Maybe five years."

"And your parents let you?"

"No, I hide it. I have a coffee maker in my closet."

"Really?"

"Can't you tell a joke? Of course they let me. Why wouldn't
they?"

He set his cup down. "Jessica, I came to a decision last night.
We have to call the police."

"We can't. Dad made me promise. Calling the cops scared
him more than anything."

"But if your parents are missing."

"Then we'll call. Let's give them one more day. I think they
went into temporary hiding."

Danny wanted to ask the obvious questions: Why wouldn't
they take you? Why haven't they called? But she didn't know the
answers any better than he did. "One more day," he said. "That's
it. If we haven't heard from them by tomorrow morning, we contact the police."

"Deal."

"In the meantime, I need to go to my surf shop today to do
some work."

The five grand from his recent surfboard sale was already
running out. He'd been emailing back and forth with a South
Beach hip-hop star named Lil Lansky, née Rasheed Williams,
who was interested in a custom board with his picture on it and
solid gold inlay around the nose and rails. Danny said he'd work
up a design.

"Do you mind going with me?"

"That's fine," she said. "I've never been to a surf shop. But first I need another cup of coffee."

* * *

"The parking lot is that way," she said when they exited the building.

"Don't need a car. We can just walk there down the boardwalk."

"That's pretty cool," she said. "Why do you call it the boardwalk when there aren't any boards?"

"Good question. I remember wondering the same thing as a kid. Technically, it's a broadwalk, but folks who grew up here still call it the boardwalk."

Reaching the shop, he noticed the missing *v* in the weathered Nine Lives sign. It now read *Nine Li_es.*

"You need to fix your sign," Jessica said.

"It just happened," he said, fumbling with his keys.

"And clean the windows. I can't even see inside. As my dad always says, you never get a second chance to make a first impression."

The windows needed more than cleaning. They needed scraping. A crust of salt covered them like burnt icing.

He had let the place go. He opened the shop five years ago with the last of the lottery money, riding a tsunami of renewed hope and motivation after reuniting with Sari. Every morning began with him squeegeeing the salt spray from the windows.

He turned on the lights and AC and flipped the *Closed* sign to *Open.*

"It's smells funky in here," Jessica said. "Like mildew."

"I haven't been here for a while," he said.

Racks of surfboards lined one wall, everything from shiny new factory models to battered rentals with a few of Danny's custom jobs scattered in between. Surfwear displayed on hooks covered the opposite wall. Two circular clothes racks and a lacquered table consumed most of the floor space. The table held board wax, surfboard leashes, Nine Lives hats and tees, a little bit of everything.

At the back, a dust-covered display cabinet held a cash register on top and scattered beach jewelry inside. Suspended from the ceiling was a vintage ten-foot longboard made of wood.

Jessica picked up one of the merch hats. "*Nine Lives Surf Shop.* How did you come up with the name?"

It was Grady's idea, back when he was worried Danny was running out of chances. "Long story. You like that hat?"

"I like the kitty in the logo."

"You can have it."

"Okay, thanks." She put it on and it plopped down over her eyes.

"Let me help you adjust the size."

"Can I ask a question? How do you expect to sell anything if you keep the store closed all the time?"

"That's a good question," was all he said before heading to the back. She followed him.

He was never into the retail side of things. His passion was shaping boards, a skill he learned in high school working at the Lost Wave Surf Shop under the tutelage of Ben Keahilani, a former surf champion from Honolulu.

"This is the workshop," he said, entering a dusty room and pulling the chain on a florescent light fixture hanging from the ceiling. He switched on the computer.

"P-U, this room is more toxic than an embalming room."

"Put on that respirator mask over there."

"How come you don't wear one?"

"I do, sometimes."

"I don't want to wear one if you don't. Why is everything such a mess?"

"I like it that way."

The walls were plastered with surf posters, board templates, and other paper detritus tacked up with push pins. Piles of saws, planers, and other tools filled gray metal shelves mounted on angle brackets. Paint and chemical containers crowded the floor space below. The back wall held up rolls of fiberglass and stacks of foam surfboard blanks.

"Look at the size of those waves," Jessica said, pointing at one of the posters. "The surfers are just little specks. They look like they're going to get swallowed. Have you ever surfed on anything like that?"

"When I was younger and braver." He spent a summer in Australia tackling thirty-foot waves at Shipstern Bluff on the southeast coast of Tasmania. They scared the hell out of him even then. So did the great white sharks that liked to hang out there.

"Hey, this is going to take me a while. Do you want to mind the store while I work?"

"Sure. I'm great at sales. Dad used to let me help families pick out caskets."

The first thing he did was search the internet for Rasheed Williams, aka Lil Lansky. Danny had heard of him, but didn't know he was such a big deal. A music blog said he took his name from Meyer Lansky, a mafia kingpin from back in the day. The old mafia bosses loved South Florida. Rumor had it Lansky once owned a house in Hollywood. A hometowner.

He called Gaspar, his airbrush artist who moved on after Danny let the shop go to seed, offering him a twenty-five percent split to do the artwork if a deal with Rasheed went through. He accepted right away. Said he'd been painting motorcycle gas tanks and would love to get back to surfboards because of the larger canvas. The man was a true artist.

He was experimenting with some new design software when the bells nailed to the front door jingled.

"Welcome to the Nine Lives Surf Shop! How may we be of assistance today?"

He smiled and listened. He couldn't make out the man's response, but Jessica's boisterous voice rang clear and distinct.

"Well, as you can see, we have a wide selection of excellent surfboards."

Mumble, mumble.

"Hold on just one sec. Let me double-check with my boss. I'll be right back."

She flew into the workshop. "Danny, what's the best board you have for a beginner, a girl? A man wants to buy one for his daughter the same age as me. It's for her birthday."

He started to stand and replanted himself. Let the kid have some fun. No one walks in off the boardwalk and buys a board on first sight.

"There's a pink seven-footer at the far end of the rack. Seven feet is a good length for beginners and the board was designed especially for women and girls by a surf champion named Sally Fitzgibbons."

"What's so great about it?"

"It's called a soft-top. Feel it and you'll see why. It's made of light foam and has three tailfins. It's stable with a rounded nose. That's the front."

"How much does it cost?"

"Four-fifty."

"Four hundred and fifty dollars? Those things are expensive."

"I think that's the price. There should be a tag on it."

"Okay."

She left the room. He couldn't help but eavesdrop.

"This is the one I recommend. It was designed by a surf champion named Sally Fitzgerald."

Fitzgibbons, but close.

"She made it especially for girls, so what could be better than that? It's seven feet long, which is perfect for beginners. It's called a soft-top. Feel here and you can see why. Believe me, she'll appreciate that the first time it conks her in the head."

Did he mention that? It's a common selling point, especially for beginner boards.

"And look: *three* tailfins. See the board next to it? It costs twice as much and only has one. Then there's this nice round nose, very smooth. And it's stable. I cannot overstress the importance of that. She doesn't want to be falling off and drowning every five seconds."

Mumble, mumble.

"Don't worry about that. Pink is super-cute for any age. At the funeral home where I used to work we had a pink casket and it was one of our most popular models."

The man asked about price.

"Regularly it's four-fifty. But since it's for your daughter's birthday and we strongly believe in girl power, I'll let it go today for four twenty-five."

She came back to the workshop. "How do I work the credit card machine?"

*   *   *

It took a couple hours, but Danny came up with a design sample for Rasheed, a tri-fin shortboard with artwork borrowed from one of Lil Lansky's album covers. It featured Rasheed standing god-like on a mountaintop, heavily laden with gold chains, muscled and tatted arms crossed, lightning flashing all around him. He knew Gaspar could bring it to life on a board.

He sent the design to Rasheed, suggesting a twenty-five thousand dollar fee. Why not? The blog said he was worth a hundred million. He recommended against the gold inlay unless Rasheed intended the board purely for display.

He shut down the computer and went out front to find Jessica sitting on a stool behind the now gleaming display case reading a *Surfer* magazine.

"I sold the stick, four bars of board wax, and a Nine Lives keychain," she said.

"Stick?" An insider's term for surfboard.

"I read it in this magazine. And I cleaned the glass on your dirty display case."

"I can tell. Thank you. You've done an amazing job. You sold more than I have in a month."

"Well, your sales would improve if you were actually here more often."

"I know. You already mentioned that. Ready to go grab some lunch?"

"Right after I finish this article," she said. "Why is that surfboard hanging from the ceiling so much longer than the other ones? There's one in this magazine too."

"It's called a longboard. Back in the day all surfboards were longboards. They're great to learn on because they're very stable, and pros can do amazing tricks on them. They're also good for tandem surfing."

"What's tandem?"

"Two people on the same board. Come to think of it, remember I offered you that surfing lesson?"

"Yeah, but ... you know, like I said."

"I remember. But if the lesson was tandem on a longboard, you'd definitely have nothing to worry about because I'd be right there holding onto you the whole time. That's how a lot of kids get introduced to surfing."

"I'll think about it. How much does that cost?" She pointed to a necklace of braided twine interlaced with puka shells.

"Why? You like it?"

"It's pretty."

"Take it."

"Don't feel like you have to give me stuff because I'm a kid or you feel sorry for me. I have money. Thirty-two dollars in my backpack at the condo."

"I don't feel sorry for you," he lied. "Consider it part of your sales commission for the day. You earned it."

He reached into the display cabinet and grabbed the necklace, helping her fasten it from the back.

She looked at her reflection in the glass display top. "Haha, I look like a surfer girl with my cap and necklace."

"Well, you don't to want be a poseur, so think about that lesson."

"I'm starving," she said.

They ate fried grouper sandwiches with hush puppies and coleslaw at a seafood joint on the boardwalk. He needed to go grocery shopping and buy some healthier, and cheaper, food.

He was about to suggest it when she said, "Can we go back and check my house again? See if anything changed since yesterday?"

"Let's do that." Still nothing from her parents.

"Except we'll be late reopening the shop."

"Don't worry about it."

*   *   *

On their second trip to Emerald Hills, he took Hollywood Boulevard and cut through on Park Road, passing within blocks of the houses and elementary school where he and Sari grew up together.

"Let's look around," Jessica said as they stepped into the gray-tiled foyer. She didn't bother to call out for her parents this time.

Danny followed her as they moved silently from room to room.

"Everything looks the same to me," Danny said when they got to a bedroom set up as a home office.

"The same but different. Look at my dad's desk. Too neat. He's messy. He doesn't straighten it like that unless my mom gets on him. She's the neat one."

"Maybe she got on him."

"I'm almost positive it was messier yesterday. And in my room, one of my Stephen King books was in the wrong place. I keep them in alphabetical order, but *Cujo* was in front of *Carrie*."

Stephen King. No surprise.

"It's like someone was looking for something and tried to make it look like they weren't here," she said.

"Maybe you misplaced it by accident."

"You always doubt me."

"I just don't want you to worry unnecessarily."

At the kitchen threshold, she stopped cold. "Now can I worry?"

She was pointing at the dry erase board. Someone had erased her message. She ran for the answering machine. "It's unplugged again." She popped open the top. "And the tape is gone."

Danny thought about the two messages he left. Did he mention Jessica on them? And did he say, *Jarrod, this is Danny*? Or *Jarrod, this is Danny Teakwell*? If he gave his last name, they'd be easier to track down if someone was looking for her.

They checked the doors and windows. No sign of forced entry.

"I wonder how they got in," Jessica said after they relocked the house and sat in Danny's Hyundai with the windows down and AC blasting, waiting for it to cool down.

Danny was more worried about who *they* were than how they got in. "Do you think it's possible your parents came home between yesterday and today?"

"Why would they do that without telling me?" she said.

Why would they do a lot of things? He was torn between worrying about them and being insanely pissed off at them for leaving their daughter in this situation.

"I don't know," he said. He raised the windows and turned down the roar of the AC. It was time. "Hey, I know we said we'd wait until tomorrow before calling the police, but the day is pretty much over."

"It's only three o'clock. We have to wait. You don't understand. You didn't see the petrified look on my dad's face when he told me not to call them."

"Don't take this personally," Danny said. "You know I like your dad, but do you think maybe he didn't want you to call the police because he's involved in something he shouldn't be? Some kind of crime or something? Just throwing it out there."

"I doubt it. Dad's honest. He never took advantage of people by trying to upsell them stuff they didn't need, which is easy to do in our business. He even got a national award for excellence."

"Well, the only other possibilities I can think of are even worse, and you and I can't solve this on our own. The police have powers and resources we don't have."

"I know what you're saying, but I don't want to go against my dad, what he said."

"I respect that, but circumstances might have changed since he said it. Your parents might be in trouble. Hopefully not, but just in case, we shouldn't sit around wasting time."

"I guess you're right."

He jammed the car in gear and burned rubber out of the driveway before she could change her mind.

*　*　*

The police station was a multi-story concrete block with few windows. Painted gray, it could double as a giant mausoleum. He glided into a parking space and turned off the motor. "Ready?"

"No," Jessica said.

"Don't worry." He'd thought about it on the way over, the best course of action. "I know a detective. We'll ask for him and make sure he knows whatever we say needs to be kept confidential."

Detective Emilio Rodriguez, who hunted and threatened to shoot Danny on sight five years ago when he was a supposedly dangerous fugitive. They made up in the end. Rodriguez admitted he made a mistake and Danny didn't hold grudges.

He pushed open the car door as his cellphone trilled. The damn things were a nuisance. Last week he almost plowed into a woman talking on one straight through a red light.

He dug it out of the deep front pocket of his board shorts. All in all, he wasn't in a good mood when he pushed the answer button and said, "What do you want?"

"Danny, this is Jarrod Jewell."

Chapter 10

"**WELL, IT'S ABOUT** time," Danny said. "Where are you?"

A hollow laugh. "Where am I? In big trouble. That's where. I'm sorry for the delay in calling. It couldn't be helped."

"Are you okay."

"At the moment? Yes."

"How about your wife?"

"Same."

Jessica tugged his arm. "Is it my dad?"

"Yes. He's okay. Your mom too."

"Dad! Let me talk to him."

"In a minute. I need to talk to him first, privately." He restarted the car and turned the AC up. "I'll be right back. You stay here."

He found shelter from the blazing sun in a spot of shade offered by a tall skinny palm. "Alright, I'm alone," he said.

"How's Jessica?" Jewell said.

"How's Jessica? She's confused and worried about her parents, who she thinks abandoned her. Didn't you get my messages? You ask me to take care of your daughter, then disappear? What the hell is going on?"

"You have every right to be upset. I apologize again."

"By the way, we're in the parking lot of the police station right now about to go inside and—"

"No, don't do that!"

"Let's start with that. What is up with you and the police?"

"Probably best if I start at the beginning."

And so he did. He was home mowing the lawn when two men in black suits showed up unannounced, the *big guy* and the *scarecrow* he called them. They asked if they could go inside to discuss some funeral business.

"Right out of the blue, they offered to buy Slagger-Jewell. It caught me by surprise. I brushed them off, said I appreciated it, but could never sell our family business. My father had died only a few days before. The big guy offered more money. When I said thanks but no thanks and tried to show them the door, he threatened me."

"How?"

"Said if I refused to sell, he'd kill us all. Me, Jessica, and Julie, my wife. Said he'd cut us into a hundred pieces and feed us to the fish. If we called the police, it would be a thousand pieces, and done slowly."

"He just up and threatened you? Just like that?"

"Just like that, like a switch flipped. It seemed obvious that was his backup plan from the beginning. And it didn't come across as a bluff. So to answer your question, that's 'what's up' with the police."

"What do you know about the two men? Jessica already told me what they look like."

"Not much. I know the big guy's in charge."

"What about the other one? The scarecrow."

"He stayed quiet the whole time, but seemed even scarier somehow. Maybe it was the look in his eyes, like he wanted to skip any negotiations and go straight to the cutting-into-pieces part."

"He didn't say anything?"

"One word. When I resisted, the big guy asked him in Spanish what he thought they should do. I minored in Spanish in college, knew it would be good for the business in South Florida. He said, *Matarlos*. Kill them.

"I said I had to think about it, talk to my wife. The big guy said think fast. I won't lie. I was terrified, mostly for Jessica and Julie. When he called two nights later, I agreed to sell. They came back the next day with the legal papers to sign. I got a wire transfer from a bank in the Caymans that night."

"They paid you?"

"Yes, and a fair price. That's what makes the whole thing even weirder. Never tried to lowball me. It seemed like they just really wanted Slagger-Jewell."

Shouting from the car: "Danny, what's taking so long? I want to talk to my parents."

"Just a couple more minutes."

"Give it to me straight," Jewell said. "Is Jessica okay?"

He felt bad for yelling at the guy. Who wouldn't be scared?

"Like I said, she's worried and confused, but she seems to be holding up. She's a tough kid, as I'm sure you know. Why did you send her away? Why not take her with you?"

"After we signed the papers, I thought the danger was over. I was sick about giving in and selling the business, but my family's safety was all that mattered to me."

"What happened?"

"My dad gave me a copy of his will years ago. With everything going on after he died, I hadn't got around to looking for it. The night I agreed to sell I found it in a file cabinet.

"Turned out he left Jessica a thirty-percent interest in Slagger-Jewell in a trust. I called the big guy the next morning to tell him, hoped he'd see a complication he didn't need and go away."

"I guess he didn't."

"No such luck. He sent someone to pick up the will copy, a blond guy with glasses. When the big guy and scarecrow came with the papers to sign that afternoon, he said his lawyer had come up with a work-around about the trust."

"The health, education, and maintenance thing. Jessica told me."

"That and a document saying Jessica consented to everything. I had to make her sign it. I never felt lower in my life, but kept telling myself, *My family is safe. My family is safe.* I thought for sure that was the end of it."

"What happened?"

"He called the next day. Said he hired a new lawyer, making a point of noting his previous one was now practicing from the bottom of the ocean. The new lawyer said Jessica's consent form was worthless. She also had doubts about whether a probate court would approve of me selling her interest under the maintenance provision."

Pretty much what Fink had said.

"Hurry up," Jessica yelled.

Danny held up a *Just a second* finger.

"He told me to stay put while they figured out a solution. That's when I sent Jessica to her Aunt Rosie's. Julie and I sat at home waiting. A black SUV kept cruising by our house. It was obvious they were watching us. I started thinking, what if they can't figure out a solution? Then what? So we took off."

"Where are you?"

"In a hotel up in Boca."

"Why didn't you take Jessica?"

"We were planning to come get her once we knew we were safe."

"And?"

"We're not. They attached a GPS tracker to our car and found us within an hour."

Yelling in Spanish in the background.

"What's that?" Danny said.

"I'm at a payphone in the back of a convenience store next to the bathrooms. I told them we needed some supplies. There's a guy waiting outside for me in a car. I ditched my cellphone at the beginning so they couldn't track my calls to you and Jessica, and they took out the room phone at the hotel. That's why I haven't been able to call sooner."

"Where do things stand right now?" A pint-sized shadow suddenly appeared behind him. "Hold on, Jarrod. Go back to the car."

"I'm going to die of old age by the time you let me talk to my parents, which means they'll have already been dead for like three decades."

"Just a couple more minutes."

"That's what you said two hours ago."

"It was more like a couple minutes ago, but this time I mean it. Please go back to the car. We're almost done."

She grumbled and stomped back to the Hyundai, leaning against the side with her arms crossed.

"I'm back," he said.

"Is she being difficult?" Jewell said. "She has a reputation for it."

"No, especially given the circumstances. Go ahead."

"Where things stand is they offered me a new deal, which like the old one, they made clear was a deal I couldn't refuse."

"Stop there. Who exactly is *they*?"

"Definitely not just the two guys. There has to be a bigger organization behind them."

"Like a mob organization?"

"Seems like it."

"Why would they want to get into the funeral business?" Danny said.

"Not sure. Maybe the same reasons mobs have always infiltrated legitimate businesses. Gain respectability, launder money, avoid taxes. Meyer Lansky once bragged the mafia was bigger than U.S. Steel."

Lil Lansky's namesake.

"So what's the new deal?" Danny said.

"Let me preface it by saying feel free to call me a coward. I already think it."

Jewell explained the big guy ordered him and his wife to stay at the Boca hotel while they prepared a new forged will that omitted Jessica's share and left everything to Jewell.

"They want me to file it with the probate court. Since I'm my father's only survivor, they don't think anyone will question it. It won't hurt Jessica. I'm going to deposit thirty percent of the purchase price in a custodial account in her name. After that, the big guy said we're free and clear. I think he's being straight about it. In the meantime, we're being well-treated."

"How long is it supposed to take?"

"He said it could take a week for the forgery to be prepared. So I'm asking if you could possibly take care of Jessica until then."

"A whole week?"

"I wish there was another way. It's too dangerous to bring her up here."

"*Dan-nee.* I'm not getting any younger."

"Almost done," he said with a faux smile. "Look, Jarrod, I know you're caught in a bad situation, but are you sure this is the best way to go? If you call the cops, they might be able to come rescue you."

"Too risky. Who knows how far the reach of the organization extends? Or how quick they'd be to kill us if the cops showed up? And what about after? The people guarding us are just flunkies. The big guy and scarecrow only show up when they need something. We'd always be targets."

"But—"

Jewell cut him off. "I don't know if you're married or have kids. Maybe you don't understand. I have to do whatever I can to protect Julie and Jessica. Unfortunately, because I'm a mortician and not an action hero, giving in seems like the easiest way out."

Danny did understand, partly. In his frenzied search for Sari five years ago, he not only would have done anything, he pretty much did.

"Okay," he said. "I'll take care of her, but I'll leave it to you to explain it to her. Does anyone know she's with me?"

"I hope not."

Danny thought again about what he might have said on the

missing answering machine tape. "One more thing. Someone was in your house. They unplugged the answering machine and took the tape, and erased a message Jessica left for you on the whiteboard in the kitchen."

"Probably so there'd be no evidence around if someone came to check on us."

"Jessica thinks they were searching for something."

"The original of the old man's will. They're obsessed with finding it so they can destroy it."

"Do you know where it is?"

"They've been pressuring me with the same question. I lied and said I didn't know if the original even existed. But I do. Do you remember me telling you back when we met about my father liking to take naps in a casket?"

"I do. It was pretty unforgettable. As was your father."

"He loved that casket, even had it customized. With memory foam for his back and a hidden compartment to keep certain things private."

"What kinds of things?"

"Viagra the size of horse pills and a nineteen sixty-six issue of *Playboy* featuring Jane Fonda. He had a thing for her."

"Why are you telling me this?"

"Because that's also where he kept his will. I figure as long it remains missing, it might give my family some extra protection. It could unravel the Slagger-Jewell sale and start a chain reaction. Once I file the forgery, we're expendable if they can find and get rid of the original."

"You said you believed the big guy was being straight with you."

"I do, but there's no guarantee. Besides, he's just one guy."

"Where's the casket now?"

"That's a big problem. Still in the embalming room at Slagger-Jewell, unless they've already thrown it out."

"That is a big problem. So to be clear, you have no clue about who the two men are?"

"None. They didn't use names and all the documents said Snowbirds in Paradise Funeral Services, LLC."

"And no guess about why they would go through so much trouble to acquire Slagger-Jewell?"

"Only what I said."

"Alright. Hold on while I get Jessica."

"One last thing," Jewell said.

"I know. Don't call the police."

Chapter 11

LUIS CARMILLION SAT in the new Brickell Avenue office suite for Snowbirds in Paradise Funeral Services taking in the turquoise panorama of Biscayne Bay. He breathed deeply, imagining the salty sea air outside, but enjoyed the off-gassing of the formaldehyde from the new furniture just as well. It made him feel at home.

Scanning a list of his recently acquired funeral homes, he smiled. Baltimore, Boston, Philly, Newark, and New York. And Slagger-Jewell, up the road in Hollywood, made six. The last piece of the puzzle. The crown *Jewell* so to speak.

He gazed down at the boats in the marina. They looked like toys from the thirty-seventh floor, including his Boston Whaler. A good fishing boat, but every self-respecting criminal syndicate executive needed a yacht. He already picked one out, a sleek sixty-one foot Bertram with royal blue stripes along the bow and gunwale.

He'd buy it as soon as *El Grande* got up and running. That's what he called his master plan. *The big one.* Ideas were what brought him this far, but he could stack them all together and they'd pale next to *El Grande*, one of the great crime innovations of all time.

Luis had grown up poor in Colombia. His mother cleaned houses; his father did landscaping. As a child, he hated seeing them work so hard for peanuts. So he studied hard in school, like they taught him, aspiring for a better life.

It didn't work, not even after he earned a university degree in mortuary science, an interest sparked when he attended his abuela's open-casket funeral and noticed she looked better dead than she ever did alive. The degree got him a job as an assistant embalmer at a funeral home that paid the equivalent in Colombian pesos of seven bucks an hour.

He drove cabs on the side to make rent. One night he got sent to the swanky Hotel Casa. A classy guy with slicked-back black hair and a smooth-as-silk shave climbed in back. His crisp, tailored suit must have cost a bundle.

Luis felt the man's eyes on him. Each time he checked the mirror, the man was still staring. He was wondering whether to be concerned when the man said, "Parcero, how would you like a job that pays fifty times this one?"

He'd heard it all as a cabbie, everything from drunken confessions to sexual propositions. Lots of hustles, but never a job offer. He laughed it off. "Sounds good to me. That include a pension? Health benefits?"

"You think I'm joking. How many jokers you know stay at the Casa and pay ten thousand dollars for a Brioni suit?"

"You don't even know my qualifications."

"But I do. You're a frigging giant."

Although average height, Luis weighed three hundred and fifty pounds and was built like a tank. The job offer was to be a *sicario*—hitman—for a drug cartel.

Luis didn't want to offend the man, emphasizing his firm belief that senseless murder had its place in civilized society, but explained he wasn't a violent man by nature. Not wanting the opportunity to slip away, he changed the subject to chemistry. His background studying mortuary science, he asserted, made him an excellent candidate to work in a drug-processing lab.

He got the job. Lab technician didn't pay as much as hitman, but Luis's ideas and ambition impressed his bosses. He moved steadily up the organizational ladder. Life was good, but he remained restless and discontented. He had long dreamed of living in America.

As a chubby toddler in an adult-size diaper, his father used to sing *Only in America* to him while he danced around their tiny living room. With its Latin percussion and horns, the 1963 hit by Jay & the Americans became his anthem. Learning the band members weren't Latino but four Jewish kids from Brooklyn did nothing to dampen his ardor for the peppy tune.

He spent many long nights working on ideas that might convince the capo to send him to the Land of Opportunity. When the answer finally lit up his brain, he was convinced it was destiny. Who would have guessed that attending his abuela's funeral as a child would be the key to punching his golden ticket?

Now here he was, living the life in Miami, ready to implement *El Grande*.

A knock on the door interrupted his reminiscence.

"Just a minute," he said.

He pulled on his eyepatch. He didn't need it; his eyes worked fine. But it made him look scarier. True to what he told the man in the Brioni suit that first night, he wasn't a violent man, but learned quickly that violence is to drug-trafficking what salt is to cooking. Essential.

To avoid it, he relied on fear as a tool of persuasion. It turned out to be the most powerful weapon of all. People will do anything if they're afraid enough and they're a lot more afraid before they die than after.

"Come in," he said when he got the eyepatch adjusted.

A blue-eyed man with blond bangs and horn-rimmed glasses burst through the door. "Buenos días, Jefe!"

It was his Ivy League accountant, Chad, from Connecticut. Luis believed strongly in a diverse workforce and encouraged the cartel to hire greedy, conscienceless workaholics without regard to race, gender, or sexual identity.

He appreciated Chad's enthusiasm and work ethic, although he suspected the accountant's coke habit played a role in both. He noticed a questionable white smudge on the lapel of his black suit as he took a seat.

Luis made everyone in the organization wear black suits, men and women alike. They added class, dignity, and authority all at once. They also made you sweat bullets in Florida's summer swelter, but in his business employees didn't complain about dress codes or work-life balance or anything else. The only way to leave a cartel is on a slab.

"You're looking awesomely fearsome, Jefe," Chad said. "Have you killed anyone today?"

"Not yet."

Luis had never killed anyone. To hide that embarrassing secret and bolster his ability to induce terror, he paid his barber in Bogotá to spread rumors of his murderous nature. In one story, he gouged the eyeballs out of ten men and ate them from a platter on toothpicks like hors d'oeuvres.

The idea worked so well Luis hired a pulp-fiction writer to compile the stories into a little book, *The Legend of Luis*, that he spread around Bogotá.

He was blessed with the natural gifts to make the legend believable, principally his impressive bulk and a sawtooth scar down his cheek from an exploding vat of ether back in his lab days. He perfected a Tony Montana glare practicing in the mirror. He was no Al Pacino, but he did have the real scar.

The eyepatch helped too. When people asked about it, he said he lost the eye in a street battle with ten men, the ones whose eyeballs he gouged out and ate in revenge.

"I have those numbers you asked me to run," Chad said. "I did them for *un ano completo*."

Luis loved South Florida. The beaches, balmy winters, corruption. But like everywhere, the Gold Coast had its issues. Hurricanes, traffic, and possibly most annoying, gringos who attempted to speak Spanish to show they were with it.

"Chad, the Spanish word for *year* is *año*—not *ano*. For Christ's sake, you just told me you did the numbers for *a complete anus*."

"Lo siento, Jefe!"

Luis squeezed the bridge of his wide nose. "Just explain what you came up with. In English."

"Sí! I mean, yes, sir."

Chad laid out the estimated operating costs for the first year of *El Grande*. Not cheap. More than ten million dollars, although most of it went to buy the six funeral homes, a nonrecurring expense.

Yago—his *teniente*—couldn't grasp why he insisted on making fair market value offers for them. "Bossman, lowball 'em and make it clear it's *plata o plomo*."

Silver or lead. A negotiating strategy sometimes used back home to facilitate bribes.

Yago had no vision or business sense. Crude and ruthless, he never outgrew his beginnings as a sicario, even after landing the plum job as Luis's second-in-command, an assignment he suspected was born of nepotism. Rumor had it Yago's father was parceros with the capo.

All the funeral home transactions went smoothly except the last: Slagger-Jewell. He selected it because of its out-of-the-way location up in Hollywood, close to I-95, the main Northeast corridor. But he fell in love with it from the loads of five-star reviews. Maintaining an excellent reputation was key to the success of *El Grande*, another point Yago was unable or unwilling to comprehend.

They approached Jewell Sr. first, who said he'd sell Slagger-Jewell when coconuts grow genitals. When increasing the offer didn't help, Luis turned to one of his go-to threats. Sell or he'd be cut into a hundred pieces and fed to the fish.

"My blood is fifty-percent formaldehyde," he cackled. "Good luck finding a fish willing to eat me."

It caught Luis off guard. The first time threats had failed him. He should have taken it as an omen to move on to another funeral home, but Yago was watching his every move. Any sign of weakness could prove fatal, an occupational hazard. It was too late to turn back.

Yago wanted to kill the old man right there. They compromised by giving him twenty-four hours to think about it.

Then he up and died the same night, in bed at his condo. The death certificate listed the cause as *Natural cardiac arrest*, but Luis wondered if Yago had something to do with it. He maintained a zero tolerance policy for insubordination, but never raised the issue. Truthfully, he was a little afraid of the man.

After Jewell Sr.'s death, they went to Junior, which was easier, but still messy. He too resisted selling, but had a family to protect and caved in the face of the same threat his father laughed at, maybe because Luis put extra oomph into his presentation. He practiced it the night before, concerned he was losing his touch for threatening mutilation.

But it had been nothing but problems since. A kid with a trust, crappy legal advice, a missing will, and now they were basically holding Jewell and his wife hostage. A complete frigging mess.

He told himself over and over that *El Grande* was worth all the trouble. Besides, nobody was actually getting hurt ... although he did still wonder about the old man.

Chapter 12

JOHN PRINE SANG *Please Don't Bury Me* at low volume on the CD player on the drive back from the police station. Danny tried to read Jessica's thoughts but she was inscrutable.

"That's a funny song," she said at the end of Prine's plea to spread his body parts far and wide on his demise rather than be placed in the cold, cold ground. "My favorite line is the deaf can have his ears if they don't mind the size."

"That is a good one. So how was your conversation with your dad?"

"Meh," she said.

"Did you get to talk to your mom too?"

"Mm-hm."

"Did your dad explain anything about what's going on?"

"He said he was on a business trip that came up suddenly and my mom wanted to go with him. He supposedly lost his phone and that's why they didn't call before."

Weak, but Danny couldn't think of a better explanation short of the truth.

"He said they didn't take me because it was really boring and I'd have more fun here. I didn't believe a word of it. For one thing, he doesn't even have a business anymore. But at least they're okay. He said I could keep staying with you until they get back. Is that true?"

"It is."

"He said it could be for a whole week," she said.

He felt her studying him for a reaction. "One week, two weeks, whatever it takes," he said. "Sorry you got stuck with me. I haven't been much fun." He'd been a dud.

"I've had fun."

"You said at your grandpa's funeral you still play softball. Have you ever been to a Marlins baseball game? They play an afternoon game tomorrow."

"Baseball's boring. Softball's a million times better. The games are shorter, the action's faster, and girls don't spit. Can we go back to the surf shop instead?"

"Now *that* sounds boring, but sure, anything you want."

"Do you have any more of those *Surfer* magazines?"

"Probably about a hundred at the condo. I used to collect them. Why?"

"I want to learn more about surfboards."

"Ah, you must be thinking of taking me up on that lesson."

"Not really. I want to see how much stuff I can sell tomorrow, but I need to know more."

*   *   *

The last remnants of the setting sun washed the sky in red and orange as they entered the Tradewinds. A hearty "Hello, Jessica!" rang out. It was Grady, standing inside the rectangular bar wearing a soiled apron and washing glasses.

"Hello, Mr. Banyon!"

"None of that Mr. Banyon stuff. I'm just plain ol' Grady. You keeping this miscreant out of trouble?"

"I don't know what miscreant is, but I'm watching him like a hawk," she said, getting a good laugh from everyone at the bar.

Her hair sprayed like cornstalks from under her Nine Lives Surf Shop hat. She was carrying a stack of *Surfer* magazines Danny retrieved from a closet. She immersed herself in them as soon as they got home from the police station. He told her some of the issues were collectors' items that couldn't leave the condo.

"That's fine," she said. "But I can tell you from experience that all the stuff people save and collect during their lives just gets thrown in the trash when they die, unless it's worth selling. Which ones don't you want me to take?"

He knew she was right. What the hell was he saving them for? He couldn't remember the last time he looked at one. "Never mind. Take any you want."

They sat at their original wobbly round table near the front windows. Shannon came over and laid out laminated menus. "Well, if it isn't two of my favorite people."

"Hi, Shannon," Jessica said.

"I like your necklace," she said.

"Danny gave it to me. Well, actually I earned it."

Danny glanced at the menu, which he knew by heart, and asked if Jessica liked calamari. She asked what it was.

"Fried squid. It's better than it sounds."

"Fine with me. I'm not a picky eater. Gramps once challenged me to eat a chunk of vein and I was going to do it."

Shannon said, "A vein? Like in a piece of steak or chicken?"

"No, it was human, but I think he was just teasing. He was a little tipsy. He liked to drink brandy in the embalming room when he was doing makeup."

"Her family owned a funeral home," Danny explained. "We'll have the calamari, hold the veins, and a veggie platter."

"Drinks?"

Danny ordered a beer and Jessica got water again.

Shannon returned carrying Danny's beer and a root beer in a frozen mug she set down in front of Jessica.

"Everyone needs a little beverage excitement in their lives. Just so you know, we save these mugs for our special friends," she said with a wink and moved on to greet some new customers.

"I can see why you like this place, Danny. It's like that TV show my parents watch on reruns. Everyone knows your name."

"*Cheers,*" Danny said.

"Cheers!" she said back, raising her frosty mug. "Now, let's talk surfboards."

She opened a spiral notebook and clicked on a Slagger-Jewell ballpoint pen. The funeral home had more merch than his surf shop.

"Let me see if I have this straight," she said, "There are basically four kinds of boards in terms of materials: soft-top, polyurethane, epoxy, and wood."

"That's right, although you don't see a lot of wood anymore."

"What kind do you make?"

"Poly and epoxy." He explained some pros and cons of each as she took notes.

"In terms of shape," she said, "We have shortboards, fish boards, fun boards, and longboards. What do most people use?"

"Most experienced surfers use shortboards. Beginners are better off with longer boards. They're easier to catch waves on and easier to ride once you do. Fish boards are ..."

As the interrogation wore on he began to suspect her obsession with the shop was a way to distract herself from her reality, a coping mechanism.

"That's enough knowledge for one night," he finally said. "How about we go for a walk on the beach and head back up to the condo?" He loved the beach at night as much as in the daylight.

They strolled along the shoreline carrying their shoes. Stars stitched the sky. A gibbous moon striped the dark water like a flashlight beam. Wavelets swashed their feet. At first Jessica ran from them, back and forth like a sandpiper.

She eventually relaxed and settled in alongside him, giggling. "The sand is so squishy it goes right through my toes. Are there any fish here that could bite us? Sharks or barracuda?"

"Just land sharks."

The joke fell flat. "There's no such thing as land sharks," she reprimanded. "You shouldn't joke with people about sharks. That's another thing that scares me about the ocean."

"Sorry."

They were walking in silence to the soothing swoosh of the surf when Jessica, gazing skyward, said, "At my grandpa's funeral, you said you don't know what happens after death. Does that mean you don't believe in heaven?"

"I'd like to, but I've always been kind of an agnostic."

"You mean an atheist?"

"They're different. Atheists don't believe in a god. Agnostics don't disbelieve. We're just not sure because it can't be proved."

"Honestly," she said, "I don't see how anyone can be a hundred percent sure. Lots of people say they are, but whatever. I'm *pretty* sure. I mean, just look at the beautiful stars and ocean. Isn't that proof?"

He wanted to ask if she believed in reincarnation because he was wondering about the possibility the short person glopping through the sand next to him had lived previous lives. The term *old soul* gets thrown around a lot. He finally understood what it meant.

"Did Sari believe in heaven?"

"As I mentioned before, I don't want to talk about Sari."

"Can you tell me why? You love and miss her. Why wouldn't you want to talk about her? I don't understand."

He must have stayed silent longer than he realized.

"Sorry I brought it up," she said. "You don't have to talk about her. I was just curious."

He was *afraid*, dammit. He kept Sari and their life together walled off. If the wall cracked, he'd be flooded again. If she was so damned smart, why couldn't she see that? ... Wait. Did he just think that? *Get a grip, Teakwell. She's twelve years old!*

"She did believe in heaven," he said. "She was raised in a devout Catholic family and was a person of deep faith."

"I know she's there, in heaven."

"Oh, really?" he said, hair prickling on his neck. "And just how do you know that?" It came out harsher than he intended.

"Because anyone who was special enough for you to love them has to be in heaven."

Chapter 13

"**MOVE THAT FILL LIGHT** to the left, just a smidge," the director said. "I see a shadow from his nose. Now bring the hair light up in back. I want a halo effect."

The lights illuminated a four-hundred pound actor named Nick, hired to play the role of Luis in a promotional video for Snowbirds in Paradise Funeral Services. Nick's enormous frame in his black suit popped against the white back drape.

"Sound check," the director said. "Say something, Nick."

Luis stood off to the side, listening to the actor recite Hamlet as the video crew steered a boom mic into place.

Yago stood next to him, pale and lofty, like Lurch in the old Addams Family TV show, another American import Luis grew up with in Bogotá. Who knows? Maybe it helped stimulate his interest in mortuary science.

"Why are we wasting so much time and money on this crap?" he said.

"I've already explained the plan to you more than once," Luis said, swallowing his irritation.

Yago's lack of buy-in to *El Grande* was getting beyond tiresome. If he were anyone else, Luis would threaten to cut his tongue out to shut him up. But he worried Yago might call his bluff.

"Quiet on the set," the director said. "We're ready to roll."

A woman cracked a clapboard in front of the camera. "Snowbirds in Paradise, take one."

"Action," the director said.

"Hello," Nick said, leaning into the lens with an earnest smile. "I'm Louis Carmen, president of Snowbirds in Paradise Funeral Services. I'd like to talk to you today about a subject we find far too easy to avoid." His dimples tightened. "Death."

Except for the girth, Nick, with his reddish hair and pink skin, bore no resemblance to Luis, but he reasoned a güero would go over better in the Northeast marketing campaign. The pseudonym, *Louis Carmen*, was growing on him. If he ever decided to anglicize his name, it might be a good choice.

"Is someone you love a snowbird?" Nick said. "Each year, thousands of Northeasterners migrate to the sunny beaches of Florida, leaving behind not only the snow and ice, but their families and memories."

Luis nodded, pleased. For a guy they found on a freelancer website for unemployed actors, Nick had some chops.

With a prayerful tilt of the head, "But what will happen to your snowbird when they depart this earthly world? The reality is most people are laid to rest where they pass away. Oh, maybe you'll travel to Florida occasionally to visit their final resting place. Or maybe you won't. Either way, it's not a satisfying arrangement for the interment of one so dear.

"But you may say, 'We'll just cremate Mom and bring her ashes home.' Let's be precise about what that really means."

The cremation issue was a tricky one, both for *El Grande* and the funeral industry in general. More and more people were abandoning religious burial tenets in favor of cremation, primarily to save money. But jars of ashes weren't going to help Luis.

"What you're really saying is, 'We'll stick dear old Mom in an oven at fifteen hundred degrees and burn her hair, organs, and other tissue to a crisp.' The breasts you suckled as a baby, the hands you held learning to walk. 'Then we'll sweep her bone fragments into a pulverizer and grind them into small pieces.'

"It's hard to imagine a more undignified ending to your loved one's physical embodiment in this earthly world. The major religions of our world have many differences, but one thing Christian, Jewish, and Muslim faiths agree on is respect for the human body and its proper disposition through burial.

"I stand before you with good news! Neither you nor your loved one need accept such an unseemly fate because Snowbirds in Paradise is revolutionizing the funeral industry. We bring your loved ones back home where they belong."

Nick paused to let the words sink in. Luis had to hold back a cheer. *Brilliant* was the only word that did justice to his idea for *El Grande*.

"You heard me right. From our headquarters in South Florida, we'll properly prepare and transport your dearly departed snowbird to any of our five northeastern funeral homes, in Baltimore, Boston, Philadelphia, Newark, and New York. From there, arrangements can be made to have them laid to rest at a cemetery of your choosing."

"And the good news gets even better. Other services can arrange to ship a person's remains, but do you really want your loved one banging around in a rail car or the freezing bowels of an airplane with the Amazon packages? As if we didn't already have enough regrets for all the times we treated them like crap."

"Cut," the director said. "Treated them like crap?"

"That's what the teleprompter says," Nick said.

Luis wrote the script himself, laboring over it for a month. He was proud of the final product, but conceded the line needed tweaking.

"How about we change it to *all the times we weren't there when they needed us*?" the director said, looking to Luis, who nodded his assent.

Nick reread the line, then said with extra pep, "It's not too late to make it up to them. Bring your loved ones home in style and class! We'll make their final road trip one to remember, a sweet ride in one of our luxury hearses.

"Picture them, homeward bound, rolling through the countryside in air-conditioning, listening to the soundtrack of their life on our premium twelve-speaker sound system. They'll think they died and went to heaven."

He smiled at the joke and turned solemn again.

"There's one more matter I need to discuss with you. Our most special feature. Americans are getting larger all the time. It's a fact. Thirty percent of us, including yours truly, meet the definition of obese, a percentage expected to increase in coming years.

"Most funeral homes remain unequipped for supersized funerals, which require special caskets and hearses. When long-distance transport is required, you may be charged by the pound, adding insult to your sorrow.

"At Snowbirds, we respect plus-size decedents. Not only do we refuse to punish them with extra charges, we give them discounts. You heard me right. And get ready: *The larger your loved one, the bigger the discount.*

Nick delivered the news wide-eyed with his palms turned up, as if even he couldn't believe it.

"I know what you're thinking. That sounds too good to be true. Why would they do it? The answer is standing before you.

"I know all too well the discrimination suffered by the weight-and-width challenged under the tyranny of thinness that pervades our society. In founding Snowbirds in Paradise, I decided that death, at least, was the time to put an end to it."

Luis's heart swelled with pride. He wrote those words through watery eyes. People made fun of his size from the day he was born. When his mother sent out birth announcements with his picture, his aunt returned a card saying, *¡Es muy bonito, para un gordo!*

On his second birthday he weighed sixty-eight pounds. Taunts, name-calling, side glances, he suffered them all the way through childhood and into his teens before he grew so big no one dared.

That his new criminal enterprise would benefit a marginalized class to which he belonged almost made the tens of millions of dollars he stood to reap from *El Grande* secondary.

Nick was wrapping up. "Call 1-800-555-DEAD today to learn how Snowbirds in Paradise can bring your departed Florida snowbird home where they belong. Thank you for listening."

The director stood and said, "Cut. Nailed it in one take. Great job, Nick."

Luis applauded. He'd make sure Nick got a nice bonus. *El Grande* was finally coming to fruition. But Yago ruined the moment.

"This is bullshit," he grumbled and stomped out.

Something had to be done about him. Luis just wasn't sure what.

Chapter 14

THE THICK SUMMER AIR was already heating up as they strolled down the boardwalk the next morning. Jessica left a trail of crumbs from a breakfast bar she was eating, causing a riot among a gang of seagulls.

She was unusually chatty, making him wonder how many cups of coffee she had before he got out of bed. She was in the middle of explaining a retail epiphany she experienced when she woke up.

"It was right there the second I opened my eyes. That's a strong sign of a good idea. A lot of people on the boardwalk are tourists. They're not going to buy a surfboard to take back to Iowa or wherever."

"Not likely."

"*Bu-ut*, they would probably love to go home with some cool beachwear, especially surfer clothes. Everyone thinks surfers are cool. Are you with me so far?"

"Yes, I'm managing to follow," Danny said.

His suspicion the surf shop had become a vehicle for her to avoid the weight of her world had elevated to a firm conviction. It didn't require a psychology degree to figure out.

"Good, because I recommend we hold a big sale on all the clothes, starting today. I'll take care of everything."

"Sounds good."

"And we should put some of the rental boards out front. I bet a lot of tourists would love to brag they went surfing on their vacay, but probably don't even know you can rent a board."

"Also good." He didn't want to burst her bubble by pointing out that the summer tourist season was winding down. "How about this? You take charge of the store and do whatever you want. I need to stay in back and start work on a new custom board."

"Lil Lansky's?"

"That's the one."

Jessica knew all about him and got excited when he mentioned it. *"Livin' and Lovin' on I-95* is one of my favorite songs," she said.

Rasheed approved the board design and agreed to the twenty-five grand. Danny apparently offended him by asking if the board was only for display. *I'm a surfer, dawg.* He talked him out of the gold inlay, saying the extra weight would put a drag on the board, offering instead to have Gaspar paint his neck chains in twenty-four carat gold leaf.

"Before you get started on that," Jessica said as they reached Nine Lives, "we need to clean these windows."

He glanced at the glacier of salt and said, "Not now."

"If not now, when, Danny?"

If not now, when? Something in her tone made the question sting like an indictment. *You want an honest answer? Probably never.* Oh, hell, he was losing it again. She was talking about window cleaning, not him getting his life together. Or was she?

"Fine," he said. "We'll do it now."

He dragged out the hose, brush, and squeegee while Jessica filled a bucket with warm sudsy water. It was going to be a chore.

They were laboring away at it when a voice from behind said, "Looks like you have a new helper, Danny."

Octogenarian Helena Quintero, sunbaked skin thick as leather, sailed past on her canary-yellow beach cruiser, pet iguana perched on her shoulder.

"And she's a good one!" he called after her.

"You sure do have a lot of friends," Jessica said.

"Not really. More like acquaintances."

"I only have one. She lives a few blocks from our house. Her name is Gloria but she likes to be called Gigi."

"I'm sure you have more friends than that."

"Not really. The people at the funeral home liked me, but they were a lot older and more like family. I get along better with adults than kids. I don't know why."

Danny had a good guess. Friends had carried him through his darkest hours. Everyone needed them. "Would you like to have more friends?"

"I wouldn't mind it."

"Any reason why you think you don't?"

"The other kids think I'm weird. They call me names like *Elvira* and *the weird funeral home kid*. It started in the third grade when we had to make a science presentation and I did mine on embalming.

"I brought some props, including a trocar. It's a hollow tube that's pointy at one end, like a shish-kebab thing. You use it to puncture the thoracic and abdominal cavities to suck out any fluids and gas before pumping the dearly beloved full of formalin, which is basically just formaldehyde and water."

"That's more detail than I needed to know, but go ahead."

"I was demonstrating on a doll leftover from my childhood. Her name was Angie. When I punctured Angie's stomach, some wimpy boy fainted. The teacher cut me off to call an ambulance right in the middle of my presentation. *Then* I got in trouble for bringing a weapon to school."

"The shish-kebab thing?"

"Mm-hm. Do you believe that?"

"Well, I think you probably have more friends than you realize, but in the meantime, you can definitely count me as one."

The windows shined with new car showroom brilliance when

they finished. Danny couldn't believe the difference. It had been that long.

"So *there* are your business hours," Jessica said.

They appeared like magic on the door as the salt glaze melted away.

"I was wondering where they were. Here's a tip. If you tell people you're going to be open at a certain time—"

"I should be here. I know."

"Why does it say closed Monday and Tuesday?"

"Because even when I was sticking to the hours, I didn't want to work seven days a week, and a surf shop has to be open on weekends."

"That's reasonable."

Inside, she gathered supplies from the workshop to make signs for her sale, dragging out a heavy roll of packing paper Gaspar used to catch overspray when he was airbrushing.

"Good luck," Danny said as she exited. He shut the door and settled in at his computer.

He needed to refine the design measurements for Rasheed's board to fit his height, weight, and skill-level. The math took concentration, which was in short supply because it sounded like Jessica was undertaking construction out front.

Just as that settled down, shouting brought him to his feet. He ran out to see Jessica standing at the propped-open front door accosting a senior on the boardwalk.

"Good morning, ma'am! Have you ever wanted to look ten years younger without surgery? Surfwear is the answer. And you're in luck because we're having a flash sale today."

The sun filtered through enormous hand-painted signs posted in the front windows. *Surf's Up! Prices Down! 30% Off All Aparel.*

Bless her heart. It just wasn't a great time of year to sell beachwear. He appreciated the missing *p* in *Apparel*, anything to remind him she was just a regular kid.

Back in the workshop, a leaf blower fired up outside. He shut the window and slid Warren Zevon into a portable CD player, cranking it up.

An hour of calculations later, he printed the spec sheets and fastened them to the wall, then set an epoxy foam blank on his DIY shaping rack and began outlining the design in pencil. Warren was singing *Poor Poor Pitiful Me* at full volume. He reached to turn it down and heard multiple voices out front.

Now what?

He swung open the door and stopped. The store was filled with people mulling around checking out clothes, more customers than he'd seen in a year.

"Those look so cute on you," Jessica was saying to a pear-shaped woman modeling a pair of loose beach pants with slits at the ankles. "You know what would go perfect with them? This top."

Danny waited until the woman left for the dressing room before approaching. "Look at this crowd. You need any help?"

"I've got it," she said.

He chuckled all the way back to the workshop. As soon as he picked up the pencil again, she stuck her head in. "Some guys want to rent surfboards. How does that work?"

He went back out and helped with the rental paperwork for four excited college kids from Michigan.

"Great job," he said as they ran out to fight over the boards in the rack Jessica had dragged out front. "Those are the first boards I've rented in a long time. How's your sale going?"

"Not bad. So far I've sold five-hundred and eighty-two dollars in clothes and accessories."

"You're kidding. That's fabulous."

"Thanks. No surfboard sales though. I've tried to sell one to every person who came in. I hope I didn't waste my time learning all that surfboard stuff for nothing. ... Have my parents called today?"

"Um, no."

"I didn't think so."

"What do you say we break for lunch? You've been working hard. And check it out, the business hours even say we close for lunch."

They walked down to the Flicker Lite on A1A, purportedly owned by relatives of Al Capone. Danny and his buddies consumed a reservoir of beer there growing up.

"I don't understand why we have to wait for my parents to call us," she said between bites of the Italian sub they agreed to split. "Why can't we just call them?"

"Remember? Your dad said he lost his cellphone."

"Even if that's true, they're staying at a hotel. So they have a room phone."

"You're right ... I'm not really sure," he said. He wanted to tell her the truth, believed she deserved to know and, being her, could handle it. Playing dumb felt like lying.

An hour later, back at the shop, he was finishing the outline on the foam blank when Jessica flew in, breathless. "Someone's out there asking for you."

"Who is it?" Recent events had upped his paranoia.

"A woman. A really cute one."

Danny trailed her out front, where a woman with sun-bleached hair and freckles was browsing the surfboard racks. Mid-thirties he guessed, in shorts and a tank top over a one-piece swimsuit. Her long arms and legs showed off the taut muscles of an athlete.

"Danny Teakwell?" she said.

"That's me."

"Hi. I'm Erin Delonia. I'm visiting from California and thought I'd stop by. Actually, I've stopped by a couple of times but your shop was closed."

Danny felt Jessica's *I told you so* gaze boring into him.

"Sorry about that. What can I do for you?"

"I just wanted to say thank you," she said.

"Thank you? I'm not following. Do we know each other? ... Wait a second. Erin Delonia. I know who you are. You won the surf competition at Huntington Beach last year, the big one. I read about it."

"I did. And I was riding one of your boards."

"No sh— Seriously?"

"Yep. Bought it at a shop in San Diego. The owner swore it was one of the best boards he'd ever ridden and he was right."

"He's famous for his boards," Jessica said. "Right now he's making one for a *major* hip-hop star."

"You sure are lucky to have such a talented father," Erin said. "And you even get to work together. That's awesome. I'll bet you're a good little surfer. My dad first put me on a board when I was seven. How about you?"

Jessica's face tightened. "Um ..."

"Well, actually," Danny said. "We're not related. She's just staying with me while her parents are out of town."

"Oh, well, that's nice too."

"What brings you to South Florida?"

"I work for a beachwear company as a sponsor-slash-spokes-model. We have a booth at a clothing expo going on in Miami Beach this month."

"Cool," Danny said.

"I'll tell you what would be cool," Jessica piped. "You two going surfing together! Think about it. She's a surfing champion and you made the board she won the championship on. It was meant to be."

"I'd be up for that," she said. "Although I've noticed you don't have many waves here."

Danny laughed. "Yeah, I picked the wrong place to open a surf shop, but this is where I grew up."

"He lives right on the ocean, in a penthouse," Jessica said.

"It's kind of a dump. They call it a penthouse because it's on top."

"How about it?" Erin said. "We could grab a couple of those rentals out front."

"Oh, sorry. I, uh, can't leave her alone."

"Of course you can, Danny. I'm the one running the store. You just sit around in back."

"I just wouldn't feel comfortable about it. Sorry."

"I understand," Erin said. "I'd feel the same way about my nieces. Do you have a pen? I'll give you my number."

Jessica raced to bring her a pen and sticky note that Erin scribbled on and handed back.

"Maybe we can get together. I'm here for a couple weeks and have a lot of free time. I only have to show up for special events. I'm staying just up the beach with a girlfriend."

"Yeah, sure. Maybe," Danny said.

"Okay then. Well, good to meet you. You too," she said to Jessica.

"Likewise," Danny said, feet nailed to the floor as she walked out.

"Good grief," Jessica said as soon as the door clicked shut. "What is wrong with you?"

"What are you talking about?"

"When was the last time a beautiful surfing champion walked through your door and propositioned you?"

"She didn't proposition me."

"She gave you an opening big enough to drive that oversized hearse we saw through and you acted like she was poisonous."

"I was perfectly nice."

"You started out okay, but when she took me up on my surfing suggestion you froze like you just died with your eyes open, which happens a lot by the way. More than thirty percent of people die with bilateral ptosis, incomplete eye closure."

Another fun death fact he could have lived without knowing.

"Danny, can I say something without you getting mad at me?"

"Of course. You can say anything you want to me. I don't get mad. I'm sorry if it sounds that way."

"You asked why I don't have more friends. One reason is because I tell the truth. A lot of people don't want to hear the truth, even when they ask for your opinion. They want to hear what they already think. When you tell them something different, trying to help, they don't like it.

"My only friend, Gloria who likes to be called Gigi? She appreciates it. One time she got a new dress and asked if I liked it. I said no because it was the color of puke. She took it back and got one that was a lot better."

"The big difference here is I didn't ask for your opinion." He had an idea where this was going.

"I think you chased her away because of Sari, and I also think Sari would have wanted you to hang out with her."

He had shut his brain down from even thinking about other women since Sari died, feeling like it would be a betrayal of her memory, but of course Yoda Jr. was right again. *Keep your heart open. Be willing to let someone else in.* Sari's own words.

"Thank you for your thoughts on the matter. I'm just not ready for anyone else," he said.

"You know, having fun with a person doesn't mean you have to marry them."

"Again, I appreciate your thoughts."

"So you're not even going to call her?"

"I'll think about it."

"Yeah, right," she said and marched off in a huff to rearrange her window display.

Chapter 15

FINK CALLED SAYING he had "big, big news" and wanted to meet at the Tradewinds at five.

Danny and Jessica were waiting in a booth when he swaggered in wearing a rumpled dress shirt with sweat rings the size of dinner plates under the armpits and bug-eye sunglasses with blue-mirrored lenses.

"Where's Shannon?" he said, taking a seat.

"Good to see you too," Danny said.

"Oh, right. Always nice to see Batman and Robin. How are you?"

"Honestly, things have been better. There's a lot going on right now."

Craning his neck, "That's good. So where is she?"

"Shannon's off tonight. Are you listening? Take off those glasses. I feel like I'm talking to The Fly."

A new server named Tulia came over, in white cutoffs and a Foo Fighters tee. Grady introduced her when they came in. Her shiny black hair and almond-shaped eyes gave her an exotic look. She was a fan of dragons judging by her several fire-breathing tattoos. Young, just twenty-two.

"You want something?" she said to Fink.

"No thanks. Just had a couple shooters in my car." He raised his palms defensively. "Not while I was driving. After I got here." Tulia rolled her eyes and walked away.

"You're supposed to order your drinks inside the bar. It's a business," Danny said.

"Saves a few bucks. Money's tight."

"Alright, so what's the *big, big* news?"

"Can we talk in private?" he said.

"Outside? In my condo?"

"I mean just you and me."

"Oh. Um, Jessica, would you mind sitting at the bar for a few minutes? I'm sure Grady would enjoy the company."

"Is this about me and my family? I'm staying. I already know you're hiding things from me, Danny. You talked to my dad a long time yesterday and all I got was some made-up story about a business trip. They're my parents and it was my funeral home, well, at least thirty percent of it. I have a right to know."

He agreed. Her father wasn't going to like it, but the time had come. "It's true. I have been hiding things. I wanted to protect you. We did, your parents and I. Everything I know is bad news. Scary news."

"Well, I already assumed it wasn't tidings of great joy, and you know me well enough to know I'm not a scaredy-cat—except for the drowning thing. I'd rather know the truth than be surprised later. I can deal with it."

He believed her. "Okay, prepare yourself. You too, Fink. I learned a lot talking to her father yesterday. Here we go ..."

"He didn't want to sell, but agreed to do it because the two men threatened to hurt your family." He left out the cutting-in-to-pieces details. "They said if anyone called the police, the harm would be even worse. That's why he's been adamant about not calling them."

"I figured it was something like that. So who are those two men?" Jessica said.

"Your dad doesn't know."

"I do," Fink said. "That's part of my news. The guy in charge is named *Luis Carmillion*. He's listed as president and CEO of Snowbirds in Paradise Funeral Services, LLC."

"Must be the big guy," Danny said. "Her father said he was in charge. Excellent work, Fink. How did you find out? I thought the names were hidden because of that legal loophole you were drooling over."

"I called a guy in the state corporate records department and told him if he didn't cough up the info, I'd tell his wife about the time he cheated on her."

"How did you know about that?"

"Just assumed. They've been married ten years."

"Isn't that kind of a ridiculous assumption?"

"Guess not. He gave me the info. I have another big discovery, but I need the internet to show you. Wouldn't it be nice if these phones had an internet connection? Maybe I should invent that. I could be a billionaire."

"Yeah, maybe you should. While we're waiting for it to happen, let's go up to the condo."

Upstairs, they huddled around Danny's iMac at the dining room table, Fink at the controls.

"Alright, Sherlock," Danny said. "What's the big discovery?"

"The website for Snowbirds in Paradise went live today." He typed in the URL. "Get ready. This is some wild stuff." He clicked the enter key and an extremely large man in a black suit popped out against a white background.

"Hello," he said. "I'm Louis Carmen, President of Snowbirds in Paradise Funeral Services. I'd like to talk to you today about a subject we find far too easy to avoid. Death. ..."

"Bizarre," Danny said when the video ended. "That's not the guy who came to your house, is it?"

"No," Jessica said. "Big enough, but definitely not him."

"Maybe his body double," Fink said. "*Luis Carmillion. Louis Carmen.*"

"Ah, good catch," Danny said. "I guess this explains the over-sized caskets and hearse we saw during our spy mission."

"Mm-hm," Jessica said. "Click that box at the top. *Plus-Size Discounts.*"

The window opened to a picture of Louis Carmen pointing to a chart and saying into a speech balloon, *Paying it forward with this gift to you, my fellow well-upholstered friends.* The chart said:

PLUS-SIZE DISCOUNTS*

200+: 10 percent

250+: 30 percent

300+: 50 percent

400+: 75 percent

500+: Free!

*Discounts based on body weight in pounds, unclothed, on arrival.

Danny said, "Jessica, as our resident funeral expert, what do you think of all this, their business plan?"

"It's actually not a bad idea. A lot of people really do leave their families behind when they move to Florida. We planted plenty of them. But the discounts don't make sense."

"How so?"

"The more someone weighs, the higher the expenses. Not only the casket, you need special lifting equipment, more staff, more embalming fluid, more everything. They'll lose money for sure. And that's not even including the cost of gas."

"Maybe this Carmillion guy has a genuine soft spot for other, um, large people, like the actor said."

"Yeah, Danny," Fink said. "And he teaches kittens to pray in his spare time. These are not do-gooders. I saved the most important piece of information for last."

"Why?"

"I don't know. I just did. Remember Dizbo Skaggs? My investigator?"

"The shady one?"

"They don't come any shadier. That's what makes him so good. He has connections everywhere. He got a Miami detective to look up Carmillion. Said he has a clean criminal record, but is a known associate of a South American drug cartel called *Los Loppers*."

"The Loppers?"

"Yeah. He said they're newish, trying to make a splash. Their calling card is beheading people," he said, slashing a hand across his throat.

"What's wrong, Danny?" Jessica said. "You just made a weird noise."

He'd come this far. "Your dad thinks everything is mob-related and drug cartels are a type of mob. So if these are the people who ..." His voice trailed off.

Her hazel eyes focused sharp as razors. "People who what? Where are my mom and dad right this second? The truth."

"Are you sure you want to know?"

"Of course I want to know."

"Remember a couple nights ago we were here talking about a possible legal snag in the sale of Slagger-Jewell?"

"My trust?"

Danny nodded. "According to your father, this Carmillion gentleman got a new lawyer who said the consent form you signed isn't valid and the health, education, and maintenance thing might not fly in court."

"See?" Fink said. "I do know the law! That's exactly what I said. I mean, I wasn't completely sure, but I raised it."

"You did," Jessica said. "Good job, Fink."

Fink beamed like he just won a spelling bee trophy. His first ever note of approval from her. She had that effect on people.

"That's when they sent you to your Aunt Rosie's," Danny said. "Then they got spooked and decided to go into temporary hiding at a hotel up in Boca Raton. They were going to come get you, but the bad guys found them and ..."

How do you tell a kid her parents are being held hostage by people who allegedly specialize in decapitation?

"And?" she said.

"They're kind of ... keeping them in place."

"What does that mean?"

"Sounds like he's saying holding them hostage," Fink said.

"Hostage!"

Danny glared at Fink. He was trying not to say that. "They've been asked to stay at the hotel until a new will is prepared," he said. "A forgery that leaves out your trust. Your dad agreed to file it with the probate court. He's only doing it to protect your family. Carmillion said once it's filed everyone is in the clear."

"Maybe it's time to call the police," Jessica said.

"Not surprisingly, I recommended that to your father, but he rejected it. He's convinced that going along is the safer route. He said they're being well-treated and it's just a matter of waiting a few days before everything is resolved. Your thirty percent of the money will be put in a separate account for you."

"I don't like it, but as long as my parents are safe. That's all I care about. What about the real will, the original?"

"Technically, it's missing. The bad guys are looking for it. That's probably why they were in your house."

"What if they find it?"

"That could be a problem," Danny said.

"Big problem," Fink said. "Once your father files the forgery, if Carmillion and friends find the original, your parents become superfluous. Wait, is that the right word?"

"Fink," he said.

"*Disposable.* That's better."

Danny kicked him under the table, not to get his attention, which expired every five seconds, but to hurt his shin.

"Ow!"

"Disposable!" Jessica said. "We need to find that will. You said it was *technically* missing? What does that mean?"

"Your dad knows where it is, but it's impossible to access."

"Nothing's impossible if you set your mind to it. Gramps taught me that. Where is it?"

Chapter 16

THE HYUNDAI COASTED to a stop on a dark slice of asphalt behind a pool supply company, sandwiched between a dumpster and cinderblock wall painted glossy white. On the other side of the wall was the former Slagger-Jewell funeral home. It was late. The only signs of life were occasional passing cars and the Denny's lights across the intersection.

One second, possibly less, after Jessica pried loose Danny's final secret—that the original will was hidden in her grandfather's nap casket—she insisted they go retrieve it.

Fink annoyed the hell out of him by egging her on, saying it could be *lights out* for her parents if the bad guys found it first, before adding the *good news* that being beheaded is probably a quick way to go.

"I really think this is a mistake," Danny said, turning off the motor.

"It's not," Jessica said. "We need that will."

"We could get arrested for trespassing and breaking and entering."

"You're looking at things their way. You need to look at them our way. I'm still a thirty-percent owner of Slagger-Jewell, meaning they're the trespassers." She held up a jangly bracelet-size ring of keys. "And we're not *breaking* into anything."

"What if they have guards or security cameras?"

"We already saw that the only vehicles in the parking lot are hearses. We never had cameras because who breaks into a funeral home? What are they going to steal? A casket? Corpse? And even if they plan on putting in cameras, they probably haven't had time to do it. It's only been a week."

"They could have changed the locks."

"Only one way to find out," she said and got out.

He willed himself to join her. Stars sprinkled the clear sky and the sweet scent of night-blooming jasmine drifted through the humid air. Buzzing cicadas provided a soothing background track.

A perfect South Florida summer night—for a walk on the beach. Only the absurdity of the moment prevented him from giving in to fear or good judgment. They were dressed in cheap black clothes and baseball caps they bought at a twenty-four hour Walmart. They looked like a father-daughter assassin team, or Nancy Drew and Inspector Clouseau.

"Follow me," she said. "I know every inch of this property. Do you have the backpack?"

"Yes, Jessica. I'm wearing it on my shoulders. Are you sure you won't reconsider?"

"Danny, I'm trying to avoid a little thing called my parents getting their heads chopped off. Boost me over this wall."

He hoisted her over the top and followed behind, landing in the shadow of a gumbo-limbo tree.

"I don't see any cameras," she said.

He didn't either, but that didn't mean they weren't there.

"Follow me," she said, zigzagging through shadows until they reached the back side of the building and a set of metal double-doors.

"These are the doors for loading and unloading clients. They lead straight into the embalming room and ... darn."

"What's wrong?"

"They changed the lock."

He almost blurted *Great!* "That's too bad," he said. "Let's get out of here."

"This way. I know another door and I'll bet anything they didn't think to change the lock."

They crept along the back wall, sheltered from the high-mounted flood lights pouring into the parking lot.

"Right here," she said, ducking into an alcove. "This door goes to a storage closet full of junk. No one ever uses it. Get out the flashlight and shine it here."

He complied.

"I knew it! Same lock."

She tried several keys before one fit. It took Danny's help to wrench the lock open. Even then, layers of paint held the door in place.

"It's no use. It's painted shut," he said.

"You've got muscles. What did that man at Snowbirds call you? Strapping? Let's go, Mr. Strapping. You can do it."

Ten minutes of prying, pulling, and grunting later, Danny landed on his butt as the door surrendered with a screech like a wounded seagull that momentarily silenced the cicadas.

"Success! Good job! Give me the light. I'll lead."

He felt like the adult should lead, but she knew the place. He picked himself off the asphalt and handed over the flashlight.

"Watch your step. Don't trip over that case of arterial."

They emerged from the closet into a long hallway lit only by *Exit* signs above the doors at each end.

"Keep your head down in case they do have cameras," Jessica whispered. "The embalming room's this way."

Danny remembered. He got a tour five years ago, not the kind of thing one easily forgets. He followed her to a metal door where she selected another key and unlocked a deadbolt. "I thought so," she said. "They didn't change the inside locks."

They entered a large windowless chamber smelling of bleach, just like the last time he was here. The air was cool but not cold, just like last time, when he expected to walk into a freezer. He eased the door shut and re-bolted the lock.

The place had creeped him out even in broad daylight with the lights on. In the dark it felt like a scene from a horror movie.

Jessica swept the room with the flashlight, halting the beam on one of the stainless steel embalming tables. The first time Danny laid eyes on them he wondered why they were set at an angle before noticing the drains at the bottom.

"Lookee there," she said. "They already have a customer, a big one."

A white sheet covered a massive bulge. A pair of wide flat feet attached to thick hairy ankles stuck out the end. Danny half expected Alfred Hitchcock to rise in the circle of light, pull down the sheet and say, *Good eee-vening.*

"This way. Gramps kept his nap casket in the nook where he did his makeup work."

When Danny first met Jewell Sr. he was putting makeup on a corpse named Sally, telling her she looked lovely and asking if she wanted a shot of brandy.

They crossed the room and rounded a corner into the nook. Jessica stopped. "Shoot. It's not here."

"Oh, well. We tried. Let's beat it."

"Danny, you're never going to reach your full potential if you give up so easily. Let's look around. They must have moved it. But where? It wouldn't be in the display room. Too nicked up."

"They probably threw it out," Danny said. "Your dad even mentioned that."

"It was a classic Silverado, stainless steel. No reason to throw it away. Follow me."

They traipsed around the embalming room until she said, "Aha! I was right." Resting on the floor in the harsh glare of the flashlight was a shiny silver casket pushed up against the wall. She tugged open the lid, half of it. It was split in the middle.

"They're using it to store casket pillows in. Not a bad idea. Keeps them clean."

She bent down and began unloading the pillows. "Did my dad say where this hidden compartment was?"

"No. Here, let me help. Give me some light."

He kneeled and began probing the red satin lining with his fingers, including the old man's memory foam, hurrying, but taking enough time to make sure he didn't miss a spot.

"There's nothing here."

"You missed a spot," Jessica said. "Right there."

"Still nothing. Any idea how much this thing weighs?" he said.

"Close to two hundred pounds. It's stainless steel."

That ruled out underneath. Ninety-eight-year-old Jewell wouldn't have been able to access his Viagra and Jane Fonda pictorial. Not much left but the ends. He studied them. The foot-end was thicker than the head-end. He knocked on it. Hollow.

"Point the light here." He felt for a latch and found one. A spring-loaded end piece slid up, spilling out the contents.

"Awesome!" Jessica said. "That looks like the will right there."

It was, resting a under a bottle of 100 mg Viagra pills. Danny couldn't believe it. They had defied common sense and won. He grabbed the will. "Let's put things back the way we found them and get out of here," he said.

"Take that other stuff too. It belonged to gramps. What is it?"

"I'll explain later," he said, stuffing everything into the backpack. "*Now* can we leave?"

"Why are you always in such a hurry? We need to investigate."

He forced a tightlipped smile. "Jessica, I know this place still feels like home to you, but it isn't. We're inside a building—illegally in all likelihood—run by people who extorted it from your parents with threats of violence and who are currently holding them captive. Are those good enough reasons to get our butts moving?"

"Actually, no. I think they support my argument for more investigation. Why would criminals do all those things just to own a funeral home? There has to be more to it. This might be our only chance to find out."

One of my teachers wrote in my progress notes that I can be difficult. "What exactly do you want to investigate?"

"That dearly beloved over there."

"Why?"

"Because he's enormous and the whole plus-size discounts didn't make sense to me from the second I saw the video. Why charge less for something that costs more? It'll only take a minute."

*   *   *

"Are you okay? You don't look too good. Try not to puke. We don't have time to clean it up. Hand me those scissors."

Danny pinched a pair of scissors from a row of diabolical-looking chromium instruments neatly laid out on a workbench next to the embalming table. They were both wearing latex gloves from a box on the same workbench, a one-stop embalming shop.

Jessica snipped stitches from the swollen gray-blue belly of a dead man whose family had apparently taken advantage of the plus-size discounts, so wide his sides hung over the table edges. Danny swallowed a gag reflex as the wound split apart, expelling a potpourri of embalming chemicals and decomposing flesh.

Why was Jessica opening the man's abdomen? Danny had asked that very question a few minutes earlier in a state of agitated disbelief when she announced her intention.

"Remember that trocar I got in trouble for bringing to the third-grade science presentation? The shish-kebab thing? It's for puncturing small holes to suck out liquids and gases—"

"I know, before pumping in formalin, a mixture of formaldehyde and water. I remember my embalming lesson."

"When they're done, the embalmers insert little plastic buttons to seal the holes."

"Very considerate of them. And the point is?"

"Do you see any little holes with plastic buttons in this man?"

"Unfortunately, no. I see a poor soul whose entire chest and belly have been carved open with a knife or saw and sewn back shut."

"There's your answer. Morticians don't cut people open. Coroners do if there's an autopsy, but not morticians."

"Maybe someone did an autopsy on him."

"Not likely. Feel here." She grabbed his wrist and pressed his palm against the man's chest. "Don't worry. He's not coming back to life. How does it feel? Soft and spongey, right?"

"Mm-hm," he said, yanking his hand back and wiping it on his pants.

"That's because the breastbone and ribs are missing. Coroners usually replace the breastbone. And he shouldn't be this bloated. Like I said, liquids and gasses get sucked out with the trocar."

"Bottom line, please. Since we're in kind of a hurry."

"We've been wondering why a drug cartel would want to get into the funeral business and I think the answer has something to do with this dearly beloved."

He was still recovering from the exchange when she said, "We're ready. Hand me the spreader."

"This?"

"Those are forceps. The thing next to it. And bring the flashlight closer. I don't want to cut any more stitches than necessary because we have to sew him back up. We don't want them to know we were here."

The only things they agreed on all night: less stitches and not letting the reputed decapitators know they had been there. He leaned in with the flashlight. The HVAC clicked on, practically giving him a heart attack.

"What do we have here?" she said, prying apart thick walls of flesh. "Looks like plastic." She stretched the gap wider. "Yep. blue plastic filled with some kind of stuffing."

"Is that unusual?"

"We'll see. When organs are removed—which, again, usually doesn't happen—it's common to stuff the cavities with filler so they don't collapse. Usually it's cotton or wool, but not wrapped in plastic. Scalpel," she said.

He located one and held it out.

"Danny! Never hand a scalpel to someone blade first."

"Sorry, doctor. This is my first operation."

She let the comment pass and made a small incision in the plastic, sticking her pinkie finger through it.

"It's not stuffing. It's powder. See? That's abnormal."

And in that moment, everything came together. "We need a sample of it," he said. He pulled another glove from the box on the workbench. "Scoop some of it into this."

"Drugs, right?" she said.

"That would be my bet."

"Give me an eye cap."

"A what?"

"Eye cap. In that box that says *Eye Caps*. They go under the eyelids to keep the eyes shut, but it will make a good scoop."

He pulled out a spiky plastic half-sphere resembling an oversized contact lens and handed it to her. She used it to carefully ladle white powder into the glove, which he rolled up and stuffed in his pocket. "Now close him up," he said. "And hurry."

"There," she said a few minutes later. "You can't even tell they aren't the original sutures."

"It's a masterpiece," he said. "Let's scram."

"We need to clean the instruments."

They were pressing their luck, but she was right. He helped her.

"All done," she said. "Put the sheet back on him and we're good to go."

He did, just as footsteps and talking filled the hallway.

They both froze.

The steps stopped at the door.

"Is there another way out of here?" Danny whispered.

"The back delivery doors. The ones with the changed lock. But maybe we can open them from the inside."

"Let's go," he said. They moved lightly and quickly as the talking outside continued.

"Dangit," she said.

The new lock was double-keyed. The hallway door started rattling. The voices were growing louder, some kind of argument.

Danny wrenched the door handle, putting all his weight into it. It didn't budge. They were trapped.

"Quick, climb on this embalming table," Jessica said.

"What?"

"No time for questions. I have an idea. Give me the backpack. Lay on your back, arms to your side."

She grabbed a white sheet from the workbench, identical to the first workbench with the same neat rows of chromium instruments. She covered everything except his head and reached for something else.

"I'm going to put these cotton wads up your nose. We do it to keep fluids from leaking out or bugs crawling in. If they come over here and pull the sheet down, hold your breath and keep your eyes closed, but don't squeeze them. Try to look natural and relaxed."

Relaxed? No problem. "What about you?"

"I'll be under the table, hidden by the sheet."

The door banged open. Danny pulled the sheet over his head as the lights flared on, his heart pounding so hard he worried it would make the sheet flutter.

"I told you it was the wrong key." A man with an angry baritone voice.

"How was I supposed to see out there? Why they gotta turn out the lights at night?" said another man, his words noticeably slurred.

"So where the hell have you been?"

"I drove down the street for a few beers. Five lousy blocks."

"You were told to stay in this room until morning."

"And do what? There's no TV, not even a couch to sit on. Why we got to guard a dead body anyway?"

"You don't ask questions. You follow orders. Comprendo?"

"Yeah, yeah."

"What's that over there?" the angry baritone said.

"Looks like they brought in another stiff."

Beautiful. And it had been such a nice night for a walk on the beach. Jessica's shoe squeaked on the concrete beneath him.

"Nobody mentioned any new bodies to me. Where'd it come from?"

"Hell if I know. I work the graveyard shift. Hey, that's a pretty good line for this place. *Graveyard shift.* I'm gonna start using it."

"Let's go check it out."

Danny was having severe doubts about his ability to look dead up close. Thanks to a lifetime of skin-diving, he could hold his breath a long time, but all it would take would be one blink, a twitch, a lip quiver.

He'd be defenseless, on his back with a pair of mobsters standing over him, one of them already in a bad mood. Maybe he should strike first. Wait till they got close, lunge for a scalpel and attack.

But waiting had advantages. They might not pull the sheet down. Even if they did, a corpse springing to life would scare anyone, probably make them jump back, give him extra seconds to locate the scalpel.

"You go check it out," the beer-drinker said. "I don't get paid to look at stiffs."

"You're such a wuss."

Danny was struggling to reconstruct the scalpel's location in the rows of instruments when something touched his side. Fingers! He nearly yelped, imagining a skeleton reaching up from a crypt.

The fingers crawled down his ribs like a spider, reaching his waistband and slinking into the front pocket of his new secret agent pants. He felt his cellphone being lifted out.

Footsteps like thudding bullets pounded the concrete floor. The angry man was on his way.

In the second he had to think about it, Danny decided to try to pull off the dead-man act. If he suspected the jig was up, he'd pop his eyes open with a big scary grin. When the man reacted, he'd make a move. He sucked in a deep breath and held it.

The man reached the embalming table, still berating the beer-drinker for being a wuss. Danny could hear his heavy breathing directly above him.

Just as the sheet began to lift, a phone started ringing somewhere in the building, outside the embalming room.

The sheet dropped. "Only bossman would be calling this late. I'll get it."

Baritone's footsteps retreated in the other direction. "Why are you following me?"

"I gotta take a piss. I drank four pints."

"Hurry. Then get your ass back on the job and stay there. And thank me for saving your life by not telling bossman you deserted your post to go drink beer. Haven't you heard the stories about him? He can tear a man's heart out with one hand."

The door opened and closed.

They were gone. Danny ripped the sheet off and gulped for air.

Jessica climbed out from under the table with his phone pressed to her ear, holding a shush finger to her lips. "Hi! Is this the all-night Walmart? No? Sorry, wrong number," she said and pocketed the phone.

"Let's go!" she said.

Racing into the hallway past the casket display room, they hung a left and returned to the storage closet. Danny was finding it hard to breathe before remembering the cotton wads stuffed in his nostrils. He pulled them out as they exited the back door and Jessica relocked it.

They zigzagged back to the shadow of the gumbo-limbo tree and scaled the wall, landing in the parking lot of the pool supply store where the adventure began.

Still wearing the latex gloves, Danny kept an eye on the rear-view mirror as he eased the Hyundai onto 441 and accelerated.

"Phew," Jessica said when they came to a stoplight. "The things we do for love. My parents better appreciate this."

In the stress of the moment, Danny laughed. "How did you think to do that?" he said. "The phone."

"I don't know. I just thought it."

"How did you know the number?"

"I took a chance our old number still worked, that it went along with the business."

"Weren't you scared?"

"At the beginning, but then I thought, well, I'm going to be in the same situation whether I'm scared or not, so I might as well make a choice not to be scared. I figured my brain would work better."

He flipped her spy cap off and mussed her hair. "You're something else, kid."

She reached up and did the same to his. "You too, old man."

Chapter 17

"I DON'T UNDERSTAND what's the big problem, boss-man," Yago said. "You never hear of the KISS principle? *Keep It Simple, Stupid.* Just kill 'em."

He was referring to Jewell and his wife. *You don't understand because you're a dumbass.* Luis bit his tongue and turned his gaze out the wall of glass. Easier to ignore him than get into a tangle.

High wispy clouds amplified the light of the almost full moon over Biscayne Bay, lighting up the boats in the marina. Earlier in the day, he put a down payment on the sixty-one foot Bertram yacht with the blue stripes. Now he was wondering if it would fit in the marina.

Definitely not in his current slip, already filled to capacity by his twenty-four foot Whaler. He planned to give it to Chad as a bonus after the yacht arrived. One of the gringo's side duties was keeping it up and ready to go for whenever Luis got the urge to escape and go fishing. The coke-loving accountant had been a top-notch boatman on his college sailing team.

"If you ask my opinion, the whole reason we're in this mess is because your *El Grande* plan is too complicated," Yago said. "We're drug-runners. You got us running funeral homes. What was wrong with the old ways?"

Luis explained—again—that *running funeral homes* was going to solve the cartel's single biggest problem: safely moving large quantities of cocaine from South Florida, where it arrived from South America, to their distribution hubs in the Northeast.

People are surprised to learn the costs of transporting large quantities of illegal drugs within the United States are five times higher than the costs of getting them here. Bribes, lawyers, everything cost more in America. But the biggest expense was lost product due to arrests and seizures.

Luis said, "In the last six months, the 'old ways' have cost the organization four hundred kilograms to traffic stops, vehicle inspections, and other busts. Assuming no one screws up"—*like you* stuck to the tip of his tongue—"*El Grande* will stop those losses."

"But why you got to go overboard on everything? You got your funeral homes now. Just stuff the hearses with coke. Cops aren't going to stop a hearse."

"Cops might be less likely to stop a hearse, but there's no guarantee it won't happen. It probably will. That's why I built in back-up protections in case one system fails, like NASA."

"Nasa? He with Medellín?"

"The National Aeronautics and Space Administration. Let me go through this one more time. Hopefully the last time. If the cops don't stop one of our transport hearses, all is good. But suppose they do. Someone, like you, might argue, hey, just put the coke inside a casket."

"That's what I was thinking."

"I know. After all, who's going to open a casket? *Someone*, that's who, especially someone with drug-sniffing dogs. But no one, not even the DEA, is going to cut open an embalmed corpse dressed in his or her finest and accompanied by all the legal paperwork required to transport it interstate."

Luis didn't start out focused on using corpses as containers. He spent months researching and compiling a list of every coke-smuggling method on record.

Narcos hid it in secret vehicle compartments, flowers, fried fish, coffee, alpaca pillows, packages of tortillas, limes, jalapeños, and cucumbers, inside of watermelons, pineapples, tomatoes, donuts, cakes, candies, frozen sharks, shampoo bottles, coconuts ...

The list went on and on. Every method had one thing in common: it failed. He began to believe it was a puzzle that could never be solved. Then he came across the dead baby story.

It supposedly happened right here at the Miami International Airport. A woman was carrying a baby on a flight from Colombia. A flight attendant got suspicious when she tried to goochie-goo the tot and it didn't move. She called ahead to customs agents in Miami, who discovered the baby was dead. Cut open, stuffed with cocaine, and sewed shut.

The story turned out to be urban legend, which Luis suspected. For one thing, the logic was all wrong. How much coke could a dead baby hold? But it got him thinking.

He assessed his own considerable girth with a tape measure and calculated that if his organs were removed, along with the breast plate and a few ribs, there would be room for thirty, maybe forty kilos.

El Grande was born.

The key to it succeeding was that everything had to be done by the book, something Yago still didn't understand. "Why all the marketing crap?" he said. "We can make our own corpses. You need fat guys, a two-second walk on the beach and I get you as many as you want."

"Here's why. In addition to the homicide investigations that would follow, moving a corpse across state lines requires documentation. Death certificate, burial transit permit, some states want proof of embalming. Driver gets pulled over without them, it's game over."

Yago shrugged. "Guess we'll see tomorrow if it works."

"It's going to work."

Tomorrow was *El Grande*'s maiden voyage. It *had* to work. The capo trusted his idea enough to invest millions in it while voicing similar concerns.

They test-marketed a TV ad in Newark featuring Louis Carmen's video. Wasn't thirty minutes before a family called to take advantage of Snowbirds' plus-size discounts to bring their father, recently dead of a heart attack, home from Pompano. Weighing in at three-oh-five, the family saved fifty percent.

Like everything else, the discounts had to be explained to Yago due to his inability to see the big picture. "We'll lose money," he said.

That was true from a funeral transaction perspective, but there was a simple explanation for the discounts. Despite the built-in layers of protection, a degree of risk would exist in every trip north.

The probability of a risk occurring increased with repetition. It was true of any dangerous activity. You drive drunk one time, you probably make it home. Do it on a regular basis, you probably end up with a DUI arrest. Fewer trips meant less risk.

The discounts were based on elementary math. *Length x Width x Height = Volume*. The bigger the body, the more cocaine it could hold. Too many people shrivel to skin over bones by the time they croak. Maybe fit one or two kilos in them. The Snowbirds funeral directors had instructions to discourage skinny corpses by presenting their loved ones with inflated prices.

Tomorrow's virgin customer was a perfect model for his vision. The embalmers had already cleaned him out, embalmed him, and stuffed him with thirty-three kilograms of pure cocaine, a weight that would double once it reached its destination and got cut.

An assistant embalmer, Francisco from Honduras, suggested a craniotomy to remove the dead man's brain and wedge in an extra kilo. Luis rejected the suggestion on detection and dignity grounds, but promoted the Honduran to chief embalmer for his creative thinking. An idea man after his own heart.

The hearse was scheduled to pull out of Snowbirds at precisely eight a.m. Luis instructed Chad to purchase a five-thousand dollar bottle of vintage Dom Pérignon to celebrate the occasion.

Only one problem remained. The original of Jewell Sr.'s will was still missing. Yago had searched the old man's condo and the Jewell house twice. It remained a liability until found and destroyed, as Yago was reminding him once again.

"The undertaker and his wife could flip on us any time, especially if they got the original will to back 'em up," he said. "Strip away all your complications and what's left? Two people who know too much. Kill 'em and problem solved. Simple."

"And you don't think murdering them a week after they sold us their family business of seventy years would raise red flags?"

"I could make it look like an accident."

He probably could. For all his other deficiencies, Yago was undeniably a highly skilled killer.

"What about the kid?" Luis said.

"What about her?"

"She knows about the trust. Jewell made her sign the consent form we gave him. Where is she? You said at some aunt's house."

"That was last I heard."

"How would you propose we deal with her?"

"Well, bossman, like you said, she knows about the trust."

That ended the discussion. "Forget all that. We don't need to kill anyone. Jewell is cooperating. Let's get the forgery filed and keep looking for the original."

"Bet you he's got it," Yago said.

"He swears he doesn't. It may not even exist. He said his old man was always losing shit, maybe threw it away."

"I think he's lying."

"You know any polygraph examiners?" Luis said sarcastically.

"There you go again, boss. Unnecessary complexity."

"What do you suggest?"

"Torture. Never fails. Guaranteed."

Chapter 18

DANNY CLIMBED DOWN from a chair after stashing Jarrod Jewell Sr.'s Last Will and Testament on top of the kitchen cabinets. Jessica was getting ready for bed. It was almost three a.m.

He was wrung out, emotionally and physically, but it wasn't the kind of night you pop home from and fall into a quick, easy sleep. He sat at the dining room table in front of his computer and poured a shot of bourbon over a block of ice, flashing back to his conversation with Grady five years ago that led to the name of his surf shop.

Be careful, son. Even an alley cat only has nine lives.

I have two left, Grady. I've been keeping track.

Cut it to one. It was a miracle they got out of that place in one piece. Not only escaped, but found the will *and* solved the mystery of Snowbirds in Paradise. Crazy, crazy world—again. Maybe the God he wasn't sure existed had him on a five-year plan.

He held up the latex glove, fingertips laden with snowy powder, picturing Louis Carmen's video: *We bring your loved ones back home where they belong.* Failing to mention: *With their trunks hollowed out and stuffed with narcotics.*

All the pieces fit, including the plus-size discounts. That poor bloke on the table must have held a bundle.

Cocaine would be his guess. Danny had smoked his share of weed, but never messed with hard drugs, part of the surfer's credo. He opened a browser and typed, *What does cocaine taste like?*

Bitter and numbing.

He dipped his pinkie into the glove and touched it to his tongue. Bitter and numbing.

Jessica came out of her bedroom in a white terrycloth robe that reached her ankles. "I found this robe in the closet. Is it okay to wear it?"

It was Sari's. "Sure."

"Find out anything?"

"I think the powder is cocaine. Have you heard of it?"

"Yes, Danny. I also know about the tooth fairy. I'm practically a teenager."

He threw his arms up. "How am I supposed to know what you know or don't know? I was just asking." He took a swallow of the bourbon and set the glass down too hard, splashing it on his hand.

"This has been a stressful week for you, hasn't it?" Jessica said.

Maybe it was the bourbon, but his laugh snorted out his nose. "You could say that."

"Well, look at the bright side. We got the will and the goods on the crooks. Things are looking up," she said as his cellphone began trilling.

Ring. Ring. Ring.

"Aren't you going to answer that?" Jessica said.

He was debating it.

Hi! This is the police. Sorry to bother you so late. Did you break into a funeral home tonight? We're coming to arrest you.

Hi! We're vicious drug-traffickers. Sorry to bother you so late. You broke into our funeral home tonight. We're coming to behead you.

He picked it up and said hello.

"Danny, it's Jarrod Jewell."

"It's your dad," he said, pushing the speaker button.

"I'm here with Jessica," Danny said. "She's listening."

"Hi, Dad!"

"Um, hello," he said. "Why are you still up? It's three in the morning."

"We just got home," she said.

"Just got home? Where were you?"

Danny whispered in her ear, "Might not be the best time to explain."

"Just out and about," she said.

"I need to talk to Danny, privately."

"Too late. He told me everything."

Silence.

"Sorry, Jarrod. I thought she deserved to know."

"Everything?"

"Everything I know."

The force of his sigh overloaded the tiny phone speaker. "In that case, the latest update is Jessica's mother and I decided to leave the hotel where we were staying."

"You escaped?" Jessica said.

"I guess you really do know everything. Yes. A man named Yago came into our room. I finally learned their first names. The tall man is Yago. The wide one is Luis."

"Carmillion," Jessica said. "We've been investigating."

"We?"

"Me and Danny, and his friend Fink. He's a lawyer."

"Go ahead, Jarrod," Danny said. "What happened?"

"They were badgering me about the location of my father's original will."

"Don't worry. We have it," Jessica said.

"What? How?"

Danny said, "Let him talk first."

"I told them I didn't know where it was or if it even existed. They didn't believe me. So this Yago comes to our room a few hours ago with a pair of garden clippers, like the kind you use to trim rose bushes. Jessica, I don't want you to hear this part."

"It's okay, Dad. I can take it."

A pause before, "He said the surest way to get the truth out of someone is to cut off their body parts."

"That's probably right," Jessica said thoughtfully.

"He said he would begin with my toes, one by one, until I told him where the will was. He gave me thirty minutes to think about it. The minute he walked out we ran for the balcony and were able to climb down the outside fire escape ladder. Thank God we were only on the third floor."

"Good job, Dad!" Jessica said. "Mom too. All those aerobics classes paid off."

"They had taken our wallets but Julie had the foresight to hide her driver's license and a credit card in her makeup kit. We left everything else behind."

He explained they got a cab to take them to a drugstore where he bought a cheap phone with prepaid minutes and then to the Palm Beach airport where they rented a car.

"Are you on your way to get me?" Jessica said.

"Well, not right this moment."

"How come?"

"We left in such a panic we didn't have time to think everything through. Right now we're driving north on I-75. Our plan is to head to the panhandle and hide out until we can figure out the next best step. I think you might be safer with Danny. I hope you understand."

She knocked her heels against the chair legs. "Yep."

"Are you doing okay?"

"Mm-hm."

"How about you, Danny?

"Hanging in there," he said.

"So you really have your grandfather's original will? How?"

"It's a long story, but we have it," Jessica said. "Can I talk to Mom?"

"Of course. Jessica wants to talk to you," he said, followed by muffled talking.

Her mother finally came on. "Hey there, darling!"

Danny hadn't exchanged two words with Julie Jewell but it was easy to recognize the counterfeit sunshine squeezed into her voice. She sounded like someone struggling to keep it together.

"Mom! I miss you. Danny doesn't know how to give good-night hugs … and I just miss you."

"Oh, Jess, darling. We miss you too. So, so much." Her voice cracked and Danny heard short, breathless whimpers before Jewell apparently took the phone back.

"Me again. Your mother's not in a great place right now. I'm sure we'll be seeing you soon. Stay strong, sweetie."

"Yeah, you too," she said and got up and walked away.

"Give me the short version of how you found the will."

"She's gone, Jarrod. She went to her room."

"Damn, I screwed up again. I keep making one bad decision after another. Just when I thought I was getting some nerve back, Yago came in with those clippers. We didn't do a lot of clear thinking. Just ran."

"Escaping was a good decision," Danny said, leaving out his opinion that they should have escaped in the direction of their daughter.

He gave Jewell a heavily redacted explanation of how they found the will and solved the mystery of why a mob wanted to get into the funeral business.

"Corpses stuffed with drugs. I wouldn't have guessed that one. But how did you—"

"Jarrod, dawn's coming soon. I'm tired and you must be too. I'll give you the details another time. I do have one more thing to tell you. We're going to the police in the morning and I'm not interested in hearing any more of your protests about it."

Silence again before, "I wish you wouldn't do that."

"It's time." Beyond time. "You're safe now. Things are getting out of control here. Lay low and you should be okay."

He made sure he had the number for Jewell's new burner

phone, ended the call, and walked down the hall. "Knock, knock," he said.

"Come in."

Jessica was lying on the bed on her back, straight as a board, staring at the ceiling. Like a corpse. He shook the image away.

"How are you doing?"

"Fine and dandy except for the fact that even my own parents don't love me. That leaves Gloria who likes to be called Gigi and Norma Pollinuk from the funeral home, and I'm not even sure about them."

"Of course your parents love you."

"*Pfft.* They're going to the panhandle without me. They'll probably stay in Destin at the Slackwater, my favorite hotel. We went there on a vacation once. It has a pool with a water slide, a game room, and free hot dogs."

"They're not going on vacation. Remember, they've been threatened and held hostage. I'm no expert, but I'm guessing they're traumatized."

"I would have gone and got them."

"They're not as strong as you. I'm not sure anyone is." He didn't mean to say it. It slipped out.

"You are."

A weak laugh. "No, not me."

"You were brave tonight."

"It was all an act. I was scared to death. I told your dad we're going to the police tomorrow. He wasn't happy about it, but I decided to do it. You okay with that?"

"I guess. Do you love me, Danny?"

"Huh?"

"I'm trying to think if there's anyone I could add to my list."

"Well, love can mean many different things. I have tremendous fondness for you."

"Fondness? Whatever."

He thought about her question as he wrestled to get settled in his bed. He had no idea what love meant when it came to a kid. And he didn't want to love anyone, couldn't bear the thought of letting someone in and losing them again.

Sari would have liked her. He was sure of that. They were talking about having a child when the docs dropped the hammer that her cancer was terminal. She wanted a girl. He asked what kind and she said, *That's a silly question. Obviously, a girl who could take over the world.* That would be Jessica Jewell.

Exhaustion overcame the tornado swirling in his head and he fell into a deep sleep.

*   *   *

His eyes popped open. Sounds in the condo. He sat upright and listened. Something out there. He picked up the baseball bat he kept by the door and stalked into the hallway. The sounds were coming from Jessica's room. He stood at the door.

Weeping. Long mournful sobs. They tore at him, but there was also some relief. She'd been repressing everything since the moment she walked into the Tradewinds.

Knowing her, she would want to be left alone, but that didn't mean it was the right thing to do. She went to bed wondering if her own parents loved her.

Cracking the door, he saw her small frame curled under the covers in the center of the queen-size bed, clutching something to her face. In the moonlight filtering through the sheer curtains, he made out what it was.

Snoopy, sentimental Sari's favorite stuffed animal from childhood. The famous beagle was perched on her pillows the first time he visited her bedroom when they were ten years old. Jessica must have searched the whole closet to find him.

The crying stopped abruptly. She knew he was there.

"What do you want, Danny? I'm sorry if I woke you up."

"Nothing to be sorry about. Is it okay if I sit on your bed?"

"Mm-hm."

Wet blotches darkened her pillowcase. He didn't know what to say. Everything that came to mind was trite. *What's wrong?* Everything, obviously. *Is there anything I can do?* Like what?

"I see you found Snoopy."

"He was in the closet. I wasn't being nosey. I was just looking for something. Is he yours?"

"No, he belonged to Sari, ever since she was a little girl."

She wiped Snoopy's head with her pillowcase and held him out. "Here. I got some snot on him. Sorry. It'll wash out."

"You keep him. Sari would want you to have him."

"Are you sure?"

"Very."

"Okay. You can go back to bed. I'm all better now."

He doubted that. "Hey, I wanted to clarify something. You asked if I loved you. Let me explain it this way. If someone was trying to hurt you and the only way to save you was by giving up my own life, I would do it. Does that sound like love?"

"I don't know. Maybe."

Chapter 19

"**WELL WELL WELL.** Danny *Teak*well. A blast from the past."

Detective Emilio Rodriguez sat behind a gunmetal-gray desk chewing on a toothpick. He never grew tired of spitting out Danny's last name, even after his status evolved from most-wanted fugitive to hometown hero five years ago. Always snazzy, he wore a mauve suit with narrow lapels over a light-blue dress shirt with a spread collar. His skinny tie, held in place by a gold clip, featured tiny pink flamingos on a navy background.

Danny and Jessica sat in mismatched guest chairs in front of the desk, one black vinyl, the other brown fabric. It was early afternoon. They slept in after their late night invading the funeral home.

"Long time no see," Rodriguez said. "How's lottery life been treating you?"

"You know what they say. Easy come, easy go. Thanks for agreeing to meet with us. This is Jessica."

"I never knew you had a daughter."

"She's not my daughter, just staying with me for a few days at her parents' request. She's in trouble. Her whole family is. That's why we're here."

"Let's hear it," he said, leaning back and planting his gleaming alligator loafers on the desk.

He showed surprising patience as Danny unspooled the

story of the two men who threatened the Jewells into selling their family funeral home, until he got to the parts about Snowbirds in Paradise, Louis Carmen's marketing video, and the plus-size discounts.

"Hold on," he said. "You lost me. What does all that have to do with the Slugger funeral home?"

"Slagger-Jewell," Jessica corrected.

"Everything," Danny said. "There's a lot to fill in, but I'll cut to the chase. We think it's all part of an elaborate drug-smuggling scheme."

"Who's *we*?"

"Me and Jessica."

"So you decided to take on a partner this time, huh? Sort of a Mulder and Scully thing. Are aliens involved?"

"Remember, Detective, you didn't believe me last time either."

"Alright, go on."

"We think a South American drug cartel is behind it and that they're using Slagger-Jewell as the staging point to distribute cocaine to five funeral homes in the Northeast."

"There's that *think* word again. You got any evidence?"

"We do." He pulled out a zip-top bag containing the glove with the white powder and tossed it on his desk.

Rodriguez opened it and tasted the powder. "That's cocaine alright. Very pure cocaine. This from your personal stash?"

"Danny doesn't use drugs," Jessica said indignantly.

"He's making a joke," Danny said. "I think."

"I hope he's a better detective than a comedian."

Rodriguez shot her a look, brushy eyebrows stitched together. "Where'd you come across this?"

Danny let out a half-hearted laugh. "Well, you know, it's kind of a strange story." One he dreaded telling because he knew Rodriguez wouldn't believe it. "We found it last night while visiting the newly named Snowbirds in Paradise funeral home. You see—"

"It was inside a dead body," Jessica said. "They're smuggling it in corpses."

The detective spit out his toothpick and returned his feet to the floor. "This some kinda hidden camera prank, Teakwell? You trying to get back at me for making a reasonable mistake five years ago you were a psychotic killer?"

"It's true," Jessica said. "I personally got that powder from the abdominal cavity of a dearly beloved we found last night on an embalming table."

"Dearly beloved?"

"Her euphemism for corpses," Danny said. "She's the undertaker's daughter. This corpse was an extremely large dearly beloved. Probably three hundred pounds. That's why I mentioned the plus-size discounts. They're part of the scheme. The bigger the bodies, the more coke. At least that's the way I figure it."

"Me too," Jessica said.

"I'll play along," Rodriguez said. "So, Jessie—"

"Jessica."

"Excuse me. Why were you inside a funeral home your family no longer owns poking around the abdominal cavity of a dearly beloved? I guess that's two questions."

Danny said, "Go ahead, tell him."

"Okay, but it's complicated. My lawyer and I believe I still own a one-third interest in our funeral home. So that's the first thing. We had to find my grandfather's original will before the cartel kills my parents and—"

"Whoa," Rodriguez said. "That does sound complicated. For now, let's fast forward to how you happened to be exploring the insides of a corpse."

"Oh, that part's short. I just cut him open with a pair of surgical scissors."

Danny jumped in. "He had already been cut open and sewed shut by the cartel people. All she did was snip a few stitches."

"From what we could tell, his body cavities were completely

stuffed with that white powder," Jessica said. "Even the ribs and breastbone were missing."

Rodriguez looked around like he was still searching for a hidden camera. Danny didn't blame him. It was all true. He'd lived it. But hearing it spoken in official quarters, *prank* was almost a compliment. It sounded insane.

Danny ran his hands through his hair. "Detective, I know it sounds bizarre. It *is* bizarre. If you let us fill in the gaps, it will make more sense."

"Hold on," he said, picking up his desk phone. "Audrey, I have a drug sample that needs analyzing. How soon can we get it done? Mm-hm, got it right here." He set down the phone.

"Before you go on," he said, "how long have you known about this alleged scheme?"

"We've been trying to piece things together for about ... "

"Five days," Jessica said.

"Why didn't you come sooner, instead of burglarizing a business?"

Danny said, "That's where I'm going next and why it's crucial that everything we're telling you needs to be kept confidential. I already mentioned the people who extorted the funeral home threatened her family."

"What kind of threats?"

Danny looked at Jessica. "I didn't tell you these details. You want to hear this?"

"You keep asking me that. It's getting annoying. I want to know everything."

"Well, according to her father, they threatened to cut her family into a hundred pieces if they refused to sell and a thousand pieces if they went to the police."

"A thousand?" Jessica said. "That seems excessive. Even a hundred. I mean, seriously, two is enough. Separate head from trunk. End of story." Turning to Rodriguez, "This cartel is known for cutting people's heads off according to one of our sources."

"Sources?"

"Yes, we've been investigating."

"Teakwell, why is this kid here with you and not her parents?"

"Like she said, it's complicated. If you'll just bear with us ..."

Danny explained the will situation and the attempt by Jessica's parents to flee, only to be tracked and held hostage at the hotel in Boca.

"Her parents were cooperating, willing to go along to get this behind them. The cartel guys said they were preparing a forged will for her father to file in probate, one that left out Jessica's thirty-percent interest. But they were still looking for her grandfather's original will to get rid of it."

"Getting complicated again."

"I can simplify everything," Jessica said. "To find the original will, they threatened to cut my dad's toes off. So my parents escaped down a fire ladder and are hiding in the panhandle."

"So this is all real? You're not putting me on?"

"It's real," Danny said.

"Where is this will? Does anyone know?"

"We have it," Jessica said. "That's why we went to the funeral home last night. My grandpa hid it in his napping casket. He died two weeks ago, right before everything started happening."

"Napping casket?"

"That part's not important," Danny said, afraid they might lose him again.

"What's all this about a cartel? Where did that come from?"

"Our lawyer," Jessica said. "Bennie Finkel."

"Finkel! That clown's still masquerading as a lawyer?"

Danny said, "He's legit now. Just passed the bar exam. He got access to Snowbirds' corporate records. They show a *Luis Carmillion* as president. A Miami detective told Fink's investigator Carmillion has ties to a South American drug cartel called Los Loppers. Apparently, their trademark is decapitation."

"Never heard of them. Teakwell, how does a surf bum like you get involved in another shitshow like this?"

"Danny's not a bum," Jessica said. "Quit insulting him or we'll take our case to another police department."

"Don't worry, young lady. If your story pans out, I'll be calling the feds. DEA and FBI. They'll take over whether I want them to or not. We don't have the resources to investigate international drug cartels."

"What should we do in the meantime?" Danny said.

"*Nothing.* No more private investigating. You'll be hearing from either me or the feds. I can't guarantee how long it will take. Things aren't going to happen overnight. You have a way to contact her parents?"

"I have the number they called from last night. They bought a cheap phone with prepaid minutes at a drugstore."

He handed Danny a pad and pen. "Write it down, along with your contact info."

"If you talk to them, be gentle," Danny said. "They're scared out of their minds."

"If your story is verified, and that's a big *if,* they could be eligible for the federal witness protection program. Jessica too. In the meantime ..." He paused and looked at Jessica.

"Go ahead and say it," Danny said. "You heard her. She wants to know everything."

"Very well," Rodriguez said. "In the meantime, there's a good possibility people will want to take her into state custody if she's not reunited with her parents soon."

"Uh-uh. No way. I'm with Danny. My parents are the ones who wanted me to stay with him."

"I didn't say for sure it's going to happen. Just wanted you to be aware of the possibility."

"Well, I'm saying for sure it's *not* going to happen. I'm not going anywhere."

"Sorry, kid. It won't be up to you."

"Danny won't let them take me, will you, Danny?"

Danny sensed panic vibrating through her thick shield of bravado. He knew it wasn't going to be up to him either. "Detective, would there be any way around that happening?"

"Sure. Just get yourself appointed as her guardian. Kidding. That ain't gonna happen. Get her back with her parents."

Chapter 20

LUIS SAT WITH YAGO and Chad watching the security video on a wall-mounted monitor in the Brickell conference room. The wall of glass overlooking the bay was curtained to block out the sun glare.

Still not much to see. Just two grainy shadows in black with a flashlight creeping down the main hallway. They stopped at the embalming room, unlocked it in seconds, and disappeared inside.

"Dammit, Chad," Luis said. "Why is it so dark in there? And where are the outside cameras?"

Chad squirmed in his seat, eyes glued to his computer screen, blond bangs plastered to his forehead with sweat. "Sir, the only lights operating at the time were the emergency exit signs. The previous owners set the lights to shut off automatically at night, presumably to save energy. That issue has already been fixed.

"As for cameras, the security contractor couldn't get started until yesterday because his truck was in the shop. The only cameras installed so far are this one and one monitoring the front door."

"But they didn't come in the front door, did they, Chad?"

"No, sir."

"Then how did they get in? I thought we changed the locks."

"They entered through a backdoor the locksmiths missed. It was old and painted over. And we didn't change the inside locks. We talked about that, remember? You said there was no point."

Luis sputtered, "Camera installers with no transportation, locksmiths who miss locks. Where do you find these people?"

"They were on *Carmelita's List*, the cartel's list of approved contractors. I can show it to you. It's right here on my computer."

"Forget it. Tell me this. Where was the person assigned to stay in the embalming room all night?"

"He lied at first and said he only left to use the bathroom, but the hallway camera showed him leaving for two hours. He told his supervisor he went down the street to a bar. Needless to say, he's been terminated."

Employee termination had two meanings in Luis's world. He preferred not to know which one applied, so didn't ask.

"The good news is that nothing in the embalming room looked disturbed and the first shipment went out as scheduled without a hitch. Eight a.m. on the dot."

"The timestamp on the video shows they were in there for almost an hour," Luis said. "What the hell were they doing? And what was this bullshit I heard about a disappearing second corpse?"

Yago slumped in his chair with his long legs stretched out. "I told you to put a camera in the embalming room. You never listen to me."

"And I told you that only morons record video of themselves committing crimes carrying potential life sentences."

Chad said, "Most likely, the second corpse was the intruders trying to hide."

"Not just trying. They did it. Who were these two? One's either a dwarf or a kid. And how could they have keys to the locks?"

"Got to be the Jewell kid," Yago said.

"I thought she was only twelve. What is she, some kind of ninja?"

"Only thing that makes sense. Has the keys and knows her away around even in the dark."

"Assuming it was her, who was with her? Obviously not her father. You only lost him yesterday."

Yago straightened in his chair. "Hey, I didn't lose him. I wasn't in charge of security."

"You had to go and threaten to cut the man's toes off. He was cooperating. No wonder he climbed down the fire escape. I never authorized torture."

"I told you it was the best way to go."

"And I ignored you. It's time you start learning about chain of command."

Yago's insubordination was getting worse and setting a bad example. Couldn't let people like Chad see him getting away with disobeying orders and mouthing off. But his options for addressing it were limited, especially if his uncle really was pals with the capo.

"Let's work on something constructive," Luis said. "Do we have any idea where Jewell and his wife are?"

"Not at the moment," Chad said. "We checked and they didn't go back home, but that's about it."

"I told you we shoulda killed 'em," Yago said.

"One more *I told you so* and I'm throwing you through that window. It's thirty-seven floors to the ground."

Yago raised his palms in mock deference.

"Chad, find someone to enhance this video, see if we can get a better look at these two. Yago, do whatever you can to find Jewell and his wife. But hear my words. Do not harm them without my okay. That is a direct order. Is that clear?"

"Yeah, bossman. It's clear," he said with a yawn.

Chapter 21

THEY WENT TO the surf shop after the meeting with Rodriguez. Danny called Jewell's new phone as soon as they arrived. It went to voicemail. He left a message explaining what they had done.

"I gave the detective your number so be expecting a call, either from him or the DEA or FBI. I'm not sure when it will be, but hopefully soon. Call us back when you can."

Danny pocketed the phone and walked back to the workshop. Jessica followed him.

"So what's our next move in the case?" she said.

"You heard the detective. He said to hold tight, no more private investigating."

"I know he said that, but what are we going to do?"

"Listen to him."

She didn't like that answer and was about to object when Danny's phone chimed. "This might be your dad. Hello?"

"Danny, it's Fink."

"What's up?"

"I need your help. My fitness hearing with the state bar is this afternoon and I need a character witness."

"You're just now looking for one?"

"I had some, but they all backed out when they found out they'd be under oath, even my parents. I'm really in a jam."

"When and where is it?"

"It's starts in an hour, in Coral Gables."

"That doesn't even give me time to change. I'm wearing a t-shirt and shorts with flipflops."

"I don't care if you show up nude. If I botch this hearing, I can't practice law."

"Alright. Give me the address. I'll head there right now."

He put down the phone. "That was Fink."

"I gathered."

"He needs me as a witness at his fitness hearing. You'll have to go with me."

"You're going to close the store again? I can run it."

"I don't doubt that, but I can't leave you alone with everything that's going on."

From the moment Jewell called with the news of their hotel escape Danny had re-upped his vigilance. Would they try to come after Jessica? It wouldn't make any sense. She's just a kid. Still, he stayed alert.

"Maybe I could get Erin to help."

"Erin?"

"Delonia. The surf champion. We still have her number."

"We're not going to do that and don't have time to debate it. Let's go."

*   *   *

The hearing was at the Coral Gables Branch Court on Ponce de Leon. An accident on I-95 slowed them down. They arrived just in time to see Fink being placed under oath.

They sat in back. Three hearing officers, two men and a woman, occupied a long table in front. A court reporter sat off to one side.

The woman in the middle was obviously in charge. Her name plate said *Beviak*. Everyone was dressed in business clothes except Danny and Jessica, who looked like they just strolled in off the beach, which they essentially did.

"Mr. Finkel," Beviak said. "I will be asking you several questions and remind you that you are under oath. As you are aware, you are here today because of your prior unauthorized practice of law. Do you admit or deny that?"

"Admit, Your Honor."

"I'm not a judge. You can call me Ms. Beviak. And your unauthorized practice of law was not simply an isolated incident. Is that correct?"

"Correct," he said. "I ran a full-service law firm." The hearing officers winced in unison.

"Without a license."

"Correct."

"Without taking the bar exam."

"Correct."

"Without attending law school."

"Correct."

"What could have possibly possessed you to do such a thing?"

"That's an easy one, Judge, I mean, Ms. Beviak. For as long as I can remember, I've had a passion to pursue justice."

It took effort for Danny to keep a straight face.

"Admirable," she said. "But why did you not take the necessary steps to do so lawfully?"

"I faced a number of obstacles. I intended to go to law school, but when I looked into taking the LSAT, I found out you had to go to college first."

"Let's stop there. I see from your records that immediately before enrolling in law school you received a bachelor's degree in sports management from Geckelstein University. Where is that located?"

"No idea. It was all online."

"And you managed to obtain that degree in a mere twelve months."

"It was what they call an accelerated program. But it was legit. I'm sure you have my certified transcript."

"I do. I'm looking at your course list. *Online Betting 101. Advanced Fantasy Football.*"

"That one was a killer, believe me. Geckelstein has very high academic standards."

"What about this? *Bonus or Bribe: How to Stray the Line.*"

"I'm glad you mentioned it. It was an elective. Solid proof of my commitment to the rule of law."

"Yes, well, why didn't you begin your undergraduate route when you initially learned you needed a bachelor's degree to attend law school?"

"My passion for justice was so strong, so powerful, that I just couldn't hold it back. Like an orgasm you want to delay when you're choking the chicken, if you get my drift. Sometimes no matter how hard you try, you can't help letting go. For men, that is. I'm not sure how it works with the ladies."

"What's he talking about?" Jessica whispered. "Why do the judges look upset?"

Danny opened his mouth but no words came out.

"As I said, I faced a number of obstacles. The undergraduate degree was just one of them. I've been a victim of discrimination my whole life."

"What kind of discrimination?"

"You see this red hair? Are you and the other hearing officers aware they used to burn redheaded people at the stake for being witches?"

"That was centuries ago."

"And we've never recovered from the scars. I also have a severe learning disability. Attention Deficit Disorder."

"What does that have to do with practicing law without a license?"

"Huh?"

"I said what does that have to do with practicing law without a license?"

"Oh, yeah. See how severe it is? I forgot what we were talking about."

Jessica groaned.

"Mr. Finkel, none of this is a justification for opening a law firm when you're not a lawyer."

"I beg to differ. Moreover, I respectfully ask the panel to quit living in the past. It's psychologically unhealthy."

He foraged through a pile of papers. "Allow me to read an excerpt from a respected medical journal. *When living in the past becomes a person's dominant focus, it can inhibit moving forward to develop new interests and relationships.* The same article notes that *nostalgia* was recognized as a mental illness all the way back in the seventeenth century. I say it's time to look to the future."

Danny had to give Fink credit. He delivered this meritless argument with all the verve and vigor of Clarence Darrow defending the Scopes trial.

"Are you completely mad?" Beviak said.

"I don't know about completely, but yeah, I'm a little ticked off."

"Mr. Finkel, I'm confident I speak for the entire panel when I say nostalgia is not the emotion evoked by your blatant disregard of all relevant rules in deciding to operate a fulltime law firm without attending law school and taking the bar exam."

"He seems to get in trouble a lot," Jessica whispered.

Danny nodded.

"Once again, that was in the past. When I realized the error of my ways, I closed my law firm by my own volition."

As Danny remembered it, he closed it because he felt the heat closing in.

Beviak rubbed her eyes and said, "Do you have any evidence to offer on your behalf?"

"Indeed I do. If I may." He stepped out of the witness chair and moved front and center. "I brought with me today my star client from my unauthorized practice of law days ... and his little friend," he said, noticing Jessica for the first time.

"You are looking at Danny Teakwell. Five years ago he was charged with a gruesome murder involving cutting off a man's penis and drilling his eyes out. He also won the lottery. I'm sure you recall this celebrated case. It was in the headlines every day. But in case you were living under a rock, allow me to refresh your memories ..."

Fink went on to describe the whole sordid mess. Jessica hung onto every word, narrating in a hushed voice: *Wow, Danny. You did that? So that's how you got shot.*

"Thank you, Mr. Finkel. We are aware of the case, as well as the illegality of your representing the defendant in it."

"Well, let's just hear what that defendant has to say about my illegal representation. Ladies and gentlemen, I present to you, here today in Coral Gables for the first time, my character witness. Danny Teakwell!"

It came out like Ed Sullivan introducing The Beatles.

"Go get 'em, Danny," Jessica said, clapping.

He pushed himself up and reluctantly made his feet move toward the witness chair. Why did he agree to this?

Beviak told him to raise his right hand and extracted his word to tell the truth, adding a warning that lying under oath is a felony.

Fink asked if he could approach the witness.

"You may, but leave out the theatrics."

"Of course. Please state your name for the record," he said.

"Danny Teakwell."

"How long have you known me?"

"Since high school."

"And isn't it true that I was and remain the best friend you ever had?"

"Um, we're definitely friends."

"And isn't it true that even in those tender years of youth, you saw my true character?"

"Well, yes."

"Please give the panel your opinion of my character," he said smugly.

Danny measured his words, wanting to avoid committing

perjury while also not hurting Fink's case. "I would describe Mr. Finkel as a person who ... always means well."

"Distinguished panel, did you hear what he said? Under oath? He said I *always* mean well. Not just sometimes. Not even most of the time. *Always*."

Leave it to Fink to convert his lukewarm endorsement into the testimonial of the century.

"What can you add to that, Mr. Teakwell?" he said.

"I wouldn't even know where to start." True. "You have too many qualities to list." Also true. Many of them were bad qualities, but he had a lot.

"Thank you. Allow me to take you back in time, to the terrifying year of nineteen ninety-five. There you were, framed for murder in a diabolical revenge plot. Scurrilously labeled *The Lottery Lunatic* in the press. Facing the electric—"

"Enough," Beviak said. "We get the picture."

"Isn't it true the state was seeking the death penalty in your case?"

"Yes."

"Mr. Teakwell, when you had given up all hope, when you were convinced you were a mere bus ride away from being strapped to Old Sparky, who did you turn to for help?"

"For my lawyer? You."

"Yes. *Me*. And please tell the panel how *me* did."

"He did great, honestly. All the charges were dismissed." Most of it had to do with Danny's exploits, but Fink definitely performed above the expectations of someone who skipped law school.

Fink echoed, "*All* the charges were dismissed. Because of my excellent legal representation—unauthorized though it may have been—an innocent man was spared. Free to fully pursue life, liberty, and happiness in this great nation of ours. Isn't that right, Mr. Teakwell?"

"I suppose."

"Mr. Teakwell, could you please tell the panel how rare it is for a lawyer to get a defendant off on a first-degree murder charge?"

"You're asking me?"

"Hold on, I wasn't finished. Then please ask the panel members if any of them has ever successfully represented a criminal defendant in a capital case."

"Halt. We've heard enough," Beviak said. "Thank you, Mr. Teakwell. You may step down. Is that it, Mr. Finkel?"

"Just one more thing. I would like the record to reflect that since the day I passed the bar exam, I have been paying penance for my previous sins by devoting myself to rendering pro bono service."

"To whom?"

"The most vulnerable of our society. Children." He pointed at Jessica. "Specifically, to that adorable, lovable, innocent cherub sitting right there."

"In what capacity?"

"As a trusted legal advisor in a matter most delicate. Attorney-client privilege prevents me from discussing the details, and I, of course, would never consider breaching such an important rule of professional ethics."

"Is this true?" Beviak asked Jessica.

She stood up. "Yes, ma'am. He's been very helpful."

"Mr. Finkel, we will take this matter under advisement. You will be notified of the result. In the meantime, you are permitted to practice law. This hearing is adjourned."

Chapter 22

"**I KILLED IT,**" Fink said, taking a swig of beer and smacking his lips. "I mean, I don't like to brag, but the truth cannot be denied."

They were at the Tradewinds, seated at the bar. Fink insisted he wanted a real celebration after the hearing. It was Friday happy hour and the place was packed. They drank pints and ate Goldfish from a bowl.

"I wouldn't get my hopes up too soon," Danny said. "Let's just keep our fingers crossed."

"Are you kidding me? Did you see the looks on their faces when I turned the tables on them with that living in the past argument?"

"Yes. Yes, I did."

"And having Jessica there was a stroke of luck. How could they not love me after seeing the mug on that kid?"

Danny kept an eye on her as she zipped back and forth wearing one of Shannon's server aprons tied to her waist, helping deliver food orders and clear tables. Shannon and Tulia offered to share their tips with her, but Jessica turned them down.

Grady came over and put coasters under their glasses. "That girl's a ball a fire, ain't she? Any word from Goebbels yet?"

"Goebbels?" Fink said.

"Grady's nickname for Rodriguez," Danny said. He still held a grudge against the detective for breaking down Danny's door five years ago and hauling him away in shackles with Grady hollering *Gestapo!* "Not yet, but he said nothing was going to happen overnight."

"How's she holding up?" Grady said.

"Outwardly, she seems okay, almost weirdly so, but she keeps a lot of things locked up."

"Hm, reminds me of a fellow I know," Grady said, removing his captain's cap and scratching his coarse white hair. "Can't quite place him, but definitely someone I know."

Subtle, Grady was not.

Fink swaggered to the jukebox and inserted some change. On his way back to the bar, an indelible bass riff began playing.

"MC Hammer?" Danny said.

"That's right, baby. Watch this. All I need are the baggy pants. *Please Fink, don't hurt 'em,*" he wailed and began wildly thrashing his arms while attempting to scissor his legs to *U Can't Touch This.*

Jessica came running up breathless. "Danny, look who I— What's wrong with Fink? Is he having a seizure?"

"Dancing," Danny said. "What's the matter?"

"Look who I found!" She pointed to the bar table near the front window where they usually sat. "It's Erin, and she's alone."

Fink stopped gyrating. "Who is that? What a hottie! She looks like Michelle Phillips just stepped out of a Mamas and the Papas album cover. That blonde hair, long and lean, and—"

"Fink, shut up," Danny said.

But he was right. Erin was a beauty. He hadn't really noticed it at the surf shop, probably because he was staring at his shoes. The Michelle Phillips comparison wasn't far off. She looked like an older version of the women Danny used to dream about listening to Beach Boys songs as a kid, a California girl to the core.

"She just sat down and ordered something from Tulia," Jessica said. "Go over and talk to her."

"About what?"

She did a face-palm. "You'll think of something. Go."

He stayed glued to the bar stool.

"Tulia," Grady said, sliding a glass of white wine across the bar. "For the lady by the window."

Jessica said, "Danny will take it over there. Won't you?"

A guttural laugh from Grady and smirky smile from Tulia. Fink said, "Don't tell me you're going to abandon me two celebrations in a row."

With all four of them staring, he summoned the courage to pick up the wine. "I'll be back in a minute."

"Just be yourself," Jessica said as he shambled toward the table.

His relationship coach was a tween mortician. He really needed to rethink life.

"Erin? Hi. I'm Danny Teakwell. We met at my surf shop."

"I remember. You blew me off."

"Sorry it came out that way. I, uh, brought the wine you ordered." He put it down.

"I'm just messing with you. Have a seat. You work at this place?"

"I spend enough time here to qualify for overtime pay, but no. Just friends with the owner. I live in the building. How's the expo going?"

"I hate it. I'm a surfer, not a spokesmodel. But it pays the rent."

"How are you liking Hollywood?" That was the best he could come up with? Next he'd be asking, *What's your sign?*

She said it was a nice escape from Miami, no glitz and less traffic. "I like your beach, despite the pitiful waves. It's peaceful. I've been taking strolls after work and stopping in different places to check them out. Tonight I picked this place."

"I'm glad you did. I really do want to apologize for acting weird at my shop. It had nothing to do with you."

"None of my business. Just so you know, I was only looking for a friend to hang out with while I'm here. A surf buddy would have been even better."

Jessica appeared at the table wielding a pen and order book.

She had two additional pens clipped to the pocket of her apron, imitating Shannon. "Erin! I thought that was you. I'm Jessica. We met at our surf shop. What a nice surprise. Do you need anything?"

"Well, hello there. Danny didn't tell me you worked here." She picked up the menu. "Is the food any good?"

"Not really. It's greasy and the kitchen is filthy. The date on the last inspection sticker looks like it was written over with a pen. Danny, don't tell Grady I said that, but you know I don't lie. Especially to Erin."

Erin laughed and looked at Danny.

"It's your basic bar food," he said. "I haven't inspected the kitchen lately, but have no reason to doubt Harriet the Spy here."

"In that case, I think I'll pass," Erin said.

"Danny, two things," Jessica said. "Grady wants to know if you want another beer and Fink is acting drunk and looks like he's going to start crying if you don't invite him to join you."

Danny hesitated before deciding he couldn't inflict Fink on Erin. The memories of the day's hearing were too fresh. "I'm here to celebrate my friend's court case with him."

"Go celebrate," Erin said. "I just stopped in for a glass of wine."

Jessica's stare was burning a hole in him, bringing back her lecture at the shop. *I think you chased her away because of Sari, and I also think Sari would have wanted you to hang out with her.*

And he liked her. What were the odds of that? "Hey, tomorrow's Saturday. Do you work on weekends?"

She put her palms together. "No. Thank you, Lord."

"You up for a challenge?"

"Always. What do you have in mind?"

"Tackling the death-defying waves of Hollywood Beach."

"Haha. I'm always up for surfing. On one condition. Jessica goes with us."

Jessica's pen clattered to the floor. "In the ocean?"

"That's the best place," Erin said.

"We can't do it. We have to keep the shop open. Sorry," she said. "Danny, did you want that beer?"

"I'll come get it. You're not allowed to serve alcohol. It's against the law."

She flipped her order book closed and marched away.

Erin fanned herself with the menu. "First you blow me off, then she does. What is up with you two?"

"That girl might be the most fearless person I've ever known, with one exception. She has a phobia about the ocean and drowning. I've been trying to talk her into a surf lesson but she keeps dodging it."

"Ah. Well, we all have our fears."

"The thing is, I think she really wants to do it."

"Don't pressure her. She'll come around in her own time. How about just you and I go?" she said.

"Sounds good. Do you mind going early? If I don't open Nine Lives on time, my business manager over there might fire me. She's been helping me get the shop back on track, get *me* back on track." All while her own life was falling apart.

"That seems like a good opening to ask a question, if you don't mind."

"Ask away."

"What's eating you? You've been twisting that napkin into confetti since you sat down. And then there was that day at the shop. Is there something about me that makes you nervous? That's the vibe I get."

He looked down at his lap, covered with a snow flurry of shredded napkin bits. He debated taking the easy way out by lying, but she deserved better.

"You're the first woman I've met, even as a friend, since my wife died a year ago. Breast cancer. Hearing myself say it, I realize it must sound ridiculous. Poor, poor pitiful me."

"It doesn't sound ridiculous. It sounds honest. I'm sorry about your wife. Truly. What was her name?"

"Sari."

"That's a pretty name. My little brother, Kevin, died in a car accident when he was only fifteen. It was ten years ago. I still think about him every day. Nobody gets it. They all expect me to get over it."

He felt something move inside him. Looking into her ocean-green eyes, he fought off the temptation to turn away. "I'm really sorry about Kevin."

Jessica reappeared. "I changed my mind," she said. "I want to go surfing, but I don't know how and I'm afraid of the ocean. There, I said it. Knowing Danny, he probably already blabbed it to you."

"Are you sure?" Erin said.

"Mm-hm. I've felt like a total fraud selling surfboards."

"Okay, we're on," she said. "Don't worry. We'll start you out with a lesson on dry land. Then when we hit the water, you'll be in good hands with two of the best surfers in town."

"Can we try tandem first?"

"Of course," Danny said. "I'll be holding onto you the whole time."

"I mean Erin and me."

"Oh. Well, of course."

"You know how to swim, right?" Erin said.

"Mm-hm."

"Have you ever ridden a skateboard?"

"Yes, I have one. I'm pretty good. I can't do any tricks, but I have good balance."

"Great, there's a lot of similarity. Other than balance, the hardest parts of surfing are catching the wave and what's called the pop-up. That's where you get off your belly and stand up. We're not going to worry about that tomorrow. It takes more than one lesson."

"Then how will I stand up?"

"Like Danny said, I'll be holding onto you and I'll help pull you up. Don't worry about your form or how you look. Just have fun."

"Okay."

"I'll give it to you straight. There's a chance we'll fall off the board and you might swallow some water. It won't hurt you though."

"Do I have to wear a life vest?"

"If Danny has one and you want to, but I don't think you'll need it."

"Good. I don't want to look like a baby."

"Danny, I assume you have a longboard we can use."

"Absolutely. I have a nine-footer at the shop that will be perfect."

Grady called from the bar. "Jessica, could you give me a hand washing some glasses? This place is hopping tonight."

"Sure, Grady! I gotta go. See you tomorrow."

Danny couldn't stop smiling. "Do you have kids?" he asked as she trotted away.

"Not me. Why do you ask?"

"You were just so natural with her. It's like you already figured her out. I know that girl and she's going to want to be perfect right off the bat."

She laughed. "I was exactly the same way."

They arranged to meet at Nine Lives at eight. "I still have your number. Let me give you mine." Danny scribbled his phone number on her napkin since he had torn his to pieces.

"I'll look forward to it," he said, and meant it, which surprised him. He glanced over at Fink, talking to Shannon. "I better go help my friend celebrate, and rescue the server from him."

"So he won a big court case today?"

"Not exactly."

*   *   *

They didn't get back to the condo until after talking an intoxicated Fink out of celebration mode and into taxicab mode. The cab sped away with him hollering *I killed it!* out the window.

His celebration reached a low point, literally, when he got down on one knee to propose to Shannon and couldn't get back up, spuriously blaming it on an old football injury. Shannon was a good sport, laughing it off and saying she'd keep it in mind if she ever got divorced.

Danny emptied his pockets on the kitchen counter as Jessica poured a glass of orange juice. His phone showed a missed call. The jukebox must have drowned it out. He recognized the number.

"Looks like your parents called and left a message." He turned on the speaker and played it:

"Danny, I haven't heard from any law enforcement people yet, but I'll keep you informed. We're at a hotel in Destin. It feels safe, at least for now. Give our love to Jessica and tell her we'll be home as soon as possible. Oh, and Julie asked if you could give her a goodnight hug. Tell her it's from her mom. And once more, from the bottom of our hearts, thank you for taking care of her."

"Destin! I knew it," Jessica said.

"At least they're safe," Danny said. "That's the important thing. You ready to hit the sack? We're supposed to meet Erin at eight."

"Definitely. I'm tired."

"How are you feeling about your first surfing lesson?"

"Excited, but a little nervous."

"Focus on the excitement part. You trust me, right?"

"Mm-hm."

"And you obviously trust Erin, since you asked her to be your tandem partner."

"Mm-hm."

"So you have nothing to worry about. Neither of us would let anything happen to you."

"What if a riptide carries me a mile out to sea?"

"That's not going to happen, but if it I did, I'd swim a mile out to sea and get you."

"Can you really swim a mile?"

"I can." He spent a few years doing Ironman triathlon relays with a couple of buddies, handling the swimming leg: 2.4 miles.

"That's pretty cool. Did I hurt your feelings picking Erin as my tandem partner?"

"No, of course not ... okay, maybe a little, but it's silly."

"I thought so. The only reason I did it is because I have a feeling I'm going to fail and I never want to fail you. I like Erin, but she's not you. Once I learn, we can go surfing all the time."

He swallowed what felt like a mouse stuck in his throat. He knew their time together was running out, one way or another. "There's no such thing as failing in this. Remember what Erin said. It's all about having fun."

"Of course. Drowning is more fun than a barrel of scorpions."

"No pressure. You can change your mind in the morning if you want. I'm going to go get ready for bed. You need to do the same."

When he came out, she was standing in the hall wearing Sari's robe over her pajamas, arms stretched out. "I'm waiting," she said.

"For what?"

"My hug from my mom. The one my dad told you to give me."

"Oh, okay."

He leaned forward for another long-distance shoulder tap, adding a squeeze with his fingertips.

"Ow! My mom doesn't have crab claws for hands. You need hugging lessons," she said and retreated to her room.

Chapter 23

"ARE YOU OKAY?" Danny said, standing in the foamy swash at the shoreline patting Jessica on the back.

"*Ack, ack, ack.* Do I look okay? I'm puking my guts out and probably have a concussion. *Blechhh.*"

"It'll go away in a few seconds. Just stay bent over like that. Do you really think you have a concussion?" The longboard whacked her in the back of the head after she wiped out.

"No, but I can see why people like soft-tops."

"Is your daughter okay?" asked a woman navigating the shoreline with a baby in a sling.

"She's not my— She's fine," he said as Jessica belched again. "Just swallowed a little water."

"Fabulous," Jessica mumbled. "Now I'll be the laughingstock of Hollywood Beach. I told you I would fail."

"Get out," Danny said. "You did great."

She did, right until the end. Erin handled the tandem surfing to perfection, pulling Jessica to her feet and keeping her balanced ride after ride, not falling even once. He marveled at her skill while also noticing she looked amazing in a swimsuit.

He expected to see a burst of joy on Jessica's face the first time she stood up, but she was all steely concentration. After the successful tandem experience, she insisted on making a solo attempt, which didn't surprise Danny.

They both told her to stay on her belly and not try to stand. After a couple smooth rides, Danny said it was time to go in.

"One more time," she said. Straddling the board, she waited patiently for the right wave. Paddling with fury, she caught it like a pro, Danny surfing alongside congratulating her.

But cresting the wave, she decided to stand. The board promptly flipped and she went underwater as the tailpiece swung around and hit her. Danny dove in and pulled her up quickly, but she was already gagging.

Her retching eased and Danny stopped patting.

Erin said, "Danny's right. You were a champ. Wiping out and swallowing seawater happens to the best of us. I've probably swallowed half the ocean."

"And I've swallowed the other half," Danny said. "You're not a real surfer until you've wiped out."

Jessica rinsed her face and stood up straight. "I guess I did do pretty great, all things considered. I wish my parents could have seen it. They would never believe it."

Back at Nine Lives, Jessica headed to the workshop to change.

"Thanks for giving her that lesson," Danny said. "It was a blast to watch."

"I enjoyed it. Always like to help girls get into surfing. It's still too much of a boy's club. I admire her. She faced down her fears."

"She's pretty special," Danny said.

"You two are close. That's obvious. I'm curious. Why is she staying with you? Where are her parents?"

"The answer to that would fill a book, and I can't talk about it without her permission. I can say it's not a good situation. In fact, it's a terrible situation. There's a lot going on."

As if on cue, his phone started ringing from the top of the display case.

"I'm sorry. This is rude, but I better get that." He scooped it up and said hello.

"*Teak*well. It's Rodriguez."

"Hello, Detective," he said, shooting Erin a *This is what I was talking about* look. "What's the word?"

"Couple things. First, that powder you brought in tested out as one-hundred percent pure cocaine."

"That doesn't surprise me."

"Maybe this will. I called the number you gave me and talked to Mr. Jewell. He refuted your extortion story. Said he sold the funeral home of his own volition for a fair price."

"Please tell me you're joking."

"Unfortunately not. What's more, he said they're not hiding out from murderous drug traffickers. Just taking a little vacay on the white sands of Destin."

Jessica came out of the workshop untangling her wet hair and read his face. "What's wrong? Who's that?"

Danny held up a finger. "Did you ask him why they didn't bring their daughter on this little vacation?"

"I did. He said he and the wife just needed some alone time."

"Do you believe him?"

"Not really. His voice sounded strained. But the bottom line is that if he's not objecting to the sale, there's no extortion case to investigate."

"What about the cocaine?"

"I need you two to come back and go through the whole story with a recorder running. I can't go to the feds and say a child just happened on it while cutting open a body at a funeral home, especially with her father disavowing the extortion. I need all the details."

"I understand. When do you want to do it?"

"Monday afternoon, three o'clock. I have my kids this weekend and my ex won't be picking them up until then."

"We'll be there."

He ended the call, shaking his head. "That was Detective Rodriguez."

"I figured," Jessica said. "What did he say?"

Erin said, "I should get going."

"I'll call you later," Danny said. "Thanks again. It was really fun. Wasn't it, Jessica?"

"Yeah. Thanks, Erin. What did he say?"

*　　*　　*

The day passed somberly. They were both having a hard time coming to grips with her father lying to Rodriguez. Danny worked on Rasheed's board while Jessica moped out front.

"Let's just be honest about it," she said earlier. "My dad is a coward. Here we are taking all the risks and he's probably lounging in a beach cabana at the Slackwater eating the free hotdogs."

Danny didn't argue this time. He had tried all along to see things from Jewell's point of view, giving him the benefit of the doubt, but couldn't do it anymore. Giving into the original threats was probably a mistake, but understandable. Going along with the forged will plan may have made sense when they were captives, but not after they got away.

Now he wasn't even answering the phone. They tried to call five times.

He was measuring the rails on Rasheed's board with a caliper when he noticed Jessica in the doorway, slumped against the frame.

"How's Lil Lansky's board coming?" she said lethargically.

"It's getting there."

"Can I ask a favor?"

"Shoot."

"Can you call Fink and get him to meet us again at the Tradewinds?"

"Fink? What do you want with him?"

"I need to discuss a legal matter."

"What kind of legal matter?"

"I want to sue my parents."

*　　*　　*

Hungover and still limping from his bended-knee proposal

to Shannon, Fink drank water. "Let me get this straight," he said. "You really want to sue your parents."

"That's right. You said I might have a claim against them for breaching their—what was it called?"

"Fiduciary duty."

"Run that by me again," Danny said.

"Trustees under a will owe a fiduciary duty to the beneficiaries of the trust. That includes a duty to protect and manage the assets in the beneficiary's best interests."

"Selling my thirty percent of Slagger-Jewell to criminals was not in my best interest," Jessica said. "Danny, show him the will."

He handed over Jarrod Jewell Sr.'s Last Will and Testament. They had already explained the bizarre night at the funeral home.

Fink whistled through his teeth as he flipped pages. "I still can't believe how you found this thing. You realize this is just a copy, right?"

"We made it at Kinko's. The original's in my condo," Danny said.

Jessica said, "That will makes my grandfather's intentions crystal clear. He owned half of Slagger-Jewell. My dad owned the other half. They bought out Mr. Slagger's interest from his family a long time ago when he died.

"My gramps left twenty percent from his half to my dad, giving him a total of seventy percent, and thirty percent to *my dear, beloved granddaughter, my sweet little Artie.* Look at page nine, paragraph four."

"Artie?" Danny said.

"He liked to call me that because I always helped him drain the dearly beloveds' blood and inject arterial fluid into the carotid artery. Isn't that a cute nickname?"

"The cutest," Danny said.

Fink scanned the page. "You're right. Sounds clear."

"Not only that. He says in the same paragraph it was always his intention I would take over Slagger-Jewell when my father retired."

"Danny, what do you think?" Fink said.

"I'm not a fan. They're her parents. What would be the point of a lawsuit?"

"*Cha-ching*," Fink said, sandpapering imaginary bills between his fingers. "We might even be able to get punitive damages for making her sign that bogus consent document."

"*No-oo*," Jessica said. "Money's not the point at all."

"Then what would you hope to accomplish?" Danny said.

"To make them come home. They'd have to if they were sued, wouldn't they, Fink?"

"Assuming we could serve them with process, but we'd have to know where they are."

"I know exactly where they are. They're living it up at the Slackwater hotel in Destin."

"They could also refuse to appear, but then we'd be able to get a default judgment against them without having to go through a trial. I'd lower my fee in that case."

"What fee?" Jessica said.

"Lawsuits are a lot of work. I can't do it pro bono. I'd handle it on what's called a contingency fee basis. That's where you don't owe me anything if we lose, but I get a percentage if we win."

"How much?"

"Forty percent."

"Forty! That's robbery."

"Alright. For you, I'll do it for a third, plus expenses. That's standard."

"Still a rip-off. Twenty percent and not a penny more."

"Twenty percent! That's nothing. I have to front all the costs of litigation. I'll need to take out another loan. It'll cost me five hundred bucks just to get Dizbo Skaggs to drive to freaking Floribama and track down your parents so the sheriff can serve process on them."

Danny waved his arms. "If you two don't quit arguing, I'm sending you both to timeout. You're getting way ahead of things.

Jessica, you have every right to feel mad at your parents and want them to come home. But do you seriously want to sue them?"

"Mm-hm. And Snowbirds in Paradise too. I want my funeral home back. It's time to go on offense."

"There's an idea," Fink said, brightening. "Add Snowbirds as a defendant. Go for the deep pockets."

"Deep pockets?" Danny said. "How about deep graves? Did you forget who we're dealing with here?"

"Don't tell me you're chicken too?" Jessica said.

"Let's try this first," he said. "When we get ahold of your father, we'll try to talk him into changing his mind and cooperate with the authorities."

"You mean *if* we get ahold of my father. Okay, but it's going to be his last chance."

"Can I hang onto this will copy in the meantime?" Fink said. "I want to study it."

"If you swear to keep it confidential and locked up."

"Of course. I'm not stupid."

Chapter 24

YAGO ENTERED the Jewell house in Emerald Hills the same way he got in when he came to look for the old man's will. Through the front door with a key. He got it the night he visited Jewell Sr. to inject him with succinylcholine.

The muscle paralytic was a thing of beauty, nearly untraceable, not that you have to worry much about autopsies when a ninety-eight-year-old kicks it. The key was hanging on a hook in the kitchen with a tag that said *Junior's House*.

He was at the end of his rope frustration-wise and the house key reminded him of one more reason to be pissed off. The only one in the Jewell family not causing problems was the old man. Why? Because he was dead. Simple.

His doubts about bossman grew daily. He conceded the idea for the Snowbirds operation, though overly complicated, wasn't terrible after the first delivery went smoothly. The stiff was safely buried in a Newark cemetery after being disemboweled of his cargo.

What *was* terrible was bossman risking the whole operation going down the toilet because he was unwilling to eliminate the problem of the Jewell family.

It didn't make sense. He knew the killing stories. Bossman made sure everyone did. *The Legend of Luis* and all that crap. But he never saw any proof. Just the opposite. Every time he suggested murder as an easy and obvious solution, he got rejected.

He was beginning to think the big man was all talk, a gasbag of empty threats.

Yago, do whatever you can to find Jewell and his wife. They never would have got lost if bossman had listened to him in the first place. Just like with filing wills, dead people don't climb down fire escapes.

Then he had the nerve to *order* him, like he was some kind of flunky, not to hurt them even if he did find them, and did it right in front of the little gringo Chad.

He was sick of being disrespected. From now on he was doing things his way. He'd fix the problem himself. If bossman gave him trouble, he'd go over his head, lay it all out for the capo. Explain how the *idea man's* peace-loving ways came *this close* to blowing up the entire Snowbirds in Paradise operation.

Unfortunately, the undertaker and his wife could be anywhere. Jewell had peed his pants when he threatened to trim his toes with the clippers. He might have run all the way to Orlando pulling wifey by the hand. There was nothing to track. No vehicle, no phone.

Doing a walk-through of the house, everything looked the same. They hadn't come home.

The morticians kept the place hot as on oven. He cranked down the thermostat and plunked into a massive glove-leather recliner in the living room—to think. One arm had a touchscreen. He tapped it with a latex-gloved finger and the cushions started vibrating. A massage chair.

His back had been killing him. He hurt it years ago lifting a body into an incinerator.

He played with the controls until he found *Sensual Soothing.* The vibrations became rolling undulations. He cranked a knob to full, closed his eyes, and laid back. Not bad. It was almost like being at one of the spas in West Dade.

A half-hour later, his back felt better, but he was no closer to formulating a plan to find the Jewells than when he arrived. No point wasting more time hanging around. He climbed out of the recliner and stretched.

He was halfway out the door when *Bango!* A much-better-than-Luis's idea came to him. He resented that Luis always got credit for being the idea man, like he was the only one. Yago had ideas. Good ones, like the one he just thought of, without all the complications.

Sitting in his steaming black SUV, sweating buckets in his black suit, he worked through the details. Didn't take him long. Just needed to make a phone call and do some shopping. Simple. Wiping perspiration from his stinging eyes, he decided his first stop would be the T.J. Maxx he passed on the way in. He was done with black suits.

Chapter 25

SUNDAY AT THE SHOP had been slow, aggravating Jessica's already pent-up vexation. Her father still hadn't called and continued to ignore their calls, even after she left a desperate voicemail plea.

Danny spent the day sweating under a dust mask, smoothing Rasheed's board with a sanding block. Jessica helpfully observed it was *finally* looking like a surfboard.

Around noon she suggested they call Erin and invite her to lunch. Danny liked the idea but said, "How do we explain what happened yesterday when the detective called? She's definitely going to be wondering."

"I guess we can tell her the truth. I trust her. I have a good instinct about people. Just like I did with you back in the old days."

Danny laughed. "The old days? You make it sound like we've known each other for a hundred years."

"Maybe we have, Danny."

Erin said she just finished a five-mile beach run and was famished. She met them at the shop and they walked to Luno's Lobster Trap. Danny had been going there since he was a kid selling lobsters he bagged diving. As always, Luno gave him a rousing greeting.

"Everyone loves Danny," Jessica said.

Jessica ordered a grilled-cheese sandwich. Danny and Erin shared the catch of the day. Mackerel, broiled to perfection.

Jessica took the lead during a dessert of Luno's famous Key lime pie with real whipped cream.

"Thanks again for the surfing lesson, Erin. It was awesome. I should have listened to your advice and not stood up and almost drowned. So, you're probably wondering what happened when Danny got that phone call before you left."

Danny was used to her directness, but it caught Erin by surprise.

"Well, I did wonder. It didn't sound like good news, but please don't feel like you have to explain it to me."

"We do feel that way. Because we like and trust you."

We. It had become a regular thing with her, Danny noticed, referring to them as a unit.

Erin listened intently to Jessica's recounting of the bizarre events, occasionally glancing at Danny with an incredulous *Did that really happen?* look. Each time, he nodded resignedly.

"So now I'm going to sue my parents," Jessica said when she got to the end. "To make them come home."

"Well, that part is still up in the air," Danny said.

When they parted after lunch, Erin gave Danny a quick good-bye hug. Sunday night, he found himself thinking about it and drifted off to sleep on a cloud of warm thoughts.

He woke up Monday morning to overcast skies and their looming meeting with Rodriguez to go over the cocaine story. It rained all day. Their late afternoon drive to the police station was as gloomy as the weather.

"There's a parking spot," Jessica said, pointing.

Danny pulled the Hyundai in and turned off the engine. "Ready?"

"I guess. I'm not even sure what the point is anymore. If we're not helping my parents or trying to get our funeral home back, why do I care if someone's smuggling cocaine? It's no skin off my nose."

Danny vaguely remembered his grandmother saying that.

They were greeted by Audrey, Rodriguez's assistant, a sixty-ish woman with silver hair cut in a smart pixie. She led them to his office where the detective sat behind his desk sculpting his nails with an emery board, looking sharp in a tan poplin suit over a tight-fitting black tee.

"*Teak*well," he said. "Hey, kid. Make yourselves comfortable."

They sat in the mismatched guest chairs.

He set down the emery board and fiddled with a tape recorder. "Jessica, as I told your sidekick, I need to get the complete story of your cocaine adventure on record. You okay with that?"

"Yes, but first things first. What exactly did my father say when he called?"

"He denied any extortion and said the sale was on the up and up. It was a short conversation. When I tried to ask questions, he said he was running out of minutes on his phone."

"He lied to you," she said. "Because he's scared."

"He wouldn't be the first person. I don't disagree, but I need a victim to investigate a crime."

"I'm a victim. I own thirty percent of that funeral home."

"I should have been more precise. I need a victim *witness*. Did you actually hear the threats?"

"No, but my dad told Danny about them."

"Which leaves us with double hearsay of a story the original speaker denies. Inadmissible as evidence. Let's focus on the cocaine right now. If we could nail them on that, it would lead back to the extortion. I need every detail of your funeral home visit. Ready?"

"I suppose," she said.

He picked up his phone. "Audrey, hold my calls. No disturbances. Teakwell, close that door."

Danny reached back and swung the door shut. Rodriguez started the recorder, giving the time, date, and place. "This interview is with Danny Teakwell and Jessica Jewell. Who wants to go first?"

"I'll go," Jessica said and began the unabridged version of the funeral home caper.

"... So after climbing over the wall we found a backdoor that my keys still fit and—"

"Hold it right there," Rodriguez said. "You broke in?"

"No, as I was just explaining, I found a door my key fit."

"But you didn't have permission from the owner to enter."

"I *am* the owner, one of them. Remember? The extortion? The will? The thirty percent? Are all adults ADD or something? It's like nobody ever listens to me. Danny's the same way sometimes."

Danny saw pressure cracks in her armor.

"I understand, but the property records currently list Snowbirds as the lawful owner."

A knock and Audrey popped her head in.

Rodriguez stopped the recorder. "What is it? I said I didn't want to be disturbed."

"I think this might be important. Your calendar says you're meeting with Jessica Jewell and there's a man named Jarrod Jewell on the line saying it's critical he talk to you."

"Put him through," Rodriguez said. "Well, this should be interesting. I'm putting it on speaker." He pushed a blinking button. "Jarrod Jewell?"

"Yes, it's me."

"What a coincidence. I happen to be sitting in my office this very moment with your daughter and her surfer pal. You're on speaker."

"Hello, father," Jessica said. "How nice of you to call."

Danny gave her an *Easy does it* pat on the arm.

"I—I'm sorry, to everyone, but especially to you, sweetheart. Detective, I lied when we talked. I did it out of fear, to protect my family. But her mother and I spent the weekend taking stock of the situation and came to a decision. We're ready to come home and tell the truth.

"Jessica, I wanted to call the detective first, before I could change my mind again. I was going to call you and Danny right after this."

"Why did you ignore our calls?"

"Because I was ashamed. Blame it on me, not your mother. She's the one who convinced me we had to take a chance and do the right thing. I hope you can forgive me."

The pendulum of Danny's feelings for Jewell swung yet again. This wasn't a conversation for public consumption. When Rodriguez reached to turn the recorder back on, he shook his head. Rodriguez frowned but backed off.

"Of course I forgive you. I love you, Dad."

"Again, I'm so sorry. We're leaving in a little while, but it's a nine-hour drive, so we won't be home until after midnight."

"You might want to stay away from your house," Rodriguez said. "Get another hotel."

"We need some things, including my heart medication. Julie's credit card is maxed out and we're wearing the same clothes we escaped Boca in. We'll scout it out first. If it's clear, we'll hide the car in the garage and spend the night there. Jessica, we'll call you first thing in the morning and arrange to pick you up."

"How about calling her second thing in the morning?" Rodriguez said. "After you meet with me. I want to get your story on record before, like you said, you can change your mind again. Eight a.m. My office."

"We'll be there. Is that okay with you, Jessica?"

"Definitely. I don't want you to change your mind either. I'll be waiting with Danny at the Seabreeze Towers. It's on the beach. We'll be downstairs in the restaurant. I'll be all packed up and ready to go. Can't wait to see you and Mom!"

"We can't wait to see you either. And thank you again, Danny."

"No problem," he said.

"Once again, my apologies," Jewell said.

"Don't be too hard on yourself," Rodriguez said. "From everything I've heard, you had good reasons to be scared. Still do. Be careful."

Rodriguez hung up and turned the recorder back on. "Let's pick up where we left off."

With renewed verve, Jessica resumed her play-by-play of the wild night at the funeral home, Danny adding footnotes as necessary. Rodriguez had no doubt seen and heard a lot in his career, but the tale managed to raise his eyebrows more than once. It took more than an hour to get through it.

He patted them both on the back as he walked them to the elevator. "With this recording, the cocaine sample, and your parents' story—which I also intend to record—I'll have a solid-enough case to take to the feds that won't get me laughed off the police force. Hallelujah."

On their way back to the beach, Danny said, "Now aren't you glad you didn't file a lawsuit?"

"Yeah, I feel kind of silly about that. It's going to be so awesome to see them!"

She turned quiet after that. Danny reached for the radio.

"Danny?"

"Yeah?"

"What do you think will happen to us once my parents come home? *Us* us."

"I assume we'll just go back to our regular lives."

"We'll still be friends, right?"

"Of course."

"Will we get to see each other?"

He didn't like the answer, but knew she wanted the truth. "You'll be busy with school and your family and I'll be busy with the shop and ..." He had nothing to follow *and*. "Just, you know, everything."

"Maybe I could still work at the shop on weekends."

"You'll have much better things to do after you get back to a normal life."

"I wish you could be part of my family. You can come to our Thanksgiving and Christmas dinners."

"Thanks. We'll see."

Chapter 26

"SO WHERE ARE THEY?" Jessica said, arms stretched around her backpack, even more puffed-out than when she arrived by the addition of Sari's beloved Snoopy.

"Same answer as ten seconds ago," Danny said. "Probably still in the interview."

She dragged him down to the Tradewinds promptly at eight, ignoring his insistence that her parents' interview with Rodriguez could last for hours. The Tradewinds didn't open until eleven. Danny had a key, but didn't need it. Grady was already inside cleaning fish after another successful surfcasting session.

In the two hours that passed since, Jessica compulsively poured down coffee until, on requesting another refill, Danny shook his head at Grady, who got the message and said he ran out.

"Try calling them again," she said.

"Go for it," he said, handing her the phone.

"Come on, come on. Pick up." Cheeks deflating like a pufferfish, she set the phone down. "No answer. Let's call the detective."

"Not yet. Relax."

She got up and pressed against the front windows.

"Don't worry. I'm keeping my eyes out," Grady said from inside the oak bar.

When his phone finally rang, Danny exhaled relief. "Here we go," he said. "I bet they're calling to say they're on the way."

"Yay!" Jessica said.

He snapped it up. "Jarrod?"

"*Teakwell*," Rodriguez spit. "Where the hell are they? I've been sitting here waiting for two hours."

Jessica squeezed his arm with both hands, nails digging into his skin. "My dad sounds excited. Tell them to hurry!"

He closed his eyes and lowered chin to chest. "We thought they were with you. We haven't heard anything."

"Oh no, not again," Jessica said, letting go and plowing her forehead into the backpack.

"Well, that's it," Rodriguez said. "I give up on these people. If they ever make it home and want to talk, let me know. Later." The call ended.

Still face down, Jessica said, "I can't believe it. They wimped out again."

"Let's go out to your house," Danny said. "Maybe they got in so late they overslept."

"You don't believe that."

"Come on. Let's go check it out."

*   *   *

Jessica walked woodenly to the door of the Emerald Hills house and stuck her key in the lock, Danny following close behind. They stepped into the gray-tiled foyer.

"Hello?" she said. "Mom? Dad?"

No reply.

"Someone's been here," she said.

"How do you know?"

"The air. It's freezing. Look." She pointed to the thermostat. It was set at sixty-eight. "My parents are energy misers. They usually keep it at eighty." She raised it back up.

"Well, maybe after all they'd been through, including a nine-hour drive, they wanted to luxuriate."

"What's luxuriate? Does that mean have sex?"

"No. It means to relax, in luxury."

He followed her as she inspected the house, starting with the master bedroom suite. "Nobody luxuriated in that bed. It's still made."

"They could have made it when they got up."

She went into the bathroom and opened the shower stall. "Dry," she said. "Mom loves her showers."

"They were probably in a hurry this morning."

"Please stop. I know you're trying to make me feel better, but it's not working. If they were in a hurry, it would have been to get to their meeting with the detective, which they never did. And none of their stuff is here."

"You're right."

In the living room, she found crumbs on the seat of the enormous leather recliner. "Those weren't there before. I don't think."

Her bedroom was next. She said it looked the same. Then came the kitchen.

"You smell that?"

Danny sniffed. He did. "Smells like somebody cooked something. Can't tell what."

She opened and closed the refrigerator, examined the counters and then the trashcan, which was empty. "If someone was here, they did a good job cleaning up."

Danny followed her into the garage. "There," she said, pointing at the floor. "That clinches it. Someone was definitely here."

A drying puddle of water, precisely where an automobile AC would leak condensation.

"I can't figure it out," she said. "It's like they were here, but not here. But if they were here, why would they drive all this way and not show up for the meeting with the detective, or even call us?"

"I don't know."

"Unless it was someone else. Follow me."

She marched to the spare bedroom with the shag carpet. Danny waited by the door as she entered.

"This bed isn't made up right," she said. "My mom keeps

everything perfect. The comforter is lumpy and the edge is crook-ed. And don't say you'll take my word for it, because it's true."

She went into the bathroom. He heard an "Aha!" and she came out pinching her fingers.

"Someone else was here and this is where they stayed. Whoever it was, they were careful to cover their tracks, but left an important clue behind in the shower. This hair."

Danny leaned in to study it and recoiled. Short and curly, it looked like a pubic hair. "That looks nasty. Put it down."

"It's just a hair. Don't be such a baby. I'm saving it for evidence."

"Evidence of what? That someone once used that bathroom?"

"My mom is an obsessive cleaner. I think this is new."

She sealed the hair in a sandwich bag and said she was ready to go. They made it back to the foyer, almost to the door, when she gasped and froze.

"What in the world?" She pointed at a wicker tray on a narrow console table. "Look! Look!"

"I'm looking, I'm looking. At what?"

"My mom's wedding ring." She picked it up. "You know what this means don't you?"

"Um, how about you tell me."

"They definitely made it home! This is one-hundred percent proof. A, Mom always wears her wedding ring, even to bed. B, no way would I have missed it on our first two trips. They must have stayed in the spare room last night for some reason. That pubic hair must belong to my mom or dad."

Danny fought to unsee the image. "Why would they come all the way home and not show up to meet Rodriguez, or call?" he said.

"That's the mystery question. Call the detective and tell him what we found."

He punched in Rodriguez's number. "It's going to voicemail. Detective, it's Danny Teakwell. I'm here with Jessica at her home. There's evidence someone has been here and Jessica thinks it was her parents."

"*Knows,*" she said.

"We wanted to let you know. Call back when you can."

He pocketed the phone. "Let's get out of here."

"I'm taking the ring and hair with me."

"As you wish."

Back at the condo, they ate turkey sandwiches and apple slices for lunch. Danny tried to raise her spirits, reminding her not to jump to conclusions, that they really didn't know anything. "Maybe they got what they needed from the house and went to a hotel," he said. "Like the detective suggested, and accidentally left the ring behind."

"Then why haven't they called?"

"There could be a lot of explanations," he said, although he couldn't think of any that were plausible. "Or maybe you're wrong and they didn't come home."

"I guess that's possible."

"Let's do something to take our minds off it."

"Like what?"

To his surprise, the only suggestion she took him up on was going tandem surfing.

He afforded himself three luxuries when he won the lottery: the condo, a vintage Fender Telecaster he played every weekend at the Tradewinds with his band, *Scurvy,* before Sari got sick, and a Greg Noll longboard from the sixties he kept parked in a corner of the dining room because Hollywood's waves were too puny for it. They changed into swimsuits and wrangled the board into the elevator.

Concentrating on "not drowning," as she put it, the outing seemed to temporarily capture her attention. She was more confident than the first time out. Danny focused every bit of energy on ensuring they didn't wipe out.

When they plodded out of the surf onto the beach a couple hours later, Danny carrying the board under one arm, the western sky behind the Seabreeze Towers was the color of a ripe plum.

"You know, Danny, you're almost as good as Erin."

"Thanks."

They rinsed and toweled off at the boardwalk shower, pulled on dry shirts and shorts over their suits, and walked across to the Tradewinds. Danny leaned the longboard against the wall next to the mounted marlin. The impaled pink underwear had been removed, replaced by a red clown nose stuck to the tip of the fish's sword. The usual weekday crew was assembling.

"Hi-De-Ho!" said John the Diver.

"*Oh, Dan-nee-boy,*" crooned the D'Angelo brothers. "And lest we forget to mention, *Oh, Jess-i-ca.*"

"*Oh, D'An-gel-los,*" Jessica sang and cracked everyone up.

All the regulars knew her by now. Grady swore he hadn't told a soul about her situation, but it was obvious everyone felt protective of her. That was the Tradewinds way. Your family is my family.

They sat at the bar. The surfing helped work out some of the stress, but it had been another hard day. Danny was tempted to order a couple of shots, but went with a light beer instead. He'd been reducing his alcohol intake since Jessica showed up, a side-benefit of responsibility. Jessica went all out and got root beer.

The TV mounted at the end of the bar was tuned to the local news, the sound muted. Sports report. Danny read the closed captions while Jessica chatted with Tulia.

The Marlins lost again. Almost football season. Time to watch the Dolphins lose for a change. Only a couple weeks until the first preseason game.

That made him think about Jessica and the new school year. Shouldn't someone be worrying about those kinds of things? *Where were her parents?*

Otis Redding poured his soul into *Try A Little Tenderness* on the jukebox as Jessica quizzed Tulia about her ink. "I want to get a tattoo," he heard her say. "A big one, of a casket or a surfboard. Maybe both."

The TV captions were explaining that the Dolphins first-round draft pick was injured in practice and would be out until at least mid-season. They have the worst luck.

Jessica nudged his shoulder. "Tulia wants to know if it's okay with you if I get a tattoo."

He looked at Tulia, who shrugged. "That's not within my caretaking jurisdiction," he said. "But the answer is no. It's illegal."

Sports ended and the TV switched to a breaking news report, showing video of an industrial-size tow truck pulling a red compact car out of a canal on thick chains. A ticker crawled across the bottom of the screen.

Man and woman found dead after car careened off Alligator Alley into canal last night. Police investigating "terrible accident" ... Man and woman found ...

Alligator Alley. An eighty-mile strip of I-75 slicing through the Everglades, the only southern connector between Florida's east and west coasts. Danny remembered when it was a two-lane road where hundreds died in head-on crashes. Widening it to four lanes with a median in the eighties made it safer, but it remained a dark no-man's land at night, lined by canals on both sides with few lights and stops in between.

Jessica tugged his shirt. "Tulia says things are only illegal if you get caught."

"What?" This time he glared at Tulia, who was twirling her hair with a ringed forefinger and holding back a laugh. Normally he'd be up for the joke, but wasn't in the mood.

"She's just messing with you," he said and went back to the TV, which had switched to the weather report. Forecast: another week of hot muggy days and nights.

He finished his drink. "Let's go. I'm worn out. You must be too."

"I am."

Chapter 27

THE ALARM WENT OFF just as Danny entered the embalming room. He turned and ran but there was no way out. Rounding a corner, a cold gun barrel to his head stopped him. The man holding it was wearing a black suit. He said something Danny couldn't make out because the alarm kept ringing. And ringing ...

He opened his eyes with a start. Just a dream. His cellphone was chiming on the nightstand. The bedside clock said 4:42. It was still dark outside. He grabbed the phone. "Yeah?"

"Danny?"

It was Rodriguez. The detective had never called him by his first name before.

"It's me."

"You alone?"

Something in his voice made Danny hold back a wiseass answer to what seemed like an obvious question. "Yeah. I'm in bed."

"I have bad news, for the girl. Terrible news."

He ratcheted upright, a shiver running down his spine.

"I hate to even say it over the phone, but I figured it would be better if you told her before she heard it somewhere else."

"What is it?"

"Her parents are dead."

The words thudded his brain like a blunt object.

"You still there?"

"I'm here. What happened?"

"Their vehicle went off Alligator Alley into a canal. The Florida Highway Patrol thinks it happened yesterday in the early morning hours. Her parents didn't make it out of the car. It appears they drowned."

"I saw that on TV. A red compact? How do you know it was them?"

"The wife had her driver's license in her pocket. They ran the license plate. The car was rented in her name at the Palm Beach airport a week ago. They called me because I put in a missing persons alert for them yesterday after they failed to show up, just in case. No positive ID on the male yet, but I'm assuming it was her father. Pudgy? Curly brown hair?"

"That's him," he said. "They must have been on their way home from Destin. Seems strange they skipped the turnpike interchange and stayed on I-75. Shorter and they could have avoided driving Alligator Alley at night. They're Floridians. They would know that."

"Well, it's stranger than that. They were driving west when the vehicle left the road."

"West? Toward the gulf? That doesn't make sense."

Rodriguez stretched out a yawn. "Sorry," he said. "The state police woke me up a half-hour ago. I have a theory. They got scared as they closed in on home, chickened out, and turned around. They were close. The accident happened inside the Broward County line, west of Plantation."

"Did you get the message I left yesterday?"

"About going out to the house?"

"Yeah. It seemed pretty clear someone had been there. We were thinking it might have been a stranger. Then Jessica found her mother's wedding ring on a table, which convinced her they made it home."

Rodriguez said, "Maybe so, in which case my same theory applies. They got home, fear took over, and they decided to split again."

"Maybe. But given everything that's happened, are you convinced it was an accident?"

"No. That's the preliminary conclusion, but no one involved knows the backstory yet."

"I just thought of something," Danny said. "I didn't see a fence in the video clip. I thought the state fenced both sides of the highway to protect the panthers." Florida panthers, the official state animal, were endangered. Vehicles regularly killed them as they attempted to cross Alligator Alley.

"There are still gaps. This happened at one of them."

"Coincidence?"

"Beats me. Don't worry, I'm going to try to get someone's attention before all the evidence is destroyed."

"Why would it be destroyed?"

"A lot of it already has been. Not intentionally. Drag a car out of a canal on chains with a big-ass tow truck and you already ruined a crime scene. Tire tracks, body positioning. Gone."

"Why weren't they more careful?"

"The responders assumed it was an accident. Reasonably, I'd say. Not the first car to leave the road, that's for sure."

"Can you order autopsies?"

"My jurisdiction ends at the city boundaries, but I know who to call in the county sheriff's office. Now that I have the recorded cocaine story, I'll also call my contacts at the FBI and DEA. Fair warning. Anyone who's interested is going to want to interview you and Jessica."

"Makes sense."

"Alright, I gotta to go. There's a lot to do and I still haven't had any coffee. Tell Jessica I'm sorry. You too, Teakwell."

"Okay, thanks. One more thing. You probably have a lot of experience breaking this kind of news to people. Any suggestions for the best way to tell her?"

"Be direct. Don't beat around the bush. Just be yourself. It's obvious that little girl is very fond of you and vice versa. Which brings me to another unpleasant topic. I mentioned it before as a possibility. Now that her parents are dead, it's a certainty. Prepare yourself. Her too. People are going to want to take charge of her."

"Take charge how?"

"Take her into state care while they try to find a relative to place her with."

"She only has one. A great aunt who doesn't want her. Uprooting her right now would be a trauma all by itself. She won't want that. You heard her in your office."

"I'm sure you're right, but I have no control over it. Just wanted to give you a heads-up."

He said goodbye and set the phone down, sitting at the edge of the bed in the dark with his bare feet planted on the cool ceramic tile.

Sari, what should I do?

He didn't expect an answer, wasn't that far gone. When she died, he talked to her a lot, so much he thought he was losing it. A therapist, Melanie Holley, told him it was a common reaction to death and grief.

Follow your heart, Danny. It will lead you to the right place.

That's what Sari would say. He didn't have to imagine it because it was her standard advice for almost everything that mattered.

Don't overanalyze. Wait until she gets up and ... no, she'd be furious. *You knew my parents were dead and let me sleep?* But waking her up would be worse. *Wake up. Surprise! Your parents are dead.*

He was still deeply immersed in not-overanalyzing when the sun came up. He brewed a pot of coffee and took a mug to the balcony where he sat staring at the kaleidoscopic horizon. He decided to wait until she got up and settled before—

From behind, "You're up early."

She stood at the patio doors, hair in a mess, Sari's robe wrapped around her. It made her look so small.

"Um, yeah. You too."

"I always get up this early. That's why I'm already up when you get up."

"Ah, that makes sense."

"I hope so. I would be worried if it didn't. It's not very complicated. I need coffee."

She retreated and he followed her inside, watching her stand on her toes to reach a mug in the cabinet. She filled it from the carafe and started back to the patio.

Danny stood in her way.

"Let's go back out," she said. "The sunrise is my favorite time of day. That's why I get up so early. If I ever decide to become an artist, which I'm pretty sure I will, it will be my first painting. That's after I learn to play the guitar, and surf, I guess. Hey, I just got an idea. I'll tell my parents I need surfing lessons and we can still be friends that way."

A thousand needles pierced his chest. "I need to talk to you," he said.

"Talk away." She moved to skirt around him to the patio.

"I'd rather do it inside. Can you come in the living room with me?"

Her eagle eyes narrowed, but she followed him to the couch and sat beside him. Danny stared straight ahead, searching for the right words.

"Why are you acting weird, Danny?"

Be direct. Don't beat around the bush.

He turned to face her. "I got a call early this morning from Detective Rodriguez."

"Oh, brother. Don't tell me. My parents ran all the way to Canada this time."

He lowered his chin, blinked, and met her eyes again. "It's much worse. He called to tell me that your parents ... are dead. They were in a car accident the night before last."

He didn't know what reaction to expect, but he did expect a reaction. There was none. Just a vacant stare.

"Not all the facts are known, but apparently their car went off the road and into a canal. I can't even tell you how sorry I am. There are no words."

Still nothing.

"Did you hear what I said?"

"I heard. But you're wrong. My parents are fine." She picked up her coffee and walked to her bedroom. He expected the door to slam, but it eased shut soft as a breath.

Should he leave her alone? Her room opened onto a small side balcony. He didn't think she would hurt herself. She was too strong. But he couldn't take a chance. He walked to her room and rapped lightly on the door.

"Jessica?"

"Go away."

"Could you open the door?"

"*Please* go away."

"I can't. I need to make sure you're okay. I'm responsible for you."

The door flew open, banging off the wall with a shudder. "You are not *responsible* for me. My parents are responsible for me. You're no one to me. *Go A Way!*" This time the door slammed, in his face.

His instinct was right. She was too strong to hurt herself, and definitely too strong to be pushed.

"Take your time and let me know if you need anything. I'll be here waiting."

It felt easier sharing through a closed door. "Not because I feel responsible for you. That was another stupid thing to say. Maybe I was covering up my own feelings. Maybe we're alike in some ways."

Silence.

Follow your heart, Danny. "And in case you think you can out-wait me, you can't. No matter how long you decide to stay in there, I'm going to be here. Forever if that's what it takes."

He turned and made it two steps when the door opened again and she ran to him. He wrapped his arms around her and held on, swallowing his own tears as she sobbed into his shirt.

Chapter 28

SHE WANTED TO KNOW everything, of course. He said he didn't have much information, but recounted his conversation with Rodriguez, leaving out the part about the state taking charge of her. It wasn't the right time.

"As of right now, it's being treated as an accident."

"They were murdered," Jessica said. "I know it. And I'm responsible."

"That's silly," he said and regretted it. Survivor's guilt. Danny felt it when Sari died even though he knew it was irrational. Common, not silly. "Why would you think that?"

"Because I wanted them to come home. If they stayed in Destin, they'd still be alive."

"Your dad said they wanted to come home to set things right."

"My fault."

She was going to need help. He stopped seeing Melanie Holley months ago, but still had her number.

Rodriguez called after lunch asking if they could attend a two p.m. conference meeting at his offices to discuss the case. Danny asked who would be there.

"Not sure. More people than I would like for something like this. The feds are interested in the coke-trafficking and the county sheriff's office is investigating the deaths. The good news is we have everyone's attention, which might not last long because there are too many cases out there and not enough cops."

Jessica didn't want to go. "I'm not in the mood," she said, flopped sideways on her bed, hair covering her face, hanging onto Snoopy.

"I can call him back and explain you're not ready. I'm sure you're not. No one could be. But here's the deal. Rodriguez said evidence is already disappearing. He also said law enforcement attention to your family's case might not last long. I know you. You're going to want answers. Me too. This might be our best chance."

"That is a very persuasive argument, Danny. Maybe you should have been the lawyer instead of Fink. I'll go, but only on the condition you do all the talking."

"No problem," he said, estimating the arrangement would last less than thirty seconds.

*　　*　　*

"Welcome, everybody," Rodriguez said. "This is Teakwell—Danny Teakwell—and Jessica Jewell."

They had just entered a windowless conference room and sat at one end of an overly crowded oblong table. Eight people, including Rodriguez. Five men and three women. Too many.

"Let me start by saying, Jessica, we are all very sorry about the loss of your parents."

A stony nod.

"The reason it looks like a convention in here is because multiple agencies are interested in investigating what you and Danny have told me and, of course, your parents' deaths. Given the circumstances, everyone has agreed to handle your case with the utmost confidentiality."

Jessica tapped Danny on the shoulder and whispered, "Tell them I said thank you."

"Jessica asked me to convey her thanks."

Rodriguez paused awkwardly. "Okay. Well, to avoid making you relive everything, we just finished listening to the recording of our interview. I've also explained the extortion and will situations. But there are still questions. I'd like to go around the table and have everyone introduce themselves."

A county homicide detective, highway patrol investigator, trauma therapist, DEA agent ... Danny forgot name after name. The last person to speak was a burly man facing them from the other end of the table.

"Good afternoon, Jessica. I'm Special Agent Winton Munroe. FBI." His thick neck, butch haircut, and broad flat nose reminded Danny of an old-school football coach. His cheeks were red and puffy, like someone who drank too much. Or maybe it was because his tie looked tight enough to choke someone.

"I'm in charge of this investigation," he said. "I'll begin by stressing that although there are suspicious circumstances based on the information you provided to Detective Rodriguez—which has yet to be verified—there is no evidence as of now that your parents' deaths were anything but an accident."

Danny glanced at Jessica, wriggling in her chair and biting her bottom lip, maybe thinking the same thing he was. He heard *anything* as *nothing*. Nothing but an accident. Like an accident would be no big deal. *Which has yet to be verified*. Like he was already doubting them.

"Well," Danny said. "I suppose it depends on how you define evidence."

"Excuse me," Munroe said. "I'm talking to the girl."

"Excuse me," Danny said. "First of all, *the girl* is named Jessica. Second, she just experienced a horrific trauma and asked if I would do the speaking."

"Who exactly are you, Mr. Tickwell?"

"It's Teakwell. Who am I? Exactly? That's an existential question I think we all struggle with. I haven't figured it out completely."

He never reacted well to assholes. It was a character flaw. A high-pitched helium chirp escaped from Jessica.

Munroe's cheeks darkened to raspberry. "I'll be more specific, sir. What exactly is your relationship to Jessica? Are you a relative?"

"No."

"I understand Jessica has been living with you throughout this ordeal. How did it come about that you are housing her?"

Housing her? He made it sound like pet-sitting. "Her parents asked me to take care of her while they were away."

"Do you have any proof of that?" Munroe said.

"Hold it, hold it," Jessica said, waving her arms. "Murderers killed my parents and instead of trying to find them, you're interrogating my best friend? Seriously? Are you really in the FBI?"

Danny was impressed. Her vow of silence lasted an entire minute.

"Yes, I really am," he said with a fake smile.

"Could I see your identification, please?"

Munroe scanned the group for support. When none came, he grudgingly unfolded a black wallet and held it up.

"I can't see it from here. Would you mind passing it down?"

He did so with his jaw clenched.

Jessica spent an overly long time studying it, looking up several times to check that his face matched the picture. The message of her takedown was clear, to Danny at least. Loyalty was a code they shared. Don't mess with my friend.

Danny snatched the wallet from her fingers and handed it to Rodriguez, who sent it back down the table.

"It's okay, Jessica," Danny said. He knew the FBI agent wasn't the only one wondering about their relationship. Searching his phone before they left the condo, he found the voice message from Jewell explaining they were in Destin and felt safe *for now*. "Yes, I do have proof. I have a message from her father on my phone. Would you like to hear it?"

"I would," Munroe said.

He held up the phone and pushed the speaker button. "*... and Julie asked if you could give her a goodnight hug. Tell her it's from her mom. And once more, from the bottom of our hearts, thank you for taking care of her.*"

Hearing her dad's voice brought a stiff upper-lipped sniffle from Jessica. He patted her shoulder. The woman who introduced herself as a trauma therapist, thin and pale with flaming red hair, watched with an appreciative smile.

"*There,*" Jessica said. "Are you satisfied? Now let's get back to the case. You said there was no evidence it wasn't an accident. Wrong!"

Danny felt the meeting turning. Munroe and the others were about to learn who was really running it.

"My parents were murdered," she said. "It's clear as day. You want evidence? There's plenty."

"Such as," Agent Munroe said.

"*Such as* people from a drug cartel extorted my father into selling our family funeral home by threatening to chop us into pieces and feed us to the fish. I'm not in the FBI, like you claim to be, but that seems like very good evidence."

"That's not—"

"Excuse me. I'm not finished. Then the same people took my parents hostage and threatened to torture my father by cutting off his toes with a pair of garden clippers. Again, good evidence. Do you disagree?"

"Well—"

"Then we found out they're using our funeral home to smuggle drugs inside of dead bodies and even brought you a sample."

"I've heard all that. What I meant is we currently have no physical evidence from the accident itself to show they were homicide victims."

"Would you like hear my theory about how it happened?" she said.

He turned his palms up. "Go ahead."

"Danny and I went to our house after my parents didn't show up to meet with the detective, like they promised. Someone had been there."

She laid out the supporting facts: AC turned down, crumbs

on her dad's recliner, smell of cooked food in the air, and the puddle of water in the garage.

"At first I thought it was my parents, but no one had used their bedroom or bathroom that night. At least it didn't look that way. But it did look like someone had used the guest bedroom because the bed wasn't made up right. So I decided there must have been a stranger in the house.

"But when we were leaving I found my mom's wedding ring, which she never took off except in the shower. So I changed my mind again and thought my parents came home. Except why would they stay in the guest room?"

She turned to Danny. "Do you see where I'm going with this?"

"I do," Danny said. "It was both. There was a stranger *and* your parents came home."

"Exactly. Danny's very smart," she said. "Sometimes you wouldn't know it because he's a surfer and some people don't think of surfers as being smart."

Danny's stifled laugh came out as a snort.

"Here's what I think happened. The stranger was waiting for them when they got home. He somehow killed them and drove their car out to where it went into the canal. Or maybe he killed them after they got out there."

"Interesting theory," Munroe said.

"An autopsy should let us know," she said. "If they really drove off the road, they would have drowned and their lungs will be filled with water. You are doing autopsies, right?"

A balding man next to Rodriguez spoke up. The homicide detective from the county sheriff's office. "Yes. Autopsies have already been ordered."

"Good. While you're at it, could you do an autopsy on my grandfather? He died a few weeks ago, right before this whole mess started. Don't you think that's suspicious, Danny?"

"Maybe, but didn't the death certificate say it was natural causes?"

"Yeah, but there was no autopsy."

"Let's stay focused," Munroe said. "Is there any other relevant information you have right now regarding your parents' deaths?"

"Yes. I have a sample of the suspect's DNA."

"Oh, really?" Munroe said. "You already have a suspect, do you?"

"Well, obviously the suspects are the people in the cartel. But my specific suspect is the stranger in the guest room."

"Like Colonel Mustard in the library?"

Jessica looked at Danny, bewildered. He whispered, "He's teasing you. It's from a game called Clue."

"Danny just informed me you're mocking me. That is an evil thing to do to a child who just lost her parents."

Nods and furrowed brows around the table. She knew how to work a crowd. A dark-skinned woman next to Munroe—the DEA agent—whispered something in his ear.

"Forgive me," Munroe said. "I just don't share your certainty about the events. Please tell us about your DNA evidence."

"It appears to be a pubic hair. I found it in the guest bathroom and sealed it in a plastic bag. Danny said it could have been there before, but he doesn't know how obsessive my mother was about cleaning."

Munroe opened his mouth, but the DEA agent cut him off and pleasantly reintroduced herself as Special Agent Timberly Jenkins. "Thank you for that information, Jessica. If it's okay with you, I'd like to move on to the cocaine you found in the funeral home …"

Rodriguez closed the meeting with a confidentiality reminder. Everyone agreed it was best for now to stick with the official position that the deaths of Jarrod and Julie Jewell were an accident.

Almost everyone. Jessica had the last word. "Objection!"

Chapter 29

"DANNY, JESSICA, hold up a second."

It was the redheaded woman from the meeting. They had just reached the parking lot.

"I'm Allie Dearden, the trauma psychologist. Do you have a minute?"

"Sure," Danny said.

"Would it be possible to talk to you alone?" she said.

"Anything you say to me, you can say in front of her."

"Are you sure?"

"He's sure," Jessica said.

"It involves a rather delicate matter."

"That's okay. I'm not delicate."

"Well," she hesitated. "First of all, I probably shouldn't be telling you this, so please don't out me. Before you arrived there was a discussion regarding what to do about Jessica."

"What does that mean?" Jessica said.

"I think she means where to place you, now that your parents are gone," Danny said.

"That again? I already told Detective Rodriguez I wasn't going anywhere. I belong with Danny. We're a team."

"Was a decision made?" Danny said.

"Not final, but the consensus was to take her into state care."

"Ha!" Jessica said, but it came out more like a wounded cry than a laugh.

"I admit I was leaning the same way when I learned she had no close relatives. But studying you both during that rather horrid meeting, I realized it would be exactly the wrong thing to do, especially right now."

"Finally, someone with a brain," Jessica said.

"Unfortunately, I'm not the one who will be making the decision."

"What do you think we should do?" Danny said. "Detective Rodriguez mentioned a guardianship once, but he was just joking."

"I'd give it a try," she said. "The sooner the better. I'm not sure how long they're going to wait and I don't think you made a friend today in Agent Munroe."

"No, I don't think so," Danny said.

"You'd need to file an emergency petition. Do you know any lawyers? If not, I could give you some names. I work with a lot of them."

"We have a lawyer," Jessica said. "Benjamin Finkel."

The thought of putting something this important in Fink's hands made Danny's gut cramp, but Fink had got him through his murder case, where the stakes were also high. And at least they could trust him.

"Thanks for the warning," he said. "I'll call my lawyer friend as soon as we leave."

"I'd help if I could, but there's probably no time. I'd have to do a full psychological evaluation and write a report."

"That's very kind of you."

"*Very* kind," Jessica echoed. "If Danny didn't already have a girlfriend, I'd try to fix you up. Assuming you're unattached and like boys, of course."

"Girlfriend?" Danny said.

"Erin."

"She's not a girlfriend." He turned to Allie, who was suppressing a smile. "Sorry."

"I'm tired. Let's go home," Jessica said, and started walking to the car.

Allie motioned for Danny to stay behind.

"Here," he said. "Take the keys and I'll meet you at the car. Lock the doors. I'll be watching." He waited until she slap-stepped away. "What's up?"

"It hasn't really hit her yet," she said.

"I know, but it's also her personality. Her strength of will is like a force of nature. I'm worried she'll keep everything bottled up until it breaks loose and falls on her like a ton of bricks."

"I'm glad you realize it. She's lucky to have you."

"I don't know about that, but thanks. I called a therapist I saw after my wife died. She has a lot of experience with grief issues. Melanie Holley."

"I know Melanie. She's great."

"She said she'd be happy to see Jessica. Now all I need to do is convince the force of nature to go. About the guardianship, you know how these things work. Do you think we have any chance at all?"

"Honestly, it will be an uphill battle with you not being a relative."

"And being a single man with no kids?"

"That won't help."

She dug into her purse and handed him a business card. "I work for the county, but keep a small private practice going. That has my cell number on it. Don't hesitate to call if you or Jessica want to talk."

He pocketed the card. "We really appreciate your support. I better get going before she drives off without me. Patience is not one of her virtues."

On the drive home he called Fink, who was shocked to hear about Jessica's parents and wanted to know everything. Danny said he'd fill him in later. The priority was getting an emergency guardianship petition filed.

"I'm not expecting a freebie, Fink. I'll figure out a way to pay you."

"I'll get right on it. We'll have to meet in person. I'm sure the forms require a lot of personal information about the applicant—that's you."

"Can you come to the condo tonight? Around seven? Or we could come to your place."

"Your place is fine. See you there. Tell Jessica I'm sorry."

They ended the call. "Fink said he's sorry about your parents." She nodded.

"Hey, I need to talk to you about something. Have you ever had a counselor?"

"I went to summer camp once. There was a counselor for every cabin. I never went back because, once again, the kids thought I was weird. They wanted to make hair scrunchies and I wanted to dissect a dead squirrel we found in the woods to determine the cause of death."

"Actually, I'm talking about a mental health counselor?"

"You think I'm crazy?"

"Of course not. She does grief counseling. I went to see her after Sari died."

"Did she help?"

"I'd say so."

"I don't think I need a counselor."

"Sometimes it's hard to realize when you do."

They were closing in on the intracoastal bridge when she said, "Uh-oh. I just remembered something."

Danny prepared his frazzled nerves for another jolt. "What is it?"

"We didn't open the surf shop today."

Chapter 30

LUIS STOOD ALONE in the Brickell conference room watching the evening news on the wall monitor as he worked to extricate his fist from the hole he just punched through the wood-composite table. On the monitor, a jumbo tow truck trawled a red compact car out of a canal.

He saw the same video yesterday, but didn't pay attention to it. Just another car accident. He paid attention now. Streaming across the bottom:

Police have identified the bodies of a man and woman whose vehicle veered off of Alligator Alley into a canal as Jarrod Jewell Jr., 43, and his wife, Julie Jewell, 40, of Hollywood ...

Pictures of Jewell and his wife stared back at him from the top corner of the screen. Jewell's face exuded affability. His wife looked like the kind of woman who always smiled. A nice couple. A dead couple.

Damn Yago!

It had to be his doing. Too much of a coincidence, just like the old man dying the same day he refused to sell Slagger-Jewell.

Yago had specifically said he could make it look like an accident, which would mean he violated a direct order to not harm the Jewells if he found them. The cartel's HR manual included execution as a potential disciplinary measure for disobeying a superior's order.

He ruined everything. The whole mess could have been put

to bed by now if Yago hadn't screwed up in Boca by threatening to cut Jewell's toes off. The forger came through with a gem of a new will. All they needed was for Jewell to file it and everyone could have gone on with their lives.

Of course he had to do it just when all the pieces had finally come together. The second payload, to Baltimore, went as smoothly as the first. The client was a woman, nowhere near the size of the first guy, but she qualified for a ten-percent discount. He promoted Francisco to CEO of Snowbirds-Hollywood for coming up with the excellent idea of tucking an extra kilo in her enormous bosoms.

Another shipment was scheduled for tomorrow, to Philly. Tipping the scale at just over five hundred pounds, the customer was the first to qualify for the full free ride. His family was ecstatic.

Now all of *El Grande* hung in the balance. He looked at his watch. Yago was ten minutes late for their meeting, probably intentional, more defiance.

When he finally strolled in, he was dressed in baggy tan cargo shorts, a pink polo shirt, and a ridiculous floppy hat with a drawstring pulled tight around his chin. His long pale legs stretched like stilts from the bottom of the shorts.

"What the hell is this?" Luis said.

"My new look. Like it?"

"You look like an egret on safari. You know the dress code."

"I decided to make my own. We're in Miami. We should be tropical. We look like undertakers in those black suits."

"We are undertakers."

"Black is too hot. And the lady at the T.J. Maxx said I looked good in pink. Never knew it." His eyes pointed to the hole in the table. "Doing some remodeling, bossman?"

Something was off. Insubordination was one thing. This felt closer to mutiny. Why was he pushing it? He had to know there would be consequences.

"Sit down," he said. "Let's talk about the Jewells."

"Yeah, let's do."

"Did you kill them?"

"I did."

"I ordered you not to hurt them. You put the whole enterprise at risk. What do you think the capo's going to do when he finds out?"

"Probably promote me. Stead of giving me shit, you should be thanking me for saving your ass."

"You killed the man who was going to file the forged will that would have fixed everything."

"You and me, we always see things from a different point of view. Why worry about a forged will when now we don't got to worry about any will?"

"The police will investigate the deaths."

"I saw the news. They're calling it an accident, just like I planned it."

Luis bit down on his anger. "Tell me exactly what happened."

"First, you told me to do whatever I could to find them, but didn't give me a crystal ball. So I moved in and waited for them. Figured they had to come home sometime."

"You moved into their house?"

"Just for a couple nights. It wasn't bad. No swimming pool, and I stayed in a crappy room with gold shag carpeting. But Jewell had a sweet massage chair and a new HD TV to go with it."

"And you don't think you left evidence behind?"

"I wore gloves, cleaned the place, put everything back like I found it, just like when I searched for the will. Just like when I killed the old man. I'm a professional."

"So you did kill the grandfather."

"I did, and what happened? Nothing. They ruled it natural causes. You're too blind to see it, bossman. You're the one who's been risking everything."

"How did you stage this *accident*?"

He said he was dozing on the recliner when the Jewells arrived home sometime after midnight.

"I hid my car in the garage and unplugged the door opener, so they came in the front. I surprised them with a gun and they started crying and begging. It was embarrassing, people got no self-respect. I wanted to shoot them right there, but it would have ruined my plan."

"Which was?"

"*Perfect.* That's what it was. But unlike you, Yago never gets credit for his ideas."

"If they ever extended beyond killing, I'd be more impressed."

Yago's face darkened. He made a quick move for his waistline and Luis drew back, expecting a gun, but he just adjusted his cargo shorts.

Smiling through thin bloodless lips, "Bossman, maybe you oughta talk less and listen more when I'm explaining. We poured a few shots of vodka down their throats, mixed with some oxycodone we got at a pill mill in Fort Lauderdale, just enough to make 'em pass out. Who knew they had a drug habit, right? We planted the vodka bottle on the floorboard and stuck the bottle of pills in the console. Made sure their fingerprints were on both of them."

"We?"

"You know I believe in keeping things simple. But there was no getting around it was a two-man job to move them and their car out to Alligator Alley, push it in the canal, and have a ride back. So I called Javier."

"Who. Is. Javier?"

"My gardener. I promised him an easy thousand bucks for a couple hours work. Javier's a good man. Reliable, hardworking. A magician with hibiscuses. You shoulda seen my lawn this summer. Looked like the cover of a magazine."

"So in order to eliminate two witnesses, you added a new one. This was your perfect idea? Now we have to worry about your gardener."

"Bossman, you keep underestimating me and, I'll be honest, it upsets me. Of course we don't got to worry. I strangled Javier as soon as we got back in town. Dumped him in a rock pit with some cinderblocks tied around his waist. No one's gonna miss him. His family's still in Mexico."

Not just a cruel sonofabitch. A psychopath. Disgust swelled in his chest, not just for Yago.

In his deepest well, Luis knew early on he wasn't cut out for cartel work. He had a conscience, or used to. Over the years, he managed to keep his distance from the mayhem, like the button-pushers who launch cruise missiles. All they see when it hits is a puff of smoke on a screen.

This was different. A family. And there was no denying his own fault. He should have picked a different funeral home at the beginning when the old man refused to sell.

"So, anyways, bossman, I've been doing some thinking and decided it's time to make some changes around here."

"You decided?"

A knock on the conference room door. Chad peeked in. "You wanted to see me, Jefe?"

"Ten more minutes."

Luis waited until the door closed. "What kind of changes?"

"For starters, from now on we hold equal rank, equal partners with equal pay."

"Are you out of your mind?"

"I'm not finished. I'm sick of black SUVs, black everything. I want a new company car, a Porsche, red, and not one of the cheap ones. Most important, I don't ever want to hear another insult coming out of your mouthhole as long as you live. Got that? There'll be other things. Like I said, those are starters."

"You realize you just signed your own death warrant."

"Who's gonna carry it out? Not you."

"I've been patient long enough," Luis growled. "Don't forget who you're dealing with. I could snap your neck in two seconds without working up a sweat."

"Maybe. But you won't. See, that's a difference between us."

"Are you really that stupid? Haven't you heard the stories from back home? I was a killing machine."

"Yeah, I heard those stories, and that's what I think they are. Stories. Like the time they say you burned down a house fulla screaming women and children because the music was too loud. I did some asking around the neighborhood. Turns out that house was empty and the owner torched it to collect the insurance."

"You need to fact-check your sources," he said, although it was indeed one of the rumors he paid his barber to spread that made it into print in *The Legend of Luis.* "Once I tell the capo about all this, you'll be lucky to live out the week."

"Let's call him right now. I think it's gonna be the other way around when he learns how you risked the cartel's investment because you like to play nice-nice with everybody. He might even assign me the job."

Luis strained to keep his Tony Montana glare going, but Yago's words rattled him. He was worried he might be right.

"Or," he said, "we could work together and neither of us gets hit. We might make good partners. We got different skills. That's my offer. Your choice."

Luis rubbed his stubble and turned his gaze out to the bay. "I'll think about it."

Yago stood to leave. "While you're thinking, keep in mind there were only four people on this planet who could blow up your precious *El Grande.* Now three of 'em are gone, all thanks to Yago."

"Who's the fourth?"

"The kid."

"Send Chad in on your way out."

He paced the conference room and evaluated the situation. He couldn't give in to blackmail, not even to salvage *El Grande.*

Or could he? For three years he'd devoted every waking minute of his life to painting his masterpiece.

He would think about it. In the meantime, he wanted to find the kid. Probably with the man from the funeral home. Who the hell was he? Enhancing the video showed only that he was tall with blond hair.

Chad knocked again, holding a notebook. "Are you ready for me, Jefe?"

"Come in and shut the door. Is the next delivery still on schedule."

"Yes, sir. Eight a.m. tomorrow. The client is a giant. The embalmers had to roll two tables together to get the job done. Francisco stuffed him with sixty-four kilograms. A new Snowbirds in Paradise record."

"Keep tabs on it. Make sure there are no snags."

"Yes, sir."

"And as soon as you leave this room, call Francisco. He's in charge of Hollywood now. Tell him tomorrow is the last shipment until further notice. The second the hearse rolls out his only mission is to erase every trace of the operation. Sterilize the place from top to bottom."

"Is this because of the *accident*? I saw the news."

Luis nodded. "We need to be prepared in case there's an investigation. Got it?"

Chad scribbled on his pad. "Yes, sir. Is that all?"

"No. I have an assignment for you."

Chapter 31

THEY HUDDLED once again around the dining room table. The surfer, the barrister, and the junior mortician. This time to fill out the forms for the emergency guardianship application. Jessica sat at the end of the table clicking keys on the iMac. A dead fern hanging on a chain swayed rhythmically in the ocean breeze coming in from the balcony.

"Jessica, pay attention," Fink said. "This is important."

"I'm listening."

"Before we get started, I want to make sure you understand the gravity of what we're trying to do. If this petition is granted. Danny will have all the rights and responsibilities of your parents, including the power to manage your assets."

Typing as she spoke, "My only asset is my savings account and I'd rather manage it myself. It's taken me three years to save four-hundred and twenty-three dollars and sixty-three cents."

"You'll be getting an inheritance. Probably your parents' entire estate. Danny would have the power to control it."

"Will he be able to boss me around?"

"Yes."

"Can he make me go to bed early?"

"Go to bed, take out the garbage, eat liver. Anything a parent could do. Are you okay with that?"

"I suppose. As long as he doesn't let the power go to his head."

"Okay," Fink said. "Then here we go. A lot of these questions are easy. Does the applicant have any physical disabilities? No. Mental illness? No. How long have you been in this condo?"

"Going on fifteen years," Danny said.

"That's good. A stable residence. History of alcohol abuse?"

"Nothing there's a record of, but I can't say I never abused it."

"Yes you can," Jessica said. "This is no time for complete honesty."

"She's right," Fink said.

"What happened to your devotion to the truth?" Danny said.

"Well, I—"

"Not you, Fink."

"Desperate times call for desperate measures," Jessica said. "My dad said that. I'm pretty sure he made it up."

Danny thought it was Hippocrates, but didn't correct her.

"So that's a *no* to alcohol abuse," Fink said. "Drug abuse?"

"I've smoked some weed, but that's it. I haven't done it for a while. I could pass a drug test."

"No drug abuse," Fink affirmed. "Oh boy, this next one's a beaut. *Has the applicant ever been charged with a felony?*"

Danny had to laugh. "Other than first-degree murder? Nothing I can think of."

"We have to specify type of offense, location, and final disposition. *Murder, Broward County, Charge dismissed.*"

"Can't we explain it a little better than that?"

"I'm sure it'll come up at the hearing. The form only gives us one line. Let's see. No previous guardianships, no bankruptcies—"

Danny laughed again. "Not yet."

"Danny, there's nothing funny about this," Jessica said, not looking up.

"Those are embarrassed laughs, not funny laughs."

"Don't distract him," Fink said. "Employment. Surf shop owner. Education?"

"High school and a year at Broward Community College."

"Weak. Anything else?"

"I took a CPR course when I was a lifeguard in high school," Danny said sarcastically.

"*Advanced medical training*," Fink said as he wrote.

"He's also an expert surf instructor. I'm a witness," Jessica said. "Don't worry, I'll leave out I almost drowned the first time."

"And you know everything about fishing and diving," Fink said. "And boats. I remember you were always fixing Grady's." Danny watched him scribble *Extensive nautical expertise*. "Not much, but it's something."

He was already feeling hopeless when Fink said, "Alright, now we get to the heart of it. The whole ball of wax rises like the phoenix or goes down the tubes on this next question."

"Isn't that like three mixed metaphors?" Danny said.

Fink ignored him. "*Specify applicant's relationship with the alleged ward*."

Danny was stumped. "Friends?"

Jessica moaned, not looking up from the screen. "We can do better than that."

Fink said, "If only we could write *Uncle* or *Brother* or something. This is what's going to kill us, not to sound pessimistic."

"No, that doesn't sound pessimistic at all," Danny said.

"What can I say? Guardianship law favors blood relatives, pure and simple."

"Danny can be my fictive kin," Jessica said.

"Your what?" Danny said.

"I'm looking at it right here in the Florida guardianship statutes. '*Fictive kin*' means *an individual who is unrelated to the child by either birth or marriage, but has such a close emotional relationship with the child that he or she may be considered part of the family*."

"Why do you always have to be such a showoff?" Fink said.

"*Fictive kin*. Interesting. So there's a chance?" Danny said.

"About as much chance as you winning the Lotto a second time," Fink said. "But again, don't lose hope."

"I can't imagine why I would."

"So what do you want me to put down?"

"How about, *Close relationship akin to family?*"

"Good enough. We're going to have to go through it all in court anyway. What's your answer when the judge asks, *How long has this close relationship akin to family existed?*"

"About ten days," he said. They were doomed.

"Wrong," Jessica said. "We met when I was seven and I've always felt a special kinship to you."

"Really?"

She hunched her shoulders. "I don't know, but that's what I'll say if the judge asks."

They finished the paperwork and Danny asked if Fink wanted to stay for dinner.

"What are you having?"

"Veggies. Stir-fried."

"I'll pass."

Feeling a guilty weight of responsibility on their way home from the meeting with Rodriguez and friends, he stopped at Publix and stocked up on healthy food.

Fink packed the papers in a faux leather vinyl briefcase with a tear down one side.

"I'll file everything first thing in the morning. It's an emergency petition so be ready for a hearing on short notice. Have your clothes out. No t-shirts or flipflops. We need to get Aunt Rosie there too. As the only living relative, she has to testify she's not on board with being a caretaker."

Jessica had called Aunt Rosie that morning to deliver the news about her parents. She hadn't exaggerated about her hearing impairment. "No, Aunt Rosie," she shouted. "I don't know your neighbor Fred. I said Mom and Dad are *dead. D-E-A-D.* That's right. In a car accident. Don't worry, I'm fine. ... Thank you for the birthday wish, but I turned nine three years ago. ..."

"Alright, I'm outta here," Fink said.

They went to work preparing dinner, cutting up and stir-frying the veggies.

"Cooking," Jessica said, hacking an onion with a carving knife. "My mom used to say she liked it. I think she was lying. It takes too much time."

"Slow down. Be careful with that knife."

"I guess it could be fun once in a while, but every day?"

Danny saw an opening and took it. "You know, Fink raised some good points. This really is a huge decision, for both of us. It's terrible it has to be made in a hurry. Are you absolutely sure about it?"

"Are you saying you don't want me?"

"Of course not. It's just that ..."

He'd been thinking about it all day. Seriously taking care of a kid was a totally different undertaking from temporarily *housing* her, in Agent Munroe's words. Her new school year was getting closer every day. He had no idea what needed to be done.

His long pause took the shine out of her eyes. "I get it," she said. "It's a big responsibility on you. It's okay if you don't want to do it, but I need to know now because I don't have a lot of time to make other plans."

"I want to do it. Okay, here's the truth. I don't have enough faith in myself that I can do it right, and it's too important to screw up. I don't know anything about kids."

"Don't worry, Danny. I have enough faith in you for both of us. And I know all about kids. I'll teach you. The veggies are burning. You have to keep stirring them."

"Are you sure you wouldn't rather be in a foster home, with parents, and maybe brothers and sisters?"

"With strangers? Are you kidding? With the luck I've been having, they'll place me with child molesters or terrorists, maybe child-molesting terrorists."

"And you've totally ruled out Aunt Rosie?"

"Danny, be real. You heard our call."

"What about your friend Gloria? Maybe her family would like to take you in."

"She likes to be called Gigi, and her parents are ancient. Her mother didn't have her until she was forty-seven. They're practically on Social Security already."

"I just want you to consider all the options." In truth, there weren't any good ones.

They spent the evening watching TV from the couch. Danny was dozing in and out when the nightly news came on.

Tropical Storm Josie, the first storm of the season, was forming east of the Caribbean. Al Gore selected Joe Lieberman to be his running mate for president. The Queen Mother celebrated her hundredth birthday from the balcony of Buckingham Palace ...

Then he heard, "In local news, authorities have identified the victims of the tragic Alligator Alley drowning accident as ..." His eyes popped open and he reached for the remote, but Jessica was gripping it with both hands.

It was the same video clip of the tow truck pulling the car out of the canal. "It wasn't an accident," she murmured.

She hadn't talked about her parents all day. Danny decided to force the issue. He wriggled the remote from her fingers and turned off the TV.

"Let's talk," he said. "Tell me how you're doing. And please don't say fine."

"Why not?"

"Because it's impossible for you to be fine. Your parents are dead. I'm sorry to be so direct about it, but that's what you taught me."

"Obviously, I don't mean, like, fine-fine. I'm not. My heart is broken in a million pieces. Would you rather I fall apart? Would that make you feel better?"

"Of course not. I'm just worried that holding everything inside might not be the healthiest thing for you."

"You don't talk about Sari. How come?"

She got him again. "Because I hold everything inside and it's not the healthiest thing for me. But at the beginning, I cried every day."

"I can't do that right now. Don't you see? You heard Fink. He thinks we're going to lose in court. Then what? I could be spending tomorrow night in some kind of institution. I have to keep it together. If I let my feelings out now, I'll drown, and you know how I feel about that."

"Well, let's think positively. We're going to try our best to win."

He meant it, but the words rang hollow. Why would a judge award guardianship of a child to him? A former murder defendant with little education, no wife, no experience raising children, barely able to support himself.

"Let's get a good night's sleep in case the hearing is tomorrow," he said. "We'll need all our energy. If you need anything during the night, don't worry about waking me up."

"Okay. Same here."

Chapter 32

HE TWISTED and turned for an hour before realizing a good night's sleep wasn't in the cards. He was staring at the ceiling when loud pounding on the front door jolted him out of bed.

Jessica met him in the hallway. "Who do you think it is?" she said.

"No idea."

He went to the door with Jessica attached to his hip. "Who's out there?"

"FBI. Special Agent Munroe."

"It's almost midnight. What do you want?"

"Open the door."

"Not until you tell me why you're here."

"Open the door or we'll break it down."

He cracked it open. "May I help you?"

"I'm here with Deputy Marshall Marshall of the county sheriff's office."

Danny examined the deputy, skinny with acne scars and a wispy mustache, looking like he still belonged in high school. He wore an evergreen uniform with a silver badge. His thick black belt was loaded with crap that probably weighed as much as he did.

"Your parents really named you Marshall Marshall?" Danny said.

"Yeah," he said, looking chagrined.

"What do you want?"

"We have a signed order from the probate judge directing us to seize one Jessica Jewell and take her into protective custody," Munroe said.

Jessica shrieked. "Oh no you don't." She ran to her room and slammed the door.

"Let me see it," Danny said.

Munroe stuck a document in his face. Danny grabbed it and skimmed it over.

"Endangered minor?" he said. "This is bullshit. Our lawyer will be filing an emergency guardianship petition in the morning. We'll see you court."

He handed back the document and tried to shut the door, but Munroe lowered his beefy shoulder into it and shoved his way into Danny's living room, the deputy tagging behind like a puppy.

"Bring us the girl," Munroe said.

"Shove it."

"Do you want to be placed under arrest?"

"Not particularly."

"Then out of my way." He marched to Jessica's bedroom and tried to open the door, which was locked.

"Agent Munroe," Danny said. "What gives the FBI jurisdiction to break into my home? I'm no lawyer, but since when are guardianship issues part of federal law?"

"*He* gives me jurisdiction," he said, nodding to Deputy Marshall Marshall, who shifted uncomfortably from one shiny black-shoed foot to the other. "I'm here to assist the deputy."

"Go away!" Jessica shouted.

"We have a court order to take you into protective custody," Munroe said.

"I'm already in protected custody. Danny's. He's my guardian. You have no right."

"Well, honey, bad news. A guardian needs official legal documentation."

"Okay, hold on."

A minute passed before a piece of lined notebook paper slid under the door. Danny picked it up. "It says, *I hereby officially declare Danny Teakwell to be my official legal guardian.*" Below her name, she wrote *Official Signature.*

"That's not going to cut it, honey," Munroe said. "Unlock the door or I'll have to break it open."

"Quit calling me honey! I'm not your honey."

He grabbed the doorknob.

"Let go of that door! I'm changing my clothes. I knew you weren't in the FBI. Are you a registered sex offender?"

Deputy Marshall Marshall reared back like the door had suddenly turned radioactive. Even Munroe jerked his hand away.

Danny tried not to smile. The girl could think on her feet at the speed of light and always knew the right buttons to push.

"Agent Munroe," Danny said calmly, stepping in front of Jessica's door. "It seems we've reached an impasse."

Munroe's ruddy face resembled an exploding cartoon thermometer. He puffed up his chest and balled his meaty fists. Danny crossed his arms and stood his ground.

"Unless you intend to break in on a half-clothed child, in which case we will seek criminal charges and sue you until the end of your most likely greatly shortened career, you will leave right now. As I said, our lawyer has already prepared an emergency guardianship petition that will be filed in the morning."

"Let's go, deputy," he said. "You can bet we'll see you at the hearing."

"Can't wait," he said with more bravado than he felt.

The deputy tipped his cap apologetically and followed Munroe out the door.

Chapter 33

FINK STOOD BEFORE Probate Judge Helena Strazinski dabbing his eyes with a tissue. Danny saw him squirt the artificial tears from a small bottle when he stopped by the counsel table and pretended to peer deeply into a law book, but he used too much. It looked like someone hit him in the face with a water balloon.

They were in a courtroom at the Broward County Judicial Complex in Fort Lauderdale, a modern multistory building a stone's throw from the New River.

Danny and Jessica sat side by side at the counsel table wearing the same clothes they wore to her grandfather's funeral. Danny his navy blue wedding suit and Jessica her black sleeveless dress, the only one she packed when her parents sent her to Aunt Rosie's.

"Forgive me, Judge," Fink said, mopping his face with his sleeve. "I'm simply overcome every time I think of the terrible tragedy that has befallen this angelic child and the ugly future awaiting her if my client's guardianship petition is denied."

Strazinski, gray-haired with stooped shoulders and a scabrous complexion, continued wearing the scowl she set in place the moment the hearing began. She granted Fink's request for an emergency hearing almost immediately, which, combined with the scowl, Danny took as a bad sign. The order Munroe thrust in his face the night before bore her signature.

"Look at her," Fink said. "So young and lovely, not unlike yourself, Your Honor. Has anyone ever told you that except for that wart on your chin you bear an uncanny resemblance to Audrey Hepburn?"

"Who's Audrey Hepburn?" Jessica whispered.

"A famous actor," Danny said.

"Mr. Finkel, you are out of or—"

"But I digress. Back to our beloved ward, Jessica Jewell. It's almost impossible to believe that just a few days ago she was running through a meadow flying a kite and chasing a butterfly, not a care in the world."

"What?" Jessica said.

"*Shh,*" Danny said.

"Now here she is. Shattered. Orphaned. Forsaken. Yet in this darkest hour, when all else has been extinguished, one light continues to burn brightly for her. One savior remains. One great man has arisen."

"Is he talking about Jesus?" Jessica whispered.

"I wish."

"Daniel Teakwell, my client!"

"Mr. Finkel, are you done talking?" the judge said. "Because I'm done listening. Call your first witness."

"Very well. The applicant calls Ms., um, Aunt Rosie."

Using her walker as a battering ram, Jessica's great aunt barreled through the swinging gate separating the courtroom participants from the spectators. "The name is Rosemary Peligrini, you clod."

It took a minute of writhing and complaining about the lack of a cushion before she settled into the round-backed wooden witness chair.

Strazinski asked her to raise her right hand. "Do you solemnly swear to tell the truth and nothing but the truth so help you God?"

"Of course I do, but you don't have to shout at me." When Danny and Jessica picked her up on the way to the courthouse, Jessica grabbed her hearing aids from the charger and cranked up the volume.

"Ms. Peligrini, is it true you're Jessica's only living blood relative?" Fink said.

"Far as I know, although I can't swear my brothers—may they rest in peace—never slipped one past the goalie."

"And you're her Great Aunt, correct?"

"I'm not bad. I don't know about great."

"You are her mother's father's sister, is that right?"

"Hell, I hope not. That sounds like some kind of incest arrangement."

"Going back to what you said, that you wouldn't consider yourself a *great* aunt. What did you mean?"

"I never said that."

Fink slapped his forehead. "It was three seconds ago. Are you senile?"

"Mr. Finkel, how dare you insult an elder in my courtroom!"

"Sorry, Judge. I meant it as a compliment."

"What?"

Fink held up his hand. "I think we can speed this up. Ms. Rosie, isn't it true you hate children?"

"I wouldn't call it hate, but they're nasty little buggers. Except for my darling Jessica, of course. She's not nasty. Just a royal pain in the ass."

Strazinski pounded her gavel. "Thank you, ma'am. You are excused."

"Why is everyone shouting at me?"

Fink's next witness was Grady. Danny asked him to be a character witness. He showed up in a worn houndstooth sports jacket with his unruly white hair neatly trimmed.

"Could you state your name and occupation for the record?" Fink said.

"Grady Banyon. I own the Tradewinds Bar and Grill on the Hollywood Beach boardwalk."

"Tell the court how and when you came to know the applicant?"

"Which one's the applicant? Danny or Jessica?"

"Danny."

"I've known Danny Teakwell going on fifteen years now. He's been a friend and a regular at my business establishment the entire time."

The judge interrupted. "A regular? And your business is a bar? Is he a heavy drinker?"

"He's been known to have one too many on occasion. That's true of a lot of good people. I meet them every day."

"Would you say he has an alcohol problem?"

"No, Judge, I'd say he's human. Is he flawed? You bet. He'll tell you that himself. I'd be more worried about him as a guardian if he claimed to be perfect. I can say this, with God as my witness. If I ever had a child who needed caring for, there's no person on this earth I would trust more than Danny Teakwell."

Jessica nodded along.

"And if I hadn't been told to keep this hearing confidential, there would be a dozen people lined up waiting to tell you the same thing, to explain about all the times Danny helped them when they were down and out. We're talking about a man who would give you his last dollar if you needed it."

Fink showed the surprisingly good judgment to quit while the going was good. "I have no further questions for this witness."

Danny's pulse sped up as Grady stepped down. He was next. He drained a paper cup from a water cooler and crumpled it into a ball.

"Believe in yourself," Jessica said. "Like I believe in you." The words comforted him until he noticed she had her fingers crossed on both hands under the table.

The judge administered the oath and told him to be seated. Facing the courtroom, he wasn't surprised to see FBI Special Agent Winton Munroe and Deputy Marshall Marshall sitting together. But he didn't expect to see Detective Rodriguez, looking natty in a silvery sharkskin suit, or Allie Dearden, the trauma psychologist, red hair sprayed over her shoulders.

Fink asked him to state his name for the record.

"Daniel Teakwell."

"Mr. Teakwell," Judge Strazinski interrupted. "I have been patiently holding my tongue waiting until we got a chance to meet. Do I understand correctly that last night you defied an endangered child order of this court to surrender Ms. Jewell to the protective custody of law enforcement?"

Danny was wondering why it hadn't been mentioned earlier. He had hoped it slipped through the cracks. "Well, Your Honor, the thing is—"

"The thing is I'm the one who defied it," Jessica said, standing. "And no, you do not understand correctly."

She pointed at Munroe. "That disgusting man who claims to be with the FBI broke into our house at midnight. The only person endangering me was him. He kept calling me *honey* and tried to break into my locked bedroom while I was undressed."

Munroe's mouth fell open and the color drained from his crimson face, leaving it a sickly shade of pink.

Strazinski said, "Sir, please stand and identify yourself."

"Winton Munroe, Your Honor. Special agent with the FBI."

"Is what the girl said true?"

"No, of course not. We did go to Teakwell's condo to execute the order, but the rest is completely false."

"Who is we?"

"I accompanied Deputy Marshall Marshall here."

"Why is the FBI interested in a guardianship, a matter of local law?"

He glanced around and saw Rodriguez. "I'm sorry, Your Honor, but the answer to that question is part of an ongoing confidential criminal investigation."

"I'll tell you why," Jessica said. "Because yesterday we had a meeting and he got all ticked off and acted like a whiny little baby just because I asked to see his identification. Everything I said is true. You can ask Deputy Marshall."

"Please rise, deputy. Is what the girl says true? Did Agent Munroe refer to her as *honey*?"

"Uh, yes, Judge. Twice, I believe," he said, wispy mustache twitching.

Munroe stared down on the scrawny deputy like he wanted to wrench his neck.

"Did he attempt to break into her room while she was undressed?"

"Well, he did threaten to break the door down if she didn't unlock it, and she did say she was dressing."

"Your Honor," Munroe sputtered. "It wasn't like it sounds. As you noted, we had your lawfully signed endangered child order."

"Forgive me for interrupting, Judge." It was Allie Dearden, standing in a soothing green pantsuit that complemented her red hair.

"Dr. Dearden? What are you doing here?"

"I also have an interest in the wellbeing of Ms. Jewell," she said. "I attended the same meeting yesterday as Agent Munroe. Deputy Marshall, who signed the affidavit in support of the endangered child order, was not present."

"I just signed what he gave me, Judge," the deputy said, pointing at Munroe. "He said he's from the FBI."

"I am from the FBI, you idiot."

Allie continued, "Not only did I not see anything suggesting Jessica is endangered by Mr. Teakwell, I left the meeting believing the opposite is true. That she is in a safe and stable place, which is incredibly important right now."

"Thank you for that opinion," Judge Strazinski said. "Agent Munroe, I will deal with you later. Mr. Teakwell, back to you ..."

Fink led Danny through his background, spending an inordinate amount of time on his short-lived prowess as a high school baseball star, neglecting to mention he got kicked off the team.

"Why did my client pursue baseball? Not to win championships or trophies, which he did, but for one reason and one reason only." He put a hand over his heart. "To prove through our national pastime that the American Dream lives on and to set a wholesome example for the troubled youth of Broward County. Isn't that true, Mr. Teakwell?"

"Well, that's two reasons and I don't think either—"

"Thank you, Mr. Teakwell," he said.

Jumping forward in time, he promoted Danny's thirty seconds of dumb luck picking six numbers to win the lottery as if he had invented penicillin. The fact that he squandered away the money didn't come up.

Then he said casually, "And five years ago you were charged with first-degree murder, but the charge was dismissed. Moving on, you opened your surf—"

"Whoa, back up," Strazinski said. "I saw that in your application, Mr. Teakwell. I have to say, I can't remember ever granting a guardianship to a person who was charged with first-degree murder."

"I would imagine that's true, Judge. But as Mr. Finkel said, the case was dismissed. I was innocent."

"There must have been some basis for the charge," she said.

"No. There wasn't," said a man's voice from the back of the courtroom.

Everyone turned to gaze at Emilio Rodriguez, adjusting his lavender pocket square as he rose from his seat.

"My, my," Strazinski said. "Another surprise guest star. Long time no see, Detective. What is your interest in this matter?"

"I'm the one who pursued the murder charge against Mr. Teakwell. I figured it might be a big deal in a guardianship proceeding and wanted to be here to clear things up."

"Please do."

"A psychopath committed the murder and framed Teakwell for it. I'm embarrassed to admit I fell for it. Teakwell was being too humble just now when he said he was innocent. He wasn't just innocent. He was a hero in my opinion."

Fink jumped out of his seat. "A hero indeed. A giant of a man whose shoes can never be—"

"Mr. Finkel?"

"Yes?"

"Close your mouth and sit down. Continue, Detective."

"Teakwell went through hell and back to track down a woman

the psycho had kidnapped. Sari Hunter, his childhood sweetheart, who he ended up marrying. He not only saved her life, but
apprehended the real killer in the process, taking a couple of bullets that almost killed him."

"Ah, yes. It's coming back," Strazinski said. "Lottery winner
framed for murder. It was in the news for a month."

"That's the one, Judge."

"Very well. Thank you for clearing that up."

"One more thing, if I could. Anyone who knows me will say
I'm a coldhearted sonofabitch, excuse my language. Who am I to
argue with such a compliment? But I'm also a father who loves
his kids. I've seen these two characters together. They make quite
a pair. There's a definite bond there, a fierce loyalty. I can't explain where it comes from, but it's real. Thank you for letting me
interrupt." He sat down.

Jessica flashed Danny two thumbs up.

"Mr. Teakwell, you certainly seem to have your share of
supporters."

Grady jumped up, "That's what I was telling you, Judge. I
could bring in a busload more."

"Everyone loves Danny!" Jessica piped. "Except for the alleged FBI agent."

"Enough. Everyone remain seated and do not speak out of order. Mr. Teakwell, let's move on. Tell me why you're interested in
being Ms. Jewell's guardian."

"It started when her parents asked me to take care of her for a
few days after they got in some trouble. The trouble involves the
criminal investigation referred to by the FBI agent."

"Why did they ask you?"

"Excellent question. I asked them the same thing."

"Because they trusted him," Jessica said.

"That's what they told me," Danny said.

"How did you come to know them?"

"I visited her family's funeral home when doing some research during my case." He left out that the research involved a

dug-up grave with a body missing. "That's how we met. Then she brought me a hamster in the hospital when I was recovering from the injuries mentioned by the detective."

"Because I didn't want him to be alone," Jessica said. "That was before he married Sari."

"Jessica," Strazinski said gently. "You will have your own chance to speak after Mr. Teakwell. Okay?"

"Okay."

Danny said, "That was all five years ago. Just recently she invited me to her grandfather's funeral."

Fink stood. "Take note, Your Honor. Five years. That's longer than most marriages."

Strazinski waved him back down and returned to Danny. "Go on."

"When she first came to stay, I felt responsible for her, of course, and still do. But she also grew on me. Like the detective said, there's some kind of symbiosis there. It would probably take a psychologist to understand it. Maybe we're both lost souls of a sort.

"Sometimes I'm not sure who's helping who more. My wife, Sari, died of cancer about a year ago. This probably won't help my case, but I sank into depression. Jessica's been a positive influence on me. She's an unusual person, a special one. I admire the heck out of her strength and intelligence."

"Aw, thanks, Danny. Oops. Sorry, Judge," Jessica said, making a zipper-slash across her lips.

Strazinski said, "What makes you qualified to be Jessica's guardian?"

"In a perfect world, I'm sure I'm not. I don't have a partner, don't have kids. I don't make a lot of money. But her world is the opposite of perfect right now. I can promise you one thing. You could never find anyone who would try harder to protect her or do right by her."

"Thank you, Mr. Teakwell. You may step down."

An unusually subdued Fink stood and announced, "Your

Honor, for our last witness, the applicant calls Jessica Jewell."

Strazinski swore her in and told Fink she'd handle the questioning. "Jessica, I'm terribly sorry about your parents. I'm also sorry you're having to go through this proceeding. Everything would be much easier if you had close relatives."

"I don't need close relatives ... except my parents. I have Danny."

"Yes, well, that's what we're going to talk about. Why do you feel Mr. Teakwell is best-suited to be your temporary guardian?"

"Because we belong together, like you already heard."

Danny detected the familiar note of exasperation in her voice and hoped she didn't accuse the judge of being ADD and not listening.

"I'd like to hear it from your side."

"Danny understands me. Most people don't. He treats me like a regular person, not like a child."

"Anything else?"

"He doesn't think I'm weird, which most people do. Or if he does, he doesn't act like it. I don't know if anyone thinks you're weird, Judge, but trust me, it's not fun."

"I wouldn't think so," she said, face softening.

"He's also very patient. If you knew me, you'd know that would be a job requirement for my guardian. I can be difficult sometimes. My teacher even put it in writing."

Her voice started to crack. "And he—he's kind. To everyone, not just me. And humble, like the detective said. He doesn't even know how great he is. And he needs me. He ca—can't run his surf shop without me." She blinked and twin tears broke loose, one winding down each cheek.

Strazinski handed her a tissue. "Thank you, Jessica. I apologize in advance for this next question. It's my responsibility to ask it. Has Mr. Teakwell ever done anything inappropriate around you?"

"Inappropriate? What do you mean?"

"Has he ever touched you?"

"Touched me? ... Wait a minute, I know what you're getting at. That's sick! The answer is a big fat *no*. He wouldn't even give me a goodnight hug after my mom asked him to."

Vulnerable Jessica vanished. "Frankly, I don't understand why we're even having this hearing."

"Because I face a difficult decision and need input to make sure I do the right thing," Strazinski said.

"Why is it anyone's business except mine? I don't go around trying to tell you who can be your guardian. It should be my choice."

"Unfortunately, the law doesn't allow minors to make that decision," she said.

"Well, I plan to write the government about that, believe me. In the meantime ..." She looked at Danny, who was pushing air down with both palms, mouthing *Easy, easy*.

"I'm sorry, Judge," she said contritely. "It's been a hard week."

"I understand." She looked to the back of the courtroom. "What was that you were saying about fierce loyalty, Detective? I've heard enough. The court hereby appoints Mr. Teakwell as Jessica's temporary guardian. A written order will be forthcoming."

Jessica leapt to her feet pumping her fists. "Whoo-hoo! Best judge ever! Thank you!" Strazinski dipped her head to hide a smile.

Danny motioned Jessica back into her chair. "Thank you, Your Honor," he said.

"Mr. Teakwell, there are several obligations guardians must fulfill. You and your lawyer can meet with my clerk to discuss them."

Fink stood and bowed. "Your Honor, it has been one of the great pleasures of my budding legal career to make an appearance in your court."

"Mr. Finkel, I wish I could say the same, but it would be a lie." She banged the gavel on the bench and said court was adjourned.

Fink's face drooped.

Chapter 34

CHAD SAT IN the back pew of the church in Hollywood Hills. *Hills?* The neighborhood was flat as a pancake, like the rest of Florida. He kept his face buried behind the funeral program as people filed in. His assignment from Jefe was to find the Jewell kid and the man who broke into the funeral home with her.

No better place to do it than her parents' funeral service. They were easy to spot, even in the packed church. The girl sat in the front row between an old biddy with a walker and a lanky blond guy who looked late thirties. Had to be the one in the video.

Jefe ordered him to keep the assignment a secret. Getting more specific, he said he would tear Chad's heart out if he mentioned it to Yago. Chad had never been to Colombia, but knew the stories. *The Legend of Luis* was on the new employee required reading list.

He sensed the power struggle brewing between Jefe and Yago and wasn't sure what to do about it other than stay clear and try to pick the winner before it was too late. They both scared him to death.

For now he'd stay with Luis. He was still the boss and Chad appreciated his commitment to diversity in hiring. Most important, he controlled Chad's employee benefits.

His parents didn't understand when he left his job at a Big 4 accounting firm in New York and moved to Miami to work for a chain of funeral homes. He explained that in an epiphanous moment he knew his life's calling was to make death a better experience for people.

The real epiphany was the interview revelation that the Snowbirds employee benefits package included free cocaine.

His addiction began the first time he tried it, at a party in grad school. He fell in love with the euphoric sense of accomplishment it brought him without having to do anything to earn it. He'd spent his whole life as an overachiever doing things the hard way.

He twitched impatiently through the preacher's eulogy and scripture reading, keeping a watchful eye out for Yago. If he happened to be looking for the kid on his own, this would be a logical place.

When the preacher instructed the mourners to open their hymn books, he slipped out to his SUV, readying his camera with the telephoto lens behind the tinted windows. He'd get some good pictures and try to follow them home.

*   *   *

"This stinks," Jessica said when the family funeral limousine reached the Westbrook Cemetery. "You spend your entire life owning a funeral home and when you really need one, you have to go to a competitor."

The limo's passengers included her and Danny, Aunt Rosie, Norma Pollinuk, the longtime assistant at Slagger-Jewell with whom he'd had a run-in five years ago, and Gloria, who reminded Danny she liked to be called Gigi when they were introduced. They sat facing each other in the backseats.

"It's so unfair," Gloria said, black hair parted in the middle, framing her dark eyes and milkwhite face. "You didn't even get to embalm them like you always wanted to do when the Big Sleep arrived."

It was becoming clear to Danny why the pair had bonded as

friends. But he agreed with her. Knowing the Jewell family history, it really did seem unfair.

"There's a bomb?" Aunt Rosie said. "Get me the hell out of here!"

"Em*balm*, Aunt Rosie. Not bomb," Jessica said. Rosie left her hearing aids at home.

Norma Pollinuk sat cattycorner to Danny, wearing a pillbox hat and long-sleeved mid-calf dress accessorized with a cameo pin at the neck, hands folded primly on her lap. She stayed silent the entire ride, opening her mouth only when the limo glided to a halt on the grass alongside the *Jewell Family* mausoleum, a freestanding granite structure with ornate iron gates and a domed top.

"Mr. Teakwell, I want to apologize for being rude to you five years ago," she said. "Thank you for taking care of Jessica."

"No problem."

"At the time I thought you were a lowdown, dirty-dealing, scumbag prick. I apologize for that too."

"Prick means ..." Gloria said, pointing to his groin.

"Thank you, Gloria."

"Gigi."

"Right." He again said no problem to Norma Pollinuk.

"Look at all the people," Jessica said wistfully. "I never knew my parents had so many friends. Most of the ones I met were dead."

Her parents' caskets were already set up on gurneys, ready to be placed inside the mausoleum. Exiting the limo, Jessica explained that her grandfather built it fifty years ago. "It has six crypts," she said. "Three stacked on each side. If Rosie wants in, we'll probably use five of them, so there'll be an extra one for you if you want."

Danny just said thanks. No point telling her he intended to be cremated or that she'll most likely have a partner and kids of her own someday. He sat next to her in a row of chairs reserved for the family party. Everyone else had to stand.

The cemetery service was brief. The director of the competing funeral home said a prayer and talked a little about Jewell, commenting that he was a shining star of integrity and uprightness in the mortuary business.

After the service, several people approached Jessica to express their condolences. Most just gave Danny odd looks, but one woman said, "And who might this be?"

"My court-appointed guardian," she said.

"Oh," the woman said, surprised. "Are you a lawyer?"

"No, he's a surfer."

When anyone mentioned *the terrible accident*, Jessica's lips tightened. She was furious the county sheriff's office was still calling the deaths an accident. Danny had to remind her that's what was agreed on at the meeting.

"Over my objection. They're going to owe me a huge apology when the autopsy report comes out and proves it was murder." The report was due the next day.

After the service, as the caskets were being loaded into the mausoleum, Jessica said she wanted to go inside and spend some private time with her parents. Danny understood and took it as a good sign she might be starting to come to terms.

What he didn't understand was why she insisted on bringing her backpack and why it clanked each time she moved it.

*   *   *

Chad sat in his SUV watching from a distance. Cocaine addiction was a terrible thing, he thought, snorting a line from the dashboard as he watched the girl disappear inside the mausoleum. It changed your values. All you cared about was getting more coke, not nice people getting killed, not even kids getting orphaned. Except he did care a little, which was why he kept snorting the lines.

The mourners were dispersing. He couldn't stay there alone. He merged into the line of cars leaving the cemetery, parking around the corner so he could spot the limo when it came out.

It took almost an hour. He followed it back to the church, where the kid, blond guy, and biddy stepped out and squeezed into a blue Hyundai.

The old lady was probably the aunt. The man and girl looked a little alike. A brother? Too old. Maybe an uncle.

Chad snapped a picture of the license plate and followed the Hyundai as it left the church and headed east. After a couple miles it veered around a circular park, jotting right then left before stopping in front of a square pink house with rusty aqua hurricane shutters yawning from the windows.

He noted the address and drove past looking the other way. When he came around the block, the Hyundai was gone. He cursed and snorted another line.

*   *   *

Danny ran to the bathroom to pee when they returned to the condo. He'd been holding it for hours. He came out to find Jessica's head buried in the cabinets under the kitchen sink, clanging around in his toolbox.

"What's up?" he said.

"I borrowed some of your tools and was just returning them."

"Why did you need ... what's that?" He pointed at a zip-top bag containing a gray slab that looked like a beef tenderloin gone bad.

"Oh, this?" She picked up the bag and slid it into the freezer. "Just part of my grandpa's liver. So what should we do for the rest of the day?"

"Nice try. How and why is your grandfather's liver in my freezer?"

"It's not his whole liver. Just a slice. But it's a fair question."

"Let's hear the answer."

"It started when Agent Munroe blew me off at the meeting when I asked if they could autopsy gramps ..."

The more she thought about it, she said, the more convinced

she was that the cartel killed her grandfather. "It's just too much of a coincidence that he died right when this started."

"Well, he was ninety-eight."

"I saw him a couple days before and he seemed fine. And, yes, I know the death certificate said natural cardiac arrest, but when someone that old dies, people just assume it's natural. We did too, me and my parents."

"Were there any injuries on his body to suggest someone hurt him?"

"Nothing obvious, but all it would take is a needle prick and the right kind of drug or poison."

"So this is what you were doing in the mausoleum? Extracting body organs from your grandfather."

"No, not just that. I wanted to see my parents one last time and give them goodbye hugs. I didn't tell you about grandpa because you wouldn't have let me do it. Also, defacing a corpse is a serious crime and I didn't want you to be an accomplice."

"That's very thoughtful of you."

"However, I personally believe that since my family owns the mausoleum, we also own the contents, which would include grandpa."

"Let's hope we don't have to test that theory in court. Why the liver?"

"That's where any drug or poison would be metabolized."

"How did you, you know, cut him open?"

"With your wire clippers."

Danny last used them to run speaker wire through his attic space to his bedroom. He had a hard time wrapping his head around the image. "Did you just leave him like that?"

"Of course not. I wouldn't do that to gramps. I borrowed your caulking gun too. It had half a tube of window and door sealant in it. It was even gray, so it sort of blended in with his skin."

"You caulked your grandfather shut?"

"It wasn't like I had a suturing kit available. The caulk has a twenty-year guarantee. It'll last longer than he does."

"Didn't it make you feel bad cutting him up like that?"

"Why would it? I'm trying to help him by catching his killers. He'd do the same for me. What's the problem?"

"Let me count the ways. First, you're going completely by speculation. Second, as you said, it might have been a crime. Third, did you think it all the way through? How do you plan to get your liver sample analyzed for drugs or poison?"

"Once the autopsy comes out and the police know my parents were murdered, it shouldn't be hard to convince them gramps was too and get them to test it."

"How will you explain why you just happen to have a slice of his liver handy for testing?"

"I'll say we extracted it during the embalming to keep as a memento. You won't rat me out will you?"

*   *   *

Sunset brought Danny and a bottle of Red Stripe out to the balcony to soak up the view and healing air. The sun washed the water in a golden sheen.

Jessica came out to join him, plopping with a bounce on the stretched-out rubber bands of the old patio chair. "Did you like my parents?"

"Of course. I never got a chance to know your mom, but she seemed really sweet. And I liked your dad a lot."

"Mom was sweet. I'm more like my dad."

"Apparently a lot of people liked them. The church was packed."

"Yeah, that was nice," Jessica said. "I wonder if my parents got to watch the service. Have you ever wondered about that, whether Sari can see you and hear you?"

"I have. I even talk to her sometimes, mostly at the beginning, not so much anymore."

"Do you think you'll ever get to see her again, in an afterlife? Even though you're a, what's it called?"

"Agnostic. And yes, I think about it all the time, which I guess makes me a hypocrite."

"Everyone thinks about it. We used to comfort our customers by saying it would happen, but honestly, we had no idea if it was true."

"You hungry? We never really ate lunch and it's about time for dinner."

"Not for anything healthy, but I could eat pizza again."

"Sounds good to me."

"Should we invite Erin? Or maybe Allie. I liked the way she stood up for us today. I didn't know she was a doctor. My mom always said to marry a doctor. The detective too. And of course Grady. He's the best. He loves you so much."

"He loves you too."

"Maybe he could be my unofficial guardian grandfather."

"I'm sure he'd happily accept the appointment."

"And Fink could be my weird uncle. What is wrong with him?"

"I think he tries too hard."

"That judge looked like she wanted to crack his skull open with her gavel. Maybe we should invite them all to dinner."

"Let's save it for another time."

"Okay. Just you and me then. *The Guardian and His Ward.* Sounds like the name of a C.S. Lewis book."

Chapter 35

"**DROWNED?**" Jessica said. "Are you sure?"

"That's what it says," Rodriguez said.

They were in his office going over the autopsy report. He started with the bottom line. Cause of death.

"I—I wasn't expecting that. Drowned. Poor Mom and Dad."

"I'm afraid the results are even worse than that."

"Nothing's worse than drowning. Do you know what happens? You hold your breath until you can't, then you breathe even though you know there's nothing to breathe but water. Your lungs fill up and your heart starts beating super-fast trying to find more oxygen. But there isn't any, so it gives up."

"Drowning is not a good way to go," Rodriguez said. "Let me know if you want to hear the rest. You're not going to like it."

"I want to hear."

"The autopsy found no signs of external injuries except abrasions from the seat belts and airbags. The coroner concluded the cause of death was ... well, I'll just read it. Brace yourself. *Conclusion: Accidental death by drowning caused by loss of vehicle control, most likely attributable to alcohol and opioid intoxication.*"

"What?" She sprang from her chair and ripped the report from his hands. "This is a crock. Danny, did you know about this?"

"I didn't."

"My mom only had a glass of wine once in a while and my dad didn't drink at all, and they definitely weren't drug addicts.

246

Whoever prepared this report is either a liar or incompetent, probably both. They were murdered."

"Jessica," Danny said, prying the report from her fingers and giving it back to Rodriguez. "Let's listen to what the detective has to say."

Jessica stayed standing.

Rodriguez said, "Given everything that's gone on, I still think there's a good chance they were murdered."

"More than a good—"

He held up a stop-sign hand. "But I can't ignore physical evidence. There's something else. Investigators found a vodka bottle in the car along with a pill vial containing opioid tablets. Your parents' fingerprints were found on both items."

"Impossible!" Jessica said.

"Could it all be a setup?" Danny said. "What about other physical evidence?"

"Like I told you before," Rodriguez said. "Evidence disappears. The tow truck wrecked the scene when it dragged the car out before anything could be examined."

"More incompetence!" Jessica said and began pacing rapid ovals around the guest chairs, passing between Danny and Rodriguez on each lap.

"Any highway cameras?" Danny said.

"The car left the road on a dark patch in the boonies."

"Where there happened to be no fencing."

"That's right."

As Jessica completed another loop around the chairs, Danny blocked her path with a foot pressed against Rodriguez's desk. "Please sit down."

She complied with a glare.

Danny said, "What about these black boxes in cars? I read they can tell things like the speed a car was going before an accident."

"Event data recorders. They'll probably be in all cars someday, but they're still new. Not many models have them, including her parents' rental car."

"Have you had a chance to search Jessica's home?"

"We did. No sign of forced entry. The inside looked undisturbed."

"Any fingerprints or DNA?"

"I'm sure there's plenty of both in there, but they can last for years. It's a big house where a lot of people have no doubt come and gone. We'd need to know whose prints or DNA we were looking for."

"I already know," Jessica said. "And I have their DNA. The hair I found. I told everyone at the meeting, but as usual no one listened to me."

"I remember your hair. Remind me why you think it belongs to a viable suspect?"

"Because it was in the shower of the guest bathroom no one uses."

"No one's ever used it?"

"Sometimes my parents' friends when they came to visit, and Aunt Rosie. But like I said at the meeting, my mom is insane about cleaning, especially bathrooms."

He opened his mouth, closed it and flattened his hands on the desk in surrender. Danny knew the feeling.

"Fine. Bring me your hair and I will ask if it can be run through the FBI's CODIS system, a DNA database of convicted felons."

"I also have—Ow!"

Danny jabbed her with an elbow, harder than he meant to, before she could blurt out she was the proud owner of a chunk of her grandfather's liver. He wasn't sold on the soundness of her legal theory that it's okay to cut up dead family members based on property rights.

"One step at a time," he whispered.

She nodded. "What are you going to do about the fake autopsy?"

"It's not fake," Rodriguez said. "The conclusion could be wrong, but the bloodwork showed the presence of alcohol and opioids in both your parents. I have to consider all possible explanations. It's my job."

"What other explanations could there be?" Danny said. "You heard her. Her mom rarely drank and her dad didn't drink at all. And they didn't use narcotics."

"Maybe they were engaging in behavior they normally wouldn't. They'd been through a lot."

"Bull," Jessica said.

"Jessica," Danny said. "I know you're upset, but you need to calm down."

"Don't tell me what to do. You're not my father. Quit trying to be."

Rodriguez arched his eyebrows and continued. "Another possibility is her parents had preexisting drug and alcohol issues they concealed. Kids are often the last to know."

"That does it. I'm out of here." She jumped up and stormed out.

"That didn't go well," Rodriguez said.

"It wasn't your fault. Sorry she was so rude. She's obviously under a ton of stress. But I agree with her about the autopsy conclusion. I don't believe it was an accident."

"I didn't say I believe it either, but I can't disregard an autopsy report. Here's some good news to share with her. The DEA is working up a search warrant application for the Snowbirds in Paradise funeral home based on the information and cocaine sample you provided. It could bust things open. Keep your fingers crossed."

"I will." He glanced over his shoulder. "I better go after her."

"Teakwell, don't let those comments get to you."

"I expected some kind of backlash. She hasn't even begun to process things."

"Well, if you were having any second thoughts about being her guardian, here's a perfect example of why you're the best man for the job. I wanted to smack the kid, figuratively speaking. She could use some counseling."

"I've suggested it. You can probably guess her response."

"*I don't need any counseling.*"

"Almost her exact words."

"I feel like I'm always the bearer of bad news, but let's assume, hypothetically, her parents were murdered. Have you considered the possibility she could be in danger?"

"Of course. I think about it every time we're in public."

"You own a gun?"

"What do you think?"

"Laidback surfer dude? I'd guess not."

"Good guess. I hate guns."

"You might want to learn to love one."

Danny expected to find Jessica waiting in the reception area, but there was only Audrey, typing on a computer behind her desk.

"She took the elevator," she said.

Danny found the stairs and sprinted to the ground floor. Jessica was in the parking lot slouched against the Hyundai.

"Look," he said when he reached the car. "I know I'm not your father. You don't need to remind me. But I am your legal guardian. You said you wanted it that way. I'm asking you—no, I'm *telling* you—do not leave my sight again while this mess is going on."

She wrinkled her nose and climbed in the car. He turned on the radio when it became apparent she had no intention of speaking. Robert Plant was singing *Stairway to Heaven*.

"I know this song," she said halfway through. "Someone requested we play it at their father's funeral."

"Do you want me to turn it off?"

"No, it's fine. The title's good, but the words don't make any sense for a funeral."

"You're right."

When it ended, she said, "I'm sorry, Danny. I behaved like a child in there."

"Well, you are twelve."

"Like a rotten child. I didn't think it was possible to feel worse, but I did. Having the autopsy say it was an accident and smear my parents like that, as drunks and drug addicts. You think they were murdered, don't you?"

"Yes. I think the detective believes it too, but he has to go by the evidence. He gave me some good news to share with you. Well, there's no such thing as good news right now, but I think you'll appreciate it. The DEA is working on getting a search warrant for Snowbirds in Paradise based on our story. He said it could blow everything open."

"That is good news. So, just to be sure you know what I'm apologizing for, I didn't mean that stuff I said about not telling me what to do and not being my dad. You can order me around all you want."

"I'll keep that in mind."

"So you forgive me?"

"Of course. On one condition. You let me make an appointment for you with a therapist."

"Ah, very tricky. That's fine. But I don't want to see a stranger. Can you call Allie?"

He thought about it. It made sense. She already knew the whole story. "I'll give it a try."

Chapter 36

"I HAVE SOME good news and not-so-good news, Jefe," Chad said from across Luis's desk, on which he noticed his boss had replaced the mug warmer and fidget toy with two large handguns.

"I don't like bad news, Chad. Start with the good news."

Chad handed him a stack of 8 x 10 photos. "This is them, the girl and the guy from the funeral home break-in."

Luis sorted through the pictures. "These are nice, Chad. Where'd you learn photography?"

His face flushed. "From admiring a neighbor of mine in the next condo building through the windows."

"So who's the guy?"

"I don't know his name. He only moved in a month ago."

"Not the neighbor! The girl's friend."

"Well, sir, that's where the news turns less good. I followed them—diligently—from the church to the graveyard, back to the church, and across town to a house on Van Buren Street near Young Circle. Did you know the streets in Hollywood are named after presidents?"

"Fascinating. What happened?"

"They stopped at a house. I was right behind them so I passed by, didn't want them to notice they were being followed."

"Sounds good so far."

"Here's the bad news. When I came back around the block,

the car was gone. They were with an old lady. Probably the aunt. My guess is they dropped her off at the house and kept going. I do have pictures of the license plate. Here's a good shot."

"Doesn't help us. Vehicle records aren't public in Florida."

"If you want, I could ask Yago to break in and torture the old lady to get the information."

"We're not going to torture any old ladies. Stay away from Yago." He bent in to study the picture. "What's this, on the back bumper?"

Chad leaned in. "Looks like a sticker."

"I can see that. What does it say? Do we have a magnifying glass around here?"

"Not that I know of, but the digital versions of these are on my computer. I can find the image and enlarge it."

"What are you waiting for?"

He jumped up and ran out, returning a minute later with his open laptop.

"Here it is," he said. "The sticker says *Nine Lives Surf Shop, Hollywood Beach*."

"That's a lead at least."

"Does that mean I get to keep my heart?"

"For now."

"Awesome. Can I ask a question?"

"What?"

"What do you plan to do when you find the girl? Kill her?"

"I haven't decided yet."

*　　*　　*

Danny made an effort to simulate normal life for the two of them in the days following the funeral.

Rasheed's board was ready for Gaspar to start on the artwork. Two new custom board inquiries arrived via email. Feeling additional pressure as a guardian to earn a sustainable living, he responded quickly with preliminary sketches.

He was entitled to compensation under Florida guardianship law from Jessica's estate for his *services*, but didn't feel right about accepting it. Fink speculated her inheritance would be sizable. Property records showed they got more than a million dollars from the Slagger-Jewell sale.

The financial relevance of her grandfather's will was essentially moot. Without a will, his estate would go to Jewell as his only child. Her parents' joint will left everything to Jessica.

The will remained key evidence of a murder motive, but Danny didn't know what that was worth after the autopsy report. He pinned his hopes on the Snowbirds search warrant Rodriguez mentioned. If the DEA finds a body stuffed with cocaine, everything will tie together. The extortion, drugs, and murders.

His duties as guardian included managing Jessica's assets and filing regular accountings with the court. Not only had he proved to be a terrible money manager in life, just like with the compensation, controlling her assets felt wrong to him. He decided she was mature enough to manage them herself.

"Once the money comes in, and it's probably going to take a while, keep track of every penny so we can file the reports, and don't tell anyone I turned everything over to you. They'll fire me as guardian."

"I won't. And don't worry. I'm very frugal. I do need some new school clothes though. Can you loan me the money until the inheritance goes through?"

"I can *give* you the money."

"I want to pay my own expenses. It's only fair, especially since, you know, you're basically broke."

Danny called her middle school and learned that seventh grade started in ten days. He got through to the principal, explained the situation, and arranged a meeting. On arrival, she showered Jessica with condolences, took her time examining Danny's guardianship order, and gave him some papers to sign.

Jessica stayed silent until reviewing the class schedule. "Didn't you get my request to include mortuary science in this year's elective curriculum?"

Fidgeting, the principal put on a polite smile and said, "We considered it and decided there wasn't sufficient demand."

"That's because you never spread the word. I suggest sending out a survey explaining—"

Danny patted her knee. "How about we let this one go?"

Jessica nodded and the principal looked at Danny like he was her new best friend.

Allie Dearden was happy to meet with Jessica. They had their first therapy session that afternoon.

"How'd it go?" Danny asked when she came out.

"Fine, but bad news. She can't be your girlfriend because she already has her own girlfriend. So we're back to Erin."

"Why are you so intent on finding me a girlfriend?"

"Would you rather have another hamster? Also, did you know she's not a real doctor?"

"She has a Ph.D. in psychology," Danny said. He saw it on her business card. "That's a doctoral degree."

"She can't cut people open. I asked her."

"No, and I'm sure she wouldn't want to."

"I don't think you should be allowed to call yourself a doctor if you can't cut people open. Live ones."

"You're entitled to your opinion. What else did you talk about? If you want to share. If not, that's fine."

"I don't mind. First, she expected me to do all the talking. I thought I was going to be able to just sit and listen."

"That's how therapy works."

"She wanted to get me talking about my parents. I think she wanted me to cry, like you did."

"That's not exactly accurate."

"She said I need to get in touch with my feelings. I said it was easier to not think about them."

"I'm guessing she didn't agree with that approach."

"Nope. Said they're going to come out one way or another and it's better they come out in a healthy way."

"Makes sense to me."

"Fine. We'll have a cryfest. I'll cry about my parents if you'll cry about Sari. You need to get in touch with your feelings as much as I do."

"Did Allie say that?"

"She didn't need to. Ask anyone who knows you. Just make sure to tell them you really want to hear the truth. Otherwise, they'll try to be nice and say, *Oh, no, Danny. You're perfect. We love you. You don't need to change anything.*"

He laughed.

"Ask Grady. He'll tell you the truth."

"No doubt."

"I'll bet Erin would too, once she gets to know you a little better."

"I wouldn't waste time thinking about Erin. She's lives in California. Her stay here is only temporary."

"Like mine?"

"What do you mean?" he said even though he knew exactly what she meant.

"Facts are facts. It's in your official title. *Temporary Guardian.* What's going to happen to me when temporary ends?"

"Let's not think about that right now."

"See? You're worse than me!"

Chapter 37

"**BOSS, WE GOT** a big problem," said Francisco, chief embalmer and newly installed CEO of the Hollywood Snowbirds in Paradise Funeral Home.

"What now?" Luis said.

"A bunch of DEA agents are at the front door with a search warrant. What do you want me to do?"

Yago! "You sure they're DEA?"

"They got badges, vehicles, even drug-sniffing dogs."

"Not much choice then. Cooperate. Did you clean the place like I instructed?"

"A hundred percent. All the bleach we used in the embalming room, you need a respirator to breathe in there."

"Good. Any clients?"

"Just an itty-bitty granny. I took her in yesterday in case someone came around looking for jumbo-size corpses stuffed with white powder."

"You're a genius, Francisco. I'm leaving the Brickell offices now and heading that way. We need a local criminal defense lawyer, pronto. Any ideas?"

"I saw a billboard down the street. Guy named Bennie Finkel. Calls himself *The Hammer.*"

"Call him. Say we'll give him ten grand in cash if he gets there in ten minutes."

*　　*　　*

The DEA agents, some in body armor and carrying assault rifles, swept through the funeral home, herding the occupants into the lobby, all of whom wore black suits except for a trio in white lab coats.

Special Agent Timberly Jenkins led the search team. "Everyone stay calm and don't make any sudden movements. What's this?" she said, pulling open the suit jacket of the man nearest to her.

"A Glock."

"Anyone else armed?"

Everyone raised their hands except Fink.

He had just walked in. He was eating an early lunch at McDonalds when his phone rang. The caller said only that the feds were about to execute a search warrant at their place of business and his boss was willing to pay ten thousand dollars in cash to any criminal defense lawyer who could show up in ten minutes.

Big Mac in hand, Fink ran out of the restaurant saying, "I think I can fit that into my schedule. Give me the address."

"You got experience in criminal law, right?"

"Got a man off on first-degree murder charges. Not many lawyers can claim that."

"Alright."

Squeezing into his prized Pontiac Firebird Trans Am, he brought the turbocharged V-8 thundering to life. *Vroom, vroom, vroom.*

Big men needed big motors. He sped through red lights and drove on the sidewalk to get around a delivery truck, just in case the client was wed to the ten minutes. Only when he swerved into the parking lot, almost rear-ending a K-9 van, did he see the Snowbirds in Paradise sign.

He shut down the engine and weighed the titanic conflict of interest awaiting him inside.

These were the people who extorted Jessica's family! Probably murdered them! ... On the other hand, maybe they had troubled childhoods and weren't to blame. No rule says you have to like your clients. His ethics professor at Frogleman taught him that.

But he did like Jessica, sort of, and she was already his client! And Danny his best friend! ... Then again, it's not like they had a formal agreement or anything, and he wasn't getting paid. As for suggesting she bring a lawsuit against Snowbirds, that was just bar talk.

Mostly, he really, really needed the ten grand. He kickstarted his new practice with what was left of his student loan money. The damn government was already hounding him about it. They actually expected him to pay it back. WTF! And yesterday he missed the first payment on the bank loan he took out to get the billboard.

He decided there was no harm going inside and checking out the situation, play along until he figured things out.

So far, the only thing he had figured out was that the dark-skinned woman in the trim blue suit was in charge and concerned about the pistol-packing workforce.

"Alright, everybody," she said. "Let's try another class participation exercise. Everyone with a concealed carry permit raise your hand."

No hands went up.

"Tut, tut. Florida law requires one. We're going to confiscate your weapons for everyone's safety. We appreciate your cooperation."

As the agents moved toward the congregation, the front door burst open, smacking Fink in the spine. He fell to the floor and looked up to yell profanities and threaten a lawsuit against the negligent person responsible.

His lips clamped when he saw a man who had to be Luis Carmillion. Big enough to play nose tackle for the Dolphins, with an eyepatch and scar down his cheek. A trim man with blond bangs and horn-rimmed glasses followed closely behind.

Fink's first thought was he had gotten himself into one helluva mess. His second was that the eyepatch was pretty cool. Maybe he should get one. A lawyer with an eyepatch would definitely look tough on billboards.

"You the lawyer?" Carmillion said, looking down at him.

"Bennie Finkel at your service," he said, rubbing his spine.

"Get off the floor."

Fink climbed up and extended a hand that Carmillion ignored.

"What are you waiting for? Do something."

A reasonable request, although he hadn't seen the ten grand yet. The obstacle was they didn't teach this kind of stuff in law school. He had no clue what to do. When a DEA agent removed a handgun from a gentleman's belt holster and the man objected, he decided to wing it.

"Hold it," Fink said. "Stop right there. You have no right to seize that man's firearm. It would be an obsequious violation of his constitutional rights."

"You mean obscene?" said the woman in charge.

"Maybe."

"Who the hell are you?" she said.

"Who the hell am I? I could ask you the same question."

"I'm Special Agent Timberly Jenkins. DEA."

All eyes were on him: DEA, Carmillion, the blond guy, the black suits and the white coats. Even the dogs were staring.

"I the hell am Benjamin Finkel. Attorney at law."

"Do you represent these people?"

"Well, I haven't see the ten—" He felt Carmillion's glare. "Yes."

"Then by all means, please do share with us the provision of the constitution you believe is being violated here."

"Well, the Second Amendment, obviously. Also the Third, Fourth, possibly others."

"The Third Amendment? No quartering of soldiers without the consent of the owner? I went to law school, counselor. The Third Amendment has never been invoked in the history of this country."

Take charge. You're a big man. You have a turbocharged V-8. Vroom, vroom!

"And I say it's about time! Are you not soldiers with your body armor and assault weapons? These fine people pose no threat. Look at them." He waved to the collection of glowering men and women in black suits, all of whom could have been posing for their Most Wanted poster.

"Gentle as lambs. If I had children, I'd hire them as babysitters. In fact, if they'll give me their numbers, I'll call them the day my firstborn pops out of the ... well, you know where they pop out, obviously."

"You're actually licensed to practice law?"

"Currently." He hadn't heard from the state bar since the fitness hearing. "I'm sure you're aware employees do not need a carry permit inside a private business and I'm confident these law-abiding citizens would never carry their weapons in public. They have every right to keep and bear arms for self-defense and the defense of their customers."

"The corpses need protection?"

"So now you're saying the dead, the most defenseless among us, have no Second Amendment rights?"

Jenkins rolled her eyes.

Luis interrupted. "It's not a problem, counselor. Everyone, calmly place your firearms on that side table. We have nothing to hide, Agent Jenkins. We will cooperate fully."

"Thank you," Jenkins said. "You must be Mr. Carmillion."

"That is correct."

"Finkel," Carmillion said. "Shouldn't you ask to see the search warrant?"

"Yes, I was just getting to that. Agent Jenkins, may I see the search warrant?"

She handed it to him.

"Does it look in order?" Carmillion said.

Fink had never seen a search warrant and was surprised it was a single-page form with a few blanks filled in. "Far as I can tell," he said. At the bottom it mentioned cocaine and cited some federal statutes. "They're looking for drugs."

"On what basis?"

The conflict of interest raised its ugly head. Most likely because Danny and Jessica found an enormous corpse in their embalming room stuffed with blow.

He was relieved when Jenkins answered, "The probable cause affidavit is under seal by court order. Where's the embalming room?"

Luis pointed down the hall.

Jenkins said, "Time to go to work everybody."

An agent with *K-9* on the back of his jacket warned everyone to remain still as he huddled with the dogs and their handlers. He said *Find!* and all three canines lunged at the blond guy in glasses, barking and snarling.

"Chad, go wait in the car," Carmillion growled, muttering something about a cut in employee benefits.

The search ended two hours later with the DEA team departing empty handed, wearing looks of frustration and disappointment. The dogs seemed to hang their heads in shame as they padded sluggishly up the ramp into the van.

When they were gone, Carmillion brought Fink to his office. He wedged himself behind a desk and waved Fink into a leather guest chair that squeaked each time he nervously adjusted his sweat-soaked rear end.

"Ninety percent of what you said in there sounded like complete bullshit," Carmillion said. "But I like your style. Just the kind of lawyer I want. An attack dog."

"Thank you," Fink said.

"How would you like to be on retainer as the Broward County lawyer for Snowbirds in Paradise?"

As the mobster cracked knuckles the size of tractor bolts while waiting for an answer, several significant facts coalesced in Fink's brain for the first time:

(1) In all likelihood, the probable cause for the search warrant came from Danny and Jessica.

(2) The only reason he was sitting in the funeral home was because the man in front of him threatened to chop Jessica and her family into pieces and feed them to the fish if they didn't sell it.

(3) The same man most likely murdered her parents and would probably kill him without giving it a second thought if he knew of the conflict of interest infecting the day's legal matters.

Fink coughed. "Well, that's very tempting, but—"

"We pay well and in cash. I'll throw in a five-thousand dollar signing bonus."

Fifteen thousand! "Can I think about it?"

"For two seconds. Aggressive lawyers are a dime a dozen in South Florida. Easier to hire than fast-food workers. I passed billboards on the way here for *Sheldon the Shark* and *Tammy the Terminator.*"

He could work around the conflict. No reason he couldn't walk and chew gum at the same time. Just compartmentalize. Build a firewall between Snowbirds and Danny and Jessica.

"Okay, I'm in."

He drove home with his good angel repeatedly stabbing his bad angel in the heart and a paper sack stuffed with fifteen thousand dollars resting on the seat next to him.

*　　*　　*

FBI Special Agent Winton Munroe was sitting at a sidewalk table in South Beach cracking open a crab leg, juices spattering his plastic bib, when his phone rang. He wiped his hands on a cloth napkin and snatched it off the table.

"Munroe."

"It's Jenkins."

"How'd it go?"

"*Nada.* That's how it went. We spent two hours there with a team of seven agents and three dogs."

"No large bodies full of blow?"

"No large bodies and no blow. Just a skeletal female elder. We brought along a forensic pathologist, who examined her and said the only incisions were from normal embalming. All their paperwork was in order. Licenses, etc. He said the place seemed legit."

"What about the dogs?"

"The embalming room reeked of bleach. The canines couldn't wait to get out of there."

"And the rest of the place?"

"The dogs alerted at an employee who arrived with Carmillion after we got there. He promptly departed and we weren't sure whether the search warrant covered him, so we let him go. They perked up a few other times but we didn't find anything. Let's face it, it's South Florida. Trace cocaine is on pretty much everything, including ninety-five percent of all cash."

"That damn kid! She led us on a wild goose chase. I never believed her cockamamie story about cutting open a dead body."

"I agree it sounded crazy, but I didn't get the feeling she was lying. And they did bring in the pure sample."

"Probably from surfer boy's personal inventory. I think the kid is nuts. Maybe she's delusional, convinced herself it really happened. She didn't want her parents to sell their funeral home, so she claims they were extorted, even though they got more than a million bucks for it. She's in denial that her parents were closet alkies and druggies who recklessly drove into a canal, so she insists they were murdered."

"You're a psychologist now? What about the guy? He said Jewell told him the whole extortion story on the phone."

"Probably lying to protect the girl by backing up her fantasies."

"I don't know how you can be so certain. They both sounded credible to me. This couldn't have anything to do with her embarrassing you, could it?"

"Of course not. I'm a professional."

"So what do you suggest we do?"

"I'm in charge of the investigation and I'm calling it off."

Chapter 38

IT WAS LATE in the day. Danny was listening to a Miles Davis CD while attempting to make his first-ever shrimp casserole when Rodriguez called his cellphone.

"Teakwell, I'm on my way home from work. Can you meet me at the Tradewinds in fifteen minutes. Without Jessica."

"What's wrong now?"

"I'd rather tell you in person."

Danny stuck the casserole in the fridge and went to Jessica's room. She was stretched out on the bed talking to someone on the landline. From the conversation he picked up, it had to be Gloria who liked to be called Gigi.

"You're right," Jessica said. "I've never seen a well-dressed zombie either."

"Jessica," he said. "Grady needs a hand with something. Stay in the condo. I won't be gone long."

She waved goodbye and kept talking. "Here's something else," she said. "Why does every zombie have a leg disability? Just once, I'd like to see one who could take off running really fast. That would scare the crap out of people!"

Danny heard her friend's cackling all the way down the hall.

Pre-happy hour, the bar was nearly empty. Danny sat alone at a booth, turning down Tulia when she asked if he wanted something to drink. Rodriguez arrived carrying a newspaper and slid and into the booth.

"Have you seen the afternoon paper?" he said.

"I've been busy making a casserole."

He slapped it on the table. Danny grimaced at the headline:

Autopsies of Hollywood Couple Show High Levels of Alcohol, Drugs at Time of Drowning Accident

"This sucks. How did they get hold of the autopsy reports?"

"Someone must have leaked them," Rodriguez said. "Autopsies are public records, but not when they're part of an active criminal investigation."

"Which this obviously is," Danny said.

"Well, yes and no."

"What does that mean?"

"The DEA executed a search warrant at the Snowbirds in Paradise funeral home yesterday. They didn't find anything."

"Nothing?"

"The place was clean as a whistle. The embalming room reeked of bleach. From everything we know, whoever's running the show, probably Carmillion, isn't stupid. They would have expected some kind of investigation after the deaths."

"So they wiped the place clean. That's evidence of guilt, isn't it?"

"Unfortunately, our friend Special Agent Munroe sees things differently and he's in charge of the investigation. Or was. I just heard from him. With the autopsy calling the deaths an accident and the unsuccessful search, he accused you and Jessica—and me—of wasting his time on a snipe hunt. He called off the investigation."

"No frigging way. What about the extortion?"

"It's basically your hearsay word against the fact that Snowbirds paid fair market value for the funeral home. Munroe thinks you and the kid are in cahoots."

"Cahoots for what? Is he out of his mind?"

"He thinks she's delusional and you're lying to protect her."

"What about Jewell's phone message, the one where he

thanked me for taking care of Jessica? I played it for everyone at the meeting. He said they were at a hotel in Destin and felt safe, *for now.* Those were his words. *For now.* Then he called your office and said he lied to you because he was scared and was coming home to set the record straight."

"Munroe has a theory about that too. He thinks Jewell was a druggie who decided to dump his daughter on you while he took his wife for a romp at a beach resort, and then strung us along."

"Munroe's a dick. I wouldn't be surprised if he's doing this to get back at Jessica for exposing him as a petulant fool."

"Me either. Anyway, I wanted you to know so you could share the news with Jessica. I gotta go. My lady friend is cooking us dinner. You can keep the paper."

"She's going to take it hard. You think Munroe was the leaker?"

"It wouldn't surprise me."

"What about you? Are you giving up on us?"

"I'm insulted you'd ask. Did I ever give up when I was trying to hunt you down and shoot you like a rabid dog? I'm still in, but we're back to square one. No evidence."

*   *   *

Sitting at the dining room table, Danny expected Jessica to go ballistic when he showed her the paper, but her empty eyes seemed to stare right through it. When he told her Munroe had called off the investigation, she set down the paper, stood up and walked away.

"Where are you going?"

"To bed. I'm tired."

"It's only six o'clock."

"Is there a rule for when you can be tired?"

"Let's talk."

"Talk talk talk," she said in a robotic monotone as she traipsed down the hall. "Blah blah blah, tra-la-la." Her bedroom door closed.

He ate his shrimp casserole by himself, surprised by how well it turned out, but also by how quiet and lonely the meal felt.

He checked on Jessica several times during the night. The emotional and physical toll must have finally caught up with her. She was out for the count. She didn't stir until eleven the next morning. Danny was on the balcony when she stumbled out to join him, yawning, coffee in hand.

She plummeted unsteadily onto the patio chair. "I've never slept so long in my entire life. Almost seventeen hours. Did you drug me?"

"Don't be ridiculous. I wouldn't drug you."

"My parents did, once. With children's Benadryl, even though I didn't need any. We were on a road trip. I was in a carseat crying the whole time and they were trying to get me to fall asleep and shut up. My parents confessed to the incident when I was ten."

"How did you feel about it?"

"I didn't care. I'm sure I needed the rest. You try sleeping strapped in a carseat. That's probably why I was crying in the first place."

A good sign. She sounded like herself. "Do you feel better?"

She gulped the coffee. "I'll let you know in a few minutes."

"Erin called earlier," he said. "She wondered if you'd like to go surfing, the three of us. She's headed back to California in a couple days. I told her I'd ask you and call her back."

"Aw, she wants to see you before she goes home. That's a good sign."

"No, she wants to see *us*. I thought it might be a nice diversion, like the other day when you and I went. Being on the ocean is always a good release."

"What about the shop?"

"It's Tuesday. We're legitimately closed."

"In that case, okay. I could use a little relaxation. Except I don't want to go surfing. Does she do anything else?"

"I'm sure she does, although I don't know what."

"Let's ask."

They spent the afternoon playing miniature golf. Tropical Storm Josie was tracking toward Florida, but still far enough that the sun shined brightly. Erin played mini-golf as well as she surfed, making one great shot after another, dominating both of them.

"Probably why she picked it," Jessica grumbled when she got stuck at the windmill hole, the twirling blade repelling her ball again and again.

She decided brute force was the solution, winding up and attacking the ball with a vengeance. It ricocheted off the windmill thirty feet in the air, bounced off the dinosaur at the next hole, and landed in a faux creek two holes away.

"How's she doing?" Erin said as Jessica ran to retrieve the ball.

"As well as could be expected, I guess. It's so hard to tell with her."

"It was really kind of you to volunteer to be her guardian. Says a lot about you as a person."

"She didn't really have any good choices."

"I think you're a good choice. Hey, I'm heading back to Cali day after tomorrow. This will probably be our last get-together, so I'll just spill it. When we met, I said I was just looking for a hangout friend, which was true. But even though we don't know each very well, I'm thinking I kind of like you."

"Really?"

"You sound surprised. Sorry if that was overly direct."

"Don't worry about that. I live with the Director of Direct. I am kind of surprised. I haven't exactly been at my best lately when it comes to ..."

"Getting to know someone?"

His face flushed. "Yeah, that. I like you too. It's hard for me to say or even admit to myself. I still struggle with feeling like I'm betraying Sari's memory if I have feelings for someone else. I'm kind of a mess."

"Eh, aren't we all? Have you ever surfed California?"

"Once, a long time ago."

"You should come back. I know all the choice spots. Consider this my invitation to visit. Jessica too. That girl is definitely one of a kind. Do you ever feel like you're talking to an adult with her?"

"You have no idea," he said with a laugh. "Then just as fast she'll do something to remind me she's just a kid."

"I did it! I did it!"

They turned to see Jessica jumping up and down and waving her arms, standing suspiciously close to the windmill as her ball rolled out the back.

They ate corndogs and cotton candy for lunch and headed back to the beach, saying goodbye on the boardwalk. Erin gave Danny a hug and a kiss on the cheek. Her hair smelled like orange blossoms.

"I want a hug too," Jessica said.

"Of course." Erin leaned down and gave her a tight squeeze, but when she tried to release Jessica hung on.

"Let go," Danny said. "You're going to hurt her neck."

"What would you know about hugging?" Jessica said, loosening her grip. "I'll miss you, Erin. Danny will too even if he won't say it. Are you ever coming back?"

"Not sure. Have you ever been to California?"

"Nope."

"Well, I invited both of you to come visit."

"Awesome! When are we going, Danny?"

"I'm not sure. She hasn't even left yet."

As they parted, Erin whispered, "I'm no parent, but I think that girl needs more hugs. You too." She embraced him again and he reciprocated, aware Jessica was watching with a triumphant smile.

Chapter 39

WEDNESDAY MORNING found them back at the surf shop, Danny helping tuck Lil Lansky's board wrapped in blankets into the back of Gaspar's pickup. He moved his paint shop to his garage after leaving Nine Lives. Jessica was inside the store.

"Don't forget we promised him twenty-four carat gold leaf for his necklaces."

"Already bought it," Gaspar said. "This should take me about a week."

"I know it will be amazing."

He got one confirmed order and one rejection on his two latest board proposals. Gaspar was happy to accept another twenty-five percent split to do the artwork on the deal that went through.

They waved goodbye and Danny retreated into the air conditioning. Jessica sat behind the display case, flipping through another surf magazine. She tossed it on the glass.

"It was kind of nice taking a day off yesterday," she said. "But it's time to get back to work."

"Sounds good. I thought I'd get started on the new board contract if you're up for minding the store."

"No, I mean back to work on our case."

"Oh. Well, Detective Rodriguez kind of indicated there is no case without more evidence. I don't know what options we have right now."

"Don't worry, I know. We have to do two things. First, we deliver the hair I found to the detective. He promised to run it through the FBI's DNA database."

"I'm not sure he actually promised, but okay. We can easily do that." Her conviction that the hair belonged to the killer was irrational, but sometimes when you have nothing, you cling to anything. He knew the feeling. "But let's not mention the liver yet. We're already on thin ice with law enforcement."

"It'll keep in the freezer. The second thing is more complicated," she said.

"I was afraid of that. What is it?"

"We sue Snowbirds, like I suggested before."

"For what?"

"Extortion, murder. How many things do you need?"

"I'm not sure about that. We don't have much evidence without your parents. How about we wait until the hair analysis comes back and go from there?"

"That could take months, maybe forever if Whiny Baby Munroe is in charge."

"I just don't know if a lawsuit is a good approach."

"It's worth a try. What do I have to lose?"

"Let's assume your parents were murdered. Filing a lawsuit could make you a target."

"I'm not afraid, as long as they don't drown me."

"I'm afraid for you."

"Danny, you know me. I can't give up."

He did know her. "I'll tell you what. I'll call Fink and ask him to meet to talk about it. But that's all I'm agreeing to. Clear?"

"As a bright blue sky," she said and picked the magazine back up.

*　　*　　*

"Can't make it. I'm starting candle-making classes tonight," Fink said.

"Get out. I don't believe you."

"Alright, it's kind of embarrassing, but I'm in a porn movie. Tonight's the first script read-through."

"Try again."

"Going to the emergency room to hand out business cards?"

"Sounds more like you, but I'm still not buying it. Why are you putting me off? We can meet at your office if that's more convenient."

"No! Don't do that. I'll come to the Tradewinds."

*   *   *

Wednesday being the first day of the weekend in the eyes of many regulars, the joint was already filling up as Danny and Jessica waited at their usual conference booth. Grady said he was going to start charging Fink rent for office space.

Danny sensed something was off as soon as Fink showed up. He ordered a scotch on the rocks from Shannon without commenting on how great she looked in a pair of jeans.

"How's it going?" Danny said.

"It's going," Fink said, avoiding eye contact. "So what's up?"

"I'll let Jessica explain."

"Hi, Fink. Remember when I mentioned suing Snowbirds in Paradise and you got all excited about deep pockets? Well, I'm ready."

Fink spit out his drink mid-sip. "Ready for what?"

"The lawsuit. It's time. I'll agree to a one-third fee, like you said."

"I don't think a lawsuit is a good idea."

"Why not? You liked it before."

"Um, it could be dangerous for someone. You, I mean."

"My parents are dead, my grandfather too, so I'd say things are already pretty dangerous."

"There's not enough evidence," he said. "Especially since the funeral home search turned up zilch."

"How did you know about that?" Danny said.

"You told me. Didn't you?"

"Not yet. I was getting ready to."

He tugged on his collar. "You sure? Seems like you did."

"I didn't."

"Strange. Not sure where I heard it. Maybe it was in the news."

"It wasn't. Is there something you're not telling us? First you didn't want to meet and now you know about a search we only found out about from Rodriguez."

He snapped his fingers. "Ah! I bet it was courthouse scuttlebutt. Lawyers love to gossip. Whatever, I just can't take on a lawsuit like that right now. Business is, uh, picking up."

"*Please*," Jessica said. "Just think. You could probably make a fortune."

"It's not the money. It's just that ..."

"Help me, Fink," she said, hands clasped prayer-like. "I need you. You're my only hope."

"I—I ... okay, okay. I'll do it."

With butterfly claps, "Yay for Fink! Don't worry about evidence. I have an idea about that. We sue for extortion, but in case we can't prove it, we attach my grandfather's will and take back Slagger-Jewell on the ground my father didn't have the power to sell my interest. Breach of fiduciary duty, like you said."

"Smart," Danny said. "What do you think, Fink?"

Fink drained his drink and wrestled his way out of the booth. He slapped down a twenty. "Yeah, smart. I gotta go."

"You just got here."

"And now I'm just leaving." He walked out without saying goodbye.

"What's eating him?" Jessica said.

"No idea."

Chapter 40

FINK PLODDED into his office, which looked even dingier than usual in the glare of the harsh fluorescent ceiling lights, and collapsed in the threadbare desk chair. His ensuing wail was long and mournful.

It wasn't just his vertebrae, which had been killing him since Carmillion whacked him with the door at the funeral home. It was Danny and Jessica. *Reality,* sitting right across the table.

How did he let it happen? In one frenzied moment he had sold out his best friend and a child with murdered parents. Probably his life too, which he considered putting in the plus column because he wasn't sure he could continue living with himself.

He yanked open the desk drawer and sorted through a clatter of spiraling plastic pill vials until he found the Xanax. He shook out an orange tablet and chewed it for faster effect.

Waiting for the benzo-glow to fill his veins, he searched his mind for someone to blame, ticking through the usual suspects. His parents dressed him in culottes when he was in the fifth grade. That didn't help.

Neither did the time in peewee basketball when he sank the game-winning shot for the other team, his only basket of the year, by shooting at the wrong goal.

Jenny Stetweiler crushed his self-esteem early on when she beat the crap out of him in the second grade with half the school watching. He told everyone he didn't hit back because she was a girl. It was a lie. You would never guess it by her pigtails and knobby knees, but the girl was a beast. He didn't hear the end of it until his family moved to Florida when he started high school.

If only the indignities stopped there, but they *never* stopped. Just a week ago the probate judge humiliated him in open court. To think he actually complimented her. Audrey Hepburn, his ass.

At Snowbirds, he told himself it was all about the money. Now he realized there was more to it. Sitting in the mob boss's office being praised as an *attack dog* and offered the job as a cartel lawyer, he felt like a genuine big deal. A *consigliere*! With a signing bonus!

Now the piper or chicken or whatever the hell it was had come home to roost, or rest, or maybe get paid. He wasn't sure.

He pictured the pleading look on Jessica's annoying little round know-it-all face. She *needed* him. She actually said that. When was the last time anyone needed him? Especially a kid.

Resting his head back, he asked out loud: "Are you a hero or a coward?"

He didn't like the answer so quickly chewed another Xanax. He waited impatiently, passing time counting the shotgun blasts in the acoustic ceiling tiles. His officemate had bragged about the previous occupant's pioneering technique for negotiating settlements.

Fink asked the question again and, with effort, eked out the answer he needed: *HERO!*

He would do it! ... He *could* do it! ... He might possibly do it. ... Not a chance.

You can't hurry love or benzos. For the third attempt he set the alarm on his Casio watch and made himself wait ten full minutes with his eyes closed. Tick by tock, he felt better. By the time the alarm chimed and his eyes popped open, his brain was fuzzy, but destiny clear.

Fuck you, chicken! Or piper! There's a NEW HERO in town.

He reached in the mini-fridge under the desk and grabbed a

Red Bull, using it to down an Adderall. The job in front of him required focus.

He turned on his computer and began drafting a lawsuit on behalf of his client against his other client:

DANIEL TEAKWELL, as guardian for
JESSICA JEWELL, plaintiff

–Versus–

SNOWBIRDS IN PARADISE
FUNERAL SERVICES, LLC, defendant

Maybe he was worrying for nothing. He'd file the suit in Broward. With any luck, when the process server delivered the complaint, Carmillion would send it along to his new lawyer and say *Defend it*, not noticing Fink's signature on the last page.

Of course, then he'd have to file a response on behalf of Snowbirds. That could get tricky. The real magic act would be if he had to appear in court.

Chapter 41

"CHAU," LUIS SAID and disconnected the call. He set down the phone, lifted his backside out of his custom-built double-wide chair and walked to the window.

Down in the marina, a sixty-one foot Bertram yacht was in the process of docking. One of fate's stick-in-your-eye jokes. It was the exact same yacht he put a down payment on when *El Grande* started to take off, even had the same royal blue stripes along the bow and gunwale. He had wondered whether it would fit at the marina docks. Turns out it would have.

He shifted his gaze to his Boston Whaler. With the auxiliary gas tank he kept on board, it could probably take him to the Caribbean, some place to hide out.

The person on the other end of the call was the capo. Luis called him yesterday to explain about the DEA search, but he didn't pick up. When he finally called back a half-hour ago, he knew all about it.

"Qué carajo?" he said.

What the fuck? Luis decided to tell him. The moment Yago made his proposal, he knew in his heart he could never cave into blackmail, especially by that hijueputa. He was beyond feeling moral hesitancy about killing Yago, but he was a company man, a rule follower. You can't just up and kill your teniente without going through the chain of command.

He explained to the capo that Yago had become a dangerous

rogue employee who disobeyed direct orders and exposed the cartel to risk. His unnecessary murders of the Jewell couple probably led to the search warrant. Only Luis's quick thinking to halt operations and sterilize the funeral home saved them from complete disaster.

"Now he's hinting about killing their kid. She's only twelve."

He expected a response to that. The cartel's unwritten policy was to avoid harming children. The capo stayed silent.

Luis changed gears, boasting about the success of *El Grande*. His idea had already proved to be a winner, he said, but it was a delicate mechanism with many moving parts. It needed to be steered with a sensitive touch, not brute force.

More silence. He hesitated before proceeding to the moment of truth, the point of no return.

"Capo, for the health of the organization and continued success of the Snowbirds operation, I believe it is essential Yago be dispatched, the sooner the better."

Nothing.

"I'll be happy to do the job myself if it's too much trouble," he added with more than a hint of desperation.

The capo said after a long pause, "I hear a different version from Yago. I'll think about it."

The capo was a man of few words, hard to read, especially on the phone. Luis figured the odds were 60-40 against him as to whether he really was going to think about it or whether Yago had already convinced him Luis was the one in need of dispatching.

When Yago didn't show up for their morning meeting, instead leaving a phone message—*Shoulda took me up on my offer*—he lowered the odds to 90-10.

A wave of great sadness fell upon him, not so much about the prospect of losing his life, although that was no small point. It was more about the loss of his bebito. *El Grande*.

He had nurtured it from scribbles on a piece of paper in his one-room apartment in a Bogotá slum to this, his empire on the thirty-seventh floor in Miami. Only in America. His papi would be proud.

He turned away from the bay and removed his eyepatch. Holding it in both hands like a piece of fine jewelry, he turned it over, examining both sides and stretching the elastic band.

He walked to his desk and dropped it in the trashcan. *The Legend of Luis* was dead.

Chapter 42

JESSICA CEREMONIOUSLY handed over a sandwich bag containing her infamous strand of hair to Detective Rodriguez.

"Take good care of it," she said.

"If this turns out to belong to your Aunt Rosie, they'll demote me to traffic control," he said, sealing it in a larger official evidence bag.

"How long will it take to get the results?"

"Don't hold your breath. A while. And remember, the only DNA in the CODIS system is from convicted felons." He summoned Audrey to take the bag to the evidence room.

"Can I go with her?" Jessica said.

"Be my guest."

When they were gone Danny told Rodriguez about Jessica's determination to sue Snowbirds in Paradise. "She sees it as her only chance to get justice. I understand it. The idea of those sleazebags getting away with everything isn't acceptable."

"I get it too, but it would be a risky move. The last thing she needs to be doing is calling attention to herself."

"I told her the same thing. What do you think of this angle? Her parents tried to cooperate with the cartel and still ended up dead. We've talked about how she might already be at risk. Maybe filing the suit would have the reverse effect of giving her some protection."

"I see where you're coming from. Knocking off a kid suing you for extortion could bring the house down, especially after what happened to her parents. Still a crapshoot though."

"I know. I'm trying to stall her. Maybe she'll change her mind."

"If you go through with it, please tell me you're not going to use that dolt Finkel as a lawyer."

Danny hid his wince with a shrug.

On their way out Danny asked Jessica why she wanted to accompany Audrey to the evidence room.

"It was obvious the detective has no faith in my hair. I wanted to be sure she didn't throw it in the trash."

Danny started the Hyundai. "Only five days until school starts," he said. It had been weighing on him. "About time we shop for some new clothes and school supplies."

"We'll be late opening the shop."

"You saw yesterday there's no beach business in August."

"That's no excuse. Which reminds me, you're going to need to hire a new helper when I start school, at least until three o'clock. That's when it gets out. I can still work an afternoon shift."

"You're not going to be working after school. You're coming home and doing your homework."

"Danny, do you remember the seventh grade?"

"Parts."

"Did you come home and do homework after school?"

Danny rarely did homework in any grade, but wasn't about to tell her that. "That's one of the parts I don't remember."

"I thought so." She pointed to a Target as they left the police station. "I can get clothes and supplies there."

He asked if she wanted to shop someplace more upscale. She reminded him she's frugal and intends to pay back her expenses when her inheritance comes through, which, she astutely observed, would most likely be delayed by any lawsuit seeking to unwind the Slagger-Jewell transaction.

"Sounds like a good reason to forget the lawsuit for now," Danny said.

"Not to me. Target is fine. I'm not picky about brand names. Pants are pants."

He followed her around the store, biting his tongue as she searched rack after rack to add to her growing armload of black clothes until he couldn't take it any longer.

"This is Florida. How about some brighter clothes? Add a little pizzazz."

"I can't. I made a pact with my friend."

"Gloria who likes to be called Gigi?"

"The one and only. We vowed to dress in black for the entire seventh grade."

And she wondered why the other kids think she's weird.

"How about at least trying on some brighter stuff, just to see?"

"If you insist."

"Huh," she said a few minutes later, standing in front of the mirror in sky-blue chinos under a short-sleeve tangerine blouse with a white collar and buttons. "Not bad. They go with my surfer necklace. Maybe I'm becoming a beachy girl. Okay, for you, I'll go with bright, but I'll probably lose my only friend."

She turned quiet on the drive back to the shop.

"You okay?" Danny said.

"I never went clothes-shopping with anyone except my mom. She would have liked I got some colorful stuff."

"I'm sorry she couldn't be there. Maybe she was with you in spirit, nudging you in that direction."

"That doesn't sound like an agnostic."

She was disappointed when they arrived at the shop to discover a nearly vacant boardwalk. Adding to the seasonal slump, Tropical Storm Josie was churning closer, bringing scattered showers and overcast skies.

He left her fiddling listlessly with her clothes racks and went back to the workshop to search the internet for artwork inspiration for his new client, a self-proclaimed fan of pop art and bright colors.

Thirty minutes later Jessica entered to complain there were no customers.

"I told you it's not a good season for beach shops."

"Tell me about it," she sputtered and left.

He found some links with Andy Warhol and Romero Britto images and sent them to Gaspar. *Try to come up with something in the Warhol/Britto vein, but don't copy.*

Jessica made a clomping return. "It's been an hour and no one. Not one person."

He knew she took it personally. In too many ways to count, Danny was hopelessly unequipped to be a parent. But like Jessica told Judge Strazinski, he understood her. That counted for something.

This was no way to spend her last days of summer. He shut down the computer. "I'm done here. How about we close early? We'll put a sign on the door."

She hesitated. "Okay, but only because of the sign."

The computer was still powering down when the front door jangled.

"I got it," she said. "Sit."

Danny expected to hear a spirited pitch about why the un-suspecting visitor needed a new surfboard more than air itself. Instead, an ear-piercing scream shattered the calm.

"Danny! Get the gun!"

WTF?! He didn't have a gun.

Then a gruff voice: "Anyone comes through that door with a gun is dead."

"Danny! Never mind the gun! Forget the gun!"

In three sprinting steps he stood face to face with Luis Carmillion. No mistake about it. If his size and black suit didn't clinch it, the scar did. He looked exactly like Jessica described. Only the eyepatch was missing. One hand held back his black suit jacket, showing off a large semiautomatic handgun in a holster.

Danny instinctively dashed in front of Jessica.

"Danny, move over. I can't see."

Luis let go of his coat and raised his palms. "Relax. I'm not here to hurt anyone."

"Why are you here?" Danny said.

"Yeah, why?" Jessica chimed. "Are you going to start extorting surf shops? Stuff the boards with cocaine?"

"Smart kid. I knew it from the way you broke into the funeral home. We have you both on video, although it took a while to find you."

"I'll repeat," Danny said. "Why are you here?"

"Actually, I'm not. I'm on a geolocated phone call in Miami, with a witness. This conversation isn't happening. You say otherwise?" He shrugged. "My sources tell me the feds already branded you as liars. Dropped the investigation."

Danny said, "So you came here to smirk?"

"No, I came with a warning."

"Don't tell me. Now you're going to cut me into a *million* pieces," Jessica said.

"Not a threat. A warning. I'm here to help."

Jessica chirped her helium laugh. "*Help?* Not unless you plan on bringing my parents back to life, the ones you murdered. And give us back our funeral home, the one you stole. And what about my grandfather? Did you kill him too?"

"I swear on my mother's grave I did not kill anyone or intend for anyone to get hurt. It was never meant to turn out this way."

"Liar! Danny, call nine-one-one."

The man showed the gun again.

"Let's hear what he has to say."

"My name is Luis Carmillion."

"We know who you are, mister," Jessica said. "So do the cops. Soon everyone will because we're getting ready to—"

She was about to tip off the lawsuit. Danny shook his head.

"You're obviously Jessica Jewell," he said. "And you're Danny somebody."

"Teakwell."

"This your shop? Not bad. Always wanted to try surfing, but didn't have the right figure for it. My watersport is deepsea fishing. Got my own boat. You like to fish?"

"Just say what you came to say and leave," Danny said.

"There's a cancer in our organization."

"You're a cancer," Jessica said.

Danny raised a hush finger.

"An extremely violent employee—a sicario, assassin—has gone rogue. I can't control him and don't have permission from the company to do so. I'm here to warn you the girl may be in grave danger."

"Why her?" Danny said.

"Bluntly? She's the only living connection to the Slagger-Jewell mess. Except for you, I suppose. If she goes, I'm sure you'll be joining her."

"Why are you telling us this?" Danny said.

"I'll put it this way. You're not the only ones at risk. Maybe it's not too late to redeem my soul."

"Who is this employee? How do we spot him?"

"The girl has seen him."

"The tall, goony guy you brought to our house?"

Luis nodded.

"Yago," Danny said, remembering Jewell's description of the man who threatened to cut off his toes.

He nodded again.

"What are we supposed to do with a warning?" Danny said. "How is that supposed to help?"

"Maybe not much. You got a gun?"

"No."

He slid his handgun from the holster and held it out grip first. "Take it."

"Take it, Danny!"

"I wouldn't know what to do with it."

"I'll take it," Jessica said.

"No, you won't," Danny said. "I have another suggestion. If I'm hearing you right, it sounds like you might need protection too. Have you considered flipping?"

"I'd be flipping against myself and dead before sunrise." He reholstered the gun. "If you see Yago, run. He doesn't waste time making threats. He's a pure killer, through and through."

He wiped his brow with a handkerchief. "I'm sorry," he said and lumbered back out onto the boardwalk.

Chapter 43

"YOU'RE KIDDING," Rodriguez squawked over the phone.

"Nope. Even offered me his gun."

"You sure it was him?"

"He introduced himself. The assassin he was talking about is named Yago. He's the tall guy who threatened to torture Jessica's father in Boca. He came to their house that first day with Carmillion."

"It doesn't make sense."

"Maybe it does. He was vague, but said we're not the only ones in danger, made it sound like he might be out of favor with the cartel."

"You're telling me a honcho in a ruthless drug cartel came to warn you, apologize, and offer you his gun."

"You don't believe me?"

"Doesn't matter if I do. You got to look at it from a cop's point of view. That story is way out there, sort of like cutting open a dead body and finding it stuffed with cocaine."

"In other words, there's not a snowball's chance Agent Munroe would believe it."

"I'd put the odds lower than that."

"Help me then. How do I protect Jessica?"

"The only thing I can think of is to leave town and go into

hiding."

"She's supposed to start school next week. Can't the police protect her?"

"I wish, but no. It would take a twenty-four/seven bodyguard, and even that would be no guarantee. Cops don't have the resources to protect individuals. People call us with threat complaints every day."

"I'm sure Judge Strazinski would be impressed if the new guardian skipped town with his ward a few days before school started. She'd terminate me in a heartbeat, probably put out an arrest warrant. And how long would we stay away? This has to end. What would it take to make that happen?"

"Only one answer. You need concrete evidence backing up your story. Something that would bring the feds back in. Meanwhile, I sure wouldn't be filing any lawsuit."

"I already decided that. Jessica might pitch a fit, but I'm the guardian. She can't do it without me."

"That's the spirit, Teakwell. You're the boss. She's the kid. Take charge. Tough love, buddy. Trust me. I have three kids. They spend half their lives in timeout."

Danny gave a weak laugh. "Tough love? Timeout? I thought you knew her better than that."

Chapter 44

BLEARY-EYED, FINK struggled to bring the tiny print on the pill vial labels in focus. *Not that one, not that one. There.* He choked down the last Adderall.

Mid-afternoon. He hadn't slept, spending the night powering through the lawsuit complaint, fueled by the amphetamines while sucking on the occasional benzo to take the edge off. The only healthy thing he did all night was order a Carnivore's Rapture pizza.

Eighteen straight hours of research and writing, the longest and hardest he'd ever worked. But it was finished. A forty-two page masterpiece!

Fraud, assault, battery, conversion of property, intentional infliction of emotional distress ...

He threw in every tort he remembered from law school, topping them off with a civil RICO claim he stumbled on accidentally. He blew off legal research in law school. Who knew it could be so helpful? The Florida racketeering statute allowed for triple damages and attorney's fees.

At the end he demanded $100 million in damages, then changed it to a billion. Why the chicken-and-piper not?

The more he wrote, the angrier he got, which became apparent when he scrolled through the document. It started out okay: *On or about July 18, two uninvited strangers visited the plaintiff's residence ...* But by the midpoint even he could recognize his prose crossed the line of professional pleading standards: *Then the motherfuckers had the nerve to murder my client's fucking parents!*

He went back and started editing. The drugs, no sleep, impending doom. They all made it hard to concentrate.

The moment Carmillion laid eyes on the complaint, Fink would be a walking dead man. His fantasy hope that the mobster might forward the complaint to his new Broward lawyer without noticing the signature block on the last page collapsed when he filled out the summons form.

It goes on top, first thing anyone sees, ordering the defendant to serve written defenses on *[Insert Name], Plaintiff's Attorney, whose address is [Insert Address].*

He stared at the sticky note on his computer monitor, the only thing that kept him going. *HERO!* That was how he would be remembered. A lionheart who threw everything away in a final glorious quest for justice.

His parents would be proud. For once. His joke at graduation about them hiding turned out to be true. Under interrogation they admitted it was them laughing at him from the limbs of the ficus tree.

Jenny Stetweiler would hear the news and spend the rest of her life wallowing in regret for beating him up. The law school classmates who mocked him for three years would stand in line to compete for the honor of being pallbearers at his funeral.

Best of all, Shannon would remember him with misty eyes and a pounding heart, thinking of what might have been.

If by some miracle he avoided assassination, his legal career, already hanging by a thread, would end promptly when the state bar discovered he attempted to represent the plaintiff and defendant in the same lawsuit.

The edits took an hour. He needed to hurry. The courthouse closed at five.

Hitting the print button, he waited as the pages fed into his trembling hands, which shook harder as he used a stapler to attach Exhibit A. The old man's will, the copy Danny gave him when Jessica first raised the idea of a lawsuit.

He scooped up his cheap cellphone to call Danny to tell him the big news, but the piece of junk didn't work. He slammed it on the desk and screamed as blood spurted from his thumb. Either things were shapeshifting or it had been the stapler all along.

He found the real phone in the pizza box. The bite marks on the screen brought back a hazy memory from the night before.

Danny didn't answer his call. He left a message to meet him at the Tradewinds at six.

In the parking lot, he revved the Trans Am, feeling at one with the high-pitched whistle of the turbocharger. *Charged. Dominant. Potent.*

Reaching I-95, he gunned the muscle car north, racing to get to the Fort Lauderdale courthouse before the drugs wore off and he chickened out.

* * *

"Here he comes," Jessica said, pointing out the side window as Fink's Firebird screeched to a halt next to the fire hydrant that would save the Tradewinds and Danny's condo building in the event of an inferno.

"Why does he drive that car? I bet it makes him feel more manly. I think he has insecurity issues."

Danny wished that just one time he could honestly reply to one of her tween life observations with, *You're full of crap.* "I think you're right," he said.

"What does he want to meet about?" she said.

"Not sure. His message was garbled. Good he's here though. We need to tell him we're putting the brakes on any lawsuit."

"He probably already forgot about it."

Danny expected a fight when he announced they were shelving the lawsuit idea for now. She surprised him by readily agreeing.

"Seeing that man again freaked me out. It feels different when they know how to find you. Do you think they know where we live?"

"I hope not."

"It was weird," she said. "He seemed like he was being honest, like he really was trying to help, but I don't trust him."

"Me either."

They both stared out the window. Fink still hadn't exited the Firebird.

"What's taking him so long?" Jessica said. "I'm hungry. I'm going to go ask Shannon if they can make me a chicken sandwich without all the gook on it. It's unhealthy. Don't worry, I'll put it on my tab."

"You have a tab?"

"Mm-hm. I got Grady to open one for me. You want anything?"

"I'll have the same."

"Do you want me to put it on my tab?"

"Let's not worry about those kinds of things. Okay?"

"Fine by me," she shrugged. "It's your money."

When Fink finally climbed out of the car, he appeared to be locked in a heated argument with someone, shaking his fist and mashing his jawbone. But there was no one around.

He teetered through the front door wearing the same clothes as yesterday and wobbled to the booth, hitching his pants up by the belt loops before falling onto the bench. He landed with a howl, muttering something about an aching back and the gates of hell.

"Fink, are you okay?" Danny said.

"So you finally found a new place to hang out. It's about freaking time."

"What?"

Shannon sallied up. "What can I get you, Fink?"

"Shannon! You came here too? Whoa. This is blowing my mind."

"He'll just have water," Danny said. "Fink, you're at the Tradewinds. Same place as always."

Eyes darting left and right, "You think I'm falling for that?"

Jessica returned with a magnifying gaze. Shannon must have said something. "Hello, Fink."

"Whoa! You're all here? It's like a Twilight Zone episode. I know you. You're ..."

"Jessica," she said.

"No, that's not it."

"I'm taking him upstairs," Danny said.

"I'll be up as soon as I get our sandwiches."

In his living room, he parked Fink on the couch and coaxed him to drink some water. He emptied the glass, closed his eyes, and seemed to relax.

"Now tell me what's going on? Are you on drugs? Fink, Fink."

Fink's head fell back and he released a snore that sounded like a hog drowning in mud. Fast asleep. Danny tilted him over and stuffed a couch pillow under his head.

Jessica returned with the sandwiches and spotted Fink. "Is he dead?"

"Of course not," Danny said, but checked his pulse to make sure.

"What's wrong with him?"

"I'm not sure. He fell asleep as soon as he sat down."

"Can we eat our sandwiches before they get cold?"

Two hours passed before Fink began to stir. Danny kneeled next to the couch and peeled open one eyelid. "Fink, you in there?"

The other eye came unglued. "Danny? Is that you? Where are we?"

"In my condo. Get up." He wrenched Fink upright. "What happened to you?"

"Where's Jessica?"

"Right here," she said.

He looked at her, started to speak and burst into tears. "I'm sorry," he wailed.

"For what?" Danny said.

He blubbered through the story of getting the phone call offering him ten thousand dollars if he arrived in ten minutes at an address where a search warrant was being executed.

"I didn't know until I got there. I swear."

"Didn't know what?" Danny said.

"It was Snowbirds in Paradise."

"What? Why'd they call you?"

"They saw my billboard down the street."

"What did you do?"

He slobbered, "*Garble, garble, garble* ..."

"Slow down and quit crying," Jessica said. "We can't understand you."

Danny refilled his water glass. "Here."

Fink gulped more water, wiped his dripping chin, and took a deep breath. "I went inside and started ... I started ..."

"What? You started what?"

"I started representing them," he said and the blubbering resumed.

"Who?"

He hung his head. "Carmillion, the cartel."

"You didn't! Traitor!" Jessica said.

"I am. I'm a traitor. You should just shoot me right now."

"Danny doesn't have a gun," she said disapprovingly. "But you could jump off the balcony."

"No one's getting shot or jumping off the balcony," Danny said. "Tell us exactly what happened."

Danny spent half the time listening and the other half asking Jessica to calm down and be quiet.

"It was temporary insanity," Fink offered as he finished the story of his afternoon at the funeral home with Carmillion and the DEA. "But I have good news too. That's what I wanted to talk to you about."

"Did you tell them about us, about Nine Lives?" Danny said.

"Of course not."

"Someone did. We had a strange visit at the shop today from Mr. Carmillion himself. That's why we decided to can the idea of a lawsuit. So you can take that off your plate. What's your good news?"

"Well, I— Run that by me again?" Fink said.

"Which part?"

"About the lawsuit."

"We decided to ditch it. Carmillion said Jessica could be in danger and we didn't want to increase the risk by putting a target on her."

"But ... but ... but ..." He exploded into a fresh round of tears.

"Here we go again," Jessica said.

"What's wrong now?" Danny said.

"I was up all night drafting the complaint. That's why I was so messed up when I got here."

"Sorry you went through all that trouble. We had no idea you were making it a priority. Maybe someday things will calm down and we can file it. It's going to be a while though."

He flopped on his back. "It's too late. I just filed it. That was my good news."

* * *

Commotion followed, all from Jessica. Danny suggested she go to her room until she calmed down.

"You're trying to send me to timeout? *You* go to timeout!"

"Look, Fink was trying to help us, help you. I'm not happy about it either. He should have checked with us first, obviously, but he did exactly what you asked him to do."

That got through. Her shoulders sagged. She sighed and said, "I guess you're right. I'm sorry, Fink. I just don't want to get murdered."

"Either do I," he said.

"Great," Danny said. "We're all in agreement we don't want to get murdered. See how much easier everything is when we work together?"

He felt like a real parent mediating a squabble between siblings. "Fink. I'm not familiar with the rules of ethics for lawyers, but are you allowed you sue your own client?"

"No. I wasn't thinking clearly. I think it was my medication."

"Isn't the cartel going to be upset when they learn their lawyer is suing them?"

"Oh, yeah. I'm toast."

Chapter 45

LUIS STARED at the summons. *Benjamin Finkel.* Why did the name sound familiar? ... Sonofabitch! His new lawyer! He double-checked the business card in his wallet to be sure. WTF?

Chad was the one who answered the door buzzer when the deputy sheriff showed up to serve the summons and complaint. He brought the documents straight to Luis.

"Jefe, your eyepatch. It's gone. What happened?"

"Don't need it anymore. Got a replacement eye."

Chad studied his face. "Magnífico! I can't even tell the difference."

Luis swore him to secrecy about the lawsuit, reiterating his promise to rip his heart out if he breathed a word of it, especially to Yago.

He studied the complaint in disbelief. It laid out the extortion of Slagger-Jewell, accused him of threatening to chop the family into fish chum, and called him a *blood-sucking turd.* Among a long list of other claims, it asserted the funeral home transaction was invalid because of the old man's will. Finkel even attached a copy.

They had it the whole time, the girl and the surf shop guy. *Daniel Teakwell.* The complaint was in his name as guardian for the kid. He underestimated all of them.

Ingrates. After he gave Finkel fifteen grand for a pile of bullshit and offered his own gun to Teakwell.

If he had any doubt about his future, this put the final nail in his plus-size coffin. The capo wasn't going to be happy. He was dead meat.

Most likely, so were they. All three of them. Filing the lawsuit might have been a good move if they were dealing with rational actors, an immunity shield. But Yago wasn't going to stop killing and the capo had never been to America. He didn't understand the limitations on eliminating witnesses here.

A shame. The image of Teakwell instinctively moving in front of the kid had stayed with him. Ready to take a bullet for her. They didn't deserve to die. Either did the girl's parents or grandfather. The only person who deserved to die was Yago, and maybe Finkel.

It baffled him how such a blowhard was smart enough to weasel his way inside Snowbirds. Was it a coincidence or did Francisco betray him? He's the one who suggested Finkel when the DEA showed up.

Had to be a coincidence. Chad and the Honduran were the only two people in the entire South Florida organization he trusted completely.

So what now? Run? Fight?

He picked up the desk phone and pushed a button.

"Chad, is my boat ready to go?"

"Siempre, Jefe!"

"You could just say yes."

"Where are you going? Do you need a crew?"

"Fishing and no." Might be his last chance for a vacation day.

"But the storm is coming."

"It's already here."

Chapter 46

Daughter of Dead Hollywood Couple
Sues for Fraud, Extortion in Family Funeral Home Sale

DANNY SAT at the bar shaking his head at the newspaper Grady handed him on arrival. He'd already seen it. On TV too. Reporters had been calling and leaving messages on his landline all day.

"Perfect, right?" Danny said. "Just what we needed. Our names in the paper."

"Maybe it's a good thing," Grady said. "They'd have to be crazy to try to hurt Jessica now. All fingers would point to them."

"You'd think so. The problem is they are crazy, at least one of them, according to the Carmillion dude. And so far they've been smart enough to get away with murdering her parents, maybe even her grandfather."

"Speaking of Carmillion, I doubt he's going to be stopping by for any more friendly chats. The article says the lawsuit complaint called him a *blood-sucking turd*. Is that legalese?"

"Only in Fink's world."

Jessica ambled up and climbed on a barstool. "Tulia says I should dye my hair purple."

"As a disguise?"

"No, as a back-to-school fashion statement. Can I do it?"

Changing her appearance might not be a bad idea. "Knock yourself out."

"Cool. Gloria who likes to be called Gigi threatened to choke me in my sleep at our next bunking party for breaking our agreement to wear black."

"She likes black that much, huh?"

"Yep. This should make her a little happier. Purple's her second favorite color."

If it wasn't the surf shop, it was something else. Erin or purple hair. Any diversion from her reality. *Your parents are dead!* Part of him wanted to scream it.

Maybe he did want her to cry, just like she said. Anything to let things out. He knew she was hurting. He imagined her veins bulging like a garden hose in the Florida sun.

She'd probably reply, *Sari's dead too!* He suddenly felt like a fool for all the times he'd said he didn't want to talk about her, not just to Jessica but everyone.

She was supposed to start school in two days, and looking forward to it. In a normal world, it would be a much healthier distraction than the surf shop. He hadn't found the heart, or maybe courage, to tell her it wasn't going to happen. Not now. Too dangerous.

His head had been on a swivel since Carmillion showed up, seeing potential hitmen everywhere. He considered getting a gun, but knew he couldn't master armed combat overnight. He bought a Taser instead, black with a flashlight built in. It bulged in the front pocket of his board shorts.

"Is that the article?" she said.

"Yeah." He handed it to her.

"Danny-boy," Grady said. "Come back here and give me a hand. Something's wrong with the beer taps."

"What?"

"I don't know. A thingamajig."

Grady could disassemble and reassemble the beer taps in his

sleep, but Danny got up and joined him inside the rectangular bar through the swinging gate.

"What's the problem?"

Grady whispered, "Didn't want to alarm Jessica, but there's a man outside on the boardwalk. He's been there a few minutes, trying to look nonchalant while scoping out the bar."

Danny caught a glimpse of a slight man who quickly turned away.

"The blond guy with the glasses?"

"That's the one. What do you think?"

"Definitely doesn't look like part of a South American drug cartel."

"Probably a reporter. You want me to tell him to move along?"

"No law against loitering on the boardwalk."

"Who needs laws? I'll take John the Diver with me."

At six-four, J.D. was two inches taller than Danny with more meat on him and intimidating sleeves of tatts featuring sharp teeth. Sharks, barracudas, moray eels, even a triggerfish.

"I'll go out front and see if he approaches me," Danny said. "He looks harmless. If he's a reporter, I'll say no comment and ask him to leave."

"Where are you going?" Jessica said as he exited the swinging gate and headed to the front door.

"Outside for a minute. You stay here."

She hopped off the bar stool. "I'll go with you."

"No, stay here."

"I want to go with."

"No."

"But I'm scared to be away from you."

He wasn't sure he believed her, but Shannon overheard, her face melting in motherly *aww*-ness. That and the fact the bar might close before any argument about the issue got resolved made him say, "Alright. Just hang back behind me."

A blast of sticky sand hit him in the face as they stepped out onto the boardwalk. Tropical Storm Josie was closing in, bringing wind and thick clouds that blotted out the moon and stars. The night was so dark he couldn't discern the ocean from the beach.

The blond man offered a jittery smile and made an indecisive move in their direction. He didn't look like a threat, but Danny kept his hand in his pocket on the Taser.

"Daniel Teakwell?" he said.

"Who wants to know?" Jessica said.

"I got this," Danny said. "Who are you?"

"My name's Chad."

"What do you want?"

He whispered something Danny couldn't make out through the wind.

"Speak up."

"I work for Snowbirds in Paradise," he said, eyes dancing in every direction. A film of sweat covered his face like a thin layer of machine oil. "As an accountant. I have information for you."

"What kind information? Did they send you to deliver more threats?"

"The opposite. I know what's going on. It's been eating me up inside. Then I learned about your lawsuit and decided I needed to do something. I had no idea what I was getting into when they hired me."

"What do you know?"

A couple in matching green windbreakers approached, the man grumbling, "Great planning for a Florida vacation, Estelle. Just in time for a hurricane."

"Don't blame it on me, Hal," she said. "You're the tightwad who insisted we wait for the cheap hotel rates."

"I know everything," Chad said when they were out of earshot. "And I have hard evidence to back it up. I can help her, help you."

You need concrete evidence backing up your story. Rodriguez's answer when Danny asked what it would take to make the nightmare end.

"What do you want from us?"

"Just your promise to keep my name out of everything."

"I need to know more before I can make any promises."

"Fine. But not here. Can we move down to the shore, out of the light and hearing range? If I get caught talking to you, I'm dead in two seconds."

He looked like an accountant, not a killer. "Jessica, go wait inside for me," Danny said.

"I'm coming. We're a team."

Another argument he wasn't going to win without a marathon. "You say your name is Chad? You have identification?"

"My driver's license."

"Let me see it."

"Sure, but again, can we please get off this broadwalk first?"

"We call it the boardwalk," Jessica said.

Danny glanced behind to see Grady pressed against the window, hands in the pockets of his apron. He shot him a thumbs-up and followed Chad onto the beach and into the darkness.

The whipped-up surf grew louder when they reached the lifeguard stand, but Danny still couldn't see the ocean. "This is far enough," he said, sliding the Taser from his pocket. "Driver's license. Take it out nice and easy. No sudden moves."

Chad withdrew a wallet, slid out a card and held it up. Danny could barely see his arm, much less the license. He remembered the Taser had a flashlight. He pointed it and turned it on, hoping he didn't accidentally launch electrode darts into the accountant's face.

"*Chad B. Dankworth,*" he read. "*1826 Aberdeen Way, Greenwich, Connecticut.*"

"That's where I'm from. I only moved here a few months ago."

Jessica squeezed in to see. "The picture looks like him," she said. "Quick, Chad, what's the *B* stand for?"

"Braxton. My grandfather's name. Could you turn off that flashlight?"

Danny pocketed the Taser.

"Frisk him," Jessica said, sounding like Joe Friday.

"Do you mind?" Danny said.

"Not at all. It's impossible to be too careful with these people."

"Don't skip the groin area," Jessica said.

Danny patted Chad down from wrists to ankles.

"Is he clean?" Jessica said.

"Yes, Sarge. He's clean. Okay, Chad. What do have for us?"

A crisscrossing flashlight caught them in its beam. "I told you the ocean's this way," said a man's voice. "Don't fall in, Hal. You can't swim." The couple in the green windbreakers.

"Can we move up the beach a little?" Chad said. "It's too crowded around here. I know I sound paranoid, but you should be too. I think they've been tailing me."

"That couple?"

"No, the company. First, I need that promise you'll keep me out of this."

"I'll try my best if you deliver the goods."

They walked in silence. Danny's condo building sat at the north end of the boardwalk, almost to Sheridan Street and the fifty-six acre North Beach Park, closed at night.

*　　*　　*

Chad stayed two steps ahead. Even in the exceptional darkness, a lucky break, he felt the girl's eyes x-raying him. Just the coke, he told himself.

His mother would never believe it. Her *good boy*. That was the first thing she said about him to anyone who would listen. It was true. His life's resume was a litany of good boyness. Altar boy, Maypole King of the Third Grade, high school valedictorian, captain of his college sailing team …

Does goodness die or just get buried? He wondered. It's not like he wanted to be doing this. He hated himself for it. But nothing else matters when every synapse in your brain is screaming in harmony: *More white powder! Are you deaf? We said MORE WHITE POWDER!*

He didn't like betraying Luis, but everything changed the day of the funeral home search, when he cut off Chad's coke supply after the drug-sniffing dogs went after him. By any drug-addicted logic, it left him no choice but to switch allegiance to Yago.

Yago promised him an unlimited supply. He also said he had the capo's support. That cinched it. So Chad ran and told him about the lawsuit shortly after he delivered the papers to Jefe.

"I didn't get a chance to read the complaint," Chad explained. "But it was filed by a *Daniel Teakwell* as guardian for the girl. Has to be the guy who was with her on the video. He sat next to her at her parents' funeral service."

"How come I didn't know about that?"

"Jefe ordered me to keep it secret, threatened to rip my heart out if I told you. Said the same thing about the lawsuit."

"You don't got to worry about that."

"How can you be sure?" Chad asked.

"Bossman is a paper tiger."

"What about all those stories?"

"Fairy tales. So how do we find them? The girl and man."

"I gave Jefe a lead to a surf shop on Hollywood Beach from a bumper sticker on the guy's car, but once I saw his name on the lawsuit, he was easy to find on the internet. He was charged with murder five years ago."

"No foolin'?"

"Turned out he was innocent, framed by some psychopath. He became a local celebrity when he rescued his childhood sweetheart from the wacko. Talk about batshit crazy. The psycho drilled out a guy's eyeballs and cut off his dick."

Yago froze him with a glare. "You call him batshit crazy, you call me batshit crazy. That's called *craftsmanship*. When I was a young sicario, I inscribed the cheek of every head I lopped off."

"My mistake, sir. I'm sure he was a wonderful man, like your-self. And although I never saw your, um, severed-head art, I have no doubt it belonged in a gallery."

Chad knew then he had made the wrong choice, but a wave of dopesickness swept him forward.

"One of the articles said Teakwell lives in a condo building on Hollywood Beach called Seabreeze Towers and likes to hang out at the bar on the ground floor. I can't swear the girl's with him, but it would make sense if he's the guardian."

"Nice job. Luis know about this?"

"I haven't told him."

"Don't. I'll drill your eyes out and cut off your dick. I like the way that man thought. And Chad."

"Yes, sir?"

"Luis and I got nothing in common. I don't waste time making threats."

"I won't say a word. I can trust you, right? Because if you're wrong about Jefe or the capo backing you, I'm a goner."

Yago's twisted grin didn't comfort him. He looked like the Joker without makeup. "Of course you can trust me. You and me, we're hermanos. Once I take over, you get a promotion and raise, first thing."

"Muchas gracias. Please don't forget my employee benefit."

"What benefit?"

"The coke."

"No problem."

"Do you happen to have any on you right now?"

*   *   *

Chad stopped when the lights of the boardwalk were behind them. "This is good right here." They had reached the park's edge, standing next to a dune covered with spiky palmetto scrub.

"Tell us exactly what you have," Danny said.

"Everything. Accounting records, texts, voice messages. One document lays out the entire Snowbirds business plan. Do you know about it?"

"Shipping dead bodies full of cocaine up north."

"That's it. I also have secretly recorded conversations."

"Do you have any proof they killed my parents?" Jessica said.

"Not direct proof, but I know who did it. Do you know who Yago is?"

"The tall goony guy," Jessica said.

"Right. He's the killer."

"What about Carmillion?" Danny said.

"He's the brains behind Snowbirds in Paradise. Came up with the whole idea, which has turned out to be kind of brilliant. But the killing? That's all Yago."

"That's right," said a voice behind them. "All me."

Chapter 47

"DAN—"

He spun, too late. Yago loomed in the shadows behind Jessica, towering above her with one long arm wrapped around her neck, cutting her off mid-scream. He must have come from behind the dunes, wind and surf washing out his movement.

Danny prepared to lunge, stopped by a pistol pointed at his head.

"You wanna play hero?" Yago said. "Go for it. I can snap her neck and shoot you at the same time, no problem. No one will hear a sound out in this weather."

Carmillion's words came back. *If you see Yago, run. He doesn't waste time making threats. He's a pure killer, through and through.* He considered going for the Taser but Jessica was between them, and he couldn't risk a mistake with Yago's elbow pressed against her throat.

"You armed?" Yago said.

"No."

"Chad, check."

Chad felt around. "Just his phone and this flashlight."

"It's a Taser, pendejo. Gimme. Throw the phone in the ocean."

Yago tucked the Taser in his waistband. "I am Yago. You are the famous Daniel Teakwell and Jessica Jewell. And you already know Chadsito here. Walk that way." He pointed north with his head.

"Where are we going?" Danny said.

"No questions. Get moving."

"Let go of her first."

He lowered the gun. The muzzle flashed and a bullet thudded the sand inches from Danny's feet.

"Teakwell, you don't got, what it's called? *Bargaining power.* But you're in luck because I can't walk and carry a girl by the neck at the same time."

He let go and shoved Jessica toward Danny.

"Now move."

Danny scanned the surroundings as they trudged up the beach. Dark and deserted, stormy ocean on the right, dunes and thick vegetation to the left. The park.

Chad led the way. He and Jessica were behind him and Yago brought up the rear, staying close enough to shoot them in the back but far enough that Danny couldn't make a move on him.

The skeletal outline of a dock came into view. As they got closer, Danny saw a boat. Looked like a Boston Whaler.

"We're going for a ride," Yago said. "That's our transportation."

"No no no," Jessica murmured. "Not a boat."

Chad's ruse. Yago waiting. Now a boat. They added up to one conclusion. Everything happening had been carefully planned, just like the deaths of Jessica's parents.

"If you care about your own lives, I'd rethink that," Danny said. "Look at the surf. Feel the wind. That boat could easily go under." Their odds seemed better on dry land. He doubted Yago had a roundtrip in mind.

"Well, actually, not," Chad said. "It's a Boston Whaler. It belongs to our boss." He looked to Yago and quickly corrected himself. "Former boss. It can handle conditions a lot worse than this."

Boston Whalers were legendary for being unsinkable even in rough seas, but how did an accountant from Connecticut know it? Yago was answering the question at that moment.

"He don't look it, but Chadsito here was captain of his sailing team in college. So save your bullshit."

They reached the foot of the dock. The surf repeatedly dashed the Whaler against the pilings, but Chad knew to hang rubber bumpers from the mooring cleats.

"Chad, go get the boat ready."

"Yes, sir."

He sprinted up the dock and hopped over the gunwale.

"Walk," Yago said.

Danny hesitated. His choices on where to make a stand had shrunk to three: here, on the dock, or in the boat. *Here* was the only place with room to move. If there was just some way to distract—

Blam.

The bullet splintered the dock next to Jessica. "Quit acting stupid, Teakwell. Only reason you're still alive is I'm a pro who likes to follow a plan to the end without leaving evidence."

"Like when you killed my parents?" Jessica said.

"Like that. Abuelo too."

Seething, "Whatever happens to us, you're going to burn in hell forever."

"Bad news, lollipop. We're already in hell. As I was saying, I like to follow a plan, but you got to be adaptable in my business. Teakwell, next time you don't listen, I shoot the girl in the head. Now walk."

Danny nudged Jessica and they started the trek up the dock, slick with ocean spray. Jessica squeezed his fingers.

"The water," she said in a hushed voice. "It's so dark."

"I know, sweetie."

She looked up. "Sweetie? You never called me that before."

"I guess that's right."

"You two shut up," Yago said.

Chad cranked an outboard to life. Sounded like a Merc. The running lights came on.

Danny's only possible ace in the hole was he knew at least as much about boats as Chad. Like Fink said in his guardianship application, he had *nautical expertise.* He grew up on boats, including Boston Whalers like the one they had reached.

Looked to be twenty-two, maybe twenty-four feet. The engine was indeed a Merc, with a red auxiliary gas tank parked nearby. Used for fishing, judging from the trolling rods strapped under the gunwale and the tackle box in a side storage compartment in back, next to an emergency kit.

Up front, in the sunken bow where passengers put their feet, was a stack of cinderblocks. For ballast? The coils of rope next to them suggested something else.

The boat was parked with the bow pointed at the shore. It had a dual console, which meant the captain's seat and instruments abutted the dock.

If he could get his hands on the throttle and thrust it forward after Yago got aboard, they might survive. If the hitch ropes were still attached, it would be a short ride, a few feet before the slack tightened and jolted everyone off their feet, maybe even flip the boat. If the opportunity arose after the ropes were detached, he'd do the same thing, adding a sharp twist of the steering wheel on his way to ramming the beach.

If … If … If …

"You're never going to get away with this," Danny said, eyes measuring the interior. "The cops aren't stupid. If you kill us, they'll know it was connected to Snowbirds, especially with the lawsuit pending. Even if you make it look like an accident."

"You're right," Yago said. "That's why you're going to be disappeared. No bodies, no evidence, no case."

That explained the cinderblocks and rope. Danny shuffled along the dock until he was adjacent to the captain's chair. He had to get Yago in the boat for it to work.

"You know, if you plan on putting us up front with those blocks, you're going to risk nosediving powering into a wave. You might want to get in the boat and check out the trim first." It was lame, but he couldn't think of anything else.

"We appreciate your concern for our safety, Teakwell. You're going in the back where we can keep an eye on you. Chad, grab the duct tape and get out here. It will be easier to tape 'em up on the dock."

So much for Plan A. He couldn't let it happen. Once they were immobilized there'd be no chance. He wasn't going down without a fight.

Down to one option. Not a good one. Rush Yago while yelling for Jessica to run, hope he had enough velocity after taking some bullets to knock him into the water. With any luck, she could make it across the sand and escape into the park.

Chad climbed out of the boat with a thick roll of tape. Yago stood ten feet away. If he could get him to look the other way, even for a second, his odds would increase. Danny let go of Jessica's hand and set one foot forward to get a running start.

"What the hell is that?" he said suddenly, pointing to the water with his mouth agape.

Look, dammit! Look!

Chad looked. Jessica looked. Yago didn't. Instead he slid the Taser from his waistband, said "Nice try," and pulled the trigger.

Danny was vaguely aware of someone screaming as he fell to the dock. He couldn't move, every muscle clenched in a vise. The pain felt like wasps stinging his veins from the inside. Then, as it began to subside, as his brain stopped rattling like a coin in a jar, it started all over again, the voice now shouting, *Stop! Stop!*

When the second round of agony began to fade, he opened his eyes, just in time to see Yago standing above him swinging something down on his head.

Everything went dark.

Chapter 48

AS CONSCIOUSNESS returned, Danny's first awareness was the hum of the revving Merc and sensation of bouncing on the hard deck. His second was that he couldn't move his hands or feet.

"Danny, Danny," Jessica whispered.

He opened his eyes to find the two of them propped together in the back of the boat leaned against the port side, the auxiliary gas tank across from them.

He looked down to see their wrists and ankles bound with duct tape. Each time the boat rose and fell in the chop, a fresh shower of sea spray hit them. They were soaked to the bone.

The boat was dark except for the instrument panel. The running lights were off. For concealment, no doubt. Not only illegal, but dangerous, especially on a night like this.

Chad piloted from the captain's chair, tacking slowly back and forth at an angle against the waves. Yago sat in the passenger chair, glancing over his shoulder to check on them, still holding the gun. He said something to Chad, but the motor and whooshing wind drowned it out.

"Are you alright?" Jessica said.

Their heads were practically touching.

"Yeah," he lied. His muscles were cramping from the Taser and his head throbbed from Yago's hit. "How about you?"

"I'm okay. Your head is bleeding, and your stomach. Yago hit you with the gun and tore the Taser wires right out of your belly."

"How long have we been moving?" he said. His brain was un-fogging, senses returning, a relief.

"Probably about twenty minutes."

Straightening his back, he peered over the gunwale, but saw only blackness. He had no idea where they were. He learned to tell directions by the North Star as a kid taking sailing lessons. Only problem was you had to be able to see it. Clouds still crossed out the sky.

"After Yago hit you they hurried to tape us up and dump us here. And I mean dump. Like we were already dead things."

Side by side, she looked tiny and wraithlike. Her teeth were chattering. Being wet on a boat will make you cold even on a warm night. The chattering, the tape around her thin ankles and wrists, the whole situation, made his heart hurt much worse than his body.

He failed her, when she needed him most.

There has to be a way. Think. He wracked his pounding brain for an idea while she continued talking.

"I have a confession," she said. "I'm scared. I tried not to be. Remember my philosophy? I told you at the funeral home that night when I used your cellphone. You're going to be in the same situation whether you're scared or not, so you might as well make the choice not to be scared."

"I remember."

They were leaned against the storage rack holding the tackle box he spotted from the dock. It might contain a knife he could use to cut the tape, but he needed to cut the tape before he could reach the box.

"I just can't do it now."

"Do what?"

"Are you still not listening to me? Make the choice not to be afraid. It's not working. I think it's the water. It's so dark, like oil all around us, like we really are in hell. Maybe Yago knows something we don't."

"We're not in hell," he said. It just felt that way. "I'm scared too, but we're not giving up."

He looked to the sky for answers that didn't come. Some of the clouds had cleared. He couldn't see the North Star but spotted Orion, another reliable celestial navigation marker. It rose in the east and set almost perfectly due west. It was behind the boat. They were heading farther and farther into open water.

Chad adjusted the bow again and moonlight splashed the boat, just for a moment. Danny thought he saw a glint at his feet. Something shiny.

Did he imagine it? He stretched his legs and dragged his heels back, catching onto something. He spread his knees and peered into the dark space below them.

It was a fishhook, a big one. Looked like a 9/0 with a three-inch shaft. It must have rattled loose from somewhere as they pounded over the waves. He clam-shelled his hands and pinched it with his forefingers.

"What are you doing?" Jessica whispered.

"Just stretching," he said, not wanting to give her false hope.

He worked the hook up and inside the tape, face down, concentrating on being inconspicuous while not slitting his wrists. Carmillion, the deepsea fisherman, had helped them after all. One size smaller and the hook wouldn't have reached the tape.

Jessica rambled on as he etched the barb against the layers of adhesive. Another diversion, her go-to coping tool.

"I hope Gloria who likes to be called Gigi does my eulogy. She knows me best. Besides you. But you'll be dead too. The only other person still living would be Norma Pollinuk from the funeral home. I think Gigi would spice it up. Who do you want to do your eulogy? I'm guessing Grady."

The barb punctured the outer layer. He tugged the shaft gently, like he was reeling in a fish he didn't want to lose. He needed the tear to reach the edge. When it finally did, he flexed his wrists and the tape gave way.

Danny faced Jessica and said, "What's all this funeral talk? Who was it who told me that if I give up too easily, I'll never reach my full potential?"

"Danny, you shouldn't try to make people laugh when they're about to die. ... Wait a minute, I change my mind. You should. That was pretty funny."

"Listen carefully and don't react." He explained about the fishhook. Her mouth fell open, then she stared at his wrists and her face screwed up.

"I intentionally cut the bottom, so they can't tell if they come check on us. Bring your wrists over and I'll do the same for you. Keep an eye over my shoulder. Pinch me if you see Yago or Chad looking this way."

She pinched him before he even touched her. He thought she was experimenting before Yago's voice cut through the white noise of the wind and Merc.

"What are you two whispering about?" He swiveled to face them. A widening break in the clouds let more light through, casting ghoulish shadows on his long angular face.

"Answer me? You saying farewells or plotting against me?"

They stayed silent.

"Chad, turn on the lights."

The navigation lights came on, casting eerie red, green, and white glows on the swells and white caps churning all around them. Yago stood, holding his chairback for balance while somehow managing to keep his gun calm and steady.

"Not just the running lights. I can't see."

The overhead console light came on. Pupils fully dilated in the pitch dark, the tiny bulb burnt a hole in Danny's eyes, sending pulsating arrows of pain through his battered brain before he could turn away.

Yago took two steps and stood over them. "Hold up your

hands."

Danny raised his forearms for inspection, hoping he didn't insist on seeing both sides.

"Now you?"

Jessica did the same.

Satisfied, he went back to his seat. "Cut the lights, Chad. They're killing my eyes. What's taking so long?"

"The conditions, sir," Chad said. "But we're almost to the three-mile point. Probably only five more minutes."

"How deep is it?"

"Depth finder says ninety feet."

Jessica groaned. "Ninety feet? I almost drowned in two feet when I was little. Remember? So this will be like forty-five times worse drowning."

Danny whispered, "*Shh.* We don't have much time. Give me your hands again and keep your eyes on Yago." With his own hands now free, he needed the hook only to notch the edge. His fingers did the rest.

"I'm going to do the same with our ankles, but you just saw how important it is to make it look like the tape's still attached. And one of us needs to be watching them every second."

"Do you have a plan?"

"We'll have to play it by ear, one step at a time. Here's the first thing. Right behind me in the storage rack is a fishing tackle box. It's likely to have a knife in it. I'll watch them and use my body to cover you. Reach behind me and see what you can find. But be careful feeling around. There could be all kinds of sharp hooks in there."

"What's our signal if one of them turns around?"

"I'll nudge you with an elbow. Keep the tape on one wrist so you can wrap it back around in a hurry."

She nodded. Danny twisted to face Yago and Chad, using the width of his swimmers' shoulders to conceal Jessica. Yago made a quick side glance, but returned to talking to Chad. Danny tried to listen, but could only make out "dropping anchor" and "cinderblocks."

That was enough. Time was running out.

Something clunked behind him. In his wound-up state it sounded like a sonic boom, but didn't draw their attention. "Sorry," Jessica whispered. "Okay, you can turn around. Bad news."

"What happened?"

"Nothing. The top only opens like one inch. The back hits the side of the boat. This was all I could reach without making a lot of noise."

"What is it? I can't see."

"A screwdriver."

He took it from her and felt the tip. A Phillips, long and narrow. Almost as good as a knife. "Good job," he said.

"Now what?"

"Not sure."

He considered trying to sneak up on Yago and stab him with the screwdriver, but even if he made it without getting shot first, it would be unlikely to put him down. Chad also had to be considered. Was he armed? Would he fight? He didn't look like a fighter, but didn't look like a sailor either.

"What's the red box next to the tackle box?" Jessica said.

"Emergency kit."

The winding drone of the Merc suddenly stopped. So did the boat. Chad had shifted into neutral, idling, making it easier to hear.

"This is it, sir," he said. "Three miles out."

"About time," Yago said. "Go drop the anchor. I'll take the captain's seat."

"Yes, sir, but I need to turn the running lights back on to see where I'm going. We're pointed into the current. You can just let us drift back as I let out the rope."

"Don't lecture me, accountant. I know how to drive a boat. I used to run shipments from the islands on a go-fast."

Chad got up and made his way to the bow, holding the side

rail to steady himself on the pitching deck. He opened a hatch, pulled out the anchor, and began lowering it. Yago sat in the captain's seat and swiveled it their way with the gun trained on them. They stayed still with their severed-tape bracelets in place around their ankles and wrists.

"Nice night for a swim," he said. "Although they say the water gets colder the farther down you go."

A whimper escaped Jessica's throat.

"You ever hear that old mobster saying about cement shoes, or cement overcoat? I call bullshit on it. Even quick-set cement takes a couple hours to dry, a lump that big. No killer's wasting two hours watching cement dry.

"Then you got your cinderblocks. Things were made for sinking bodies, especially in sunny Florida. Got all the water around and they got the holes to run rope through. Don't even have to pay for 'em. Just stop at any construction site and pick some up."

Danny felt Jessica tightening, shrinking. He had another use in mind for the cinderblocks: use one to crush Yago's skull. "We really don't need to know the details," he said.

"Too bad. I'm talking. You listen. Some people say, Yago, why go through all that trouble? Just shoot 'em. Because like I said earlier, I don't leave evidence behind. I'm a professional. My way, even if your bodies get loose someday and float to the surface, no bullet-holes. Autopsy shows lungs fulla water. You drowned. Simple."

He wheeled frontward and shouted, "Chad, what's taking so long?"

"The water's deeper than I thought."

Danny could see Chad through the split console and windshield, huddled on the bow with his head between his knees. It didn't look like he was still letting out anchor rope. Maybe he was seasick. Yago noticed it too.

"Hey, what are you doing?" He stood up.

Yes yes yes. Go check it out. Danny zeroed in on the captain's chair and throttle.

Yago took one step toward the bow, glanced at Danny and hesitated. Maybe the look on his face gave him away because Yago reached back to turn off the motor and pocketed the key.

His heart sank. That was it, their chance. He could have scrambled to the cockpit, hit the throttle and spun the steering wheel. Knocked them down, maybe even thrown them overboard. Not much different from his original idea.

"Are you doing what I think you're doing?" Yago shouted at Chad. "Lemme me see your face. Up close."

He grabbed Chad by the shirt. "You fucking dope addict. I told you. No cocaine on a mission. You violated a direct order."

"I—I'm sorry, sir. It was just a little bit. To calm my nerves."

"Nerves, huh? You know what gets on my nerves? You telling our prisoners that Luis is the brains behind Snowbirds. And you think I'm *goony*?"

Danny had been wishing for a distraction since the beginning. It was now or never. Only problem: he needed a new plan, in two seconds.

One came to him. A longshot, but what wasn't at this point? He tore the duct tape away and wrenched the emergency kit from the storage bin.

"What are you doing?" Jessica whispered.

"No time to explain."

Inside were the usual contents. Air horn, SOS flag, and what he was looking for. Flares. Four of them, two with orange caps, two with red. The orange were smoke flares, for daytime.

The red were pyrotechnic, SOLAS-grade. Thirty times brighter than Coast Guard requirements. Visible for miles, but that's not what gave him hope.

He grabbed one and pulled the cap off.

"I'm going to the other side of the boat and set this off. Don't look at it. It will blind you."

"Why are— Never mind."

Chad was begging forgiveness as Danny crawled to the

captain's chair. "I'll never do it again, sir. Please don't cut my employee benefits."

"Don't worry, Chadsito. You're not going to need your employee benefits anymore, not even your health insurance. Stand up."

"Wh—what are you going to do?"

"Dr. Yago is here. I have a cure for your nerves, addictions, everything."

"What is—"

Pop pop pop pop.

Holy shit! He was shooting him! *He's a pure killer, through and through.*

A wail as Chad fell backward and disappeared in the dark water.

Danny moved quickly. He shut off the running lights, plunging them back into darkness, and yanked the cord to ignite the flare. He turned his face away and stuck it in a fishing rod holder.

Yago would look. How could he not? When he did flash blindness was guaranteed, for at least several seconds, maybe even minutes. Danny would stay crouched behind the console and jump him with the screwdriver when he came back looking for them.

"*Ahhhhh!* You die!" He looked.

Then the gunfire started. Wild shots in the direction of the red glare. *Maniac!*

Danny ordered Jessica to lay flat and did the same. A plunk behind him and he immediately smelled gasoline. A bullet went through the auxiliary gas tank. Another one penetrated the console just above his head.

He slithered back to Jessica and snatched up the other red-capped cylinder. "Jessica, we need to leave this boat and there's only one way. Over the side."

"In the water? No, Danny. Please."

"I'm sorry."

There were probably lifejackets aboard, but no time to look

for them. They were already drenched in gasoline, a deepening pool of it washing back and forth as the waves rocked the boat.

Danny saw Yago's outline in the moonlight, feeling his way back from the bow. "Where are you?" he howled.

"Let's go. Get up," Danny whispered. "Hurry."

"I can't."

"Are you hurt?"

"No. My legs just won't move. I think I'll stay here. You can go without me."

He held the flare in his teeth and scooped her up, garbling, "Get on my back. I'm not going to let you drown."

He carried her over the rear seat onto the tiny swim platform and leaned against the Merc's hot cowling for support. Grasping the flare, "We're going to have to go underwater. Hold your breath when I say *now* and don't let go of my neck."

"Are you sure we have to do this?" Her voice no more than a wisp in the wind.

Danny looked out upon the sea of ink. The swells undulated like great rolls of licorice taffy. He wasn't any crazier about the idea than she was but there wasn't a choice. "I'm sure."

He glanced behind them. Yago had found his way to the split console.

Biting the ignition cord, he yanked and held the flare as far away as he could in case Yago started shooting at the new red glare, which he did. *Pop pop pop.* A hot poker burned through Danny's right calf and his leg nearly buckled.

"*Now,*" he said, tossing the flare over his shoulder and leaping into the void.

Chapter 49

THEY MADE IT ten feet before the explosion rocked the water. The shockwaves hit them like a shove in the back. When they surfaced night had turned to day. The boat was a bed of white-hot fire, pumping plumes of black smoke into the night.

"Omigod," Jessica said, spitting and sputtering. "You did it. I don't even believe it."

Danny didn't either. He looked to the sky and sent a *Thank you* to anyone or anything who might be listening.

The swells took them up and down like a fishing bob as they watched. Jessica tightened her grip around his neck. "But now what? We're going to drown and sink ninety feet. Don't take this wrong, but I think I would have rather exploded in the boat."

"Don't you ever listen to me?" he said, unable to see if she got the joke. "I told you, I'm not going to let you drown."

He was determined to keep up a brave face, even if it required lying. He had severe doubts about their survivability, but to stand any chance at all, they both needed to hold on to hope.

"How?" she said.

Good question. Even in the bad weather, someone would be likely to spot the fire and summon help, but it could take hours. The more energy he used up treading water, the less chance they had of controlling their own destiny.

He scanned in every direction. The foam-filled hulls had stayed in one piece. There was no flotsam to grab onto.

He reached down and diagnosed his calf. The bullet had grazed him, leaving a smooth gash and flap of skin. He was losing blood, no idea how much, but the longer they stayed in one place, the more likely they'd end up as shark bait.

"I'll tell you how. We're going to swim to the shore."

"Are you crazy? We're three miles out. We don't even know where the shore is."

"Sure we do. Look over there. See Orion, the constellation? That's where the shore is. We need to start moving. I'm going to do all the swimming. Your job is to hold on. Whatever you do, you can't let go."

That was his worst fear, that she'd slip into the abyss and he wouldn't be able to find her. He explained she needed to stay high on his back, so she could hang on without choking him. "It won't be easy in these waves. Do you think you can do that?"

"I'll try. I'm pretty strong."

The understatement of the century.

"Kick off your shoes to lighten the load." He did the same, then tore his t-shirt off.

"I have an idea," she said. "You could tear your shirt into strips and tie my hands in front of you. Just, you know, in case they slip."

"Good idea, but don't rely on it. You still have to hold on. Keep your head above the chop as much as you can. Don't panic if you swallow some water. I guarantee it's going to happen to both of us."

With only his damaged legs to keep them afloat, tearing the shirt into strips and securing her wrists exhausted him before they even had a chance to get started. He used the last strips to tie a bandage around the bullet wound.

"One more thing. I won't be able to talk. You shouldn't either unless it's an emergency. You'll use up energy and every time you open your mouth is one more chance of swallowing water."

"Do you really think we have a chance of making it? I want the truth."

"Of course," he said, hoping the assurance sounded less phony than it felt.

When he swam triathlons with his buddies, 2.4 miles was difficult but doable. But he trained for them and they happened in smooth water in broad daylight, without an eighty-pound weight on his back, a leg leaking blood, and muscles burning from a double-dose of Taser. Throw in a possible concussion and the odds dimmed even further.

He pedaled in a circle, a last search in case help was coming. They were all alone.

"Here we go," he said and took his first long, round-arm freestyle stroke with a two-beat kick.

He told himself only one thing mattered: the little remora fish attached to his back.

* * *

She proved adept as a first mate once they got in a rhythm, tapping his left or right shoulder if he veered off course from Orion.

Time passed, strokes passed, he lost track of both. He couldn't tell if they were making progress. Each time he climbed the rise of a swell and swam down the other side the shore felt farther away.

His muscles were spaghetti strands ready to snap. He kept going only because he had to, plowing one arm then the other into the brine, over and over and over.

With nothing else to block out the pain, he thought about Sari, wondered if she was watching. That brought him back to Jessica. Sari's dying wish: *Be willing to let someone else in. A heart has room for more than one person ...*

He swore he would try, but didn't, not until the weird funeral home kid showed up at the Tradewinds dragging her backpack.

I did it, Sari. I let someone in. Just not exactly what you had in mind.

Each time he noticed his arms flailing or kicks diminishing, he thought about how he lost the only other person he'd ever let in and dug deeper.

Getting drilled repeatedly in the face with ocean water was enough to keep even Jessica Jewell quiet until, "I see lights! We're going in the right direction!" She had seemed dubious about his celestial navigation claim.

A thousand or so strokes later she spoke again. "Danny," she said. "I know you don't want to be bothered, but there's a fin sticking out of the water behind us and I think it's a shark."

He stopped and pedaled a one-eighty. Treading water with her aboard was even more taxing than swimming.

She was right again. Of course it was a shark. The only other obstacle left would have been a torpedo.

Looked like a blacktip, six to eight feet, although hard to tell for sure in the impenetrable dark water. Common in Florida, including being the shark most likely to attack a human in a hit and run. Leaving a trail of blood for miles, his only surprise was it took so long.

"You're right. It's a shark, but don't panic."

The helium chirp. "Why would I panic? Being eaten alive is the perfect ending to drowning."

Facing her worst nightmares and able to make a joke. Her strength gave his another jolt. Danny knew how to fend off a shark. He'd done it before, although he was underwater, scuba-diving in daylight, a more even playing field.

The shark circled them and Danny twirled to stay even with it. Never take your eyes off a shark. Rule number one. A lot of times they'll go away ... but probably not with blood in the water.

It nosed in and backed away, circled again and vanished below the surface. Danny couldn't see his legs, much less the shark. Rule number two is don't thrash in the water, but it took all of his limbs moving to stay afloat.

Sandpaper skin abraded his thigh. He flinched, but stayed focused on the immediate circle around him.

The shark was there somewhere. He could feel it moving.

When its head popped up a foot away, Danny was ready.

Drawing from an energy reserve he didn't know existed, he punched, left fist to the snout, right to the eyes, with enough force that Jessica lost her grip. Her smart idea to tie her hands around his neck with the t-shirt worked. It caught and she pulled herself back up.

Standard procedure for warding off a shark. Hit them where they're most sensitive: snout, eyes, gills. It worked. The shark disappeared, at least for the time being.

He told Jessica to keep an eye out for it and resumed grinding. He wasn't sure how much more time passed before he heard, "I think I see the shoreline! We're getting closer. Hang in there, Danny-boy."

Danny-boy. Like Grady or one of the D'Angelo brothers. He would have laughed if he had the strength and his face wasn't underwater.

But not long after that he began slipping away. His arms and legs kept moving, but he didn't know who they belonged to anymore. They didn't feel like his. Didn't feel like anything. At least the pain was gone.

Jessica said something from behind a wall of glass. He couldn't make out the words. Then her voice changed. To Sari's.

I feel you coming closer, Danny.

I can't leave yet, Sari.

A warm current flowed through him. His body felt light. So tempting to succumb, just float away into the darkness. Peaceful ... serene.

Snap out of it!

He threw an arm in front of him, then the other. He was still trying to fight off the feeling when thunder shattered the sky and everything flipped. The current turned cold. His body grew heavy again, like it was being pushed down.

The water began to swirl. What was happening? Maybe he was being sucked into hell. That would be a fitting end. *You want proof, doubter? Here!* The thunder grew louder, the swirling more intense.

A sudden bright light consumed him and his confusion grew. Maybe he was caught in between, in a tug of war. Purgatory. Had he been a believer the whole time? The thunder perforated his ears.

Jessica's voice again, bigger, stronger, urgent. "Danny, Danny!" Pounding on his back. "Can you hear me? Look!"

He did. It wasn't thunder. It was a helicopter, with a searchlight.

Chapter 50

DANNY LAID in his hospital bed watching the IV drip in his right arm. That's how bored he was.

He'd been there a week and was past ready to go home. The two pints of blood he lost through the hole in his leg had been replaced and the stitched-up wound was healing under bandages. He guessed right about having a concussion, but the headaches were gone. It was his damn muscles keeping him there.

Rhabdomyolysis. He'd never heard of it. A breakdown of muscle tissue from a blood toxin called creatine kinase, or CK, triggered by extreme physical exertion or direct muscle trauma. In his case, both. The trauma came courtesy of the Taser jolts. Dangerous if untreated, but the first-responders waiting on the beach took them straight to the hospital. The only treatment is rest and continuous IV fluids.

They released Jessica four days ago. She arrived dehydrated and exhausted with an assortment of bumps and bruises but no serious physical injuries. Danny was more worried about her psychological health.

His several hospital visitors included Allie Dearden, who he had called and asked to meet with Jessica for a counseling session. She stopped by afterward to fill him in.

"This probably won't surprise you, but her self-evaluation was *I'm fine.*"

"She's still holding things in," Danny said. "That's the way she copes. The truth is too much for her to face so she relies on distractions to avoid dealing with it."

"What a coincidence," she said with a wry smile. "She thinks the same thing about you. Maybe that's one reason you two are simpatico. You have each other figured out. Just know her grief and trauma are likely to come out at unexpected times and in unexpected ways. I hope you'll convince her to keep doing counseling."

"I'll definitely try."

"You're welcome to join her."

He let the not-so-subtle hint pass.

Jessica was staying with Shannon. She called the second night with an announcement. "I'm never having a baby. All they do is waste one perfectly good diaper after another. What is their problem? I had a kitten who learned to use a litter box in three weeks."

"I don't think they do it on purpose."

"They could at least try to hold it. It's rude. And the crying! It's a miracle my parents didn't drug me more often. Nope. No babies for me."

"Well, the good news is you have plenty of time to think about it," he said.

"I already thought about it, Danny. Did you not listen to what I just said?"

The conversation put a smile on his face that lasted all night. He had no doubt Allie was right about the grief and trauma, but despite everything, she was still Jessica.

She was scheduled to start school next week after missing the first days. She changed her mind about dyeing her hair purple and talked Gloria who likes to be called Gigi out of it. "This year," she told her friend, "let's pretend to be normal girls."

"How did she respond to that?" Danny said.

"She laughed so hard she peed in her pants, then she threw up."

A lot had happened since they swam away from the burning boat. When they didn't return from their walk down the beach with Chad, Grady assembled a half-soused search team from the Tradewinds to look for them.

Someone with binoculars spotted the fire on the horizon and Grady called the Coast Guard, fearing the worst. They said they were already on the scene. There were no apparent survivors, but they would keep looking.

Danny and Jessica were only two hundred yards from shore when the helicopter discovered them and lowered a rescue basket. They would have made it, if just barely.

Detective Rodriguez had been by to see both of them, bringing the news that the DNA in the mystery hair Jessica put so much stock in matched Yago's. His charred remains were baked into the hull of the burned-out boat.

"No one believed me," she gloated. "Not even you, Danny. You should have seen the look on the detective's face when I told him about grandpa's liver. But at least he took me seriously this time. He said as soon as we can get it to him, he'll send it to a lab for analysis."

She took grim satisfaction that news reports now referred to her parents' deaths as homicides rather than a drunk-driving accident. A trucker who saw the news came forward with a dashboard cam video of his drive across Alligator Alley that night. Three seconds of it showed him zooming past the red compact rental car on the side of the highway with a black SUV parked behind it. Yago's.

Chad's bullet-riddled corpse, what was left of it after being lunched on by marine life for three days, washed up on the beach in Fort Lauderdale in the middle of a family reunion picnic and volleyball game.

The feds not only got back on the case (minus Agent Munroe, removed without explanation), they already raided the Brickell office suite. The big prize was a damning dossier found on Chad's computer, exactly like the one he described to lure them up the beach that night. Maybe he compiled it for self-protection, or maybe he had good intentions and lost a battle with his addiction.

The danger was over. DEA intelligence intercepts indicated Los Loppers had pulled up stakes in the U.S. after the feds arrested several employees and seized their assets, including the six funeral homes.

The FBI was searching for Luis Carmillion when he called from a Miami hotel and said he was hiding there under the name *Louis Carmen*—not from the law but the cartel. He surrendered peaceably and was discussing a plea deal to turn government witness in exchange for a shorter sentence and placement in the federal witness protection program.

Overnight, Danny and Jessica had become unwilling darlings of the media, who couldn't get enough about a case involving ruthless assassins and corpses stuffed with cocaine. But it was the human angle that really drew them in, the tale of the fearless guardian who saved his orphaned ward in a miraculous escape from an exploding boat three miles at sea.

Erin saw the news on CNN and called from a surf competition in San Diego. She offered to hop on a plane and come help out with Jessica, the surf shop, or anything else. But it was all covered.

Gaspar finished the artwork on Rasheed's board, capturing Lil Lansky on the mountaintop in all his virile glory. All that was left to do was the glassing. Danny called Rasheed to apologize it would be delayed a couple weeks. The next day he got a life-size flower arrangement of Lil Lansky himself, yellow chrysanthemums depicting his gold chains. The card said: *From one surfer to another, get well.*

Danny called Erin back the next night and they talked a long time. She hadn't made it to the competition finals, but shrugged it off. "You know how it is. Sometimes you get your wave, sometimes you don't."

He was struck by how comfortable she was in her own skin. Confident without pretense. Kind without overdoing it. And funny. He never got a chance to know that side of her. He was laughing at her story about a guy who tried to enter the tandem competition with his surfing cat as a partner when a nurse told him the patient in the next room complained about the noise and it was time for lights out.

"I have to go. I just got in trouble with the nurse," he said.

"Hey, I know you have a lot going on right now, but what about that trip to California?"

"Jessica's already deciding what to pack. It looks like Thanksgiving is her first real school break. Would that work?"

"Let's do it."

"I hope this doesn't sound bad, but part of me wishes I could come alone."

"There's always next time."

At the same time Danny was no-commenting every reporter on the planet, Fink was in his element, taking his bombastic blather from one cable news show to another as an *expert legal commentator*. His drug-fueled lawsuit was being hailed as a bold and brilliant tactical move. One pundit speculated *blood-sucking turd* may become part of standard legal lexicon.

Danny laid down the law when he showed up at the hospital beaming about an inquiry he received for a made-for-TV movie. "I came up with the perfect name for it. It's *Snow-Bodies Business*. Get it?"

"Get this. Tell them no and quit talking to the media about us starting right this second or you're fired and can kiss your new fame and potential contingency fee goodbye."

"Alright, alright. Touch-*chee*."

The state bar issued its ruling granting Fink's admission, conditioned on him completing five thousand hours of remedial ethics courses, which it grudgingly reduced to two hundred after Fink argued it would take seventy years to fulfill the condition. It never came out he was representing Snowbirds at the same time he sued them.

Danny shifted his gaze from the IV drip to the parenting book

Grady brought him earlier that morning. *Why Some Animals Eat Their Young: A Survivor's Guide to Motherhood.*

They both got a good laugh from the title. "You're a father and a mother now, Danny," Grady said.

"I suppose that's true. Last night I was planning a visit for us to visit Erin, the surf champion I told you about, and realized I had to work it around Jessica's school schedule."

"Next thing you know they'll be appointing you treasurer of the PTA and the whole place will go to hell."

They laughed again before Grady turned serious. "So what do you plan to do about it?"

"What do you mean?"

"What's in a word, Danny-boy? If you were a kid, would you rather have a guardian or a parent?"

"Parents, obviously, but they're dead. No way to change that."

"You know what I'm getting at," he said, and left to go open the Tradewinds.

The elevator down the hall pinged and the doors opened to expel Jessica's big voice. "He never even told me he got shot. It's a miracle that shark didn't chomp his leg off."

He smiled. Her first visit since she was released. All their conversations had been over the phone.

He listened to her steps slapping on the industrial tile as she marched down the hallway, the same purposeful steps of the unusual young girl who once brought him a hamster because she didn't want him to be alone. It evoked a sense of déjà vu from five years ago. Same hospital, same outsized media attention, even a bullet wound in his calf, although last time it was the left leg.

Maybe Jessica felt it too because she stopped at the doorway and leaned against the frame with Shannon standing behind her.

"So we meet again," she said. "Just like old times."

"Did you bring me another hamster?" he said.

"Something way better. I brought me!"

He laughed. "That is way better, nothing against good old Patches."

Shannon said she had to run some errands and would be back in a couple hours. Danny thanked her for everything she had done.

"You look a lot better this time," Jessica said, hopping on his bed. "Back then, with that tube coming out of your chest, I wasn't sure you were going to make it."

"You signed me up as your first embalming customer. I remember it well." He did. It was the same day he reunited with Sari after twenty long years. "What have you been up to today?"

Her tongue lolled out. "Taking care of a baby. What else? When are you getting out of here? I want to go home to our condo. Shannon's always busy and her husband has no idea how to talk to me. All he does is watch sports on TV."

"Hopefully tomorrow." The CK level in his bloodstream was at seventy-nine thousand units when he checked in. It had to go below two hundred. He was almost there.

"Good news," she said. "And here's some more. Grady took me to the shop yesterday to put a sign on the door saying we're temporarily closed, and guess what? While we were there, a man came in and I sold him a board! A poly. Seven hundred bucks."

"You're a natural."

"I'm just glad I didn't waste my time learning about surfboards for nothing."

He asked if she was excited about starting school on Monday.

"I am, except Gigi said our math teacher is mean as a snake."

"How so?"

"Gigi gave an answer the teacher said was wrong. She asked why and the teacher explained it. Gigi said her answer wasn't wrong, the math was wrong."

"You mean the teacher made a mistake?"

"No, the teacher was right going by the way math is done, but Gigi thinks math should work differently."

"Ah, I see. But I'm not sure that qualifies the teacher as being mean as a snake."

"It gets worse. She keeps calling her Gloria and we both know how Gigi feels about that."

He pitied the poor teachers who had to deal with Jessica and Gigi in the same class. "What's been happening at the Tradewinds?" he said.

"Not much. Everybody misses you, of course. John the Diver asked me to give you a message. He said, and I quote, *Tell him to quit lazing around the damn hospital and get his sorry ass back here.* But he meant it in a nice way."

"I'm sure he did, although he shouldn't have used curse words."

She rolled her eyes. "Fink stopped by last night. He's excited about the lawsuit. Thinks we might win a lot of money. He also thinks I'll get Slagger-Jewell back at some point. Apparently, the government can take away criminals' property and give it back to the victims."

"How do you feel about that?"

"I thought about it a lot. I can't run a funeral home because of school and the age thing, but I wondered whether I could get the old gang back together, the assistant directors and embalmers, and of course Norma. Then I decided I don't want to."

"How come?"

"That life is over. It would never be the same without gramps or my parents. You can't go back again."

"That's what Thomas Wolfe said."

"The weird guy at the Tradewinds who sits alone sharing his beer with his parrot?"

"No, that's Thomas Haney. Thomas Wolfe was a writer. He's dead now."

"Like everyone," she said. She picked up Grady's book. "What's this?"

"Grady brought it to me. He thinks I need to learn more about parenting."

"You've done a good job so far, for a beginner. Well, don't kill yourself. Remember, I'm only temporary." She tried but failed to make it come out as a lighthearted quip. "Did you ever find out how long the guardianship lasts?"

"Still not sure."

A tightlipped nod of resignation.

He sat up straight and rolled his shoulders, forward then back, a delay tactic while he considered his next words. "I've been thinking about something." He paused. "Something involving you."

She stiffened.

"It's not bad. I don't think. How would you feel about being adopted?"

Her jaw fell open. "Not bad? You're getting rid of me, after everything we've been through?"

"No, I'm sorry. I mean, adopted by ..." He had a hard time spitting it out. Sari's words shoved him forward. *Follow your heart, Danny. It will lead you to the right place.* "You know, by me."

"For real? You'd do that for me?"

"And for me."

"How long would I be adopted?"

"Well, if it went through, forever."

"Wow. Does that mean you love me?"

"Of course. You haven't figured that out by now?"

"Sort of. When I asked before, you said if someone was trying to hurt me and the only way to save me was by giving up your life, you'd do it. You proved you weren't lying. *Bu-ut,* you still never actually said it."

He cleared his throat. "I love you."

"Aw. Well, then I love you too. Would I be able to get real goodnight hugs?"

"I'll have to work up to it, but yes."

"Would I have to call you Dad? I mean, it's not like I would mind, it's just—"

"You don't have to explain. Honestly, I'd prefer Danny. Think about it. There's no rush and it's a huge decision."

"I'll say. It's probably the biggest decision I'll ever make in my entire life. I need to think really hard about it and be one-hundred percent sure."

"Absolutely."
"Okay. Yes!"

What did you think of
Funeral Daze?

THANK YOU for reading *Funeral Daze*. If you liked it, please consider posting a review on Amazon, Goodreads, or anywhere else to help spread the word. And thanks again!

You won't even believe what happened five years earlier ...

Psycho-Tropics

A TWENTIETH HIGH SCHOOL reunion in a South Florida beach town unburies the past (literally) in this dark mystery of revenge and redemption. Lottery-winning surfer Danny Teakwell seems to be living the life, but he's been hiding a terrible secret, punishing himself for two decades.

Now he's hit rock bottom. So he thinks. The ghosts from his past show up at the reunion, launching him on a mayhem-filled race through the Sunshine State to save a missing woman. He broke a vow to her when they were kids. He won't let it happen again.

The odds aren't good. He only has three days and his main allies are a pill-popping lawyer, crusty barkeep, and seven-year-old embalming expert. Heart and dark humor combine with page-turning action and a twisty plot that will keep you guessing until the end.

Editorial Reviews

"Marrying humor with suspense is not easy, but it comes across masterfully ... A truly enjoyable read." — *Writer's Digest Award for Genre Fiction*

"An engaging thriller with plenty of humor, good characterization, and a memorable villain." — *Kirkus Reviews*

"Clues are tossed out like bait, twisting and turning the storyline along ... The characters are brilliantly constructed ... The dark humor serves to lessen the tension in all the right ways before it heightens again ... Effortlessly captures the wonderful eccentricities of life in South Florida." — *IndieReader* (Official Seal of Approval)

"*Psycho-Tropics* is like riding Pipeline with a hangover. It's jaw dropping, heart thumping and addictively exhilarating, but with a hint of disorientation, dizziness and an unsettled stomach. But by the end you'll be smiling ear to ear and bursting to tell your mates how good it was." — *Surfer Dad UK*

Amazon Reviews

"A twisted, hilarious mystery with heart ... When a seven-year-old embalming expert and James Garfield, the twentieth president, play roles in solving the case, you know something different is up."

"It's got it all: action, humor, pulse-raising suspense, pathos and warmth."

"Lots of writers have stories to tell—but can't. Box has stories to tell—and can."

"I thought this was going to be a typical crazy Florida book ...

what a huge surprise. ... Great story and great characters, well told and believable."

"This book drew me in from the first sentence ... Every time I thought I figured out what was going on, I was wrong. Every time I wanted to finish a chapter and put it down, the dramatic ending would propel me to the next chapter."

"Finished the damn thing in two days. I could not put it down. This is one of the best books I have read in a long time ... The pacing was balanced, the characters were rounded and complex. Just when I thought I knew what was going to happen, the author threw a curve ball. The ending was truly a surprise."

"Carl Hiaasen on steroids."

"I am drawn to books with heavy character development. If there also happens to be a compelling story, all the better, but I've come not to expect it. It seems like most authors can't do both. This book has marvelous, complex characters, but also moves along at a fast pace and is completely unpredictable."

"My daughter heard me laughing from across the house as I read this one. Don't let the humor fool you, though. This book has serious messages about forgiveness, redemption and self-examination."

"A brilliant mystery thriller, masterfully written."

Also by Dorian Box

The Emily Calby Series
Winner of Eight Indie Book Honors

TWELVE-YEAR-OLD EMILY was a good girl from a good family in rural Georgia before the day the two men came. The only survivor of the notorious *Calby Murders*, she ran away and went missing. Ex-gang member Lucas Jackson took her in off the streets and became her family. He taught her a lot, including how to survive—and kill. *Justice. Always comes too late, but it's still justice.* His words became Emily's raison d'être.

The Emily Calby Series tracks Emily's perilous life and remarkable journey forward from the day of the home invasion to her first semester of law school. The three titles are spaced four years apart in Emily's life: **The Hiding Girl** (age 12); **The Girl in Cell 49B** (age 16); **Target: The Girl** (age 20). The books can be read together or as standalones, as each title involves a distinct plot and setting.

Emily's story is a twisty, action-packed coming-of-age adventure that will leave you cheering, cringing, crying, and even laughing. Dark and gritty, but filled with heart and hope, *The Emily Calby Series* is a testament to the boundlessness of human grief, love, and strength.

Honors and awards for titles in *The Emily Calby Series* include: Publishers Weekly BookLife Prize Semifinalist; IndieReader Discovery Award for Fiction; Best Psychological Thriller of the Year (BestThrillers.com); Feathered Quill Medal for Mystery/Suspense; National Indie Excellence Award Finalist; Best Legal Thriller of the Year Finalist (BestThrillers.com); and Readers' Favorite Awards in both Suspense and New Adult fiction.

Praise for *The Emily Calby Series*

"Dark and gritty ... an exceptional, heart-pounding story full of raw emotion, deep-seated fear, and an undercurrent of hope and innocence. Deeply atmospheric ... without peer in contemporary mysteries/thrillers." — *Publishers Weekly BookLife Prize Semifinalist*

"In Emily, Author Dorian Box has created a rarity—a teenage protagonist that is at once sympathetic, vulnerable and largely fearless." — *BestThrillers.com* (Best Psychological Thriller of 2021)

"The story that author Dorian Box has created for Emily Calby is nothing short of thrilling, but it's the masterful interplay of character, setting, and theme, along with the fast pace and high emotional stakes that make this a real page-turner." — *IndieReader Discovery Award for Fiction*

"You root for the lead, Emily, and stick with her throughout. Engaged me from the first page." — *Feathered Quill Medal Winner for Mystery/Suspense*

"A unique mix of hope, shattered innocence, pain, fear, and vulnerability ... a great, suspenseful read." — *Readers' Favorite Award for Suspense Fiction*

"What makes this book such a good read is Box's sympathetic and deeply engaging portrayal of a tough, smart girl determined to beat the odds, even when there doesn't seem to be a ray of hope anywhere. There's plenty of action too. If you're looking for a good thriller with character and substance, this one's for you." — *Andrew Diamond, bestselling author of Gate 76 and Impala*

"Stunning, captivating, heartbreaking but also heartwarming ... The characters were so alive, believable, with heart and warmth, humor and love." — *NetGalley*

"Completely demolished my expectations. ... This novel is fast-paced and action-packed but it has a profound human element that sets it apart from other novels in its genre." — *BookishFirst*

"[A] must-read thriller ... engrossing ... memorable." — *Readers' Favorite Award for New Adult Fiction*

Places, Entities, and Other Tidbits
in *Funeral Daze*

Places. Sandwiched on the Florida Gold Coast between Fort Lauderdale and Miami, Hollywood is a real place I know well because I grew up there. Like fictional Danny Teakwell, our lives revolved around the ocean and beach, from building sandcastles as kids to fishing, diving, surfing, and boating as teens. Life took me elsewhere as an adult, but I'll always miss my hometown.

Standard advice for authors is to write what you know. That's what I was thinking when I composed my debut novel, *Psycho-Tropics*, published in 2015. It's probably safe to say that *Psycho-Tropics* and *Funeral Daze* are the only two novels ever to be set in good old Hollywood.

Some specific locations described are real and some are fictional. Unsurprisingly, there is no Slagger-Jewell or Snowbirds in Paradise funeral home. Nor is there is a Seabreeze Towers, Tradewinds bar, or Nine Lives Surf Shop on the Hollywood Beach boardwalk.

The boardwalk is a roughly two-mile promenade for walkers, bikers, and beachgoers. I mention it here because in a Facebook group of people who grew up in Hollywood, I've come across passionate and at time rancorous debates as to whether it's properly called *the boardwalk* or *the broadwalk*. The technical answer is clear. It's a broadwalk, currently made of paving bricks, but we always called it *the boardwalk*.

Entities. Several government and other entities mentioned in *Funeral Daze* are real, but used fictitiously. All characters depicted as being associated with them are also fictional. I'm confident the FBI would never tolerate a numbskull like Special Agent Winton Munroe.

Tidbits. The "dead baby" story that inspired Luis's idea for *El Grande* is an actual Miami urban legend. See Kyle Munzenrieder, *Cocaine Smuggled in Dead Babies and Miami's Other Weirdest Urban Legends*, Miami New Times (Feb. 18, 2016).

Writing books set in the past presents interesting challenges. As an example, in 2000 cellphones were just becoming widespread. Being one who strives for factual accuracy, I spent hours researching what cellphone features did or didn't exist back then. Along the writing path, I originally included and had to delete references to Alexa, remote-working, fake news, and several other futuristic creations.

One useful fact mentioned in the book came via my author-friend Andrew Diamond (check out his excellent books). He said he was chatting with a former U.S. Customs agent in a bar one night at a conference and the agent mentioned it costs foreign drug cartels five times as much to move their products within the United States as it costs to get them here. I was unable to document the agent's assertion through research, but it fit the plot so I went with it.

Finally, while *Funeral Daze* is lighthearted, the toll of large-scale drug-trafficking upon producing countries in Central and South America, and on the United States as a major consumer, can't be overlooked. It was extensive and severe in 2000 and continues to be today.

Acknowledgements

READING A NOVEL draft for a friend is a "big" favor, up there with not only picking them up at the airport, but letting them stay with you for two weeks. Buckets of thanks to my daughter, Caitlin, award-winning authors Andrew Diamond and Debbie Burke, law professor Mary Pat Treuthart, and voracious reader Susan Gill (the world needs more of you) for reading and commenting on drafts of *Funeral Daze*. Their insights, suggestions, and corrections improved the book immeasurably.

My former law professor colleague, Coleen Barger, and her husband, Gary, are master boaters. Their Great Loop trip in the Calypso Poet covered more than six thousand miles and took a full year. Who knew you could leave Little Rock, Arkansas in a boat and stop by Monty's in Coconut Grove, Florida (where I lived at the time) for dinner and drinks with an old friend? Thanks to Coleen for patiently answering my many boating questions. Any errors are mine.

Thanks also to my dear friends Norma Lorenzo, a Miami immigration lawyer, for checking my Spanish usage for authenticity, and Memphis estate lawyer Russell Hayes for giving me a key idea regarding Jessica's trust left by her grandfather.

Few people have helped more with my book-publishing career than graphic artist and website developer Gary Wayne Golden. Thanks for another great cover and publishing experience, my friend.

I will always be in debt to Griffin J. Stockley, who died in 2023 from Alzheimer's disease. My newspaper reporter mother inspired me to be a writer. Grif inspired me to be a novelist. His five Gideon Page legal thrillers published by Simon & Schuster earned him the Porter Prize, Arkansas's premier literary award. He followed those with several impeccably researched civil rights history texts, earning him the Lifetime Achievement Award from the Arkansas Historical Association. As a lawyer, he spent his career fighting for those without a voice. He was a constant source of encouragement and friendship, not to mention quite a few *Wow, that was one for the books!* adventures. Rest in peace, Grif. Your presence made the world a better place.

About the Author

DORIAN BOX is the pen name for Andrew McClurg, a former law professor and the author or coauthor of seven nonfiction books, including an Amazon Editors' Favorite Book of the Year.

In fiction, he likes to combine dark themes with heart, hope, and humor. His novels have received indie book awards/honors from Publishers Weekly, Writer's Digest, IndieReader, BestThrillers.com, Feathered Quill, Readers' Favorite, and the National Indie Excellence Awards.

As an academic, he won numerous awards for both teaching and research and wrote thousands, possibly millions, of scholarly footnotes. He's been interviewed as a legal expert by National Public Radio, the PBS Newshour, the New York Times, and many other sources.

McClurg (or maybe it was Box) spent the previous decade living out his childhood rockstar fantasies singing and playing in Memphis cover bands.

Made in the USA
Monee, IL
13 August 2024

63803643R00204